AND WHEREIN YOU STAND

BOOK I

INSOMUCH AS TO DECEIVE

AND WHEREIN YOU STAND

BOOK I

INSOMUCH AS TO DECEIVE

by

WILLIAM L. BIERSACH

' Bona Tempora Volvant'

Arcadia
MMXIV

Nihil Obstat: *Huh?*

✤   Imprimatur: *Are you kidding!?!?*

ISBN: 978-0-9883537-5-6

First printing: 2014

Cover art by B. G. Callahan
Drawings signed "M.F." by the author

All the characters and events in this novel are fictitious.
Any similarity to any actual persons,
living or dead, is purely coincidental.

©2014 by William L. Biersach

AND WHEREIN YOU STAND

BOOK I

INSOMUCH AS TO DECEIVE

*As such, the sixth installment in the continuing saga
of Fr. John Baptist, the cop-turned-priest, and
Martin Feeney, his gardener-turned-chronicler,
and their tuxedo-clad comrades, the Knights Tumblar.*

Other books by

William L. Biersach

∞

Published by Tumblar House

Fiction

The Endless Knot
The Darkness Did Not
The Search for Saint Valeria
Out of the Depths

Nonfiction

While the Eyes of the Great are Elsewhere

∞

Published by Catholic Treasures

Nonfiction

Of Mary There Is Never Enough

To

Jeannette Coyne

&

Stephen Frankini

The Gospel Reading
for the
Last Sunday after Pentecost

At that time, Jesus said to his disciples:

[15] When therefore you shall see the abomination of desolation, which was spoken of by Daniel the prophet, standing in the holy place: he that readeth let him understand.   [16] Then they that are in Judea, let them flee to the mountains: [17] And he that is on the housetop, let him not come down to take any thing out of his house: [18] And he that is in the field, let him not go back to take his coat. [19] And woe to them that are with child, and that give suck in those days. [20] But pray that your flight be not in the winter, or on the sabbath. [21] For there shall be then great tribulation, such as hath not been from the beginning of the world until now, neither shall be. [22] And unless those days had been shortened, no flesh should be saved: but for the sake of the elect those days shall be shortened. [23] Then if any man shall say to you: Lo here is Christ, or there, do not believe him. [24] For there shall arise false Christs and false prophets, and shall show great signs and wonders, **insomuch as to deceive** (if possible) even the elect. [25] Behold I have told it to you, beforehand. [26] If therefore they shall say to you: Behold he is in the desert, go ye not out: Behold he is in the closets, believe it not. [27] For as lightning cometh out of the east, and appeareth even into the west: so shall also the coming of the Son of man be. [28] Wheresoever the body shall be, there shall the eagles also be gathered together.   [29] And immediately after the tribulation of those days, the sun shall be darkened and the moon shall not give her light, and the stars shall fall from heaven, and the powers of heaven shall be moved: [30] And then shall appear the sign of the Son of man in heaven: and then shall all tribes of the earth mourn: and they shall see the Son of man coming in the clouds of heaven with much power and majesty. [31] And he shall send his angels with a trumpet, and a great

voice: and they shall gather together his elect from the four winds, from the farthest parts of the heavens to the utmost bounds of them. [32] And from the fig tree learn a parable: When the branch thereof is now tender, and the leaves come forth, you know that summer is nigh. [33] So you also, when you shall see all these things, know ye that it is nigh, even at the doors. [34] Amen I say to you, that this generation shall not pass away, till all these things be done. [35] Heaven and earth shall pass, but my words shall not pass away.

—From the twenty-fourth chapter of the Gospel of Saint Matthew
Douay-Rheims Translation
(Emphasis added.)

And Wherein You Stand

Book I
Insomuch As To Deceive

∞§[Table of Contents]§∞

∞§[†]§∞

0. By, For, and About

∞§[AUTHOR'S NOTE]§∞

There is fantasy, and there is fantasy. For the Catholic, fantasy is a tool to explore reality. For the non-Catholic, fantasy is his method of being; but he calls it realism.

—Charles A. Coulombe*

OKAY, I'LL SAY IT UP FRONT: this story is by a Catholic, about Catholics, for Catholics—and anyone else who is interested. It is a metaphor for the daily battle each and every one of us faces in these modern times, hounded on all sides by hedonistic materialism in an atheistic culture. How does one hold on to the Faith left us by Jesus Christ so many years ago when the world was simpler?

Or was it?

As I search through the enchanting leaves of folklore, I find that faeries, elves, and dwarves live in a parallel universe where time and space mean something different than they do to mortal men. These creatures might, for example, lure an unsuspecting young warrior into a cramped, narrow cave—and what does he find? A sprawling kingdom with palaces and battlements and pavilions stretching for miles, not to mention an enticing but perilous princess who steals his heart. Is all this really squished inside that little cave, or has our perplexed hero stumbled

---

* From a talk entitled "Literature of Wonder," delivered at the St. Augustine Institute, St. Benedict Center, Richmond, New Hampshire, 2008.

through a portal to another world, a plane of existence where the underlying rules are different? A damsel partakes of an elven feast and falls fast asleep, awakening a hundred years hence, yet aging but a single night. Time moves differently, we are told, in the realm of Faerie.

Then I look forward to modern physics, which tells us that solid matter is really a dance of free-flowing energy, that light is simultaneously a particle and a wave, and that time can be warped and twisted back upon itself. We are told that an astronaut, under the right conditions, may embark on a journey lasting ten years, only to emerge from his spaceship having aged but a few hours. As my good friend Charles A. Coulombe recently pointed out to me, the only thing that separates modern science from folklore is Sir Isaac Newton!

Unfortunately, modern science has become something of a fairytale in its own right. Most scientists today, hypnotized by a mindset that detests and rejects all mention of a Creator, cling to the doctrines of Charles Darwin. The notion of evolution as a fundamental force permeates every discipline from microbiology to astrophysics. Even so, there are a growing number of renegades who, having peered down at the intricacies of life through electron microscopes or up at the blazing complexity of the heavens via earthbound and orbiting telescopes, shrug their shoulders and declare, "Things are not as we have been led to believe by our predecessors! Such fine-tuned complexity must be the product of Intelligent Design!" Such an intriguing idea is not met with enthusiastic curiosity and camaraderie on the part of their peers. Indeed, many such rebels find themselves denounced and hounded from their academic positions by these very peers, peers who nevertheless continue to tear out their hair and rail against the Catholic Church for having silenced their poster child, Galileo Galilei, five centuries ago.

The holders of dominant, outdated, naturalistic beliefs have the advantage of the patronage of those in power. When that power shifts, how long do you think their Godless view of the universe will survive? Come to think of it, the Catholic Church once enjoyed that advantage when the rulers of the world deigned Her useful to their purposes. Those rulers are gone, and so the Church has lost that advantage. But I'll wager She'll be around to come to the fore again someday, because She holds something that outlasts all of them: the Truth.

* * *

This opus is something of a departure from my previous works in structure, style, and subject matter. Come to think of it, so have been every one of my novels.

When I was young, I feasted on science fiction, fantasy, and tales of the bizarre. Much as I loved these genres, it was like visiting a foreign land because nothing in them seemed to have any connection with the central issues of my life, such as going to Mass and learning my Catechism. Apart from Tolkien, whose message was veiled, in all those hundreds of stories only twice do I remember plots with a Catholic center: "The Quest for St. Aquin," a short story by Anthony Boucher (1951), and *A Canticle for Leibowitz*, a novel by Arthur M. Miller, Jr. (1960). Even in the realm of gothic horror where vampires fled holy water and Crucifixes, none of their pursuers ever stopped to ask themselves why these countermeasures *worked*. None thought to consider that the religion, whose sacramentals could repel such vile enemies of the human soul, might just have something positive to offer them in their daily lives.

There came a time during my twenties, I'm ashamed to admit, when I lost heart and gave in to the ravages of doubt and dejection. I left the Church. It was then, amidst an arduous erratic search for something to fill the chasm, I chanced upon the world of the occult. I have never hidden this fact from my readers, nor would I want to. Indeed, I have often incorporated lessons learned there into my stories. Some of these concepts will come striding to the fore in this tale in ways they haven't before. I do this not to encourage my readers to delve into these perilous practices, but because they are out there, they are compelling, and the fact is that many other Catholics who have lost their grip have taken up refuge in their esoteric mists. To be forewarned is to be forearmed.

To those who insist that the mere mention of the Tarot or spiritualism or the *Lemegeton* or anything related to the occult is a moral abomination, I suggest that they not read this or any of my books. That being said, let me be clear: I am not selling these things; I am acknowledging them. They are appropriate to my plots. I use them to advance my stories. The reason I was attracted to them in the first place was that in the wake of Vatican II I'd heard too many priests and members of the hierarchy express doubts regarding the details and effects of Christ and His Gospel. After being subjected to so much uncertainty from the pulpit, it was refreshing to encounter authors who actually believed in Angels and Demons without intellectual qualms or the slightest hint of embarrassment. Their unabashed conviction was music to my ears.

But they had a lot of things wrong, dead wrong. Like atheistic scientists today, they shunned the mention of the elephant in the living room, or rather right in the middle of their magickal space: the One, Holy, Catholic and Apostolic Church of Rome, the religion from which they derived so many of their doctrines and methods. It is one of the great ironies that Arthur Edward Waite catholicized the Tarot deck, yet called the fifth card of the Major Arcana "The Hierophant" instead of what it obviously depicted: "The Pope." On a parallel but telling note, I'm reminded that C. S. Lewis, a staunch Anglican, in his memorable work, *That Hideous Strength*, resurrected Merlin and revealed him to be a Christian, but not as what he must have truly been in his time: a Roman Catholic!

But as to my story, it is quite a romp. I must say I haven't had so much fun writing a yarn in my life. It goes all over the map and careens blithely off the edge. I know some readers will get a few chapters in and ask, "Where the heck is he going with this?" I invite them to hang on and see. I repeat: this is a metaphor, an allegory about the struggle to hold onto one's beliefs against the onslaught of detractors, the claims of naturalist science, the appeal of the senses, the allure of the inexplicable, the snarls of Jansenists, and the wagging tongues of naysayers. My sincere hope is that when my readers come to the end they will get the point. I do get to it eventually. Then they'll look back and see that it was being made at every turn.

I have taken liberties with respect to California history, especially regarding the founding of Summerland and the discovery of gold in the San Gabriel Mountains. Consider this additional proof that the Los Angeles in my story is pure myth, and has nothing to do with the actual City of Angels.

As with my previous novels, I must advise gullible readers that this tale is riddled with "fool's traps." It is not intended to be an apprentice's guide to magickal procedures—that is, unless they desire to tie themselves into endless knots.

—WLB3

∞§[†]§∞

Sunday, December Twenty-fourth

The Feast of Saint Adam and Saint Eve
(The First Age of the World)

∞ **Christmas Eve** ∞

∞§✝§∞

1. More Like Marley's Ghost*

∞§[Martin]§∞

"IT'S NOT EXACTLY SNOW," observed the gardener with a shiver.

"It's a matter of perspective," philosophized the priest who was huddled beside him on the kitchen porch. "Rain, after all, is molten ice."

"And both are precipitation, but only one is snow."

"Did you really expect a white Christmas in Los Angeles, Martin?"

"According to Pierre, I'm not a pessimist. I'm a dissatisfied optimist."

---

* Preferring as I do simple, stark, unenlightening numbers for titles, I have never before assigned names to the chapters in my memoirs. Because this work is something of a group effort, and since the other participants insisted on crowning their contributions with effusive and in some cases provocative titles, and also because admittedly this opus will likely be relegated to the oblivion of the Tumblar Vault anyway, I have acceded to their wishes.   —M.F.

"Speaking of Pierre, what do you know about the soirée he's planned for this evening?"

"Only that you and I can't go inside until Kahlúa arrives."

"Honestly?"

"Honestly."

"So meanwhile we're relegated to this little porch?"

"Unless you want to sit in the garden, Father."

The priest grimaced. "I think not."

"We could use your new umbrella."

"What new umbrella?"

"The one Lieutenant Taper gave you. What else could it be? The handle is sticking out the end. I think he's confusing you with Father Brown."

"You know I never open presents early."

"So the porch it is. At least Mr. Folkstone finally replaced the bug light, God bless him."

The priest was Father John Baptist, pastor of Saint Philomena's Roman Catholic Church, and the gardener was yours truly, Martin Feeney. It had been gloomy all day and now it was dark. The garden teemed with the sound of wet fireworks.

"The sky is usually crystal-clear this time of year," said I. "I can't remember the last time it rained on Christmas Eve."

"Five years ago," said Father. "But it was just a light sprinkle. Nothing like this. I don't think it's ever been quite like—"

A zillion-volt flashbulb popped in the sky. For half a second the garden was revealed as a rain-streaked explosion of glistening foliage and drooping branches. Blades of grass wagged and ivy leaves wobbled beside the ankle-deep canal which, hours before, had been our uneven brick path. The cement birdbath near the statue of St. Thérèse had become an overflowing fountain in the middle of a pond. Trembling on the cement rim squatted a little porous stone bird, threatening to go over the falls. Then, just as suddenly, the darkness snapped back into place, plunging the plopping, tinkling, gurgling din into murky anonymity.

"Refresh my memory, Father," I said, waving my cane around for emphasis. "You're the pastor here, yes?"

"Of course."

"In fact, you own the property, the buildings, this rectory?"

"Yes."

"Then why is it that you're relegated to the porch while the Tumblars make a commotion within? What are they doing, rearranging all the furniture?"

Father shrugged. "All I know is that something has been weighing on Pierre for some days now. He hardly looked himself when he asked that we have this meeting. He was adamant that it had to be tonight. This Night of all Nights. Surely some of the fellows would like to be with their families."

"And Kahlúa is invited. To a Knights' meeting?"

"I agree that it's odd. The word 'portentous' comes to mind."

"'Crazy' comes to mine. Hold on. Did you hear a car door slam?"

"Hard to tell through this downpour."

We listened intently for a few seconds.

"There," I said. "The gate. Why would someone come 'round through the garden instead of going to the front door?"

A pair of high-pitched feminine giggles penetrated the sodden darkness.

"Mmm-HM!" came a voice. "These boots is made for wadin', and that's jus' what they'll do! How you doin', Sweetie?"

"Eek!" answered the other. "Mine are leaking! My feet are getting soaked! It's so cold!"

"Yoo-hoo!" I called. "Is that you, Madam Hummingbird?"

"Wet as rain!" she hooted back. "How's my favorite gardener-turned-raconteur?"

"Sopping!" I answered. "Who's that with you?"

"It's me!" answered her companion.

"Beth!" exclaimed Father.

The two ladies came trudging into the amber glow of the porch light, their hats sagging, raincoats shimmering, and boots sloshing.

"Well, well, well!" I greeted them. "Look what the Beast from Twenty Thousand Fathoms dragged in!"

"More like the She-Creature from the Black Lagoon," laughed Kahlúa. "Father Baptist! What are you doin' out here?"

"I was just asking the same question," said I, eyeing him up and down.

"Enough questions," said Father, milling his palms together. "You're here. That means we can finally go in."

"What?" asked Beth.

"Pierre's orders," I explained. "He's been made pastor. Haven't you heard?"

Father cranked the argumentative doorknob and we stepped aside so the two soggy ladies could enter first. Moments later we were reveling in the warmth and aromas of the kitchen.

"Just what I need!" growled Millie emerging from the pantry with a sack of confectioners' sugar in her hands. She glared angrily at the water pooling on the linoleum around our feet. Setting her burden down on the counter, she grumbled menacingly as she approached. Then she suddenly opened her arms and threw them around Kahlúa. "Lulu!" she greeted her. "You must be freezing!"

"Millie, Honey," cooed Kahlúa, embracing our housekeeptrix warmly. "There's nothing like a cozy kitchen on a night like this."

"Merry Christmas!" said Father, giving Beth a fatherly hug. "I didn't know you were coming."

"There's a lot you don't know," said Millie, disengaging from Kahlúa and glaring at him. "Do you have any idea what those ruffians are doing to your study?"

"Decorating the tree?" he asked innocently.

"Bah!" said Millie. Then she engulfed Beth. "It's so good to see you again. And so wide awake!"

"The doctor changed my prescription," said Beth. "I'm doing a lot better, although I never really was as bad off as we pretended the last time I came to visit."

"Here," barked Millie, beckoning tersely with her hands. "Let me take those wet things. Sorry there are no chairs here to drape them over. They've all been dragged into the study. I'll just drape them on the sink in the laundry room."

"Li'l Sis Liz!" proclaimed Arthur, entering through the hallway door.

"Big Brudder Art!" squealed Beth, rushing to him.

"I was afraid your flight would be delayed."

"You should have seen the mess at the airport."

"Thank-you for picking her up," grunted Arthur to Kahlúa over his sister's shoulder as he gave her a bear hug. "Beth, it's so grand to see you! This is going to be a merry Christmas indeed!"

"Hear, hear!" cheered Jonathan and Edward from the hallway.

"You stay out!" ordered Millie, shooing them as she returned from the laundry room brandishing a mop. "This floor is all wet and I'll not have it tracked through the house!"

"We'd better chuck our boots," said Kahlúa, leaning against the chugging refrigerator as she unzipped her footwear. Her raincoat came off like the curtain parting at a lavish stage production. The revealed dress swarmed with multicolored Angels against a fluorescent Milky Way background.

"Even my socks are drenched," said Beth, leaning against her brother as she followed suit. She was wearing a simple green dress with red frills. It was soaked around the collar.

Father, of course, was wearing his usual neat but threadbare cassock, and the Lads were decked out in their tuxedoes. I had considered formal attire myself but had opted for a warm wool sweater with reindeer prancing across my tummy and brown corduroy pants. Millie was wearing a shapeless blue dress with white polka dots, most of which was camouflaged by her pink-and-red checkered body apron.

"You must come in and warm yourself by the fire," said Edward.

"An excellent idea," said Father. "I take it I'm now allowed."

"As you say, Father," said Joel, squeezing his face into view between Edward and Jonathan's shoulders. "Millie, is the mead ready?"

"You get yourselves out of here and into there," snapped Millie. "Don't worry, I'll be bringing the grog in a minute."

"I'll help you," said Kahlúa.

"No you won't," said Millie. "You're a guest."

"Yes I will," said Kahlúa. "You've only got two hands and I see a dozen mugs on the dishwasher."

"Is that new?" asked Beth, pointing to Millie's month-old roll-about kitchen appliance. "I'll be glad to—"

"Lulu, you can stay," ordered Millie. "The rest of you, git!"

With that we made our way down the hallway and turned left into Father's study—or what had once been Father's study. The Lads had been busy. Gone was the handmade plaque in the gold frame that usually stood guard by the door:

> The most evident mark of God's anger, and the most terrible castigation He can inflict upon the world, is manifest when He permits His people to fall into the hands of a clergy who are more in name than in deed, priests who practice the cruelty of ravening wolves rather than the charity and affection of devoted shepherds. They abandon the things of God to devote themselves to the things of the world and, in their saintly calling of holiness, they spend their time in profane and worldly pursuits. When God permits such things, it is a very positive proof that He is thoroughly angry with His people, and is visiting His most dreadful wrath upon them.
>
> —St. John Eudes

It had been replaced with an equally provocative while not so ominous message in a pewter frame, penned with a mischievous flair:

> And the Angel said to them: *Fear not; for behold, I bring you good tidings of great joy, that shall be to all people: For this day is born to you a Savior, who is Christ the Lord, in the city of David. And this shall be a sign unto you. You shall find the infant wrapped in swaddling clothes, and laid in a manger.*
>
> And suddenly there was with the Angel a multitude of the heavenly army, praising God and saying: *Glory to God in the highest; and on earth peace to men of Good Will.*
>
> —St. Luke II:10-14

That was only the beginning of the makeover. As we squeezed into the room like so many sardines, I noted that Father's desk had been pushed into the far right corner. A white sheet had been draped upon it, and a five-foot Douglas fir placed on top. It was an uneven, lopsided tree—probably the last one sold on the lot that afternoon—but it was decorated with glee. Driblets of tinsel, sagging metallic balls, electrical lights, and strings of multicolored popcorn had been applied uproariously to the asymmetrical branches. A crystalline star with a light bulb glowing in its heart graced the top of the tree, but its weight was drawing it precariously sideways. The base of the tree was obscured by an irregular pile of odd-shaped and awkwardly wrapped presents.

Not finding it under the tree, I glanced around for the Crèche. I discovered it on the mantel over the fireplace in the far left corner. The Holy Family looked out at us from a barn made of crooked twigs and littered with excelsior hay. Some of the original figurines had been replaced along the way with mismatched pieces from other Nativity sets. Hence, two of the adoring shepherds and one of the Wise Men were giants, while the ox and the ass could have doubled as kittens. It didn't matter, of course. The point was the Child in the manger, and He was bigger than us all.

I noticed that another plaque that usually graced the right end of the mantelpiece had also been replaced. The substituted message was framed in dark wood, flanked by the hand-carved statues of Saint Anthony of Padua and Saint Thomas More who normally stood watch on Father's desk. Much as I peered, I could not make out the words from across the room. The letters seemed dark and inelegantly executed, which struck me as odd. Figuring the chance for a closer look would present itself eventually, I contented myself with taking in the rest of the room.

There were four pieces of twine attached to nails on the four walls, the other ends tied to the light fixture in the center of the ceiling. Upon these, Christmas cards of varying shapes and sizes, which had been arriving for days, had been hung along their folds. Their upward swoop added color and cheer to the room while suggesting a circus tent—at least to me. Only religious cards had been so displayed. The cowardly "Happy Holi-

days" variety had no doubt been left in their envelopes somewhere. Sprigs of holly had been wedged between some of the
volumes on the bookshelves. Three large red candles flickered
on the windowsill. The windowpane was spattered with rain, but
it was too dark to see anything of the garden outside.

Millie hadn't been kidding when she said the kitchen chairs
had been brought to the study. So had just about every other seat
in the rectory, and one I recognized as having been purloined
from the church sacristy. The small room was literally crammed
with chairs to accommodate this gathering, all facing the fireplace. The back of Father's squeaky office chair was wedged
into the near right corner. This put the musty volumes on the
shelves along the right wall easily within his reach. My own
favorite chair was positioned next to his, placing the light switch
just inside the doorway over my left shoulder while allowing
easy escape if the need should arise. Considerate, our rampant
redecorators. Just to be sure, I placed my cane horizontally
across the arms of my chair by way of claiming it. Sure, my favorite chair's twin was backed into the near left corner, and no
one else in the room would know the difference—but I would,
and I didn't want to spend an evening wishing I'd been more
assertive. The high-backed wooden chair with the cushioned
seat, the one snatched from the sacristy, had been placed between my favorite chair's twin and the doorway. Twin, cush,
fave, squeak—gottit. That took care of the back row. Three of
the kitchen chairs comprised the middle row and were more
loosely spaced, and two oddballs landed in the front row off to
the left—the area to the right being displaced by the bulk of Father's desk. The fourth kitchen chair was set sideways next to
the fireplace, way too close to the heat for comfort. Inches were
precious, so the wastebasket had been placed in the hallway just
outside the door. Details, details, it's all in the details. (If all
that was hard to keep straight, not to worry: a seating chart will
be provided in just a few pages.)

The assembly was standing in and around, chatting accord-
ingly.

"Merry Christmas, dear Chum," said Edward to Joel.

"What a year it's been," replied Joel, heaving a sigh. "If you had told me last Christmas where I'd be now, I would have said you were crazy."

"What a splendid beard you have!" I heard Beth saying to Jonathan. "I can't believe you grew that since I last saw you. What's it been, not even six weeks? Wow! And what about Stella? Is she coming tonight?"

"Her dad's big on Christmas Eve dinner at home," he answered. I didn't have to turn to see the shadow play across his face. "She might come to Midnight Mass, though."

"That will be nice," said Beth. Being a woman, she doubtless heard the sad echoes rattling around the chasm of Jonathan's heart. "And Edward, I hear you're now a concierge at a grand hotel."

"The Adirondack," agreed Edward. "You wouldn't believe the favors I had to promise to get tonight off." He lowered his voice to a whisper. "Pierre was insistent."

"That he was," said Joel, his voice likewise low. "Do you have any idea what's bugging him?"

"Not a clue," said Edward.

This interchange brought my attention to the man in question. In contrast to the otherwise cheerful ambiance in the cramped room, Pierre Bontemps stood apart, his left arm resting along the edge of the mantel. An ostentatious meerschaum pipe smoldered ponderously in his right hand. Like the other Lads he was attired in white tie and black tailcoat. Unique to him was the monocle perched in his left eye socket. Also unique to him was the grim expression on his face. It was unusual to see him standing aloof, seemingly unaware of the revelry of his companions.

A fire crackled on the hearth behind his legs. As my attention was drawn to the flames a log shifted with a puff of sparks. They swirled and waltzed magically, then darted up the chute. Normally my chair would be positioned sideways in front of the fireplace facing Father's desk, my pile of half-read books on the floor between. In their stead stood something strange indeed. It was a small metal stand about two feet high, the kind that collapses for storage. Resting on top was a marvelous wooden box, an antique by the looks of it. Dragons and winged creatures fashioned of thin burned lines danced all over its polished surface. It was about twenty inches by fourteen, and eighteen or so tall. The top four inches was a lid fastened with an ornate metal clasp with a keyhole in the center.

Wondering what had become of my books, I saw an entrance and took it.

"Merry Christmas, *Chevalier* Bontemps," I ventured as I hobbled between the chairs, wishing I had my cane. I approached him awkwardly with my right hand outstretched.

"Peace on earth, Sir Martin," he replied, switching his pipe to his left hand so he could return the handclasp. "I imagine the damp is wreaking havoc with your arthritis."

"A tad," I admitted, looking at my aching feet to avoid the chill in his eyes. "Might I ask what has become of my books?"

"Safe and sound in Father's bedroom," he replied. "Ah, Beth. So glad you could make it."

"What's with you?" asked Beth playfully as she came up beside me. She crouched and held her palms out to the waving flames.

"Me?" asked Pierre.

"He's been like this all afternoon," said Joel.

"Not exactly Scrooge," said Jonathan.

"More like Marley's Ghost," said Arthur.

They were all being playful, but Pierre did not respond in kind.

My eyes were drawn to the wooden frame on the mantel. I was close enough to read it. The message that Father usually kept there was a warning to himself:

> I do not speak rashly, but as I feel and think. I do not think that many priests are saved, but that those who perish are far more numerous. The reason is that the office requires a great soul. For there are many things to make a priest swerve from rectitude, and he requires great vigilance on every side.
>
> —St. John Chrysostom

The message that greeted me in its stead took my breath away. I read it once, then twice, then a third time. I swallowed, then I swallowed again. Finally I summoned my wits and said, "Uh, see here, Pierre, what is the meaning of — ?"

"Comin' through!" bellowed Kahlúa Hummingbird, bursting into the room with a tray of steaming mugs. One was decorated with a little Hungarian flag. That was my ginger ale. Father had decided that I'd had enough dispensations of late from my pledge to avoid alcoholic beverages. Ah well, at least it was Blue Label.

"And more besides," barked Millie, her muscular arms hefting a large metal pitcher with large, floppy potholders in each hand. She ceremoniously set it on the corner of Father's desk. A splendid time was guaranteed for all.

With that I decided not to pursue the point. Everyone grabbed their drinks and started talking at once. Everyone except Pierre.

∞§[†]§∞

∞§ † §∞

2. I Know Something You Don't Know

∞§[Martin]§∞

"IF YOU WILL ALL BE UPSTANDING," said Father.

Everyone who had settled rose again to the occasion.

"To Our Lady, Empress of All the Americas!" toasted Arthur, holding up his thrice-filled mug.

"To Our Lady!" said we all, and gulped the golden brew.

"Merry Christmas!" said Father.

"Hear, hear!" cheered the men.

"An' God bless us, every darn one!" bubbled Kahlúa, who had been enjoying herself immensely.

"If you please," said Pierre, who was still standing before the hearth. He motioned everyone to be seated with a wave of his hand.

Reclaiming my cane, I lowered myself into my favorite chair. Father was already easing himself into his office chair next to mine. Kahlúa claimed my favorite chair's twin, and Millie sat next to her across the doorway from me. In the second row, left to right, settled Beth, Arthur, and Joel. Jonathan and Edward wound up in front.

```
GARDENING TIPS: A visual aid to keep the seat-

ing arrangement straight.  Positions and pro-

portions are approximate:
```

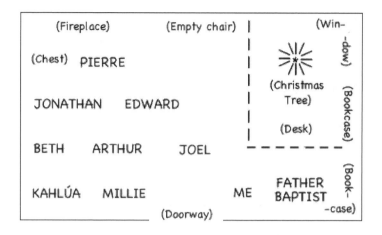

--M.F.

"So what's up?" asked Joel.

Pierre said nothing, waiting for the chatter and sniggering to die down.

"Hmmmm," rumbled Kahlúa.

"I have asked you all here for a reason," said Pierre, after clearing his throat.

"So serious," chided Edward.

"You'd think this was a wake," said Millie.

"More like a—" began Kahlúa, but a look from Pierre cut off her sentence.

We waited.

"I realize I've been acting out of character," admitted Pierre after adjusting and readjusting his monocle as he collected his thoughts. "The fact is I've been pondering how to go about this for some days—weeks—no, months, actually."

"So what's up?" asked Joel again.

His features grim, Pierre set his extinguished pipe on the mantel. "How to begin? I have something important to tell you—no, monumental. Forgive me. I've rehearsed this a thousand different ways, and now that the time has come my tongue is in a knot." When no one pounced on that one by the count of five,

Pierre continued. "I'll begin by asking you something that will seem ludicrous. Edward, Jonathan, Joel: do you remember our camping trip last summer?"

"Say what?" asked Joel.

"Camping?" asked Arthur, turning in his chair. "You never told me."

"Pierre's kidding," said Jonathan.

"I can't imagine us doing something like that," said Edward.

"It's not exactly our style," said Jonathan.

A troubled silence descended upon the Lads.

"I repeat," said Pierre, removing his monocle and polishing it against his vest. "What do you remember about camping last summer?"

"Are you saying we *did?*" asked Jonathan incredulously. "You mean, like in a *tent?*"

"Funny thing," said Joel. "While we were decorating the tree I kept daydreaming about pine trees and sailing on a lake— something I've never done. But that's not what you asked."

"I'm thinking of rain," said Edward with a touch of sarcasm. "But of course it's raining right now. You said last summer? No, I don't think so."

"This is all news to me, Pierre," said Arthur. "I, for one, don't know what you're talking about."

They fell silent again.

"For what it's worth," said Father Baptist, "I seem to remember that you all went to Spirit Lake."

"You do?" demanded the Lads severally. "We did?"

"Frankly, I hardly noticed," said Father. "It was a hectic time around here—the fallout from the murders in June. Between the incessant trips to the Chancery, harried police reports, hours of haggling in the DA's office, reporters hanging around, Monsignor Havermeyer setting up his RV in the back parking lot—"

"Where is he, by the way?" asked Joel.

"Studying his rubrics for the Midnight Mass," said Father. "I don't think he was invited to this meeting."

"He wasn't," said Pierre. "I hope he'll understand."

"What I remember, *Monsieur* Bontemps," said Kahlúa, her voice taking on a stern, officious tone, "is that you never turned in the story I assigned you."

"What story?" asked Edward.

Kahlúa snorted. "I went to a lot of time and trouble to arrange for all of you—"

"*All* of us?" coughed Arthur.

"Madam Hummingbird," pled Pierre. "I know I let you down—"

"Now *there's* an understatement," she huffed. "I can't imagine why I've trusted you since."

"Because I begged you to," he insisted. "There was a reason. I told you I would explain at the appropriate time. It has come. I don't think you'll be disappointed."

"Well," said Millie, licking her lips after a noisy sip of mead. "We're all waiting."

"Yes, you are," said Pierre. "Believe me, this is much harder than I'd imagined. I've never had trouble starting a story, but this is different. Ah, at the risk of repeating myself: how to begin?"

"Sometimes it's best to just get on with it," said I with a note of literary authority. "You can always go back and fix up the beginning later. At least, that's been my experience."

"Spoken like a true writer, which you are," said Pierre. "Okay, I'll plunge in. I'll leave it to Mister Feeney to clean up my presentation after the fact. He might want to change the names to protect the ignorant. Mister Feeney, would you kindly douse the houselights?"

"Certainly," I said, struggling to turn in my chair. The seemingly simple task met resistance from my arthritic joints. "Hang on a second. It's just—"

"Oh, here," snarled Millie, lurching to her feet and swatting the switch. As she settled back down the room was plunged into the wavering, flickering ambiance of the Christmas tree lights, bobbing candles, and crackling flames. Orange and yellow predominated, but green and red and blue had their say as well.

"Very well." Pierre gave the hem of his vest a straightening tug. "Reverend Father, Ladies and Gentlemen, and of course

Martin: To put it succinctly, I know something you don't know—or rather, I remember something that you who were involved have forgotten. It is my task this evening to rekindle your memories. What I have to tell you is so fantastic, I know you won't believe me."

"Might it have something to do with that plaque?" I asked, pointing to the frame on the mantel.

"Very good, Martin," said Pierre, taking it up and wiping the glass with his sleeve. "We have Joel to thank for inking this one. I shall read it to you:

> And thorns and nettles shall grow up in its houses, and the thistle in the fortresses thereof: and it shall be the habitation of dragons, and the pasture of ostriches.
> And demons and monsters shall meet, and the hairy ones shall cry out one to another, there hath the lamia lain down, and found rest for herself.
> —Isaias XXXIV:13-14

"How sweetly seasonal," I whispered with a shiver. "Eggnog, anyone?"

"That comes later," said Millie. "When the mead is finished."

"Lamia?" asked Jonathan. "What's that?"

"A bloodsucking shape-shifting witch," said Father thoughtfully. "From Greek and Roman mythology."

"And just what does that have to do with our supposed camping trip?" asked Edward, a mite flustered.

"Quite a bit," said Pierre. "You all know me, you know my heart. I have sworn never to lie, as have you, in the service of our knightly cause. Yet the account of the events at Spirit Lake—Gadzooks!—it would strain our fellowship beyond the limit to expect you to accept the things I have to tell you without proof. Therefore, I am going to let you remind yourselves."

With that he produced a large metal key from his vest pocket. He turned and inserted it into the lock on the antique wooden box.

"We were wondering what you had in there," said Edward.

"I have spent the last four months laboring at a task I deeply abhor," said Pierre, turning the key with a loud click. "A function I loathe being performed upon me and my efforts, I had to perpetrate upon you and yours."

"And what's that?" asked Beth.

"I have been editing your diaries," answered Pierre, raising the lid, "the accounts you all wrote of your experiences in the mountains. Not crossing anything out, you understand, but rather extracting pages and assembling them in such a way so as to produce a cohesive, collective story."

"Our *what?!*" exclaimed the Lads disharmoniously.

"Yours, too, Beth," said Pierre, dipping his hands a couple of inches within the chest and producing a double-handful of stiff off-white pages. Some slipped through his grip and settled back inside. What he held up looked like a manuscript, or part of one. Unlike what I produce in the wee hours on my trusty Underwood, the writing was executed in longhand, and the paper didn't appear to be cheap onionskin but costly vellum. If the stack was as deep as the chest, it was an imposing document indeed. "You were there," said Pierre, looking pointedly at Beth.

"At Spirit Lake?" she gasped.

"She was not," insisted Arthur.

"As were you," asserted Pierre sternly.

"What the devil are you talking about?" blustered Arthur. "I don't remember writing—"

"I know," said Pierre. "But I assure you your account is here, too, mingled with the rest. Each and every one of you—Arthur, Edward, Jonathan, Joel, and you, too, Beth—you wrote your accounts on foolscap. You did so because you were about to forget. I alone was left to remember. It was understood that the story contained herein was so fantastic you would only believe your own words in your own handwriting."

"I'm sorry, Pierre," said Beth, "but you're not making sense. I didn't go on any camping trip with you guys."

"No, you didn't," agreed Pierre. "Not precisely. Nor did Arthur, because he came up with you the following day. You and your brother joined us at Wolfram Lodge to share in our adventure. If you will be patient and bear with me, all will become clear."

"This is weird," said Jonathan.

"Beyond weird," said Edward.

"I didn't have anything to do with any of this," said Millie.

"Not directly," said Pierre. "But I know better than to ask you to leave."

"Darn right," she growled.

"At the time you were directed to write your recollections," said Pierre, "it was suggested—"

"Who directed—?" asked Edward.

"Who suggested—?" asked Jonathan.

"Please," said Pierre. "Bear with me. All will be revealed in good time. What I started to say is that it was suggested that each of you set down your recollections as fully and descriptively as possible, writing in the mood of the moment in which events occurred, rather than from your perspective and feelings when all was done—this, in order to facilitate the rekindling of your memories. That being said, it was I who proposed that you approach it as though you were writing a novel, concentrating on dialogue as much as, if not more than, narrative. It was my sense, my hope, that some day all your efforts would be gathered into a book, a grand Tumblar adventure, if you will—not necessarily for publication in the public sector: more likely to remain within our confidential archives. This you all did, and admirably. The fact is I'm proud of you, each and every one."

"Any thoughts?" I whispered out of the side of my mouth to Father.

"Many," he said with an inscrutable nod. "More than you can imagine."

"Care to share?"

"Later. For now, let's give Pierre his head. I'm curious to see where this is going."

"As I said," continued Pierre, "I have edited your memoirs. I realize this rings of Bram Stoker, the process by which he presented his story of *Dracula:* in segments penned by the characters themselves. Naturally, with so many points of view expressed by such intelligent observers, some details vary or even contradict, but overall I would say we have a complete and compelling account." He gently returned the pages into the box, leaving it open. Fortifying his larynx with a draught of Millie's heady mead, he then peeled a few from the top and held them in unsteady hands. "If you please, everyone, I shall begin."

GARDENING TIPS: With their permission and the

help of Kahlu/a Hummingbird, I spent most of

the days between Christmas and Easter inte-

grating and collating the following accounts

as extracted by Pierre Bontemps from the dia-

ries of my Friends and fellow Knights--and the

sister of one thereof--in addition to record-

ing my own narrative betwixt. Miss Humming-

bird suggested the use of different fonts to

represent each of the assorted narrators

("Chalkboard" for Arthur, "Harrington bold"

for Pierre, italicized "Papyrus" for Jonathan,

etc.), but we both complained of eyestrain

when we perused the results. So this idea was

relegated to authors' titles only. Hence eve-

rything else is presented in the "Times" font

except for my Gardening Tips, which are ren-

dered in "Courier." (By the way, as you

probably noticed, my typewriter can't produce

an acute accent; hence my resorting to the use

of the slash key after accented vowels, as in
"Kahlu/a Hummingbird," above.)

For reasons of realism and lacking any competence as an editor whatsoever, I made no attempt to correct misguided grammatical con-
structions, poor word choices, dangling parti-
ciples and prepositions, odd capitalizations
(everyone always capitalized "Hell," for instance) or the absence thereof, or run-on sentences. For the purpose of clarity and the
prevention of headaches, I did standardize the
spelling of unfamiliar names and places. As
per Arthur's insistence (see Chapter 24) I
made sure that "magick" and "magickal" in the
ceremonial or classical sense are always
spelled with a "k." To those who might question whether young men these days employ the
vocabulary these gentlemen do in their ordi-
nary speech--well, they do. What follows is a
truthful retelling of what was said and what
was read that cold, wet, stormy Christmas Eve.

                                      --M.F.

N.B.: As in my previous chronicling efforts, the names of people and places, historic as well as contemporary, from "Sheriff Brumus" to "Father John Baptist," from "Claw Junction" to the "Mythical City of Los Angeles," have been changed to protect the impertinent. For example, Averoigne is a French province in Clark Ashton Smith's stories and nowhere else --till now. Who was it who said, "Confusion is the guardian of truth"?

P.N.B.: I accede to temptation by quoting Evelyn Waugh's warning at the onset of The Loved One: "As I have said, this is a nightmare and in parts, perhaps, somewhat gruesome. The squeamish should return their copies to the library or the bookstore unread."*

∞§[†]§∞

---

* To those enthusiastic readers who, in their haste to plunge into the story, did not bother to read the Author's Note, I strongly advise them to do so now.　　　　　　　　　　　—The Author.

∞§†§∞

3. The Hookeroo Is In, Is It?

∞§[Pi℮rr℮]§∞

AN UNEXPECTED ASSIGNMENT
BY
PIERRE BONTEMPS

PIERRE BONTEMPS HERE, writing these words on 15 August, the Feast of Our Lady's Glorious Assumption, to my faithful friends and companions: Arthur von Derschmidt, Edward Strypes Wyndham, Jonathan Clubb, Joel Maruppa, and last, but not the least bit least, Beth von Derschmidt. What an adventure we've shared, but alas, you have all forgotten. I wonder how that will be for you: a gaping hole in your memory slowly receding into the roiling, murky mist of the past. It is unnerving for me, not to mention intensely isolating, to think that you have all forgotten the events at Wolfram Lodge. My hope is that one day, come December, shortly after the Winter Solstice as prescribed and agreed—dare I hope for Christmas Eve?—I will be reading this journal to you all in a comfortable setting, rekindling your synapses, drinks in hand. How I will keep my part of the bargain in the meantime, moving in your midst while knowing what you do not, I can't imagine. I pray that this account, in combination with your own journals, will produce the desired effect. All that being said, I shall proceed.

For all intents and purposes, it began when the eminently flappable Kahlúa Hummingbird, my vibrantly endowed and appareled editrix, buzzed me into her office at the *L. A. Artsy*. It was Wednesday, the 12th of July, the Feast of St. Veronica of the Veil.

"What took you?" she demanded, throttling someone's double-spaced, laser-printed submission with her bare hands as she seated herself behind her desk. The victim wasn't mine: I print my toil and sweat exclusively on yellow paper. That way the streaks and slashes of her wicked blue pencil turn a soothing shade of green on the page. "I was looking for a place to hide," I answered. "Realizing the futility of the endeavor—have you considered moving to a larger workspace with more cubicles and closets? No, never mind—I poured myself a cup of coffee, checked my e-mail, fed my half-eaten doughnut to the pigeons on the window ledge, then came directly."

"Stuff it and sit," said she, dropping the crumpled cellulose corpse unceremoniously into the wastebasket. Then she snatched up a stapled gaggle of—uh-oh!—*yellow* pages from the corner of her desk. "I said park it," she barked as she reviewed the mincemeat she had made of my sweat and toil. It's her way—

∞§[Martin]§∞

"Like heck!" interjected Kahlúa, albeit a bit late. "Imminently *what*—?"

"Eminently," whispered Beth.

"Shhhhhhh!" shushed Millie, taking up an unclaimed mug.

∞§[Pierre]§∞

—when she's riled. Zounds! Was she!

"Pierre," she said as I dutifully complied. "I've been going over the third installment of your account of the Big Kablooey at the Del Agua Mission."

"Zomtink vrong, Mein Edi-hrer?" I asked innocently, albeit pseudo-Germanically. "Zhurely you haven't run out of der blue penzils."

"Something's missing," she replied, tapping my labors ponderously with a hooked fingernail. "You were supposed to interview that priest friend of yours, the cop-turned-priest. Did you?"

"Of course," I said with a wave of my hand, thus restoring my customary identity.

"You could've fooled me," she said with a wilting glare. "Why are you protecting him?"

I shrugged vaguely. "My dear Bossess, without whom I wouldn't have money enough to fill my pipe with Borkum Riff, I don't know what you mean."

"Either he was unresponsive when you interviewed him or you left things out," she said, drawing her talon slowly down the page, making a creepy scratching sound as she did so. She looked up at me and said, "Now Sweetie, Bwana Boy, Mighty Pen: you know I hired you because of the zany article you sent me regarding the debacle at St. Barbara's Chapel last month. You obviously had an inside track. Now you're a *bona fide* reporter. This is not the time to derail."

"Reporter?" I retorted, indicating myself. "I thought I was a film and fashion critic, dumpster scrutinizer, and urban legend accelerator."

"Whatever," she sighed impatiently. "I expect you to use any and all contacts—"

"Madam Hummingbird," I countered, clearing my throat. "Kahlúa, my personal La Niña: I told you, when you took me on, that my first loyalty is to the Church."

"Father Baptist is not the Church," she huffed. "If anything, he's on the fringe."

"There you're wrong, K. H.," I insisted. "It's the hierarchy that has flown the coop. Slap-Happy Bappy is dead center. As such, he is my confessor, my spiritual director, and my friend. He expects and deserves my discretion. If he tells me not to reveal certain things, I will not cross him. The article you're clawing so severely is my firsthand account. I was there. That should be enough." I rose defiantly to my feet. "If it isn't, I'll gladly clean out my desk on my way out."

"Sit down," she said sternly. "I said sit!"

"I'm not a dog," I said, settling on my tail.

"That's a matter of perception." She tossed my article onto her desk disgustedly, then she leaned forward on her elbows. Not a good sign. "Okay, Honeycheeks, I'm a Cathoholic myself, and Hell is a place I'd rather avoid, so I'll let that one slide. I've got something better. Something particularly suited to your talents and predilections."

"Do tell," I said blithely. "You want me to review a new bar?"

"No."

"A winery?"

"Nope."

"A silent movie star's funeral?"

"Close."

"You want me to revisit an *old* bar?"

"Naw, you're getting cold again."

"What, then?"

She paused for effect, smiled mysteriously, then in a low tone resonant with cryptic significance uttered, "A reenactment."

"A what?" I groaned, blinking incredulously. "Hold on. You don't mean one of those camps where people play soldier and pretend they're in the Civil War! I'd look ghastly in either uniform. I'd—"

She shook her head. "It's not the Civil War."

"Not the O. K. Corral!" I exclaimed, half rising.

"No," she said, signaling for her unruly puppy to stay put. "The theme isn't western."

"If you're thinking World War II, the answer is equally no," I protested. "I absolutely will not don a Nazi uniform. Binkie Barnes at the sports desk would probably jump at the chance to sport a swastika, but not me."

"You're probably right about her," said Kahlúa, smiling at the thought, "but you're wrong about the premise. My, but you're jumpy today." With that she opened her top drawer and produced a glossy, folded brochure which she tossed across her blotter at me. "How's about a famous unsolved homicide?"

"Hello," I said, leaning forward in my chair. "Now you're talking. Which famous homicide?"

"Spirit Lake," she said triumphantly. "The Cassandra Ouspen-skaya murder."

"The who?" I asked, rolling my eyes. "I heard you say fa-mous."

"It was at the time."

"Uh-huh," I mumbled. "When was that?"

After pausing for dramatic effect, she answered with an air of great moment, "1896."

"Hmmm," I hummed doubtfully.

"It involved a séance," she whispered mysteriously.

"Oh," I responded with a dismissive subsidence of my shoul-ders.

"A séance held at the mountain lodge of Bartholomew W. Piaget," she persisted, spelling out his last name. She pro-nounced it a second time for my benefit with a little *esprit de Paris:* Pyah-*zhay.* "The famous oil tycoon."

"There's that F-word again," I complained. "Preceded by 'the.'"

"The W was for Wolfram," she continued. "Spiritualism was making a big splash in Southern California."

"What do you mean 'was'?" I quipped.

"Focus, Pierre. Focus," she said, tapping her temple by way of authoritative example. "You've heard of the town of Summer-land up the coast between here and Santa Barbara?"

"Sure," I said, leaning back in my chair. "The Lads and I stopped there once. We had lunch in a big old Victorian house-turned-restaurant. The waitress told us it was haunted."

"No surprise there, Typo Man," she said. "Listen: Summer-land began as a spiritualist colony in 1889. Lots of rich psychics and mystics went flitting up there on their flying carpets to build themselves a village where they could cast their runes and pester dead relatives in peace."

"Sounds charming," I said, gulping back a yawn.

"Its heyday was cut short a few years later," she continued, her syllables laced with conspiratorial sibilance, "when some dis-harmonious earthbound geologist discovered oil right under their levitating footsies. Apparently the hundreds of derricks that sprung up overnight along the beaches were not conducive to ethereal contact."

"I should think they'd make nifty antennae," I said with a wink. "Draw in great reception."

"Keep it up, Sweetie," she warned mischievously. "Bartholomew Piaget was one helluva wizard—financial, not magickal. He brokered most of the land deals that created Summerland, all the while keepin' the liddo ol' mineral rights for his sneaky liddo self. Meanwhile, above ground, property values plummeted. A lot of mediums and trance-channelers rightly blamed him for wrecking their little Shangri-La."

"One wonders why they didn't see it coming in their crystal balls," said I, feeling another whopper of a yawn coming on.

"My very thought, Pierre-*zee*-boy," she said with a smirk. "Sorry to be keepin' you from your beauty sleep, but about that time, gold was discovered in them thar bumps on the map we flatlanders call the San Gabriel Mountains, north of our fair city. Resort towns like Big Bear and Arrowhead got their start through the luck of prospectors. Well, having made a wreck of the coastline, Piaget turned his pecuniary turrets toward them thar hills and started blastin' away—well, tunnelin' actually, if you don't mind me switching metaphors. Would you believe? At one time there were eighty-seven producing mines on properties he purchased at elevations above five thousand feet."

"One can only imagine his holdings below four thousand feet," said I, "as well as the enemies he was making in both ethereal planes. Ah well, 'As above, so below,' as our Wiccan subscribers would say."

"Precisely, Pierre," she agreed. "Precisely. This will interest them, even if it bores you to tears."

"To drink, Madam Editrix," I said, raising an invisible glass. "To drink, perchance to drown."

"Hold on to that thought, my *blasé protégé*." She rocked back in her squeaky chair and flashed me one of her it's-a-comin' smiles. "Piaget was shrewd down to his toenails. Just before the gold ran out, he sold all his mines—all but one, and a couple of test holes. He and his missus of nineteen years retired to a mansion he'd been building way up in the mountains on an island at the south end of Spirit Lake—which he named, by the way, since he owned it—it, the surrounding valley, and several thousand acres of timberland all around. The one mine he didn't liquidate was on that property. He boarded it up and turned his attention toward completing his mansion. He called their humongous home Wolfram Lodge. There's a picture of it on the front of that brochure, and a map inside. You might at least pick it up and pretend to be interested."

"Right, sure," I complied without enthusiasm. "Like this?"

"Don't strain yourself, Honey," she said. "Now listen: Gabrielle Piaget, that missus I just mentioned, was something of a psychic herself. It was she who inadvertently got her rich, unspiritual hubby interested in Summerland in the first place. Although it is unclear how much she influenced his business dealings, she certainly held his attention in every other way. It is said that he built Wolfram Lodge where she wanted it, and largely the way she wanted it."

"Mm-hm," I commented.

"Things took a turn a year or so after its completion. She went sailing by her lonesome one bright summer day when a freak thunderstorm came rollin' in. The boat was found deserted, the mast burnt and twisted—struck by lightning, so the local sheriff figured. Her body washed up two days later on the north shore—the farthest point from the lodge."

"Where was Mr. Piaget when this happened?" I felt obliged to ask.

"Catching up on correspondence in his library with his personal secretary," she replied, slowing her tempo a beat above imperceptibly. "She resided at the lodge along with their full-time butler and a cook. There was also a household staff of six that did not sleep on the premises, but that is neither here nor there. There was no suggestion of foul play, if that's what you're thinkin'. The coroner's inquest ruled it accidental—death by misadventure. A mean-spirited editorial in one of the Summerland rags called it 'cosmic retribution.' Apparently Mr. Piaget thought so, too, because from then on his interests turned to the occult."

"Really," I said, adjusting my bowtie.

"Very," she said, fingering her pearls. "His wife's death hit him right in the *solar plexus*, so to speak. He became obsessed with the idea of contacting her. He started inviting prominent mediums, theosophists, mystics—many of whom he had bilked along the way—up to his mountain retreat. The usual stay was a week, during which they conducted séances and performed ectoplasmic experiments under his watchful eye. He was desperate, but he was proud, and he was nobody's fool. He despised phonies, whom he treated mercilessly if he caught them pulling strings under the table."

"He must have sent a lot of them packing then," I said, crossing my legs.

"That he did," she chuckled. "Many reputations were broken to bits at Spirit Lake."

"Just like property in Summerland," I observed.

"An interesting parallel," she agreed. "He persisted, and they kept coming. Contacting his wife remained his goal."

"It helps to have a goal," said I, nodding sagaciously.

"Enterrrrrr," said Kahlúa, mimicking a drum roll by flapping her hands on the blotter and winding up with a smack at the table lamp for a crash cymbal. You'd have had to have been there. "Madam Cassandra Ouspenskaya. Be she real—or be she just good—she got Mr. Piaget's attention. Convinced him that she could indeed contact his wife."

"Cassandra Oozie-whatzit?" I asked.

"Ouspenskaya," she said, evenly spacing the syllables for my edification. "One dark and stormy night—"

"Ah, there's an opener for you," I jibed.

"Nonetheless," continued my boss dramatically, "on one murky night during another ferocious summer thunderstorm in 1896—it was July 31st, to be exact—Madam Ouspenskaya conducted the fateful séance."

"Thunderstorms are big at Spirit Lake," I observed.

"An even better opening line, my boy," she said with an encouraging, albeit mischievous nod. "That's the spirit. There were six men present, including Mr. Piaget, and three women including Cassandra Ouspenskaya. The brochure is heavy on hype, so I phoned a friend in the 'morgue' at the *Times*. He dug up an old, old article that confirms most of it. Apparently, during the festivities, the ill-fated Cassandra did a Tarot reading for Mr. Piaget. The last card dealt was Death. Everyone 'round the table assumed he was a goner—and he soon was—but it was the medium who was found brutally murdered in the garden the following morning."

"The Death card, eh?" I said guardedly. "Sounds ominous, although it's my understanding that those in the know don't necessarily consider the Death card a predictor of doom, but rather of change or upheaval."

"Showoff," she said with a grin.

"Always," I agreed, likewise grinning. "Actually I got that tidbit from Binkie Barnes at the communal water cooler."

"Whatever," she shrugged. "It certainly meant doom for Madam Ouspenskaya."

"So the seer died instead of the seeker," I said, rubbing my chin.

"Right," said she, imitating me.

"But," I said after a moment's consideration, "you said he was a goner, too."

"In a sense," she nodded. "Madam Ouspenskaya's body was discovered on a Saturday morning, but she was killed the night before. Bartholomew disappeared sometime Sunday evening, and Arianna Marigold, the secretary, vanished between, likely Saturday afternoon."

"I'd call that a spot of change with a dash of upheaval," I admitted. "So the medium was murdered, the secretary skipped town, and Mr. Piaget chased after her?"

"So it might have seemed," she granted. "But the guests who had attended the séance assured the police that Miss Marigold and Mr. Piaget never left the lodge."

I blinked twice. "Not even out the backdoor?"

She fluttered her eyelashes. "If they did, they left no trace and were never heard from again."

"Fine host," I harrumphed, "leaving his guests to clean up and go home."

"Not right away, Wordy Wonder. The county sheriff insisted that they remain at the lodge while he and his deputies carried out their investigation. But strangely, come Tuesday morning, the otherwise dependable cook failed to serve breakfast on time. Her shredded, bloodied nightgown was discovered in her bedroom shortly thereafter."

"The nightgown," I noted, "but not the cook herself."

"Her name was Natalie Currant," said Kahlúa, checking her notes. "The window was shattered from the outside. There was blood on the floor, blood on the broken glass, but that was before blood-typing analysis, so whose blood was never determined. Her body was never found."

"Missing bodies, like thunderstorms," I mused. "I suppose the authorities never let the guests go home. They became permanent residents—ghosts, in other words."

"Oh, they all were allowed to leave," she said. "Eventually. First they were moved to a hotel in a nearby town for a few days."

"Okay," I said, "You've set me up, so I'll do the polite thing and ask: was anyone ever charged with the murder?"

"No," she said with a shake of her head. "The butler was detained for a few days, probably for appearances, then released. The incident caused quite a stir. Detectives from Los Angeles went up there to assist—the local sheriff was clearly out of his element—but they never did figure out what happened."

"Okay," I sighed. "I admit I'm intrigued. So what's this about a reenactment?"

"I'm getting there, O Great Swami," she said, thoroughly enjoying herself. "The Piaget estate was tied up in legal red tape by squabblin' relatives for decades while Wolfram Lodge fell into disrepair. The mansion and surrounding property changed sticky hands several times, but the remote location and the sheer immensity of the building and grounds made restoration and upkeep one big money hole. I understand the Forest Service considered turning it into a preserve or something, but that fell through. Then, a few years ago, this retired clinical psychologist, name of Mortimer Horehound, acquired the estate. He must have had one helluva lucrative practice and a stargazing stockbroker, because he purchased the whole kit and caboodle, refur-

bished the lodge, and for whatever reason, started staging reenactments eight times a year."

I wrinkled my brow. "Reenactments of—?"

"The séance," she almost cooed, "the murder, the disappearances."

"Ah-ha," I replied, disentangling my legs.

"The hookeroo is in, is it?" she smiled, suppressing the impulse to hug herself. "I thought so. Through one of my contacts
I learned that the next scheduled party—a group from the Upland
Paranormal Research Society—had to cancel. Not sure why. So
the slot being open, I called Dr. Horehound myself. Turns out he
subscribes to our fair rag and welcomed the opportunity, especially when I informed him of your own occult expertise."

"My what?" I protested, gripping the arms of my chair.

"The Farnsworth Case has caused a paranormal feeding frenzy,
or didn't you know?" she said sweetly. "You and your Tumbler
friends—right, Tum-*blar*, got it—were smack dab in the middle
of it. This piqued his interest. You're not professional mediums,
but you have psychic experience."

"That's overreaching a bit," I insisted.

"The *Artsy* crawls on an overreaching belly, my dear Pierre."

"You're not joking, my dear editrix."

"Never about a story," she assured me. "Dr. Horehound has
very strict requirements, although they can't always be met. I
think we can satisfy him. He prefers there to be five male guests
and one female—he and two ladies in his employ complete the
circle. Oh, and the guests must be formally attired and well-
read. Dr. Horehound is a consummate conversationalist. He
loves to interact with his guests."

"One female, you say?" I pointed to her. "So you're going
along?"

"No way," she said, swatting away the very notion. "I have a
paper to run. We'll have to find a willing damsel."

"Not Binkie Barnes!" I recoiled.

"No, not Binkie Barnes," she laughed. "We need someone
who is ... definitely *not* Binkie Barnes."

"Whew!" I sighed, wiping my forehead. "I was sweating there
for a nanosecond."

"We should all experience new things, Pierre."

"Ha ha ha," I replied in a dull monotone. Then I brightened. "You say 'guests.' Does that mean participation is free?"

"Uh, no," she cringed. "'Guests' is a euphemism. The cost—well, I'll not go into that." She heaved a Joan Crawford sigh. "I'll just have to work *my* kind of magic. There are always failed actors and fallen pop stars who want their pathetic stories told."

"They'll pay you to interview them?" I gasped in overacted astonishment. "So much for journalistic integrity."

"Remember the overreaching belly," she replied with an equally overplayed wink.

"Crawling as we speak," I concurred with a double-blink.

"You said it," she agreed. "Now: the participants must be there on the thirty-first of July—that will be a Monday—by nine in the morning. Most guests choose to arrive the day before since it's a long, winding drive up there. They are expected to stay at the lodge until Friday, August fourth. The U.P.R.S. group had planned to stay from Sunday to Saturday. Unfortunately, I don't think I'll be able to cover the first and last days. Perhaps you and your friends could contribute the cost of two nights' lodgings."

"Hold on, hold on." This was all coming rather fast. I rubbed my forehead for effect. "A whole workweek? Plus two nights' lodgings each at a swanky mountain lodge? I might be able to swing it if I lay off booze from now till then, but my friends—no, I can't ask that of them."

"I can," she said. "I'll talk to their employers. There are always inducements for cooperation."

"You sound like a Mafia hit man," I observed reservedly.

"Nothing so coarse," she retorted. "Every employer needs breaks on business supplies, arrangements for office parties, entertainment, vacation packages. I've got some connections in those areas. And free advertising goes a long way."

"In the *Artsy?*" I moaned skeptically.

"Don't be coy," she insisted, narrowing her eyes. "You know that when Kahlúa wants something, she gets it. This, I want."

"Hmmm," was all I could think to say at the moment. "Hmmm."

"As for the first and last days, this might be fun," she said. "There's an abandoned campground on the northwest shore of the lake. It's part of the Piaget estate. Perhaps you could all rough it the first night there. Maybe the last, too."

"Rough it?" I said incredulously. "I admit I was an Eagle Scout, but that was eons ago."

"Just think of it, Pierre," she said dreamily. "A séance, murder, and three disappearances more than a century old. There are bound to be ghosts in the attic and skeletons in the closets. This could put you on the map as an investigative reporter. You've got a couple of weeks to prepare, you and your pals. I'll get you access to the morgue files at the *Times*. You told me your friend Arthur is a connoisseur of old books. I'd be surprised if he didn't have the collected works of Montague Summers and Eliphas Lévi."

"If they wrote bartending guides, he surely does," I said jokingly.

"Something like that," she agreed amusedly.

"Speaking of Arthur," I said, tugging thoughtfully on my earlobe, "it occurs to me that he's expecting a visit from his sister, Beth, about that time."

"An excellent idea," said Kahlúa.

"No, wait," I protested. "Hold on. She's coming out from Cleveland for a *rest*. She's got a condition. Narcolepsy, I think."

"Well, that's perfect!" she declared with a note of finality. "Dr. Horehound is a clinical psychologist. He can keep an eye on her. Besides, what could be more restful than a pristine mountain lodge, complete with a private lake?"

"Not to mention a séance, three disappearances, and an unsolved murder," I said, frowning uncertainly.

"Pure R & R," said she as I heaved myself from my chair. "You won't know until you ask her."

"Arthur first, I should think," I said, pausing in the doorway. "When do you need to know, O Unswerving Taskmistress?"

"Yesterday, my wayworn urban legend accelerator," said my editrix, beaming like a satiated tigress. "And Pierre, relax. It's a done deal. I can feel it."

∞§[Martin]§∞

Pierre paused. He seemed to be summoning the courage to look at us—most of all Kahlúa Hummingbird, who did not look pleased.

"I don't know about the rest of you," said Arthur, shifting uncomfortably in his uncomfortable kitchen chair. "I don't remember anything about this."

"Me neither," said Edward. "Pierre, this isn't some sort of Bontempsian prank, is it? A ghost story for a cold, wet Christmas Eve, perhaps?"

"If it is," said Pierre, "then my editrix is an accomplice. Ask her."

A log shifted in the fireplace as all eyes turned to Kahlúa.

"It was five months ago," she said measuredly after fiddling with her right earring for half a dozen heartbeats. She heaved her shoulders and added, "With minor qualifications, I'll say that's pretty much how our conversation went."

"You really call him Mighty Pen?" sniggered Jonathan.

"What do you think?" I whispered to Father.

He left me hanging as he dug around in his cassock and came up with his burl pipe. "All I know," he answered finally, stuffing leathery tendrils of tobacco into the bowl, "is that I vaguely recall the Lads going on a camping trip in the mountains. As for Beth, though Arthur certainly spoke affectionately of his sister many a time, I did not have the pleasure of meeting her until early November."

"Perhaps this will help," said Pierre, setting down his pages and unfolding a glossy brochure. "Here's the advertisement for the event." He handed it to Edward.

"I say, this looks interesting," said Master Wyndham, eyeing the brochure. "It doesn't ring any bells, though."

"But if you were to propose such an outing," said Jonathan, nimbly slipping the brochure from Edward's grasp, "I think I'd want to give it a go. A week off, though, that's a kicker."

"I got it for you," bragged Kahlúa. "I arranged it for all of you."

"You satiated lioness, you," chided Millie.

"Tigress, Honey," said Kahlúa with a feline stretch. "Eminently flappable, perhaps, but a tigress nonetheless."

"Here, Joel," said Jonathan, passing the brochure. "What do you think?"

"I think it sounds fishy," said Joel, accepting the evidence gingerly. "I think I'd have talked it over with Father Baptist before committing to something so ... so questionable."

"Did we, Father?" asked Jonathan. "Consult you?"

"I can't say for sure," said Father. "You men are constantly plying me with all sorts of questions and proposals. I remember shooing you fellows out of here a number of times last summer. Things, as I said, were crazy. I had a lot on my plate."

"That's it," said Kahlúa as the document was handed to her for inspection. "That's the brochure I gave you last July, Pierre. I jotted Dr. Horehound's private number in the upper right corner. See?"

"The strings she pulled," commented Pierre melodramatically.

"Private?" asked Jonathan. "As opposed to a business number?"

"As opposed to none," said Kahlúa. "There's just an address on that leaflet. All reservations are transacted by mail."

"That's odd," said Edward.

"He wasn't pleased that I had finagled his number," said she, "but he relented because that group from Upland had cancelled and there was no one on the waiting list for that date."

"As a matter of fact," said Millie as the brochure passed through her hands, "I think they did, Father. Consult you, I mean. I remember Joel and Pierre trying to pin you down over breakfast in the kitchen. I think they were waving this at you, asking for your advice. I was busy making 'Surprise des Anges,' as I recall. You had the phone in one hand—His Nibs the Cardinal, I think—and a complaint from the Health Department about Monsignor Havermeyer's camper in the other. You were 'up's to your's ears in controverseries,' as my friend Mrs. Magillicuddy would say."

"Do you remember what I told them?" asked Father, striking a match and sucking the flame into the bowl of his pipe.

"No," said Millie. "I think you chased them out with a spatula. Or maybe that was me."

"Was I there?" I asked nervously.

"You were visiting that murdering witch in the hoosegow," she said sternly.

"Oh," I said, shrinking into my chair. "Oh, right. Could be. Then it would have been a Thursday."

"Funny," said Beth, turning sideways prettily in her chair. "I remember coming to Los Angeles in late July. It was a Sunday. I had to go to early Mass back in Ohio before catching the shuttle to the airport. Arthur had managed to take a few days off. He was going to take me on a tour of the Missions."

"Did he?" asked Edward.

"Did you?" asked Jonathan.

Arthur started to say something, then shrugged.

"That's what's funny," said Beth. "My mind's a blank. I know I don't have any photos of the Missions in my scrapbook back home, but that's distinctly what we were planning to see. And another thing: I don't remember meeting you guys until I came out here again in November."

"And that is something we won't ever forget," said Jonathan. "But this—"

"So what's next?" asked Joel. "Pierre, what happened after that?"

Pierre picked up his pages again, looked at us all tentatively, cleared his throat nervously, and continued.

∞§[Pɪɛʀʀɛ]§∞

The next two weeks were hectic indeed. To my utter amazement, my editrix came through as promised. All the Lads with the exception of Joel, who was making repairs in the rectory in exchange for room and board, were granted permission by their employers to take the impending week off. Joel hemmed and hawed for a time, then simply decided he wouldn't be missed at St. Philomena's, and that was that. It was as if the gears had been engaged in a well-oiled machine. Last minute impedi-

ments, the bane of all planned vacations, did not appear. It was
as if the thing were meant to happen, moved along by an unseen
hand.

On the morning of July 30th, the Feast of St. Peter Chryso-
logus, all the Tumblars attended Mass and received Holy Communion at St. Philomena's. I remember us assembling on the
front steps afterwards to discuss last-minute details.

"So," I said. "Everything is in order. Joel, Edward, Jonathan
and I will go in Edward's van. We'll meet at his place at two
o'clock to load our things and hopefully be on our way by
three."

"Beth's plane arrives at 6:17 this evening at LAX," said Arthur. "We'll start out in Der-von-Derschmidt-Mobile at the
crack of dawn. Barring mechanical problems, we should be
there a little before nine. I checked with the Auto Club and
there's an all-night gas station at Claw Junction, about fifteen
miles shy of the lake. Also a 24-hour café. Edward, I suggest
you refuel there en route so you'll be gassed and ready to tear
down the mountain at a moment's notice if things go sour."

"That's a good idea," agreed Edward.

"I say, are there telephones at the lodge?" asked Jonathan.

"There must be," said I. "Madam Hummingbird has conversed
with Dr. Horehound, and it wasn't via crystal ball."

"What's his shtick, anyway?" asked Joel. "I mean, why does a
retired shrink stage notorious reenactments, do you suppose?"

"My guess," said I, "dittoed by my editrix, is that he's observing human behavior in an eerie setting. Probably working on a
book."

"Great shades of *The Haunting of Hill House*," said Arthur.

"It's a guess," I repeated, "but it fits."

"You say you know how to erect a tent?" asked Joel of me.

"I was an Eagle Scout," I assured him.

"Somehow that doesn't seem like you," said Jonathan. "Who
did you bribe?"

I shrugged in reply.

"Well," said Edward, "I rented a doozy of a tent from Sports
Chalet. It's got everything but hot and cold running water."

"I assume there are facilities at the campground," said Joel, looking very worried.

"Beats me," said I. "It's on private property, so maybe not. Maybe we'll have to boil water from the lake. Come on, Lads, don't look like that. Frodo and Samwise made it through Mordor with just their knapsacks."

"But they were used to such things," said Edward. "And it was a novel, besides."

"Whatever befalls us," said I, "it will be a Tumblar adventure."

"How did you talk us into this again?" asked Arthur.

"With finesse," said I. "Okay, Lads. Let's get going. See you at Edward's at two."

And with that, we parted company.

∞§[Martin]§∞

By this time the brochure had made its way to Father and me. We examined it together. I held in a sneeze as the smoke from his pipe zinged my nostrils.

"Stir any memories?" I asked.

"Maybe," he said. "I recall the notice from the Health Department. Monsignor Havermeyer had taken it upon himself to hire a plumber to connect the outflow from his camper directly into the city sewer line. It seemed like the logical thing to do, but there was some sort of regulation against it."

"How was that resolved?" asked Arthur.

"Beats me," said Father. "I think it turned out that he'd presided at the marriage of the superintendent's daughter or something. He made it go away. That was one of the few crises that was easily resolved around that time."

"Looks like a neat place," said I, eyeing the picture of the lodge. It was an imposing rustic building, a curious mixture of rough indigenous logs and refined imported Victorian architecture. There was a structure in the near right foreground that looked like a wooden bridge. Of course, the lodge was on an island not far from the shore. The lake in front and around be-

hind looked dark and serene, perhaps a little ominous. I turned
the brochure over and started reading the pitch:

> *What befell the spirit medium at Wolfram Lodge? Was
> she the victim of a ruthless murderer, or was she per-
> haps mauled by a wild beast? Come and relive the
> ghostly events of that fateful night ...*

"Uh-oh," I said aloud.

"What is it?" asked Father.

"Find something?" asked Jonathan.

"Well, yes, kind of," I said. "Pierre, you said Dr. Horehound
stages these reenactments eight times a year. The dates are here.
They strike a bell."

"In what way?" asked Arthur.

"The event you say you attended began on July 31st. The
other reenactments are slated for September 21st, October 31st,
December 21st, January 31st, March 21st, April 30th, and June
21st."

"Yes," said Kahlúa. "So?"

"You don't see the significance of those dates?" I asked.

"Let me see that," said Father, taking the brochure and examining it closely. "Good Heavens! September 21st and March
21st are the Autumnal and Spring Equinoxes. December 21st
and June 21st are the Winter and Summer Solstices. October
31st as you all should know—"

"Is Samhain," said Joel, his face darkening. I noticed he pronounced it correctly: *Saw*-win.

"May Eve," continued Father, "is called Beltane. January 31st
is known among the Wiccans and Druids as Imbolc. July 31st,
August Eve, they call Lughnasadh." Father pronounced that last
word: *Loo*-nah-sah.

"What are you saying?" asked Arthur, rising from his chair.

"Those dates are all Greater and Lesser Sabbats," said I. "I
recognize them from a Wiccan calendar Father and I found in
Starfire's witchery shop when we were working on the Farnsworth Case last June."

"It would seem that Dr. Horehound's interests are rooted in the occult," said Father. "That, or he has a flair for the dramatic—perhaps the bizarre."

"What did you get us into?" asked Joel accusingly, pointing to Pierre.

"Quite an adventure," said Pierre. "Shall we continue?"

Talk about getting the hook in but good!

∞§[†]§∞

∞§✝§∞

4. Failure May Be Your Thing!

∞§[Martin]§∞

PIERRE SET HIS INTRODUCTORY PAGES facedown on the kitchen chair beside the fireplace. Then, with the flair of a magician at a backyard party, he turned to the ornate wooden box, leaned close, and carefully peeled five, six, seven pages off the stack within. Straightening, he stood before us, looking from Arthur, to Jonathan, to Edward. The mumbles and chair squeaks died away.

"Enough of me," he said at last. "It's time to let you tell your own stories. Normally I would insist that ladies be first, but Beth doesn't enter the tale yet. Joel?"

Even from where I was sitting, I could tell Joel was uncomfortable with the idea. His shoulders subsided, his head tilted, and he made a little sound that imparted the message: "Why me?"

"Go ahead," said Edward and Jonathan, turning and beckoning to Joel.

"It seems we're all going to be taking our turn," said Arthur, slapping him on the knee.

"You may as well lead the way," said Beth.

"Joe-well, Joe-well, Joe-well," chanted Edward in a low whisper. It was taken up by the other Lads. "Joe-well! Joe-well! Joe-well!"

With a shrug and a moan of resignation, he rose to his feet.

"Yaaaay," whisper-cheered the Tumblars.

Joel inched up beside Pierre and turned to face us. The Christmas tree lights playing on his dark complexion gave him a strange, greenish hue. His muscular Slovakian jaw was clenched so tight it looked crooked. His deep-set eyes darted every which way to avoid looking at anyone dead on. He accepted his penance from Pierre with trepidation. "Sorry, fellows," he said, almost stammering. "Suddenly I feel ... I don't know, like maybe I don't ... want to ..."

"I imagined this wasn't going to be entirely easy," said Pierre. "I could read it for you, but I think it best that you do the honors."

"I believe Pierre is right, Joel," said Father, smoke billowing from his mouth. "You're among Friends."

Joel cleared his throat and looked down at the words in his own handwriting. His eyes went momentarily wide. He spun around to examine the writing in the frame on the mantelshelf. "This is weird," he said, returning his gaze to the pages in his hands. "This is definitely my scrawl, but I don't remember ever seeing this."

"Goose feathers," grumbled Mille, hefting herself onto her feet and waddling over to the pitcher on Father's desk. After replenishing her mug with a hefty splash of steaming mead, she returned to her chair, fluffed her apron, and lowered herself like a hen onto an egg-laden nest. "C'mon, we haven't got all night."

"She's right," said Pierre. "We need to be finished in time for Mass."

"Okay," said Joel. He rattled the pages and took a deep breath. "Here goes nothing."

$$\infty\S[\textit{JOEL}]\S\infty$$

(I CAN'T THINK OF A TITLE)
BY
JOEL MARUPPA

This is the last thing I want to do. I told Pierre I'm not a writer. That's *his* thing. *He* should be doing this. The others are smarter than me, so they don't mind. Me, I got C's in English Composition. All I can say is that I'll do my best. Like the sign taped to the cash register at Hal's Groceries said:

IF AT FIRST YOU DON'T SUCCEED, FAILURE MAY BE YOUR THING!

It didn't feel right leaving Fr. Baptist to go on a camping trip. Not that I was much help, at least with his problems. Grampa Josef and I had made some progress fixing up the front room upstairs, though there were still bare wires hanging from some of the fixtures. I didn't like leaving Grampa to fend for himself for a week. Millie gives him heartburn. I almost said no to the whole thing—

∞§[Martin]§∞

"Heartburn!" growled Millie. "I'll show him heartburn!"

"Shush now," whispered Kahlúa.

"Raids the refrigerator every night. Eats everything that isn't nailed down. Heartburn indeed."

"Shhh."

"The old goat."

"Um," mumbled Joel uneasily, backing up a few words.

∞§[*JOEL*]§∞

I almost said no to the whole thing. In fact, I *did* say no several times. But Pierre wouldn't listen. Neither would the others. Not wanting to be the missing tooth (as Grampa would say) I finally agreed. If I had known what was coming, I might have gone up with Arthur and Beth the next day. Camping by the lake was one big disaster if you ask me. If I'd known what was coming after that, well, never mind.

The four of us—me, Edward, Jonathan, and Pierre—left Edward's around three fifteen in the afternoon last Sunday. Wouldn't you know, I wound up in the back with Pierre, while Jonathan got to ride shotgun. Edward had taken the backmost seats out to make room for the gigantic collapsible tent. All the room between the middle seats was crammed with camping junk. My sleeping bag was between my feet. The lanterns and backpacks and other things knocked us at every turn, and boy, there were a lot of turns as Edward tore up the mountain. I got seasick halfway there and had to ask him to stop on a turnout so I could get out. When I didn't blow chunks after ten minutes, they made me get back inside and off we went again. The road got really steep after that. Me and my stomach were on our own! At some point Jonathan and Edward had an argument about whether to take Highway 38E or 153W. I think we ended up using 46N— I'm not sure. Pierre didn't let up singing the whole way. It would have been okay if it was something I knew, but it was all Irish drinking songs and Broadway show tunes. What I wouldn't have given for a little Crosby, Stills, and Nash—or Simon and Garfunkel. Them I know. But no-o-o-o-o-o-o!

∞§[Martin]§∞

Beth giggled at that one, and Kahlúa chortled aloud.

Joel stopped. He looked nervously at his companions. They weren't laughing. From where I sat I couldn't be sure, but I don't think they were smiling. Fidgeting, Joel looked to Pierre. Pierre replied with an encouraging grin. It wasn't so much an expression of knowing as of accepting.

I felt for Joel. I'd never realized my own propensity for whining until I read the opening chapter of my own first literary attempt aloud to Father. His smile then and Pierre's just now were unsettlingly similar.

"Do go on," said Arthur.

"But—" stammered Joel.

"It's all right," said Pierre. After all, this wasn't news to any of them.

"One for all," said Edward.

"And all for booze," agreed Jonathan.

"A lot of water has passed under the bridge since then," whispered Pierre so softly to Joel I almost didn't catch it. "Have no fear. You've grown a lot in the interim. We all have."

"Okay," said Joel with an uncertain shrug. "All right. Where was I?"

∞§[JOEL]§∞

We stopped for gas at a little town called Claw Junction. There was just a gas station, a sheriff's office, a little grocery store with dirty windows, a dumpy one-story motel with the VACANCY sign on, and Howler's Café. Oh, and a hole-in-the-wall bookstore called The Raven with the shades drawn and a CLOSED sign on the door (as if books were a big draw around there). We all jumped out to stretch our legs while Edward filled his tank with regular.

"Hey," I said, "that smells good." There's nothing like hamburgers grilling in the mountains, and the smoke was pouring out of the chimney at the restaurant. "Why don't we get a bite to eat here?"

"And waste all the ground meat and hotdogs in the ice chest?" scoffed Pierre.

"Where's your sense of adventure?" asked Edward.

"Did anyone remember to bring matches?" I asked.

No one had, so I went into Hal's Groceries to get some. I bought some candy bars while I was in there, just in case. Later, I was glad I did. While I was at it, I bought a pack of ciggies to fill the engraved silver-plated cigarette case that my father presented me last June when the murder charges against me were dropped. There was supposed to be some pretense of elegance at this reenactment, so I'd brought it along. I also purchased a medium grit Arkansas sharpening stone. Grampa Josef gave me a cool camping knife when I was twelve, and it hadn't been sharpened since I was thirteen. It also had a file, two screwdrivers, and a bottle opener. I figured it might come in handy on this silly camping trip. The store was poorly stocked with few items and only one brand of each. I felt sorry for the locals who didn't have other shopping options. The lady behind the counter was eating fried chicken on a paper plate. She didn't even bother to wipe her hands when she counted out my change. I rubbed the coins against my jeans before shoving them into my pocket. Yech!

When I came back out, there was a sheriff's car pulled up behind the van, and an officer wearing those intimidating mirror glasses was talking to the guys. Just then I realized I'd forgotten the matches and went back inside. They didn't have books, just boxes of the wooden kind. When I came back out again the cop was scratching his head.

"Where'd you say you're heading?" he was asking as I came up to them.

"Spirit Lake," said Pierre.

"Really," said the sheriff. He sounded doubtful. "That's private property. What would you be doing there?"

"I'm a reporter," explained Pierre. He dug his press pass out of his wallet to prove it.

"All of you?" asked the sheriff.

"Not exactly," said Pierre. "It's my assignment, and they're going along to fill the cast. We're going to participate in a reenactment at Wolfram Lodge."

"Doc Horehound's?" asked the sheriff. "You don't look like the kind of folks that usually come up for that. Well, *you* do, but not your friends here."

I forgot to mention that Pierre was wearing a pinstriped suit and a herringbone fedora hat. Also a bowtie. Jonathan, Edward, and I were in jeans and T-shirts. Mine had Barry Manilow's face on it. Our tuxes were stuffed in a wicker chest in the van somewhere, along with a ton of "country gentleman wear" Kahlúa Hummingbird got on loan from some movie costume maker she knows in Hollywood.

"'Reenactments,'" said the sheriff, scowling. "Why people go up there just to get rattled is beyond me."

"I don't understand," said Pierre.

"The doc seemed like a suave, sophisticated fellow when he bought the place and restored the heck out of it, but ever since, upsetting people seems to be his thing. Most of the speeding tickets I issue in this town are to his guests tearing out of here, white as sheets." He eyed the rest of us disparagingly and said, "Your friends here look like they're going camping."

"We all are," explained Pierre. "Tonight, anyway, by the lake. We're moving into the lodge tomorrow."

"Hmmm, no," said the sheriff, shaking his head. "I wouldn't advise that."

"Why not?" asked Edward.

"First off," said the officer, "like I said. It's private property. You sure you got permission?"

"Indeed we do," said Pierre.

"In writing?"

"Uh, no. But my editor, Kah—, I mean, Miss Hummingbird, made the arrangements. She said it was all set."

"Sure," said the sheriff. "Sure. Maybe your lady boss wasn't aware that we've been having a problem with mountain lions."

"Mountain lions?" asked Jonathan. "Pierre, she didn't say anything about that."

"Been finding deer and small game, even the Edgars' German shepherd, all torn up something awful," said the sheriff. "Mutilated. Horrible mess. Strange, too, because whatever's killing them isn't eating them. Just hacks them up and leaves them for the scavengers."

"What do you mean 'whatever's killing them'?" asked Edward. "You said mountain lions."

"Maybe it is," said the sheriff. "And maybe it isn't. Wildcats kill for food, not for sport. Just this morning I got a call from Hal's wife. They live between here and the lake, a little nearer there than here. I drove up and found a fair-sized buck. Damnedest thing I ever saw. Throat torn out, and there were claw marks all over its back and flanks."

"That's not a mountain lion?" said Jonathan.

"Could be," said the sheriff. "Awfully big if it is. But like I said, cats eat what they kill. This carcass was just feeding the flies."

"What about a bear?" asked Edward.

"Not likely," said the sheriff. "They leave telltale signs. You guys packin'?"

"We've got backpacks and sleeping bags, yes," said Pierre.

"And a doozie of a tent," added Edward.

The sheriff snorted. "No. I mean are you carrying guns?"

"Firearms?" asked Pierre. "Why, no."

"Darn fool city people," said the sheriff, planting his hands on his fat hips. "If I was you I'd stay at Maggie's motel tonight. It isn't fancy. The beds sag a mite, but the bathrooms are clean and the water's not too rusty."

"I'm afraid we're short of funds," said Pierre. "We planned to camp to allay the cost of a first night at the lodge."

"Hoo-boy," said the sheriff. "Look here. There is a campground up there, but no one's used it for years. It's got zero facilities. I repeat: no running water, no electricity, no latrines. Zilch. And you guys don't look like you'd know how to build a proper campfire."

"I got matches," I said, shaking the box. "Surely there's twigs and branches."

The sheriff said a word I'll not repeat here. "It'll all be wet inside an hour. Do you realize there's a freak storm coming in from the north? No, you wouldn't have thought to check on that, it being summer and all. Sometimes happens after a really dry winter. They've issued a flashflood warning. Don't camp near any creeks."

"We'll be careful, Officer," said Pierre. "As I said, we don't have much choice. And I was an Eagle Scout."

"You sure as Hell don't inspire confidence," said the sheriff, adjusting his gun belt under his bloated paunch. "I'll wager if there's a fire up there, it's going to be set by lightning. Well, do what you got to do. You'll be camping on private land, outside my jurisdiction. I'm going to radio the Rangers and tell them a bunch of city boys will be camping at the lake. They'll want to know why I didn't stop you."

With that, he heaved himself into his car with a grunt. The tires screeched against the gritty asphalt as he tore out of there.

"Don't mind him," said Pierre. "We'll be all right. You'll see."

"Yeah," I said, pointing to the darkening sky. "Those are thunderheads, aren't they?"

"We'd better get moving," said Edward.

"Right," I said as we clambered into the van. I wondered if we'd come tearing through town in a few days white as sheets. "Sure."

∞§[Martin]§∞

"Hang on," said Jonathan. "You know, some of that does sound familiar."

"The storm clouds, you mean?" asked Beth.

"And the rain."

"What about the rain?" asked Pierre intently.

"I'm not sure," said Jonathan. "I keep getting these little flashes and shivers, but nothing clear. Maybe I'm trying to make connections that aren't really there."

"Because they really aren't," scoffed Edward, waving his hand around. "Of course you're getting flashes and shivers. We're in the middle of a thunderstorm right now!"

"You sound doubtful," said Pierre.

"Because I *am* doubtful," Edward assured him.

"I remember hearing the weather report on the radio that afternoon," said Kahlúa seriously. "Humongous storm, flashflood warnings, Noah's Ark sighted at seven thousand feet. I stopped what I was doing and thought, 'Yowza, Girl, what kind of a mess have you sent those poor boys into?'"

"A big one, I assure you," said Pierre. "Joel, do continue."

∞§[JOEL]§∞

We came to a Y in the road seven miles further on. The sign said DEVILS HORNS to the left, and SPIRIT LAKE – PRIVATE to the right. I remember thinking, "Either way, we lose." A dozen or so mailboxes were grouped atop a single post where the road split—proof that these lonely-seeming mountains were actually somewhat inhabited. A hundred yards further on we came to a gate. It was one of those metal tube kind the Forest

Service uses—a right triangle on its side with a latch at the narrow tip. A rusty sign bolted on the gate said, PRIVATE PROPERTY: NO TRESPASSING. Another sign on the gatepost said, END COUNTY JURISDICTION: PROCEED AT OWN RISK.

"Everyone's so welcoming up here," said Edward. Then, as Jonathan got out to let us through, Pierre broke into a song about a bunch of townspeople finding a dead body on a stormy beach. The guy's entrails fell out when they tried to carry him. It was gruesome.

Thunder rumbled as we moved on. The blacktop ended, and we found ourselves lurching our way up a rutted dirt road. I hit my head against the side window a bunch of times. So did Pierre, but it didn't stop him. Along the way, I noticed several unpaved driveways peeling off here and there and winding off between the trees. I thought of the mailboxes back at the fork and thought how "I'll get the mail, dear" meant a considerable trek up here.

About a half hour later we came around a big outcrop of rock covered with brush and found ourselves at the lake. It was beautiful, actually. We were in a valley several miles across. The slopes were covered with pine trees, all close together. The lake was larger than I had expected. The water was motionless and so dark it was almost black. The sky was filled with thunderclouds, gray and threatening. They seemed to reach down and settle darkly on the lake at the far side—right where we were going to camp. Great.

The mere sight of the lodge fills me with dread now, but the first time I saw it it looked really nice—impressive, just like in the brochure. It was built on a thirty-acre island maybe fifty yards from the shore. It was connected to dry land by a bridge built of crisscrossed logs. The bottom floor of the lodge was made of timber, with an expansive covered porch all the way around. The second and third stories were more fancy—brightly painted molding and even some stained-glass windows. There was a tower on top with a "widow's walk"—Pierre pointed it out and that's what he called it. Some of the windows had balconies with wrought-iron railings. The curtains were drawn at most of the windows, but lights were on in a few. There were also gas flames in metal cages mounted on the porch posts, the kind that never turn off. I remember thinking their propane bill must be a shocker.

"You know," said Pierre, "it reminds me of a place in Hollywood Kahlúa took me to last week. A private magicians' club called the House of Illusions."

"You think it's haunted?" asked Jonathan.

"The club, certainly," said Pierre. "This place, we'll soon find out."

"Where to now?" asked Edward as a single, huge raindrop really walloped the windshield. "There's no sign, but the road splits here."

"That way goes to the bridge and the lodge," said Jonathan pointing to the right. "I say we go left and follow the shore."

"Sure," said Edward, grinding the gears. "Why not?"

Three more large drops splatted the windshield, and off we went. It was slow going. At least the road was level now, and the lake was on my side. Pierre leaned across so his face was next to mine, and kept on singing right in my ear. The townspeople gathered up the dead guy's guts and put them in a bucket. Where does he find these ditties?

∞§[Martin]§∞

"He's got a point there, Pierre," interrupted Jonathan.

The others nodded knowingly.

Pierre put his hand on his heart as if he were wounded, and gave them a look that seemed to impart, "Let's hope Joel is as charitable with you and your idiosyncrasies."

I grimaced. This was going to be a long night.

∞§[*JOEL*]§∞

The rain began banging on the roof of the van. Soon it was quite a clatter. I could feel the beating through the arms of my seat. The road went on and on.

The first bolt of lightning flashed as we arrived at the so-called campground. It seemed to strike the far shore. The thunderclap came right behind it. It shook the van.

"What ho!" said Pierre cheerfully as we disembarked. At least that infernal song was over.

I'd been camping several times with my dad and brothers. He always found nice places with clearly marked parking spots, open barbecues, electric lights on tall posts, usually a store where you could buy firewood and basic supplies, and of course, clean bathrooms. This was nothing like that. It was basically a clearing surrounded on three sides by trees and the lake to the southeast. The branches almost met over our heads, but there was a circle of sky overhead. Well, a circle of rainclouds, anyway. There were a couple of flat stumps for tables. No benches—and of course, no faucets. There was a depression in the ground about eight feet wide. I assumed it was a fire pit, but it hadn't been used for a long, long time. It was chockfull of weeds. The ground all around was covered with a thick layer of sharp pine needles. They crunched under our feet. I remember thinking I wouldn't want to try to walk on that stuff barefoot.

"Okay, what do we do?" we all asked Pierre.

"First the tent, then a fire," he said authoritatively.

I kind of felt that one of us should start fetching twigs and branches before they got too wet to burn while the others assembled the tent, but I held my peace. Pierre was in charge. He was always in charge.

First Edward and Jonathan pulled out the ice chest. It was heavy. Then it took the four of us to heave the tent out of the back of the van. It was really heavy. It was all canvas flaps and nylon cords. We tried to spread it out, but it just unraveled into a tangled mess.

"Okay, Pierre," I said, my patience waning. "How does it work?"

He shrugged and scratched his head. "Darned if I know," he said.

"I thought you were an Eagle Scout," said Edward.

"To be sure," said Pierre. "But we used pup tents. They were a snap. This thing, I haven't a clue."

"Well, you'd better get one," I said. "The rain is really starting to come down."

That was an understatement.

"Aren't there any instructions?" asked Pierre.

"The salesclerk said it was so simple it didn't need any," said Edward.

"Here's a pole," said Jonathan. "And here's another one. Where do they go?"

Pierre just pursed his lips.

"I think it's upside down," said Edward. "Let's turn it over."

All that did was tangle the cords worse than ever. I was reminded of that dead guy's intestines on the beach. It was hopeless. And the rain got steadily worse.

As an act of desperation, I grabbed the poles and tried propping up one end of the canvas carcass. "Help me!" I yelled.

"How?" asked Jonathan.

"We can make a cave, sort of," I said.

It took a while, and the result was—to put it mildly—stupid. Sort of a canvas igloo with the opening facing the lake. I imagined the sheriff pulling up in his car, rolling down the window, and laughing his badge off.

"Great idea," said Edward as we crawled inside. "It's getting awfully cold, and I'm soaked. What about a fire?"

"We should have thought of that a half hour ago," said Jonathan.

I thought of saying that I had, but what was the use?

"I'll see if I can find something that's still dry enough to burn," I said. "It's getting dark. Why don't you guys dig out the lanterns?"

"Good idea," said Pierre. Useless!

I trudged off and started scouring the undergrowth around the tree trunks. After about fifteen minutes, I had managed to gather a fair pile of twigs and branches. The trouble was that the fire pit was exposed to the rain. There was already a puddle in the middle. And besides, what good was it going to do us so far from the tent? I certainly wasn't going to build a fire in there!

"I give up," I said at last, and made my way to the silly shelter. It was embarrassing. The poles were leaning under the weight of the wet tent, and try as we might we couldn't get them straight again. All the while, the rain was pounding on the canvas.

"What about those lanterns?" I said. "I can't see what I'm doing."

"Um, we have a wee problem there," said Pierre. "We forgot to bring kerosene."

"What?" I yelled. "Edward, I thought you went to a sporting goods store."

"That I did," he answered meekly. "The biggest and the best. Sorry, Joel, I plumb forgot about fuel."

"And the clerk didn't say anything?" I groaned. "Never mind."

∞§[Martin]§∞

"You poor dears," said Kahlúa. "What was Mama Bird thinkin'?"

"Plain idiots," countered Millie.

"Well, I feel sorry for them," said Beth.

Just then I heard a sound down the hallway. The kitchen door opened and closed. There came the flutter and flap of an umbrella, then the squirm and squeak of a peeled-off raincoat. Hesitant footsteps wandered the linoleum, probably in futile search of a chair on which to hang the wet garment. There came a frustrated grunt and the soggy plop of the raincoat on the floor, followed by the *whump-thud shick-thump* of discarded boots. Sock-muffled feet pounded to the cupboard with the squeaky door, then to the stove. The percolator rattled and clanked. I heard a long, prolonged slurp, followed by a gratified "Ahhhh."

There came a rustle and a shuffle, then footfalls creeping slowly down the hallway toward the study door. My arthritic neck wasn't flexible enough for me to turn my head to see who was approaching, but I knew it had to be Monsignor Havermeyer, freshly returned from exile in his camper in the back parking lot.

If any of the others heard him, they made no movement to indicate so.

The monsignor's footfalls slowed and ceased a few feet from the door. He was listening.

∞§[JOEL]§∞

So there we sat in the deepening gloom, wet and cold and hungry. I chewed my tongue, thinking of the hamburgers we might have had at Claw Junction.

"Well, well, well," said Pierre with his usual oblivious optimism as he rummaged around in the ice chest. He had been in charge of edibles. What were we thinking? "At least the champagne is cold," he announced. We could hear the sound of a foil wrapper tearing in the dark, followed by the distinctive pop of a cork and the splatter of foam. "Whoops," said Pierre, probably getting suds on his pants. "I had hoped to procure a bottle of Dom Pérignon 1996, but my finances forced a concession on Moët & Chandon 1990. Did we bring any glasses?"

"Paper cups," said Jonathan. "But I think they're in the van."

"Any beer?" asked Edward.

"Horrid stuff," said Pierre.

"I take that to mean no," said I.

"The ground meat is out, of course," said Pierre, setting the bottle down somewhere. "I suppose we could at least eat the wieners. They're pre-cooked."

"Great idea," I said. "Whopping great idea."

Pierre made a lot of noise attempting to tear open the nasty things, but he couldn't even manage that. Remembering my utility knife, I dug it out of my pocket and handed it to him. He tried and tried, but couldn't seem to get the blade to penetrate the thick plastic wrapper.

"These blades don't seem to be very sharp," he remarked.

"But I bought a sharpening stone in town," I assured him.

"Ah, but did you use it?"

It just dawned on me that I hadn't, when something strange happened.

"Did you see that?" asked Edward, peering out of our sopping cave into the night.

"What?" asked Jonathan.

"I thought I saw a light," said Edward.

"Maybe it's the lodge," I suggested. "Remember the porch lights."

"I don't think so," said Edward. "I would've noticed before."

"Lightning reflecting off the lake then," I said.

"No," said Edward. "It wasn't lightning. There! There it is again!"

"By Jove, I think you're right," said Pierre. Abandoning the wieners and my knife, he crawled to the mouth of our cave. "Look! There! And there!"

Indeed, there were several lights—balls of light. Three of them, then four, then five. They were floating above the abandoned fire pit.

"What did you do?" asked Edward, nudging me.

"Don't look at me," I said, nudging right back. "I didn't so much as strike a match out there."

It's hard to say how big the lights were. Perhaps the size of softballs, maybe volleyballs. They didn't look exactly solid, but they seemed to be round and glowing brightly. It was raining so hard besides. I was reminded of the time I was watching the lights of scuba divers making repairs under the Santa Monica Pier.

"St. Elmo's fire?" suggested Jonathan.

"Perhaps," said Pierre. "I honestly don't know."

"They certainly are strange," said Edward. "Maybe they're ghosts."

"That's all we need," I replied.

"Hey!" said Jonathan. "They're forming a circle. They're dancing in a circle!"

That they were. There were more than a dozen now, and they had formed a ring above the fire pit, a circle parallel to the ground. Around and around they went. Then they stopped. Then they went around in the other direction.

"This isn't natural," said Edward.

"Indeed not," said Pierre. "Look, now they're forming a pyramid!"

"Go on," said I.

"No, Pierre's right," said Jonathan. "See? There's the top, and four sides. And now the whole figure is rotating."

We watched amazed as the pyramid turned slowly clockwise, paused, then turned counterclockwise.

"I hate to admit it," said Jonathan, "but I'm getting scared."

"Me, too," said Edward.

"Steady, Lads," said Pierre. "Whatever they are, they aren't bothering us. If anything, they're putting on a show."

"Whatever they are," said Jonathan, "now they're getting all entangled."

The lights seemed to buzz around each other for a while, like a swarm of fireflies. As they did so they began changing colors— green, blue, yellow, pink, and turquoise. And then, wonder of wonders, they settled into whites and blues and arranged themselves into something that could only be called a Cross. Not an X or a T or a plus sign. A *Cross*.

"Well, Gents," said Pierre. "What do you think of that?"

The lights held that position for quite some time, as if making a point: "Hey you dumb guys huddled under that stupid tent, look at us! Look at this!"

And then, suddenly, they scattered in all directions. Some went up, some went out, and two or three came directly toward us. Just before entering our makeshift dwelling, they zoomed upward and vanished. They all disappeared, just like that.

∞§[Martin]§∞

"Incredible," said Arthur.

"Indeed," said Father.

"I can almost see it, but it keeps slipping away," said Jonathan. "I get glimpses of a Cross of lights. Blue and white, you say? I'm not sure."

"Maybe you're remembering the 'Electric Light Parade' at Disneyland," said Edward sarcastically.

"Maybe someone's just being obtuse," countered Kahlúa.

"Oh come on," said Edward, turning about to glare at her. "Balls of light putting on a show for us in an abandoned campground. You're not buying this, are you?"

"Whatever it is, I paid for it," she shot right back.

"Well, I think you got—"

"What do *you* think, Joel?" asked Beth hastily.

He looked puzzled. "I don't know. I'm reading the words here, but I'm not remembering any of it."

"It will come," said Pierre stoically. "Give it time."

"What happened next?" huffed Kahlúa. "And why didn't you tell me about this?"

"It gets better," said Pierre. "Better, and so much worse."

"Read on, Joel! Read on!" urged the Tumblars.

∞§[†]§∞

∞§ † §∞

5. *Munda Cor Meum*

∞§[*JOEL*]§∞

I DON'T KNOW HOW LONG we huddled there, peering out into the pouring night. I don't exactly remember who said it first. But once uttered it became a battle cry:

"Horehound's front porch!!!"

"But what about the tent?" complained Edward. "We can't just leave it here."

"Sure we can," said Jonathan. "We can come back and get it later. I say we hop in the van and hightail it to the lodge."

And so, dripping and shivering, we made a mad dash through the downpour. Pierre, being fleetest of foot in a crisis, made it to the van first. Jonathan and Edward were a bit slower because they decided to save the ice chest. They lugged it between them and flung it into the back. Halfway there I remembered my camping knife and lost my balance when I spun around to go back for it. It took me a while to find it in the pitch darkness under the sagging canvas. I came upon the pack of wieners where Pierre had dropped them, but decided to leave them. When I finally climbed inside the van, drenched to the bone, there was a moment of mounting horror when the engine wouldn't start. But Edward said a prayer to some saint—I forget who—and finally the motor roared to life. Whew!

"Turn on the heater!" I called from the backseat.

"Sorry," said Edward. "It hasn't worked in years."

"Well that's just great."

"You haven't noticed until now, have you? Hey, we live in a desert! Have a heart!"

"Says you," said me. Mine had turned to ice.

∞§[Martin]§∞

There was a sneeze in the hallway.

"Who's there?" asked the Lads jumping up and turning, startled.

"Just me," said Monsignor Michael K. Havermeyer stepping timidly into view. "Sorry to intrude."

"Hi, Monsignor!" waved Beth. "We thought you were studying your rubrics."

"Well," said he, clearing his throat, "contrary to what Pierre led me to believe, there really wasn't much to learn. The Midnight Mass for Christmas is basically a regular High Mass. There are no ceremonials like the foot-washings and processions during the Easter Triduum."

"What did you expect?" asked Arthur. "Blessing the Christmas tree?"

"Ceremoniously sweeping the stable?" added Jonathan.

"Washing the Baby Jesus?" chided Edward.

Chortles spread around the room.

"I honestly didn't know," said the monsignor, not amused, looking intently at Pierre. "I gather it was a ruse to keep me away from the rectory."

"Monsignor, I sincerely apologize," said Pierre, hand outstretched. "It's not that you are not welcome. It's just that you weren't involved in the things we are discussing. Oh, bosh! I've made a mess of things."

"No matter," said Father. "Monsignor, you're here now, and I think you should stay. We're a little short on chairs, though."

"No problem," said Havermeyer, taking up the wastebasket outside the door. He overturned it—fortunately it was empty— and set it down in the doorway.

"Oh, My Senior, allow me," said I, struggling to rise from my chair. "You can sit here."

"Not at all," said he, roosting himself on the narrow can. "I've often seen you humble yourself thusly in the kitchen when there weren't enough chairs to go around—you and your arthritis. As Father Baptist often says, 'There ain't—'"

"'—no humility without humiliation,'" said everyone together.

"No hard feelings," said Havermeyer, grimacing. "Erg— except where it counts. Okay, enough about me. Do please continue. I've been listening at the keyhole for some time, as it were, and I'm fascinated."

"I'm truly glad you're joining us, Monsignor," said Pierre earnestly. "I'm afraid we haven't the time to recap the situation, but hopefully you'll catch on. You enter at an interesting juncture." He lifted his chin and looked at each of us expectantly, one by one. "My Friends, with all of us sharing the same adventure— albeit with some compelling individual subplots as you shall see—a considerable amount of overlap in your descriptions is to be expected. In the interest of brevity, I have snipped and arranged sections of your narratives so that, for the most part, they don't cover the same ground. Tomorrow each of you may peruse the entirety of your own and everyone else's chronicles at your leisure. In the immediate, however, lest you suspect our Joel has been exaggerating—"

"Or inebriating," interjected Kahlúa.

"—or hallucinating," said Pierre without skipping a beat, "I think it fitting that Edward read a brief section from his own account regarding the lights that appeared at our miserable campsite. Let us see how closely their descriptions match."

"You mean I'm off the hook?" asked Joel.

"You may be seated, dear Chap," said Pierre, accepting Joel's pages and setting them facedown atop his own on the chair. "But don't get too comfortable. It's only a brief respite during which I suggest you partake of Millie's courage-stimulating tipple. You will be asked to take up the torch again shortly."

"Rats," said Joel, heading for his chair, accepting a fresh cup of mead and a pat on the shoulder from Arthur before sitting down.

"Yaaaaay!" cheered the Tumblars, clapping uproariously. "Good show, Joel!"

"My turn?" said Edward warily as the clamor died down. "I don't know about this, Pierre."

"Indeed," said Pierre, peeling three pages from the stack in the wooden chest. "That's the point. Here you go, Lad. Make us proud."

Once on his feet, Edward stood, heels to the hearth, regarding his own handiwork with those penetrating obsidian eyes of his. His expression was serious, but the Christmas tree lights playing on his face infused a playful, even elvish quality to those bird-of-prey eyebrows above his long, sloping nose. He gave the pages a startled double take; then grinned, grimaced, cleared his throat, and finally began reading.

∞§[Edward]§∞

THE BIG ALKA-SELTZER
BY
EDWARD STRYPES WYNDHAM

If no one minds, I think I'll skip the chaotic preparations and the wild joyride up to Spirit Lake last Sunday. To tell you the truth I'd rather forget the whole camping experience, and Joel already told me he's got plenty to say about that ill-fated disaster. Let him. I'd never been camping, so I had no expectations; and now that I've been, I doubt I'll ever accept another invitation. I don't blame anyone. We all fell down on that one, including Joel—though I doubt he's likely to admit it. In the midst of the madness something memorable did happen—the dancing lights—so that's where I'll begin.

There we were, soaked and shivering, huddled in our pathetic excuse for a shelter, the only edible thing a pack of cold hotdogs. Pierre put a brave face on it, declaring the champagne chilled to the proper temperature. Good old Pierre—that's something I cherish about him. But the status of the bubbly was quickly forgotten when something bright outside caught my attention. It wasn't lightning, and the lodge wasn't visible from the campground. I was sure of that. No, this luminous object had no simple explanation.

It was a sphere of light hovering over the fire-pit-turned-mud-hole. Sphere, ball, orb—these terms are all misleading, for they imply a rounded three-dimensional object. But this thing had no definite form or depth. It radiated light in all directions like a powerful light bulb, but there was no rounded surface from which or through which the light emanated. Nor was it a point source like a star. It was, in a word, inexplicable. Whatever it was, however it came to be there: there it was.

As we watched, surprised and curious, it was joined by three or four others. I'm fairly sure they didn't emerge out of the first one, but rather blossomed into existence separately in midair. We couldn't see them clearly because the rain was falling something fierce. For the same reason, I couldn't say if they made any sound. I can't even describe how big they were because, as I said, they had no solid edges. They were grouped in no pattern that I could discern. They just appeared one by one and hovered there, motionless.

Jonathan proposed St. Elmo's fire, and I, having polished off a bottle of Sandeman's port at Arthur's the previous Friday night while viewing a scary black-and-white movie from his impressive DVD collection, suggested ghosts. This phenomenon being entirely outside our experience, we could only watch, and guess, and wonder.

Lo and behold, when their number reached about a dozen, they moved smoothly and purposefully, positioning themselves to form a circle, a horizontal ring maybe ten feet in diameter a couple of yards above the ground, which proceeded to rotate clockwise, then counterclockwise, then clockwise again. I remember thinking that perhaps this phenomenon could be explained as some sort of alternating electrical discharge from the earth—great shades of Nikola Tesla!—but then they regrouped to form an equilateral four-sided pyramid, each line comprised of four lights—sharing their terminators while having two lights between. (I hope my description makes sense.) "No natural discharge, this!" I exclaimed to myself as the whole geometric form began rotating as the ring had done, the lights keeping their exact positions within the structure as it did so. I realize in retrospect that their number would have had to increase to twenty-one to produce this marvel.

At the sight of this, Jonathan expressed fear, which caused me to realize my own. This light display was the product of Intelligent Design. Of this there could be no doubt. But who would have the technology to make this happen, and to what purpose, I had no notion.

Pierre's comment to all of this: "Steady, Lads. They're not bothering us. If anything, they're putting on a show." The consummate performer, Pierre saw this unfathomable phenomenon as a theatrical event—God bless him!

Having made their point, whatever it was, the lights disengaged and proceeded to zip around each other, blooming into cheery pastel colors as they did so. This activity struck me as almost playful. Then, much to my rising awe, they arranged themselves into two straight lines, one horizontal consisting of five lights, and the other vertical of seven. (To do this, nine of the lights had to extinguish themselves, but I wasn't aware of them blinking out. Perhaps during the swarming they had merged with the remaining twelve.) The outer lights were deep blue graduating to pure white in the middle. These two lines revolved slowly around each other for a while. I thought of tango partners sizing each other up. Then, to our astonishment and joy, the horizontal placed itself upon the vertical, three lights from the apex. I can't say if the middle light of the horizontal merged with the third of the vertical, or if the one was in front of the other. No matter, they had formed a beautiful, stunning depiction of the Holy Cross—a symbol we all revered and cherished. This figure did not rotate as the others had done. It hovered there motionless, facing our tent, its significance meant only for us.

This symbol of our precious Faith stood there, daunting and frightening—and to my mind glorious—for quite some time. I couldn't help but think of Constantine's vision of the Chi Rho, and his hearing the words, *"In hoc signo vinces!"* (By this sign thou shalt conquer!) But in spite of the familiarity and implied holiness, the fact kept intruding, at least to me, that we had no idea who or what was putting on this display for us.

And then, without warning, the lights scattered in all directions at once. We ducked as several seemed to come directly at us, but veered upward at the last instant and vanished.

∞§[Martin]§∞

Edward, having come to the end of the third page, turned it over to find no more. "That's it?" he asked.

"Enough for now," said Pierre. "So tell us, what are you thinking?"

Edward considered for a moment. "I'm thinking I'm being taken for a ride. I'm confused because I don't understand why you're doing this."

"My dear fellow," said Pierre. "Those are your words in your own handwriting."

"So you say. I don't remember writing them."

"I know, but that's no reason to accuse me of malfeasance."

Edward frowned. "I didn't say that."

"Of subterfuge, then," said Pierre, tugging the pages from Edward's unwilling grip. "I knew this wasn't going to be easy, but I don't believe I deserve that from you."

"Come on," said Edward. "What would you do if I put you through all these theatrics about something that never happened?"

"I'll tell you what I think," said Kahlúa. "You boys guzzled Pierre's champagne in that messed-up tent, blew the assignment, and don't want to admit it." She spread her fingers in front of her face and added philosophically, *"In vino kablooey!"*

"Don't be too sure," said Millie, setting her mug on the floor beside the sacristy chair and wiping her mouth with the back of her hand. "I've been cleaning up after these guys long enough to know how much champagne they can handle. I think maybe they definitely saw something. Those crazy lights sound like an impossible trick, even for a prankster like Good Times."

"Why, thank-you," said Pierre, impressed by her questionable support.

"And what's with that title?" demanded Edward, pointing at the pages as Pierre laid them upon the others on the chair. "'The Big Alka-Seltzer'!?!? What's that about?"

"'Plop-plop! Fizz-fizz! Oh, what a relief it is ...'" sang Jonathan in imitation of the old television commercial. His voice faded out when no one else joined in.

"It was for the Big Bwana Boomerang Hangover the next morning," chided Kahlúa.

"Edward, all of you, I beg your patience," said Pierre, turning his attention back to the mysterious antique chest. "As I explained, your accounts overlap, and I want Joel to continue with his recollection at present. Each of you will have your turn. You'll be amazed at what you've written."

"Why can't we all just sit down and read our own accounts?" protested Edward as he settled back in his chair. "I mean, this way is so—"

"In the words of the immortal song: 'It's my party,'" insisted Pierre. "I've put a lot of sweat and toil into this, and I do believe this way—sharing our experiences bit by revealing bit—is best."

Jonathan took up the immortal song's refrain, but found himself singing alone a second time, poor fellow.

"How're you doing, Mi Señor?" I asked Monsignor Havermeyer, who was hiding his discomfiture remarkably well. I truly pitied the poor man, perched as he was on that infernal wastebasket. "Would you like some mead?"

"This coffee will do me fine," said he, savoring the aroma appreciatively. The fretful scars on his forehead seemed smoother somehow in the warm, wavering, Christmassy light. "I must take care—indeed, we all must—not to imbibe too late into the evening. Otherwise we'll forfeit the right to receive Holy Communion."

"Right you are, Monsignor," said Father, consulting the bent thing he called a watch. "I'll keep an eye on the time."

"I'm so glad I'm here," giggled Beth delightfully. Turned as she was in her chair, the flames in the fireplace danced playfully in her eyes. "This is something really ... 'special' isn't a strong enough word."

"It will do for the nonce," said Pierre, having retrieved the next set of pages from the chest. "Joel, if you will be upstanding."

"Joe-well, Joe-well, Joe-well," chanted the Tumblars again as their youngest comrade regained his feet and approached the hearth.

"I'm sorry, Pierre," he stammered as he accepted his pages. "I mean, in what I wrote about you being—"

"But he *is* in charge, Honey Babes," laughed Kahlúa. "Whatever the circs, Pierre Bontemps is *always* in charge!"

"Hurrah!" clamored the seated Knights.

"Oh, brother," grumbled Millie. "Joel, get on with it!"

∞§[*JOEL*]§∞

How we didn't get stuck on that muddy road is beyond me as we inched our way back around the lake. Edward's headlights were weak and sometimes flickered, and the rain was relentless. There was no embankment, no dotted white line to follow. Just a muddy track. But lightning was striking a lot over the lake, revealing our way.

Gradually the rain eased up. Thank God for that. The ruts appeared as puddles, so Edward did his best to avoid them. We began getting glimpses of the lodge between bends in the road. It looked so far away at first, but gradually it came more and more into view.

"I hope Dr. Horehound won't mind," said Edward. "After all, we'll sort of be trespassing."

"If he's got a Christian bone in his body he'll understand," said Jonathan.

"Maybe we should stay in the van," said I.

"It's colder inside this tin can than outside," said Edward over his shoulder. "Believe me, I know."

"It's stopped raining," said Jonathan. "That's a relief!"

Then, after a couple more turns along the shore, Pierre exclaimed, "Hold on! Wait a minute! There's another one! One of those lights!"

"Where?" I asked, leaning across and peering out his window.

"There," he said, pointing. "See it?"

Edward braked the van to a stop and turned off the engine. He and Pierre rolled down their side windows. The wind had died down to a gentle but freezing breeze that turned our breath into brief, swirling puffs. We watched in silence—a rare occurrence to be sure. Yes, there was definitely a light out there, hovering over the lake. Though it appeared to be the same size as the ones back at the campground, it seemed to be much farther away somehow. The lodge was in plain sight, maybe a mile and a half away. The reflection of the porch lights on the water was far outshined by the glare of the light in the sky.

"It's a bit hazy," said Jonathan. "I think it's just the moon."

"You're right," I said. "There's a break in the clouds."

"Quite a sight, though," said Edward. "So big and peaceful."

Hah!

Just then we heard a long, piercing cry.

"What in Heaven's name is that?" shuddered Jonathan.

"Mountain lion?" I suggested.

"That's no mountain lion," said Edward. "It sounds more like a hound."

"Well, that makes sense," said Pierre. "It's probably howling at the moon."

"There it is again," I said. "I've never heard a dog make a sound like that."

Whatever it was, it continued its yowl. Gradually its pitch got higher, changing into a terrifying shriek.

"Look at the lodge," said Edward. "Up in the tower."

We all shifted inside the van, Pierre and I looking over Edward and Jonathan's shoulders. It looked like something out of an old Frankenstein movie, the kind Arthur loves to make us watch in his living room. Irregular bright flashes, blinding white, flickered through the window at the top of the tower. An artificial storm, I imagined, created by a mad scientist to infuse a grotesque corpse with life.

The dog or whatever it was howled again—ferocious, vicious, angry—and *closer*.

"Next time a sheriff advises us not to go camping," I said to Pierre, "listen to him."

"We're safe in here," said he. "Surely it can't bite through solid steel."

"I'm not so sure," said Edward.

Suddenly the creature squealed, whimpered, growled confusedly, then fell silent.

"Zounds!" said Pierre. "The only thing missing is a screaming damsel in a diaphanous nightgown running through the night."

"And a vampire bat chasing her," said Jonathan.

"Or the Loch Ness Monster coming up and hungrily dragging us into the lake," said I.

"Be careful what you wish for," said Edward. "I think maybe we should get going."

"Hold on!" I almost yelled. "Look!"

Everyone turned their attention back to the moon. Something was happening. Moments before it had been a bright, peaceful orb poking through a break in the clouds. Now its surface seemed to be bubbling. Smokey strands of gooey white material curled off the rim, dissipating like the vapor made by dry ice. Then a bump erupted from its right side. It grew, elongated, and then detached with a soundless snap. (The word "sproing" came to my mind, but not to my ear.) It became a second, smaller ball of white light.

"This can't be happening," I said.

"Is it any more incredible than the lights at the camp?" countered Pierre condescendingly.

"They were here," I insisted. "Down here on earth, I mean, where all sorts of things go haywire. But that's the moon! It hasn't changed since God put it up there."

"Not exactly," said Edward. "It's been pummeled with meteors and space debris. The craters all over it are proof of that."

"But it doesn't flop and sputter and produce offspring!" I exclaimed.

"Well," agreed Pierre reluctantly, "not until now."

The second ball of light hung near the moon for more than a minute, like a foal hovering close to its dam. Then it began slowly circling. On the third lap it veered away, diving smoothly earthward in a long, gentle arc. As it descended it got larger and larger—and *larger*.

"This can't be happening," said Edward. I noted it was okay for him to say so without reprisals from Pierre.

"If it is, it's on every television in the world," said Jonathan. "This is one major astronomical event!"

Down it came, growing larger and larger and brighter and brighter. Its color stayed the same as the moon's—cold white, maybe a hint of pale gray around the edge. We heard the faint howl of displaced air—how close it must be!—but the thing itself wasn't making any sound as far as we could tell. The surface of the lake seemed to flatten and even depress slightly, as if an unseen force was pressing down upon it. The waves grew from their usual four or five inches to more than a foot, slopping and sploshing noisily on the pebbled shore.

"Am I seeing things?" asked Edward. "Or is it changing shape?"

"Flattening, you mean," said Jonathan.

"Yes," said Edward. "Oh, this is too much! It's beginning to look like ..."

"A flying saucer!" we all said together.

∞§[Martin]§∞

The room erupted in a flurry of groans, moans, and up-thrown hands.

"Oh, come *on* now!" scoffed Jonathan.

"This is too much!" exclaimed Edward. "Really too much!"

Joel stood there, clutching his pages, helplessly agreeing with them. Millie and Kahlúa were making noises like an endangered chicken coop. Monsignor Havermeyer cleared his throat with a chainsaw. In the midst of the uproar, Father Baptist silently and purposefully rearranged himself in his chair. As for me, well, I was enjoying myself immensely. This was going to be quite a night after all.

"Arthur!" demanded Beth. "What do you think?"

Her brother responded with a long, fluttered exhalation and a roll of his shoulders. Even his peppery gray ponytail writhed with discomfited uncertainty. "Maybe Madam Hummingbird was right about the champagne," he said unconvincingly.

"Hold it, hold it!" said Kahlúa to Pierre. "Column Slalom: this is the story you didn't turn in?"

"It is," said Pierre, standing tall and resolute.

"You mean I paid all that money," huffed his unswerving taskmistress, "called in all those favors, fretted three years off my life, for this, this—?"

"What can I tell you, K. H.?" protested her wayworn urban legend accelerator. "This isn't a ruse. It's what happened. Perhaps now you can begin to appreciate my unwillingness to hand in my assignment."

"And you'll understand my reluctance to hand over your next paycheck," she seethed through gritted teeth.

"'Tygress! Tygress! burning bright, in the dumpsters of the night ...'" recited Millie. Whether she was interpreting, interpolating, or merely misquoting William Blake was hard to say—so rarely did she cite Protestants. The point was to prod Kahlúa, and it worked.

"Not me, *him,*" she spat. "Dumpster scrutinizer, is he? He'll be trawling for his meals in them when I get through with him."

Pierre's monocle dropped from his eye at the thought.

Then Joel rattled his pages at him. "You're actually trying to get us to believe—"

Pierre halted him and everyone with a stern look and a raised hand. "Joel, Ladies and Gentlemen, I am not trying to get you to *believe* anything. I am attempting to help you *remember* that which you have forgotten. What you do with those recollections once regained is your affair. Trust me, I've got better things to do with my time and energies than to arrange such an elaborate hoax. What could possibly be my motive? Think about it. Lads, it would shatter our Fellowship. Madam Hummingbird, it would cost me my job and the pleasure of your sponsorship and tutelage. Father Baptist, it would invite your consternation and distrust, two ends I'd hate to contemplate. Mister Feeney, it would poison your typewriter against me—something I would dread till the end of my days. Millie—"

"I don't know what you're all so upset about," said our house-keeptrix, folding her sinewy arms across her bossy bosom. "Pierre didn't write this stuff—*you guys did*. None of you is suggesting otherwise. Drunk or sober, something sure happened. You don't want to remember? Close the door behind you on your way out! You don't like what you wrote? Throw it in the fireplace! But don't waste your time and mine getting mad at Bon-Bon here."

"Why, thank-you, dear Millie," said Pierre, clearly taken aback.

"Don't press it," said she, wiping her hands on her apron.

"Millie defending Pierre?" I whispered to Father. "Reality is tilting."

"I heard that," said Millie.

But it is! I thought.

"That, too," she snapped.

"So," said Pierre, indicating the antique chest. "Do we carry on or burn the lot?"

"Continue, I suppose," said Arthur. "Lord knows what we got ourselves into. We must have come through it or we wouldn't be here now. Maybe some things are better left forgotten, but I'd rather know than not. How can I claim to be an Ultra-realist otherwise?"

"Good point, I suppose," admitted Edward sourly.

"Whatever," said Joel with a raspy sigh. "I'll continue, but there's sure something fishy going on here."

"Fishy: perhaps," said Pierre in his contrived Bela Lugosi accent. "Nonsense: perhaps not."

My attention was tugged from this lively interchange by an indeterminate sound from Monsignor Havermeyer. Feeling guilty that his backside was puckered on that upturned wastebasket, I grabbed the arms of my chair and turned my whole torso to face him. He was certainly distressed, and it wasn't just from his uncomfortable roost. He had his right palm pressed against his mouth, his thumb and index finger framing his nostrils. His eyes above were wide and glaring, storms of thought tumbling around within. Beads of sweat, all the more poignant with Christmas tree lights reflecting off them, budded on his scarred forehead and trickled down the sides of his face. He mopped his brow and cheeks with a handkerchief in his left hand, then dabbed his neck with it.

"Monsignor," I whispered almost inaudibly. "Are you all right?"

His eyes swiveled in my direction. He shook his head slightly, his eyes standing still, focused as they were on me.

"Anything I can do?" I offered. "Something I can get you?"

His hand dropped from his face as his eyes fell to the floor. He gave his head a brittle sideways shake.

"Glad to assist," I assured him. "Really. You're sure?"

He gave his head a couple of micro nods. With a grunt he reached down and retrieved the coffee mug he had placed on the floor.

"At your service," was all I could think to reply as I turned myself frontward in my chair.

"I'll read on a little bit further," Joel was agreeing reluctantly, meanwhile, "but I don't like it."

"Like it, dislike it, as you wish," said Pierre. "The point is that you remember. We've opened the door this far. Do you really think you can close it now and expect to get a good night's sleep ever again?"

To a rumble of unconvinced but nonetheless captivated, albeit resentful grumbles, Joel continued.

∞§[JOEL]§∞

Even as I write these words, knowing all that has happened since, I shudder to think of that gigantic spaceship falling toward us. It was graceful and beautiful and menacing and terrifying all at once. It wobbled a little as it came to a stop maybe a quarter of a mile from us. It was wider than a football field is long, and fifty or sixty yards tall in the middle, with a sort of dorsal fin that began at the dome in the center and extended to the leftmost edge. There were no doors or landing gear, no portholes or insignias on the side, just a continuous, smooth, curved, luminous surface. This made it hard to judge size and distance, so my figures may be off.

After hovering there for several seconds—I had the creepy feeling its occupants were watching us—it slowly descended into the lake. As it touched the water the surface churned and gushed, spurting clouds of white mist. It may have been white hot or cold as dry ice. Either way, the water boiled and hissed as the ship sank slowly and steadily into the lake. When it was half submerged there was an eruption of color on its surface, perhaps some sort of reaction with the water. Ripples of red and yellow and then swirls of dark brown and even smoky black flowed up from the waterline and spread out over its contours, then swept their way up to the tip of the fin. Then it was all white again, and as such, continued to sink ever so slowly into the lake.

∞§[Martin]§∞

"I guess that explains 'The Big Alka-Seltzer,'" said Edward.

"Hey Millie, got some?" asked Jonathan.

"Vinegar, milk of magnesia, and a dash of mustard powder works just as good," said she.

"Are you serious?" giggled Beth.

"Never mind," said Edward and Jonathan together.

∞§[Joel]§∞

In a matter of seconds the water rushed in, covering the top, making a loud snorting sound. Gobs of water spewed high into the air. And that glow—an uncanny, ghostly luminousness (is that a word?)—we watched as it sank deeper and deeper into the murky depths. Water heaved out of the lake. It rushed up onto the road, foamed and slopped around our tires, then pulled back with a scary sucking noise. For a second there we thought the van was going to be pulled in, but suddenly everything got deathly quiet except for the slap of twelve-inch waves on the shore.

"How deep is this lake?" asked Edward, leaning out his window.

"I think Arthur said five hundred feet at its deepest part," said Pierre. "But that's probably a ways north of here."

"It's dimming," said Jonathan. "The light from the saucer is going out."

In about a minute the glow faded to black.

"There you have it," said Edward, sighing long and exhaustedly. "Well, fellows, what do you say to that?"

"Haven't a clue," said I.

"Words fail," said Pierre.

We sat there for quite a while, peering out the side windows, unwilling to detach ourselves from the sight which, to all intents and purposes, was a normal, beautiful, restful lake high in the San Gabriel Mountains.

∞§[Martin]§∞

Joel's voice had trailed off to a whisper as he reached the end of the page. Gulping loudly, he looked up, his eyes darting from face to face. We looked back at him. Seconds went by.

"Anyone?" prodded Pierre.

Suddenly, Monsignor Havermeyer got noisily up from his uncomfortable stool. It tipped in the process and came down sideways on the hardwood floor with a metallic *boom*. With a grunt and a groan, he backed into the hallway, turned, and stomped in his stocking feet toward the kitchen. His actions seeming to indicate more than an urge for another cup of coffee, I struggled and strained myself into a semblance of an upright posture, snatched up my cane, and hobbled after him.

"You lost me with the flying saucer," Jonathan's voice receded as I trudged down the hall. "Everything up till then was at least possible if not entirely believable. But this—this is something out of Arthur's Sci-Fi movie collection."

"Don't look at me," I barely heard Arthur say. "I wasn't in this part of the story."

I found Havermeyer, not at the percolator, but leaning over the sink, his hands gripping the edge.

"Monsignor," I said, coming up behind and placing a hand on his shoulder, carefully avoiding the pool of water spreading on the floor from his raincoat, droopy plastic hat, and floppy rubber boots which lay in a glistening heap near the garden door. "Can I help?" I asked stupidly. "Are you ill? I don't mean to intrude. If you're going to be sick and want your privacy—"

He shook his head, but continued facing the sink. I realized he wasn't looking down at the drain—a sure sign of impending regurgitation—but up at Millie's silver Crucifix nailed to the transom of the window. *"Munda cor meum,"* I heard him say several times, gasping and wincing between each utterance. *"Munda cor meum. Munda cor meum."*

Cleanse my heart, I translated to myself: the prayer of the priest at Mass before he utters the words of the Holy Gospel.

"Perhaps I should leave," I whispered.

"No," he said, cranking the faucet. He leaned over and sloshed a couple of handfuls of water on his face, then patted it with one of Millie's damp dishtowels. The spigot turned off, he rattled his head apparently to clear it, then turned to face me. His eyes were dark pools of turmoil. "Stay," he said, more of a plea than a demand.

"Of course, Monsignor," I said. Setting the tip of my cane between my toes, I rested my weight upon it as best I could. The damp coldness was indeed working its way into my aching joints. "Quite a night," I said lamely.

"In just a few short hours," he said, "I'll be saying the Words of Consecration at Christmas Mass. The Feast of the Nativity. Now is not the time for doubt."

"Doubt, Monsignor?"

He glared at me, startled that he had said such a thing. I half expected him to fumble and mumble something like, "I didn't mean it that way," but to my shock he simply said, "Yes."

A dozen of my wisest comebacks fluttered just behind my poised tongue, but this was one moment when the modicum of

Prudence I keep in some dark corner of my psyche shouldered its way to the fore. The charitable thing was to keep still and wait patiently. I was halfway through my third *Ave* when a sudden commotion came reverberating down the hallway from the study.

"You're *always* playing with our heads, Pierre!" yelled Joel. "You think you're so darn superior!"

"Hold on," intruded Arthur. "Joel, personal invectives aren't going to get us anywhere."

"Let go of me, Edward!" yelled Joel. "What did you do to us, Pierre? Pay one of your fakir friends at the 'House of Illusions' to hypnotize us?—put this wigged-out space-alien garbage into our heads?"

"Such a ploy would never occur to me," insisted Pierre. "Joel, put that down—"

Thumps and bumps ensued.

"They really don't remember, do they?" asked Havermeyer, his voice distant. "I take it that's the point of the exercise."

"Pierre gets checks for bravery," said I, "but I don't know about his timing."

"No, this is the night," said he, wringing the towel in his hands. "The Night of Nights. His timing is impeccable."

"And you, Monsignor?"

"Oh, I'll be all right, Martin," he said, apparently summoning some sort of unspoken resolve. "I have to be. It's just that—"

"Stop it!" Beth's scream ricocheted down the hall. "Listen to yourselves!"

"Men at work," mused Kahlúa. "We gotta loves 'em."

"No we don't," mused Millie right back.

There was a loud bang, followed by a sudden silence.

"Gentlemen, enough!" Father Baptist's words were low and incisive, spoken not yelled, delivered with the surety and precision of cold steel. They zinged down the hallway like an airborne circular saw. "You are dishonoring my house and besmirching your Knighthood. What has become of your Oath of Chivalry?"

"Perhaps we should go back," said Monsignor Havermeyer.

"Perhaps not," said I.

"Courage, Parcifal."

Now that brought me up short. "Monsignor?"

"I was a witness, remember?" he explained, smiling knowingly. "At your knighting. Three and ten."

"Excuse me?"

"The Ten Commandments of Chivalry," said Havermeyer, draping the dishtowel over the faucet in the sink. "I suggest you review articles three and ten. In the meantime, your place is with your fellow Knights. And mine is there at your side."

"Sitting on a wastebasket," I said dubiously.

"I repeat," he retorted emphatically.

"Okay," I conceded, "but I need a cup of coffee. How about you?"

"I'll pass," said he, patting his middle. "I don't want to face a Solemn High Mass with a full bladder."

"Good point," I said, grabbing a potholder and half-filling a cracked mug with half a handle I retrieved from the cupboard. The percolator hissed and sizzled as I returned it to the burner. "If nothing else, *Monsignore*," I said in derailed Italian, "this willa be a Christmas Vigil to-a remember."

"Maybe you could patch it up—you know, edit it together," said he, motioning me to precede him to the fray. "A fascinating chapter to add to your chronicles."

"You're talking major surgery," I said, politely deferring the honor to him. "Besides, Fantasy is not my genre."

"It isn't?"

"Hmm, I wonder sometimes."

"Just a suggestion," he said over his shoulder.

"I'll take it under advisement," I said to his back. "In any case, we'll have to survive the evening first."

∞§[†]§∞

∞§†§∞

6. Apparent Rather Than Real

∞§[Martin]§∞

"I CONFESS I'M AT A LOSS," Father was saying as Monsignor Havermeyer and I darkened the study door, more or less together. I was expecting to find broken chairs and the tree on its star, but such was not the case. Everything was pretty much as it had been, except now Father was standing at the fireplace beside Pierre. "We've waged some incredible battles together, but nothing like this." Father was hammering his words with thrusts of the pipe in his hand. "We've had disagreements and misunderstandings before, but we've never questioned each other's honesty, or doubted their integrity. Obviously something happened at Spirit Lake, something that challenged your assumptions, perhaps your very beliefs. I assume that is why you're behaving as you are, and perhaps for that reason you should be allowed some slack. But I remind you that you are Knights. I also remind you that Faith is not self-generated. It is a gift from God. Once granted, it must be nurtured, tested, and refined. Gentlemen: behold your crucible. I suggest you get a grip."

"He's in good form," I whispered to Monsignor Havermeyer as I hobbled around him in order to flop awkwardly into my favorite chair.

"Thank-you, Martin," said Father, casting his penetrating krypton-argon white laser eyes upon me.

I gulped and waved meekly from deep down in my chair.

Monsignor's wastebasket throne had rolled diagonally across the hallway, so he fetched it, placed it squarely in the doorway, and settled himself upon it with the aplomb of a warrior king.

"Now, Pierre," said Father. Discipline having been meted out and harmony restored, his voice took on the soothing overtones of Bing Crosby singing *White Christmas.* "It's your show, and Heaven forbid I should interfere in any way, but don't you think it's time to introduce a softer voice into the mix? I'm curious to see how Beth fits into all this."

"Hear, hear!" cheered Kahlúa and Millie.

Beth, who through it all had been still sitting prettily sideways in her chair, blushed sweetly. Arthur gave her cheek a brotherly pinch. She swatted his hand playfully away.

"In the dramatic sense I agree with you, Father," said Pierre. "But alas, Beth didn't enter the tale until Monday morning, July the thirty-first. We four campers—yes, yes, I use the word loosely—were the first to enter Wolfram Lodge, and we did so Sunday evening, the thirtieth."

Father withdrew with graceful dignity. His office chair croaked ungratefully as he settled back into it beside me.

"So who'll do the honors?" asked Joel, who was sitting resolutely on his kitchen chair. "I'm on sabbatical."

"And deservedly so," said Pierre, dipping into the fateful wooden box. "Ah, yes: I believe it's time to hear from our good friend, Jonathan."

"Erg," said he, rising reluctantly to his feet. Accepting his pages without enthusiasm, he looked them over suspiciously. "Hold on," he said, tapping the top sheet. "The title page isn't here."

"I explained that," said Pierre. "Since your accounts overlap —"

"Oh, right," said Jonathan, rapping his forehead. "Of course. I'm plunging in midstream. Well, could you at least tell me what title I gave my version?"

"I could indeed," said Pierre, drawing himself up. "Ahem: 'The Heart is a Clumsy Hunter—'"

"The story of my life," sighed Kahlúa.

"There, there," giggled Beth.

Twitters spread around the room.

"'—or,'" continued Pierre, "'What We Won and Lost at Spirit Lake.'"

Jonathan reacted by scrunching his eyebrows. Between his prominent forehead and the tricks played by the crosshatched shadows cast by the Christmas tree lights, he looked positively cyclopean.

"You asked," said Pierre.

"That I did," said Jonathan. "Okay, Lads and Ladies, here goes nothing."

∞§[*Jonathan*]§∞

I think we sat there in the van watching the lake for the better part of an hour. Pierre and Edward were inclined to continue the vigil until dawn, but Joel got a case of the jitters. He expressed increasing concern that the aliens might sneak up in a submersible or something and snatch us for specimens. I admit the thought nagged at me, too, but I didn't raise my voice until he broke down and started whimpering—

∞§[Martin]§∞

"Hey," interrupted Joel. "I think not."

"I'm only reading what's here," said Jonathan defensively. "I honestly don't remember writing this."

"You got *your* digs in," said Millie to Joel. "Fair's fair."

"Shoe's on the other footsie, Joely Boy," added Kahlúa. "Say, what would them aliens do with a specimen like Pierre, I wonder?"

"Don't feel bad," said Arthur diplomatically, patting Joel on the shoulder. "Under the circs I probably would have done some major whimpering myself."

"Hrmph," grumbled Joel, crossing his arms and slouching in his chair.

∞§[*Jonathan*]§∞

—so at long last, we were again and finally Horehound bound. The wooden bridge groaned and sagged as Edward eased the Wyndhamwagon slowly across. I think it was Pierre who said it was good that we'd left that waterlogged tent behind or the extra weight might have collapsed the tired old thing. The bridge was made of split pines supported by whole trunks tied to form X's beneath. I wondered what kind of ancient horse-pulled vehicles it had been made for originally, but no matter.

"You realize we're surrounded now," said Joel, looking every which way. "You know, by the lake."

"That's what makes this an island," pointed out Pierre.

Edward nosed the van up to the porch. There was a thick layer of loose gravel on the ground, so the tires made an awful racket.

"Surely they'll hear us if anyone's up," I said. "Hmm. I don't see any lights except those on the porch."

"What should we do?" asked Edward as he turned off the ignition. "We can't very well just curl up on the doorstep, can we?"

"I still think we should get as far away from here as possible," said Joel, but we would have none of that. This had turned into quite an adventure, and our Tumblar curiosity had been piqued.

"I suggest knocking," said Pierre. "That would seem the proper thing to do."

We must have looked a ragged sight, clomping our way to the west-facing front door, all disheveled and exhausted and smelling like wet rugs. It was a massive thing, the door, vertical planks held together with bands of black metal—like something you'd expect at a medieval castle. There was a large knocker in the shape of a wolf's head. Pierre grasped the snout and prepared to let go a mighty boom when a croaky voice startled us:

"And who might you be, skulkin' 'round this time of night?"

We turned to see a crusty fellow seated on an enormous wooden slab bench suspended by chains from a rafter. Though he was draped in shadow, we could see the silhouette of his tousled hair, the glimmer of the porch lights in his eyes, and the gleam of the double-barreled shotgun across his lap.

"Good evening, my good man," said Pierre, seemingly undaunted. "We're the *Artsy* party. I realize we're not expected
until tomorrow, but we were rained out of our campsite on the
northwest shore."

"Is that a fact?" said the man, cocking his weapon. "Rained
out you say. Well, that could be. You got a name?"

"Bontemps," said our fearless leader. "Pierre Bontemps. Yes,
I'm afraid we didn't come prepared for the likes of such a downpour, nor for such a threatening reception, my good man. We're
here for the reenactment."

"Ah," said the man, uncocking the gun. "I should've known.
The Master said y'all might end up on our doorstep when the
storm hit. What were you fixin' to do, sneak in and camp by the
fireplace?"

"Not at all," said Pierre, indicating the knocker he had almost
utilized. "Seeing as how we're not yet expected, and haven't the
means to pay for lodgings tonight, we sought permission to sleep
here under the cover of this most inviting porch, if Dr. Horehound wouldn't mind."

"Ha-hah! Wouldn't that be a first!" Holding the gun at his
side, the man hefted himself off the bench and onto his widely
bowed legs. The chains creaked and chattered as the bench
swung free. "Name's Grayburn," he said, stepping into the fluttering aura of the porch light. With his unkempt grizzled hair,
crooked nose, craggy face, and navy-blue pea coat with anchors
engraved on the large buttons, he looked as though he'd be more
comfortable aboard a trawler out on the ocean.

"Might you be the butler?" asked Pierre.

"Now there's a thought," Grayburn chuckled, rubbing his chin.
It made a sound like sandpaper on hardwood. "I do 'casionally
answer the front door, but mostly I'm the groundskeeper and
gen'ral handyman."

"Pleased to meet you," said Pierre with a nod. "May I present
my companions: Jonathan Clubb, Joel Maruppa, and Edward
Strypes Wyndham."

"No use introducin' yourselves to me," he said with a scornful
snort. "It's the Master y'all needs to make yer appeals to."

"The Master," repeated Edward. "Might he still be up and around?

"Haven't seen him since just after dinner," said Grayburn. "The light's on in the lib'ary, though the window curtain's drawn. He's prob'ly readin', like most evenin's."

"Excuse me," I ventured to say. "Have you been out here long? On the porch, I mean."

"On and off for a while." His eyes went all squinty. "There's a wild critter on the loose hereabouts, and I was thinkin' I might get lucky. Why you askin'?"

I pointed vaguely off to my left. "Might you have seen, um, something big and bright, maybe, you know, over the lake?"

"You mean the moon?" he said, scrunching his left eye shut as he turned his right-eyed gaze heavenward. It seemed an odd gesture since the porch roof blocked all view of the sky. "Yeah, she looked almost full a short while ago when I was checkin' the docks, least while there was a break in the clouds. They closed up since."

"Well, the moon, yes," said I, cautiously. "And perhaps something else?"

"Don't know what you mean," he said, opening both glistening eyes and aiming them at me. "There was lots of lightnin' before that. Great Queen of Cups, but that was somethin' to see! Reminds me of the Big Drenchin' of nineteen hundred and sixty-seven. I'm surprised it didn't start a forest fire."

Obviously he hadn't seen a flying saucer splash down a mile away, so I let it drop.

"Well, don't just stand there with y'all's teeth a-chatterin'," he said after a long pause. "Come inside and I'll make yer presence known. Be sure to wipe yer feet."

"Of course," we assured him, scraping our shoes on the enormous studded rubber mat.

He lumbered to the door, turned the ponderous iron knob, and led us into an impressive foyer. It was dim, but I could make out a massive chandelier overhead, and the suggestion of a sweeping staircase beyond. I could tell by the sound and feel that the floor was hardwood. There were white lace curtains to our left and right. It took me a moment to realize that both walls were comprised of a half-dozen French doors with diamond-shaped glass panes and curtains hung all over. The somber glow of a lamp and a dying fire penetrated the diaphanous setting to our right. That had to be the library.

"Stay put," said Grayburn. "I'll tell the Master y'all're here." With that he knocked on a glass panel with the muzzle of his shotgun, listened a moment, then turned the latch and slipped inside.

"Well, well," said Pierre to us. "What do you think of that?"

Before we could voice our speculations, Grayburn opened the door and beckoned us inside. "He ain't here," he said, a mite puzzled. "Make yerselves at home, and I'll see if I can fetch him."

We found ourselves in a well-stocked library. There were bookshelves all around, and oil paintings in ostentatious frames in-between. A large mahogany office desk dominated the center of the room, with a high-backed leather chair behind. There were similar chairs and knee-high coffee tables set at various angles around the place, several couches and loveseats, and a grand fireplace against the far wall with logs reduced to glowing red coals within. I counted eight thick green-tinted glass ashtrays before I decided there were more than enough of them. The floor lamp, which illuminated the room, was of the Tiffany variety, four bulbs burning at a low setting under a canopy of colorful stained glass.

"Arthur's gonna love this," I said, running my eyes along a shelf of ancient leather-bound volumes. "Hey, here's a *Latin Vulgate*, a *Douay-Rheims*, and a *King James Bible*—Mr. Feeney wouldn't like that—and hey: even a *Summa*."

"And here's a complete set of Mark Twain," said Edward. "Tennyson, Shakespeare, Dante, Homer, Tolkien, all the classics."

"And medical books," I added. "Anatomy, physiology, microbiology, pharmacology; then psychology, philosophy, and—uh oh—*The Vampire: His Kith and Kin* by Montague Summers. I think Father Baptist has that one. And *Werewolf*, also by Summers; and *Navaho Skinwalkers* by—well I'll be, it's by Mortimer

Horehound, Ph.D. Now why do you think a clinical psychologist would write a book like that?"

"Kahlúa said he was quite the conversationalist," said Pierre. "I'm looking forward to meeting him."

"Hey," Joel said, pulling a thin volume from a shelf, "here's one we studied at St. Joseph's: *Surely They Were Saved* by Fr. Micah L. Selwick, S.J."

"Really," I said. "Do tell."

"Sister Winifred was really big on it," said Joel. "She taught Transcendental Morality."

"So who got lucky?" asked Pierre. "The saved, I mean."

"Pontius Pilate, Herod Antipas," said Joel, flipping the pages wistfully, "and especially Judas Iscariot."

"Really," said Edward, who had moved to the window and pulled back the curtain revealing inky darkness without. "How so?"

"Jesus had to die to fulfill His mission," explained Joel with a lofty, authoritative air, "so somebody had to do Him in. Herod had to humiliate Him, Pilate's job was to condemn Him—to fulfill prophecy, you see. Judas didn't have any choice but to betray Jesus. It was their destiny, so naturally they couldn't be held responsible. Since they helped bring about the Salvation of Mankind, naturally they must have gone to Heaven."

"The more I hear about St. Joseph's, the more I love it," said Edward, sarcastically as he moved away from the window.

"What's wrong now?" said Joel, peering around at us warily, perhaps angrily.

"Dear Chap," said Pierre. "If Judas was destined for Heaven, what could Jesus possibly have meant when He said it would have been better if he'd never been born?"

"When did He say that?" huffed Joel, slapping the book shut and thrusting it irritably back into its place on the shelf.

"If Mr. Feeney were here," said Edward, "he'd quote you chapter and verse. I think it's in St. Matthew's Gospel."

∞§[Martin]§∞

"And you'd've been right," said I. "Sorry to interrupt the flow, everyone, but the point is well taken. At the Last Supper Jesus said and I quote: 'The Son of Man indeed goeth, but woe to that man by whom the Son of Man shall be betrayed: it were better for him, if that man had not been born.' Judas, who at the time was wearing a sign on his back that said, 'Kick me!' in Latin, Greek, and Aramaic, asked Him, 'Is it I, Rabbi?' to which Jesus answered, 'Thou hast said it.' Matthew twenty-six, twenty-four and twenty-five."

"Thank-you, Mister Feeney!" beamed Kahlúa.

"I don't remember nothing about no sign on his back," grumbled Millie.

"Right," said Joel, glowering. "Sure."

Jonathan rattled his pages for attention, and continued.

∞§[*Jonathan*]§∞

"Math—hews; Goss—spell," said Pierre, drawing out the syllables. "You see, Joel, it's not that hard. Now you try it."

"Fun—nee," answered Joel with a sneer.

"Look here," said Edward, changing the subject by pointing to the painting above the fireplace. He read aloud the plaque beneath: "Bartholomew Wolfram and Gabrielle Stonecraft Piaget."

"They don't look happy," said I.

"The rich often don't," said Pierre. "At least, not in their portraits."

"Nor in real life," said a new voice as our host strode purposefully into the room. "At least, not in their case. I trust I don't look so grim. I see you're perusing my collection. That's a good sign. I enjoy the company of well-read men."

Dr. Mortimer Horehound was attired in a full-length purple smoking jacket. A thick black scarf was wrapped around his neck, and oddly, considering the chill, I noticed bare toes protruding from beneath the hem of his garment.

"Gentlemen," he said, shaking our hands in a cordial but professional, perhaps aloof, manner. "Grayburn tells me you've had a misadventure at the campground. I saw you drive by earlier from my bedroom window upstairs. If you had stopped to introduce yourselves, I would have suggested that you spend the night here. The storm warnings were ominous, to be sure."

"Would that we had," said Pierre, jovially. "But on the other hand, we would have missed several marvels which—I think I'm speaking for all of us—we wouldn't have missed for the world."

Joel coughed pointedly but said nothing.

"Indeed," said our host, seating himself in the chair behind the desk. He indicated with a wave of his hand that we should arrange chairs for ourselves. "You were up and down the west shore. Did you happen to see a boat on the lake?"

"A boat, sir?" asked Edward.

"A dilapidated, leaky old rig," said Dr. Horehound. "Wouldn't you know, I've got two very fine sailboats and a sleek lake cruiser docked at the pier on the north side of the island. Now and then the kids from town get tanked up and 'borrow' one for a moonlight cruise with their girlfriends. I don't begrudge them the impulse—I was a frisky lad myself, once upon a time. But this is a private lake without Forest Rangers or lifeguards, and this is one Hell of a night for a beer jaunt. And what they want with that wobbly old tub is beyond me. I only keep it around because it belonged to Mr. Piaget."

"He built this place," said Joel, indicating the painting above the fireplace. "He and his wife."

"She drowned, you know, during a summer storm much like this one," said Dr. Horehound, removing a long dark cigarette with a shiny gold filter from a polished wooden case. "She went for a morning sail in that very boat. The storm moved in swiftly and caught her unawares. Lightning struck the mast, and she was apparently thrown overboard unconscious. Mr. Piaget filled scores of diaries about his attempts to contact her beyond the grave, but not a single paragraph about what happened the day she died."

"That is strange," said Pierre. "Speaking of which, might I ask if this is where we will reenact the séance?"

"Heavens, no," said Dr. Horehound. "That room lies deep within the heart of the house. Some of my guests have suggested that it *is* the heart of the house. I keep it locked at all times, except for the reenactments. But let us not get ahead of ourselves."

"Of course," said Pierre. "But as for the boat you mention, we surely didn't see it."

"I thought not," said Dr. Horehound with a sigh. "Ah, I'll have to notify Sheriff Brumus." (He pronounced it *Bruh*-muss.) "He'll have his hands full, what with the flashfloods this evening. He's a gruff sort, but he's efficient in his way, and he's all we've got."

"We've had the pleasure," said Pierre.

"He tried to dissuade us from going up to the campground," said Joel.

"And he was right, wasn't he?" said Dr. Horehound. "Would you care for a spot of brandy?"

"Would we!" said Edward.

"Do help yourselves," said our host, indicating a crystal decanter on a tray encircled with matching glasses on the corner of the desk. "You are welcome to smoke, if you wish. Try mine, if you are adventuresome."

As we did so, I took in our host. He was a large man with broad shoulders. His longish hair was dark gray with black and white streaks, and he combed it back from his forehead so that it shagged out over his collar at the nape of his neck. His eyebrows were large and not exactly bushy, but curled in such a way so as to give the impression of a sneer, even when he was smiling. In fact, his smile seemed a bit wolfish to me in that subdued light in the library. Strange, too, was the fact that his forehead was glistening with sweat, as though he was nervous (which he didn't seem) or fresh from some sort of protracted exertion (which seemed equally unlikely). His eyes were his most discomfiting feature. They seemed glassy and black—darker than Edward's, and with a glint of red (no doubt a reflection from the Tiffany lamp or the fire, but still—).

"Excuse me, sir," I ventured after a sip of brandy. "Would you perhaps be related to Mr. Piaget, or am I imagining a family resemblance?"

"Clarice asked the same thing when she was helping me move in," said Dr. Horehound, turning in his chair to gaze up at the portrait. "I suppose I should be flattered, but no. Any similarity of hairline or bone structure is apparent rather than real."

"Just asking," I said uselessly.

"Tell me," he said, striking a wooden match on the blotter and bringing it to the tip of his cigarette. He drew deeply, reveling in the experience, and exhaled slowly though his nostrils. He didn't mind keeping us waiting as he took another drag, and another. "Marvels," he said at last. "I'm interested in what so amazed you."

We looked at one another, wondering where to begin.

"We saw lights at the campground," ventured Pierre. Compared to the rest, it seemed a safe place to start. "Balls of light. They hovered and flew around, and even formed patterns."

"I wouldn't expect city dwellers to be familiar with St. Elmo's fire," said our host. "It's a common occurrence up here, especially during electrical storms."

"I'm aware of the accounts of sailors," said Pierre. "But these lights—there's no other way to put it—they formed definite geometric shapes."

"Indeed," said Dr. Horehound. "Such as?"

"Well," said Edward. "A circle for one, then a pyramid. And lastly a Cross."

Dr. Horehound paused in the middle of an exhalation of smoke, then expelled the rest with a sigh. "I've heard of such things. Anything else?"

We were taken aback by his offhanded but surgical dismissal.

As we thought it over, something caught my attention. On the edge of the desk, facing us, was an elegant glass case, maybe twelve inches wide and eight deep. On a black velvet cushion inside rested something round and metallic, two inches in diameter. A coin, I thought, or a very old medallion. On its face was a single symbol—the letter X.

"Excuse me, sir," I said, pointing. "Might I ask what that is?"

"You may," he answered, "but it will keep till morning. We were discussing marvels."

Offended, I fell silent and sipped my brandy.

"We heard a howl," said Edward. "It sounded like—well, I don't know. Being a city lad I've no real clue. But it was shrill, and seemed ferocious."

Dr. Horehound stamped out his cigarette. "That interests me. You heard this at the campground?"

"No," said Pierre. "It was on our way back here."

"A mile or two up along the shore," said Edward. "The sheriff warned us about mountain lions, but I don't think so. It didn't sound catlike to me, if you know what I mean."

"Lenore Poe," said Dr. Horehound. "She runs a little bookstore in town. I sold her the property, in fact. It had been vacant for years. Yes, her name is contrived, but I'll grant her a little wish fulfillment. She would tell you there's a Sasquatch in the area."

"Sasquatch?" I asked.

"Bigfoot," said Pierre.

"Sure," said Joel sarcastically. "Why not?"

"Well, *something's* been killing animals around here," said Dr. Horehound. "It started several months ago. The attacks come in flurries separated by lulls of several weeks. I understand the attacks have been increasing in number and savagery."

"I can't say if what we heard had any connection," said Edward. "It sure scared me, that's all I know. And it sounded like a hound. Of course—"

"Gentlemen," interrupted our host, suddenly rising to his feet. "I confess I'm tired. May we continue this in the morning over breakfast?"

"Of course," we said, also getting up from our chairs and setting down our liquor glasses.

"Grayburn will show you to your rooms," he said, stifling a yawn. "Don't worry about payment for tonight. It's the least I can do under the circumstances. If you will excuse me."

With that he walked decisively, perhaps a bit hurriedly, out of the room.

Something caught my attention as he did so: smudges of mud on the carpet. I distinctly remembered us wiping our feet on the welcome mat before entering through the front door. I couldn't be sure, but the smudges seemed to follow the path our host had taken into and out of the room. I thought to say something, but was distracted as Grayburn entered carrying an elaborate candelabrum, seven candles fluttering and billowing beefy tallow smoke.

"This away," he said, tersely. "Thorndale and I gotcher rooms fixed up in a rush while the Master was entertainin' y'all. I trust they'll be to yer likin'."

"Thorndale?" asked Joel.

"She whipped up some sam'iches and hot cocoa," said Grayburn. "Wouldn't wantcha to bed down hungry."

"Thorndale's a she?" asked Joel.

"I'm sure everything will be perfect," said Pierre.

He was nearly right, as it turned out. But not entirely.

∞§[†]§∞

∞§✝§∞

7. That Man Could Use a Vacation

∞§[Martin]§∞

"AND THAT CONCLUDES OUR FIRST NIGHT at Spirit Lake," said Pierre, accepting Jonathan's pages with polished aplomb.

"Say, you're a good writer," said Beth as Jonathan seated himself.

"Ah, shucks," said Jonathan as Edward patted him on the head.

"Indeed," said Pierre. "I must say again that I was favorably impressed with everyone's efforts. Which brings us to you, Miss Elizabeth von Derschmidt."

"Beth," corrected she.

"'Bout time," yelled Kahlúa, clapping wildly. "We've been wading in male ego long enough."

"Let the fairer half have a say," agreed Millie.

"I'm afraid you're going to be disappointed," said Beth, who nonetheless jumped willingly to her feet and made her way to the fireplace.

"Mademoiselle," said Pierre, delicately peeling her pages from within the chest and handing them to her with a flourish. "Your public awaits."

"You're all too kind," said she, accepting her account with a curtsey. "I wish to thank all the little people who helped me along the way."

"Don't overdo it, Honey," chuckled Kahlúa.

∞§[*Beth*]§∞

LADIES SECOND
(I'M NOT COMPLAINING)
BY
BETH VON DERSCHMIDT

There's so much to say, and so little time to write it. I wonder what it will be like, forgetting all the stormy and scary events of the last week. I'm hoping it won't work on me. Maybe if I bite my tongue and hold on to the images in my head really hard ... Oh well, what's my wish against the power of ... Never mind. He said that it will all come back one day, and writing it down will help. Time's a-wasting! On with it!

I can't say I was happy about the change of plans. Arthur, blessedly good brother that he is, phoned me about it three weeks ago. I was to bring my homecoming gown as well as the dress I wore to Aunt May's wedding—and all for some spooky reenactment at some mansion in the mountains. Harder still was not telling Mom and Dad. They never would have approved of me going off on a spree with Arthur's gang of merry men. In the end, it was certainly worth it. Everything turned out wildly right—well, mostly—except for ... Oh dear!

∞§[Martin]§∞

Beth looked up, puzzled and thoughtful.

"What's wrong, Sweetie?" asked Kahlúa.

"Did you write that or did you just say it now?" asked Millie. "'Oh dear!' I mean."

"What? Oh, excuse me," said Beth, coming to herself. "Yes, I wrote the words 'Oh dear!' here, but then I seem to have scribbled out the next sentence. I wonder why."

"You scratched it out?" asked Joel.

"Apparently," said Beth.

Joel seemed perturbed. "And you can't—you know—make out any of the words?"

Beth looked more closely and shook her head.

"What's it to you?" asked Jonathan, turning in his chair to look at Joel.

"Something wrong?" asked Pierre, attentively.

"No, not really," said Joel after an uneasy silence. "It just seems—"

"Not entirely optimistic as introductions go," said Edward with a touch of petulance. "And who's this powerful 'he' that said it would come back some day?"

"'It' being 'stormy and scary,'" added Jonathan with a hint of dread.

"What about the other 'it'?" added Millie. "The one you hoped wouldn't work on you."

"I don't know," said Beth. She took a deep breath and let it out nervously. Her frisky mood had completely changed. "It's a rather ambivalent beginning, isn't it? Everything turning out right—"

"'Wildly right,'" corrected Millie, "and 'mostly.'"

"Except for 'Oh dear!'" added Kahlúa.

"—and whatever it was, I obliterated. Something horrible, I fear."

"I hate to say it," said Pierre, "but there's only one way to find out."

"I'm not sure I want to now," said Beth uneasily. "But I suppose you're right."

∞§[𝐵𝑒𝑡𝘩]§∞

He was standing there when I came through the arrival gate at the airport. My first thought was how prosperous he looked. Life in Southern California had been bountiful for him. Not that it had made him rich—far from it—but he exuded a glow of happiness I had never seen in him back home. He had also gained a few pounds, but he wore them merrily. I love my brother so much, and it was grand to see him again.

"Li'l Sis Liz!" he exclaimed, throwing his strong arms around me.

"Big Brudder Art!" I replied, reaching around and giving his ponytail a good yank. Mom hates his long hair, but I think it's cute. It's certainly him.

"You're looking scrumptious!" he said.

"Watch it," I countered. "You could be mistaken for a chocolate Easter Bunny."

"How's the narcolepsy?"

"I'll tell you when I wake up."

The ride to his apartment was slow and tedious. I can't imagine living in so congested a nasal passage as Los Angeles. After a scrub and a change, we dined at an expensive place called Darby's. The chateaubriand was fantastic, and oh so fancy. Flaming Baked Alaska for dessert was too much. I was impressed when the owner, Mr. Ross, snatched up the bill and declared that our meal was on the house. Arthur, it seems, knows people.

I'm prattling.

The next morning we got up at four. Arthur made a point of praying to St. Ignatius Loyola, whose feast day it was. Having gulped down a sumptuous breakfast of sausage and eggs, and dumping the eating-ware in the dishwasher, we packed our things in the car and headed off for parts unknown. He was the captain and I was the navigator, and our ship was his battered old station wagon. As we passed the 4,000 ft. elevation marker the roads became unexpectedly dangerously wet. There must have been quite a storm during the night—and this was sunny California!

There was an interesting moment when we stopped for gas in a little mountain hamlet with the unsettling name of Claw Junction. While he filled the tank, I ducked into the grocery store for a couple of things I'd forgotten to bring. The lady behind the counter was devouring a large jelly donut, and she didn't wipe off her hands before counting out my change. Eeeew!

When I came outside, there was a sheriff with his arms folded atop his ponderous belly talking to Arthur. His face was grim and his eyes were hidden behind reflective glasses. He was doing his best to be intimidating, and he was succeeding.

"So you're with them," he was saying as I sashayed up to them. Actually I wasn't sashaying so much as dodging puddles. The sheriff didn't seem to mind me leaning close to read the engraved nameplate above his shirt pocket: BRUMUS.

"I already said so," said Arthur, pulling his receipt from the automatic pump and stuffing it into his pocket. "I don't understand your concern, Officer."

"I've seen some of the folks that go up to participate in Doc Horehound's little gatherings," said the sheriff. "Reenactments, they call them. Revisiting the scene of a nasty-ass crime. What kind of people would want to do that?"

"Our kind, I suppose," said Arthur. He was nervous and showed it. Poor guy, he'd never survive a game of poker. "I'm not being facetious, Officer. Our friend Pierre is a columnist for the *Artsy*. His editor—"

"Yeah, I looked into that," said the sheriff. "Some sort of subversive rag run by a former exotic dancer. 'Social commentary and pop culture,' they call it."

"I know nothing of Miss Hummingbird's past," said Arthur—

∞§[Martin]§∞

"Arthur's not alone there, apparently," said Millie, turning an appraising look upon Kahlúa. "Lulu, did I hear correctly?"

"Nothing to get worked up about," said Madam Hummingbird suavely. "Back then, if you wore coconuts and a grass skirt, you were an exotic dancer. Heck, it paid my tuition."

"Don't break your stride, Sis," said Arthur.

"I'm just building up steam," Beth, regaining her composure, assured him while giving Kahlúa an exaggerated wink.

∞§[*Beth*]§∞

"I know nothing of Miss Hummingbird's past," said Arthur, trying but failing to suppress the stammer in his voice. "I only know that Pierre thinks highly of her, and she of him. I researched the Piaget-Ouspenskaya case myself at the library, and while I agree that the scenario is a bit on the gruesome side, Dr. Horehound is a reputable psychologist. I have several of his books here in the car. His treatise on the roots of spiritualism and occult practices in Southern California is actually quite illuminating, incisively witty, and occasionally profound. I suspect he's conducting these sessions to glean anecdotes for an upcoming work. In a way, I'm excited at the prospect of participating in one of them."

"Yeah, sure," said the sheriff, rolling something around in his mouth. The glimpse I caught between his lips didn't look like bubblegum. "So you say. I was worried about those friends of yours, especially that dandy fellow with the bowtie. I took a ride up to the campground about three this morning, but no one was there. They'd made a mess of a perfectly good tent and left it behind. I saw their van parked at the lodge as I came back. I figure they gave up in the thunderstorm and headed there for shelter."

"I wouldn't know," said Arthur. "You say there was quite a downpour. The roadway has been wet for the last fifty miles."

"Haven't seen anything like it, not ever," said the sheriff. "The highway to Devils Horns washed out around midnight. They're predicting another round tonight."

"Sounds colorful," I butted in, tired of being ignored. "I guess there's a lot of history up here—eh, Sheriff?"

He deigned to turn his head a fraction of an inch by way of acknowledgement of my dainty presence. "And just what did you mean by that, Miss?"

"Obviously," I said, putting on my cutest smile, "with names like Devils Horns, Claw Junction, Spirit Lake, and—oh, didn't I see a sign for Witches Punchbowl thirty miles up Route 16?"

"I'd be careful about making inferences," said the sheriff, turning those mirrored spectacles fully toward me. "Folks up here mind their own business."

"And well they should," said I, sniggering. I couldn't help it. "With names like that, I don't want to know." He responded with a half-smile, so I pointed to his nametag. "Speaking of names—?"

"Brew-muss," he obliged me.

Before I could ask if he had a first name, Arthur said, "You're welcome to follow us, Sheriff Brumus, seeing as how you're so concerned for our welfare."

"I was thinking the same thing," said he, unfolding his meaty arms. "There's something I gotta check on up there anyway. I'm ready if you are."

"Got what you needed?" asked Big Brudder.

"Shampoo and hairpins," answered Li'l Sis. "I'm loaded for bear."

"Hoo-boy," said Sheriff Brumus, turning and striding to his idling vehicle.

"Why'd you invite him?" I asked as we got in our wagon.

"I don't know," said Arthur, flustered. "I figured he wants to stick his nose in our affairs, so we might as well welcome him in. Guy like that goes where he wants anyway."

The drive to the lake was beautiful, but the road was bumpy and the tires sometimes spun in the mud. All the while the sheriff loomed behind.

I admit I squeaked when Wolfram Lodge came into view. It was like something out of a time-travel novel, a mixture of Jolly Old England and the Wild Frontier. The pine log bridge creaked and sagged as we moseyed across. The water beneath seemed agitated, lots of sharp-peaked waves going every which way. I assumed it was because of the storm during the night. The parking area in front was graveled. The tires crunched and skittered as Arthur maneuvered the wagon beside an old van.

"Twelve minutes to nine," said Arthur, turning off the ignition. "We made it."

"So did the Lone Ranger," said I as the sheriff parked his car sideways behind us so we couldn't back out.

"They're here!" called a voice from the porch. "Come out, Lads! Arthur and Beth have arrived! They brought the Law with them!"

I shouldn't have been surprised, considering the dress code, but seeing that dashing gentleman in a morning coat, striped pants, and cravat was simply too much! He was quickly joined by three others, similarly attired. They looked like characters right out of Dickens as they clambered down the rough wooden steps and crunched their way toward us.

"Pierre, Jonathan, Edward, and Joel," said Arthur with a flourish. "May I present my sister, Elizabeth."

"Beth," I corrected him.

"Charmed," said Pierre, taking my hand and—of all things—giving it a peck.

The others did likewise. So these were Arthur's friends. No wonder he was so happy. I liked them immediately.

"Your names again, please," I said, so not wanting to get them confused. They heartily complied, and complied again.

"Pardon me for saying this," said Jonathan, "but you seem so wide awake."

"Told you about my little condition, did he?" said I, elbowing Arthur. "Not to worry. As long as I take my meds, I won't snore on you."

"Who're you trying to be?" asked Pierre of my brother. "Uncle Joe?"

"I was thinking Grandpappy Amos," said Arthur.

Oh, I forgot to mention that, for the purposes of a comfortable road trip and the possibility of mechanical problems, Arthur was wearing overalls—the denim kind with attached suspenders and pockets all over. I was wearing a flowered skirt and a fluffy red sweater. I figured Uncle Joe and Grandpappy Amos were references to old TV shows in which my brother and Pierre shared an interest.

"Dr. Horehound is waiting within," said Pierre as the Tumblars (what a name!) hefted our bags out of the car. "He's not the sort of host who comes out to greet his guests. He prefers to receive them in the library."

"We've got ten minutes to change then," said Arthur, consulting his watch.

"Joel," said Pierre. "Would you please escort our new arrivals to their rooms?"

"Sure," said Joel with a scowl. He'd became suddenly perturbed, though why I couldn't guess. He'd seemed so jovial a moment before. With a shrug and a sigh he took up Arthur's garment bag by the hook and draped it over his back. "Beth, Arthur, this way."

"Here, I'll help you with that," said Jonathan, taking up my suitcase. So gallant.

The floorboards of the porch groaned welcomingly as we crossed over, shuffled our feet on the immense welcome mat, and entered through the enormous front door. It was made of wooden planks with bars and studs all over, like something out of a fairytale. The foyer was breathtaking, with archways and French doors on both sides, and a huge staircase that flowed upward, then divided in two as it curved around to meet the second floor. This we climbed, paintings of all sorts of pompous people looking down upon us as we went.

"Veer to the left," said Jonathan. "Our rooms are in the north wing."

"Excuse me for asking," I whispered to him as we reached the landing. "It's none of my business, but do you guys own those getups?"

"Our tuxedos, yes," he answered with a conspiratorial wink. "But just between you and me and all these stuffy portraits, Kahlúa Hummingbird knows a guy who makes costumes for the movie studios. You've probably seen these outfits before on the big screen. Wait'll you see the 'country gentleman tweeds' we'll be wearing later."

"Arthur, you're in here," said Joel, sullenly turning the brass knob on a large oaken door.

"And this is yours," said Jonathan, swinging mine open to reveal a simply enchanting bedroom. Like a gentleman, he left the door open. Setting down my bag, he pointed to various things lest I somehow not notice them. "There's the bed, of course, and the dressing room with walk-in closet. You have your own balcony with a splendid view of the lake. The bathroom's in there—wait'll you get a load of the tub. If it's like mine, it's a veritable swimming pool. Fireplace—the logs are real, naturally. No light switches, I'm afraid. It's candles and oil lamps, at least in the guestrooms. There's electricity on the first floor, but not up here. Don't know why. You'll find matches on the mantel and the nightstand. Oh, look at me, I sound like a bellhop. I'll leave you to freshen up. But hurry, Dr. Horehound expects punctuality."

"He doesn't expect an evening gown at this time of day, does he?" I asked, testing the bed with my palms. It was yummy.

"No, but something proper to be sure," said Jonathan, heading for the door. He tripped over his feet, but righted himself with a smile. "Think Hollywood, circa 1935."

"Right," I said, wishing I'd brought more elegant daywear. Oh well, I thought, they'll kill for me this evening. For now, I'll count on my million-dollar smile.

I came swooshing down the stairway a few minutes later to find Arthur and his friends milling around in the foyer. I felt like I was descending into a luscious old movie.

"There you are," said Arthur, smiling proudly, transformed into a stately gentleman. I noticed his vest looked a little stretched across his prosperity, and made a note to dig out my sewing kit later to let it out.

"Well," I said, fluttering my eyelashes. "Shall we go in?"

"Sheriff Brumus is already chewing on our host's leg, methinks," said Pierre. "He stormed right past us and slammed the door."

"Apparently some local kids stole one of the doctor's boats," said Jonathan.

"They can't get very far, can they?" I surmised. "It's his lake, after all. This is the library? What's that across the way?"

"The recital room," said Jonathan. "There's a nine-foot grand piano in there, and a harpsichord, and even a harp."

"All in tune?" I asked, cracking my knuckles. It was unladylike, and I can't play anything but three chords on a guitar, but they took it good-naturedly.

"And that way leads to the dining room," said Edward, "eventually."

"And that, Mademoiselle," said Pierre, his voice morphing into an inept imitation of Bela Lugosi, "leads to the séance room."

"Poker, anyone?" I asked.

Before anyone could answer, the French doors to our left rattled open and the sheriff came out in a huff. "You behave yourselves," he said to us, all gruff and important. "I don't want to have to come back up here. I've got enough troubles in town."

"We'll try," I said, wiggling my fingers daintily at him.

He cursed impolitely and stomped toward the front door. As he pulled it open, he glared at us and positively growled, "Two Doberman pinschers this time: Miss Poe's, between here and the road to Devils Horns. One had its head torn completely off. I'd advise against going for any evening strolls." The door boomed shut behind him.

"That man could use a vacation," said Pierre. "Perhaps a week at a secluded mountain lake."

"Lady and Gentlemen," said a strange-looking grizzled fellow who appeared at the library door. "Dr. Horehound welcomes y'all to Wolfram Lodge."

"This is my sister, Beth," said Arthur to him.

"Tell the Master," said the terse, scrawny man before bustling off somewhere.

"I take it that's not Dr. Horehound," I said to my brother.

"Grayburn," said Arthur. "He's the irate butler. There's one in every murder mystery."

"Do come in," invited a commanding voice, and so we did.

"Oh Arthur," I gasped. "You could lose yourself in a playground like this!"

It was an immense library. What wall space wasn't crammed with old books was filled with portraits and landscapes in oil. There was a cozy fire sparking in the fireplace and a picture window facing the rickety bridge. We arranged ourselves on high-backed chairs with leather cushions around a large desk, behind which sat our host. After all the courtesies of my brother's friends, I was taken aback that he didn't stand for us — or for me in particular. Harrumph.

"Beth, Dr. Horehound," said Arthur.

"Charmed," said the doc, but he didn't mean it. "Lost something, Mr. ... uh ... Clubb?"

Jonathan, who was stooped down, dragging his fingers on the deep-pile carpet, looked up. "Not here, apparently."

"Please join us," said Dr. Horehound. "Do be seated. We'll be breakfasting momentarily, but I'd like to make a few introductory remarks. This is my home, and you are my guests— albeit paying guests. My wealth speaks for itself. I don't need your money. Experience has taught me, however, that people get more out of that which they pay for. In your case I understand Miss Hummingbird is covering expenses. Let us hope she will get what *she* paid for, albeit vicariously through you. Now, while a certain cordiality will likely ensue, we will not become, or part, as friends. That isn't the purpose of this gathering. We will be reenacting a series of mysterious and, yes, unsettling events: one grisly death and three inexplicable disappearances, the last one tinged with evidence of violence. While here, you will be afforded every hospitality. For reasons I need not elucidate, I do not employ a large fulltime household staff proportional to the number of rooms in this mansion. What servants I have are at your disposal. I remind you, however, that Grayburn, whom you've met, and Thorndale, whom you will meet shortly, are only two. This is a big house, and their duties are many. Please don't take advantage of them. They bite."

There was a moment of silence before we realized that he had made a joke. Pierre made a convincing attempt at chuckling. The rest of them less so. I just sighed and smiled.

"Although I had the original bell pull system restored during renovation," he added, "it proved to be too great a temptation for some of my inconsiderate guests."

"They got bitten," suggested Jonathan.

"Figuratively," said our host. "Too much starch in the laundry or any in the scrambled eggs can produce undesirable effects."

There was another moment of uncomfortable silence as we considered whether that was supposed to be funny as well.

"I had all but a few cords for my personal use disconnected," he said, undaunted. "Those hanging in your rooms should be regarded as quaint decorations."

We all nodded slowly and wordlessly.

"Breakfast is at nine, except for this morning," continued the doctor with an irritated sniff. "Lunch at one, dinner at six. This will be our routine for the next few days. Meals will be sumptuous, I guarantee. I'll ask that you not raid the refrigerator in between. Thorndale, my cook and chambermaid, does not tolerate forays into her kitchen. She will diligently keep a carafe of coffee on a hotplate in the dining room should you need a stimulant. There's no decaffeinated—she refuses to brew the filthy stuff. You are free to wander the house and grounds. The séance room where we will meet later is locked and out of bounds until eight tonight, at which time those of you who wish to inspect the premises may enter under my supervision. The séance itself will commence at nine. Are there any questions? No? Then let us proceed to the dining room."

"Quite the charmer," I whispered to Arthur.

"Shhh," he retorted.

Breakfast was sumptuous, as promised. I admit I overdid the sausage and biscuits. I slapped Arthur's hand when he reached for thirds on the pancakes. After all, this was our second meal in one morning.

We were joined by two women who said nothing during breakfast. Dr. Horehound introduced them as Madam Douceur (pronounced Dew-*sir)*, a channeling medium in his employ (whatever that meant), and Clarice Davenport, his personal secretary. The first was a plump little woman who reminded me of my Aunt Lorraine—no compliment there. The words "treacle," "sweet," and "nauseating" bumped together in my mind just looking at her syrupy smile. Dr. Horehound called her "E. I. D."—some sort of nickname, I supposed. The other woman was the kind of gal I would gladly run over with a truck if Arthur took a shine to her. She was a vamp, a slut, a wanton little seductress—am I being rude? She liked to tease men with her plunging neckline and wide, baby-blue eyes. A good girl knows a bad girl when she sees one. She was wicked.

There's something I noticed about Dr. Horehound that I'll mention here. While we were busy engorging ourselves, he ate very little, and extremely slowly. He'd take a tiny bit of egg or a wedge of orange and, well, suck on it a while. His lips puckered and his cheeks caved in slightly, as if he were extracting the juices out of it. Then, phase one completed, he'd chew ever so deliberately—once—twice—thrice—on up to thirty chomps or more. It took well over a minute. I timed him by the clock on the sideboard. Phase two tediously finished, he then proceeded to swallow. Only he could make this simple act into a slow, laborious, nerve-wracking process—and one can only guess at what was left to go down after all that slow-motion masticating! I've heard of chewing your food carefully, but this was something else. Then it hit me: he was savoring the experience to the fullest, just as he imbibed the smoke from his cigarettes. He was a man of deep appetites, and incredible self-control when it came to meeting them. This, more than anything else, put me on my guard against him.

"Might I ask why you hold these events?" asked Pierre as the coffee was served by Thorndale, who was rather detached and stiff, but hardly the terror Dr. Horehound had suggested.

"The fact that the perpetrator was never apprehended makes for a scenario with many possible endings," said Arthur.

"My reasons are just as many," said Dr. Horehound, lighting a cigarette, drawing smoke gradually and deeply into his lungs, and releasing it toward the ceiling in a long, unhurried trickle. "I am a student of human behavior," he said, choosing his words carefully, "and I have found the subject of death—more so the way people deal with death—intriguing."

"I read your book on spiritualism," said Arthur. "I found you to be a consummate skeptic with respect to religion."

"One has to be when dealing with whackos," said Dr. Horehound. The word startled me, coming from a professional. "Nothing in life is more final than death," he expounded, "which is why people fear it. It is a complete and irreversible severing, the slicing of cosmic scissors separating what was from what is."

∞§[Martin]§∞

I was vividly reminded of the words of Leon Blanc, *chef de cuisine* at the Willow Club in Boston, repeated by prosecutor Barry Tolman of Marlin County, to private detective Nero Wolfe at the Kanawha Spa in West Virginia, as chronicled by his assistant Archie Goodwin, in Rex Stout's *Too Many Cooks:* "Death doth not heal, it amputates." I interject this tidbit to establish, I suppose, that Doctor Horehound's insight was not original, nor peculiar to him. Hrmph!

∞§[*Beth*]§∞

"The death of a loved one," continued our host, "even one long ill and anticipating their end, leaves the survivor devastated beyond their wildest expectation for this very reason. Hence the fear, the terrible, daunting fear. I understand, on the other hand, from the way you all crossed yourselves and said a silent blessing before commencing, that you are of the Catholic persuasion."

"Correct," said Pierre.

"Your religion is permeated with death, you know," said the doctor condescendingly. "Your God died horribly, yet you believe he somehow overcame it. You eat his flesh to somehow share in his triumph.* Grisly. But in spite of your sacraments, your Extreme Unctions, you all continue to die. Do you not see the irony in this?"

It was my understanding that Joel had been a seminarian, so I assumed he would be quick to jump into such a discussion. But when I glanced his way, he seemed to be consumed with the process of selecting a cigarette from a silver case, which he then

---

* "... he somehow ... his flesh ... his triumph." In her original manuscript, Beth had capitalized these personal pronouns. Normally I, too, would capitalize all pronouns referring to Jesus Christ. However, assuming that Dr. Horehound would not, I chose, as mismanaging editor, not to impose our proprieties upon him.   —M.F.

returned to his jacket pocket. So detached was he, as he lit up, that he could have been sitting outside on the porch. In his mind, he probably was.

Arthur, however, was very much engaged. "Although you maintain an overtly cynical posture, I gathered that you had more respect for our beliefs than that. In your work on Navaho shape-shifters—"

"My graduate thesis," said Dr. Horehound with an appreciative nod. "I lived among them for two years. They regarded me with the same suspicion you are all now exuding. What secrets I learned were mostly by accident: a shaman resorting to bragga-docio when I pretended not to be impressed; one jealous healer grumbling about another's methods. That sort of thing."

"But you *were* impressed by a Catholic missionary who lived just outside the reservation," said Arthur. "You marveled that he once walked thirty-five miles into forbidden territory to baptize a dying woman."

"He was one courageous son of a bitch," said Dr. Horehound, smiling. "I'll give him that. The tribal council complained to his bishop, you know. The old sop complied, not wanting to incur public disfavor. Banished him to some toilet of a town in New Mexico. The point I was making was that the Aboriginals never took me into their confidence. You Catholics, on the other hand, are more open with your beliefs, though you surely realize that in the beginning your rites were held in secret."

"The Romans considered the Mass ritualistic cannibalism," said Arthur. "The faithful had no choice but to practice their religion literally underground, in the catacombs."

"And to this day," said Dr. Horehound, "or at least until that laughable attempt at coming clean, your Second Vatican Coun-cil, the words of consecration were uttered over altars that were but replicas of sepulchers—a revealing allusion to the good old days." He laughed at that one, the creep.

"I disagree that our religion is only about death," said Pierre. "True, it is something we all face. We pray daily in the Hail Mary that we make a good end. But there you have the real irony: the Holy Mother of God. The Blessed Virgin is our gate-way to Heaven, to eternal life. That is our goal, our purpose. If you don't realize that, then surely your research has been misguided."

"The Virgin Mother," mused Dr. Horehound. "The reincarnation of Isis, Aphrodite, the Goddess Principle."

"Wrong," said Arthur. "You can't reduce Her to such as that. If anything, those concepts, those female archetypes, are but reflections of the yearning of the pagan mind for *Theotokos*, the God Bearer."

"You really believe that," said Dr. Horehound snidely.

"With all my heart," said Arthur. I nudged him under the table. You tell him, Big Bro.

"I can see we're going to have a splendid time," said our host, rising from the table. "If you will excuse me, I have some urgent matters to attend to. Come, Clarice, E. I. D. We must prepare for this evening's festivities. The rest of you, do make yourselves at home. The storm has paused for the nonce. The weatherman predicts another round this evening. Might I suggest you visit my garden while the sun is out? The summer flowers are blooming. I hope they weren't trodden by the rain."

With that he left us.

∞§[†]§∞

∞§✝§∞

8. A Triangle within a Circle

∞§[**Martin**]§∞

"AND WITH THAT," SAID PIERRE, "our charming Beth concludes her first oration."

"Bravo!" called Millie, clapping wildly. "Bravissimo! Bra-vissie-missie-mo!"

"Well done, Li'l Sis," said Arthur, giving her hand a squeeze as she sat down beside him sideways again on her chair.

"Come to think of it," said Kahlúa, leaning forward conspiratorially, "I could use a correspondent like you in Cleveland."

"Oh?" laughed Beth. "What for?"

"I'll come up with something," said Kahlúa.

"Mead's all gone," announced Pierre, having gone to the well and found the pitcher dry.

"That's my cue to fetch the eggnog," said Millie.

"I'll help," said Kahlúa.

"No you won't," said Millie, heaving herself onto her weary feet. "You're a guest."

"You still only got two hands, Girl," said Kahlúa, swinging herself onto hers. "What is this, *déjà vu?*"

"Naw," said Millie. "You're just stuck in a groove on my broken record."

"'Ooooh in my way—a'diddlely dee, a'diddlely doo—I want to say,'" sang Kahlúa, snapping her fingers as they made their hip-swinging way down the hallway.

"'How much I need you—a'sklippety beep, a'sklippety boop—ev-er-y day,'" Millie joined in.

"So what's next?" asked Jonathan.

"I pity the next fellow," said Arthur. "Sis, you're a hard act to follow."

"What country hasn't been heard from?" asked Edward.

"Arthur!" came the resounding chorus.

"By popular demand," said Pierre with a smile. "Herr von Derschmidt: vrrrront und zenter!"

"Here goes all credibility," said Arthur to Beth. "Out der vindow!"

"Tee hee!" taunted she.

Receiving his pages, Arthur coughed behind his hand, patted his paunch, and picked up where his beloved sister had left off:

∞§[Aʀᴛʜuʀ]§∞

"Well," said I. "I'm for the library."

"No you don't," said Beth, locking her arm in mine. "Not after a big meal like that. You need to walk it off, Big Bro. To the garden with you."

"Mind if I tag along?" asked Jonathan.

"I've got my Rottweiler," said Beth, patting my stomach. "Sure. Let's go."

We went out the front door because it was the only one we knew thus far. Jonathan made a big show of opening it and bowing as Beth and I exited. The mountain air was damp, chilly, and bristling with the scent of wet pine trees. We turned right and followed the great porch around to the north side of the lodge.

The lake spread out into the valley, dark and deep, the surface still jittery from yesterday's storm. There was a picturesque boardwalk partway along the island's north shore, along with a weathered dock and four piers. Three boats rocked in the nervously surging water. Two had masts and the third, I think, was equipped with an inboard motor. At the east end of the dock was a building I took to be a boathouse. It was certainly large enough to accommodate the vessels, and at this altitude the lake probably froze in the winter. There seemed to be an extension at the far end that served as another guestroom, or perhaps quarters for one of the servants. The curtains in the windows were lacy and flowery, suggesting a woman's touch.

Jonathan seemed a bit fidgety as we stood there, taking it in. He spent a silent minute leaning against the knotty wooden handrail, gazing out at the lake. More than once he craned his neck as if to peer down at a steeper angle—to see what, I could not imagine. I chalked it up to stalling while mulling over possible avenues of approach to my sister.

"I wonder why those kids stole an old tub," said Beth as a gust of wind shifted a tuft of her hair across her face. "Why not one of those beauties?"

"Probably figured the penalty wouldn't be as great if they got caught," said Jonathan.

Beth swept her hair aside. "Why couldn't the sheriff just take a quick drive around the lake? There's no place for them to hide, is there?"

"I only glanced at Pierre's brochure," I said, "but the not-so-detailed map showed a road only going up along the west side."

"That's right," said Jonathan, pointing vaguely to the northwest. "It dead-ends at the campground."

"Oh yes, the campground," said Beth. "Can you see it from here?"

"No," said Jonathan. "The lake bends, you see, and it's too far, anyway."

"Speaking of which," said Beth playfully, "I keep hearing whispers—specifically the word, 'disaster.' What happened up there?"

Jonathan thrust his hands deep into his pockets. "You'd hardly expect us to give a detailed account of our own gross ineptitude."

"I most certainly would," said Beth.

"You don't, Arthur," said Jonathan. "Do you, Old Bean? Arthur!"

"I wish I knew how to sail," I said, charging to a fellow Knight's rescue. "This wouldn't be a great day for it, but perhaps later during our stay ..."

"I've been with Dad on Lake Erie," said Beth. "I could take us."

"Not on *that* lake," said Jonathan, wiggling his finger at it.

"Why not?" she asked pointedly.

"Trust me," said Jonathan. "I'll tell you later."

"How much later?"

"Just later, okay?"

"Whatever," said Beth, nudging me into reluctant ambulation.

The porch wrapped around the eastern or back side of the lodge. From there we beheld the garden. I'm not into flowers *per se*, but I found the scheme enchanting. In the midst of a landscape that was rocky and tumultuous, a circular area about three hundred feet across had been painstakingly leveled. Around the rim grew a well-manicured hedge about waist-high and four feet thick. Just inside the hedge was a walkway of smooth terracotta bricks. It was about ten feet wide and likewise circumscribed the garden. Within this, three straight pathways connected three equidistant points on the circular path, in other words, forming a triangle within the circle. It was a pleasing geometric arrangement that divided the garden into four sections: three slivers in which grew a wild variety of plants, shrubs, and citrus trees; and a grassy area within the central triangle sparsely dotted with rosebushes. In addition, all the walkways were lined on both sides with colorful flowers. I'm sorry I don't know the names. Beth will no doubt fill in such details in her account.

"This is charming," she said. "There must be a break in the hedge somewhere so we can look around inside."

"There," said Jonathan, indicating an entrance on the west side.

"My hero," said Beth playfully.

Jonathan smiled.

We made our way down a few wooden steps, and then along a graveled path. Growing up through the hedge, just to right of the entrance, was some sort of pale-barked sapling that formed a Y before erupting into a cover of pastel leaves. It was likely a plant that would be removed one day soon because it threw off the symmetry of the entrance—or perhaps that was the point, I could not say. Something strung between the two arms of this plant glistened brilliantly as it billowed faintly in the tender breeze. Jonathan halted for a closer look.

"Ah, a spider's web," said Beth. "It's pretty the way the rain-drops are clinging all over it."

"See how they break the bright morning light into rainbow colors like so many little prisms," said Jonathan.

"I wonder how the spider likes it," I said. "Probably not great for catching butterflies, or just getting from one end to the other, for that matter."

"Shhhh," whispered Jonathan, shutting his eyes. "Everyone make a wish."

"Why?" asked Beth and me together.

"Just do it," he said. "Trust me. Ready? Got it in your mind? Okay, here goes ..."

With his face inches from the shimmering phenomenon, he took a deep breath, held it, and blew it out in an open-mouthed puff. The web stayed intact, but all the droplets exploded into a blaze of tiny shimmering sparkles as they fell gently away.

"I've never heard of making a wish like *that*," said Beth.

"I've had pretty good results with it," said Jonathan, wiping his nose, which had gotten splashed. "Dad told me that he and Mom made such a wish the morning of the day I was conceived. They also prayed to St. Felix of Nola, which is what really sealed the deal."

Beth gave him an inscrutable smile.

"Shall we proceed?" I suggested, not wanting to get drawn in.

∞§[Martin]§∞

GARDENING TIPS: I checked, and I'll have you know that there is in fact a Patron Saint of Spiders! Felix of Nola was fleeing from Roman soldiers with an ailing friend, Maximus, during the persecution of Decius in 250 AD. At one point they took refuge in a vacant building. A spider quickly spun a web across the doorway, making it look long abandoned.

```
Fooled, the imperial forces went on by.  Felix

did a lot of other courageously virtuous

things in his life, and his tomb near Naples

became a place of miracles after his death,

but it is in his connection with that hyperac-

tive spider (no doubt divinely energized) that

he touches our story.  He died c. 255 AD, and

his Feast Day is January 14th.

                                    --M.F.



N.B.: Spiders?  Come to think of it, my little

apartment behind the rectory at St. Philo-

mena's is a shrine to St. Felix of Nola!!
```

∞§[ARTHUR]§∞

Once within the garden, I was glad that Beth had insisted that we investigate. It seemed a truly colorful, restful, thought-inducing place, even though the rain had flooded much of it during the night and drained off, leaving a layer of swirled silt over large sections of the footpaths.

"Look," said Beth, just as we entered. "Letters." Indeed, blue, red, and green marble tiles had been artistically set amidst the rectangular terracotta bricks forming letters two feet tall. "G—A—B—R," she read aloud. "Darn. The rest is covered with mud."

"Gabrielle," said Jonathan. "Bartholomew Piaget's wife's name was Gabrielle."

"Then this was her garden," said Beth. "How nice."

We followed the circular walkway in a clockwise direction. Our shoes left inch-deep impressions around the north quarter, where the silt was particularly thick.

"And here," said Beth, as we came to the eastern side. "P—H—A—E," she read, but the letters before and after were blotted out.

We veered off the circular walkway when we came to one of the straight paths. Again we found letters, mostly obliterated: "T—R—A—G—R—A," read Beth. "What do you make of that?"

"Beats me," said Jonathan. "Maybe her relatives? What do you think, Arthur?"

"Haven't a clue," said I, although something tugged vaguely at the elastic edges of my memory.

"Let's try this one," said Beth when we came to the next intersection.

"E—P—H—E—Z," read Jonathan as we walked over them. "Pretty strange names, whatever they are."

"Maybe they're places," I suggested. "Perhaps each section contains flora from a different part of the world."

Just then we came upon Grayburn. He was dressed in gardening attire—baggy jeans, rubber boots, over-sized canvas gloves. The uneven ends of his peppered hair seemed to explode from under a black wool ski cap. He was standing a few feet off the path on the wet grass, snipping plump summer roses from a thorny bush with a pair of spring-loaded clippers.

"Hi, there," said Beth, all friendly. "Whatcha doing?"

Grayburn regarded us with unwelcoming eyes, then turned his attention to the next royal red blossom. "Mornin'," he said non-committally.

"Flowers for the dinner table?" asked Beth, tightening her grip on my arm.

He shook his head.

"The library, then?" she persisted.

He positioned the clipper about fifteen inches down-stem and squeezed the handles. "The Master 'sists on roses in the séance room, Missie." He added the cut flower to the dozen or so lying on the glistening grass near his feet. "Somethin' 'bout the way it was back when."

"A touch of realism," I remarked.

He nodded tersely, his attention on his work. "It's important to him, and he pays my salary."

"We've been trying to read the words on these paths," ventured Beth. "They're mostly covered with mud."

"Happens when it rains," agreed Grayburn, whom I was beginning to regard as a crotchety old codger.

"I don't suppose you could hose them off," she suggested. "I mean, so we can see them?"

He paused to glare at her. "Now why would I wanna go to the trouble when it's gonna rain again tonight? Don't worry, Missie. I'll see to it tomorrow or the next day."

"Sorry to have troubled you," said Beth, sticking out her chin.

Grayburn gave her a look that said he was sorry that she had, too, and waved his clippers in a way that suggested we'd best move on.

"I say," said Jonathan, oblivious to the old codger's desire for solitude. "That reminds me. You said something interesting last night, you know, when we came stumbling onto the front porch."

"Oh," said Grayburn, turning back to the rosebush. It wasn't an invitation for Jonathan to proceed with his question. It may have been an acknowledgement that the event did, in fact, occur. But to my ears it sounded like the first half of an imprecation.

"Yes," said Jonathan. "You said, 'Great Queen of Cups.'"

That caught my attention. "Did he?"

"He did," said Jonathan assuredly. "I've never heard that expression. Were you perhaps referring to Mrs. Piaget?"

"Heck, no," said the gruff old bird. He abandoned his horticultural task with a protracted sigh and turned to face us. "You won't see 'em till tonight, but there'll be paintin's on the walls where y'all will be. Big ones. There's a magician with a wand, a bearded guy holdin' a lantern, a knight on horseback that'll give you the creeps, and someone saddled with a name somethin' like 'the elephant' but not 'zactly."

"The Hierophant," I suggested.

"That's it," said Grayburn, becoming more animated. "Looks like the Pope to me, but what do I know? My favorite calls herself the Queen of Cups, that's all. She's sittin' there on her throne all pretty-like with a little stream runnin' by her feet. She's holdin' this enormous goblet. She looks a bit tipsy, if you ask me. I could go for a gal like that."

"Cards from the Tarot deck," I said.

"And just how would you know about that?" asked Beth, prodding me accusingly.

"Books," I answered defensively.

"Forbidden stuff, eh?" said Grayburn, smiling sneakily.

"To some," I said vaguely, hoping for a change of subject.

"Well, y'all're in for it tonight," said Grayburn, warming to our intrusion after all. He glanced around furtively. "Maybe I'm lettin' out a cat that I shouldn't, but that Madam Oopsenkowsky, the one that ended up dead, did a fortune card readin' as part of her séance. Came up with Death, you know—that creepy knight I told you 'bout."

"Ick," said Beth. "I don't know if I want any part of that."

"It's in the ritual, Missie," said Grayburn, smiling enigmatically. "You know: it's gotta be done just like the first time—for authenticity, the Master says."

"Oh dear," said Beth.

"It's just a reenactment," said Jonathan. "Surely there's no harm."

"I don't like it," said Beth. "Would Father Baptist approve?"

"Pierre and Joel said they asked him," said Jonathan.

"And he said it's okay?"

"I guess," said Jonathan. "If he'd said no they would have said so."

"You're sure."

He shrugged.

"Arthur?" she nudged me again.

"What can I tell you?" I said. "Apparently it's all right. I'm not worried. In fact, I'm looking forward to it."

"You do that," said Grayburn, pocketing his clippers. "Well, I gotta get these in water, and then I got tons of stuff to do inside."

"I'll go in with you," I said, disengaging myself from my sister's clutches. "Beth, I really do want to peruse the doctor's bookshelves. Why don't you and Jonathan enjoy the garden?"

"Good idea," said Jonathan, offering Beth his arm.

She looked at me, a tangle of thoughts whirling around in those elvish eyes of hers. Then she turned to Jonathan and gave him a good dose of what, I don't know. Finally she accepted his arm and elbowed him into motion. Grayburn and I watched them stroll down the path, examining the partially obscured letters in the stones.

"Sweet," commented Grayburn.

"I hope so."

"Friend of yers?"

"Yes."

"I hope so, too."

I accompanied Grayburn through the break in the hedge. When we got up to the lodge, he entered through a backdoor not nearly as imposing as the one in front. I entered with him and found myself in the kitchen. Thorndale was huffing and puffing over a large pot she was stirring on the stove. She gave me a glare that reminded me of Millie.

"Pardon me," I said. "Just passing through."

"Be quick about it, then," she barked.

Yes, she was a lot like Millie.

Next stop: the library!

∞§[†]§∞

∞§✝§∞

9. Minimum Information Gambit

∞§[Martin]§∞

"WHO'S A LOT LIKE ME?" grunted Millie, entering with a new tray of mugs.

"Thorndale, apparently," said Arthur, handing his pages to Pierre. "The cook at the lodge."

"Her eggnog could *not* be as good as this!" said Kahlúa, who followed carrying a generous pot of yellow liquid. With a dramatic grunt she set it on the edge of the desk, displacing several presents, one with an umbrella handle sticking out the end. "Not no way," she insisted. "Not no how!"

"That I don't doubt," said Father, who had hefted a book from the "To be forewarned" shelf. I noticed the cover before he opened it in his lap: *Key to the Tarot: Being Fragments of a Secret Tradition under the Veil of Divination* by A. E. Waite. He paused at a woodcut rendition of the Queen of Cups. Hmm. She toted quite a goblet, all right. "So you Lads did come to me for advice," he said, turning the page.

"And you did shoo them out," said Millie, ladling the Yuletide brew into the mugs. "Or I did. Who knows?"

"Arthur, I'm surprised at you," said Edward. "Leaving your sister to wander the garden with Jonathan here."

"Says Arthur," said Jonathan sheepishly.

"Did he now?" said Kahlúa, deftly handing out mugs of eggnog. "I just knew I was missin' somethin' juicy."

"If I did," said Arthur, seating himself, "which I truly don't remember, it was with the certain knowledge that my dear sister can take care of herself."

"You'd better believe it," said Beth, punching Jonathan playfully on the shoulder.

"So what's next?" asked Joel, accepting his mug and savoring the scent of nutmeg.

"You are," said Pierre. "We come to a Tumblar powwow in the library."

"Great," said Joel, grumpily setting down his mug and heaving himself out of his chair.

∞§[*JOEL*]§∞

After lunch, we gathered in the library to compare notes—

∞§[Martin]§∞

"Was I included?" interrupted Beth.

"What? Hmm." Joel glanced down the page, then examined the next. "I don't think so."

"Harrumph."

"You was probably upstairs in your boudoir," said Kahlúa. "Makin' your pretty self prettier."

"For who?" asked Millie, settling in her chair clutching the largest of the mugs.

Beth laughed gaily.

"Enough," said Pierre. "Please continue."

Joel obliged.

∞§[*JOEL*]§∞

After lunch, we gathered in the library to compare notes. Arthur and Jonathan told us of the discovery of Piaget's wife's name on the stone path in the garden. Also the word fragments: PHAE, TRAGRA and EPHEZ. I said that'd make a cool name for a rock band, but no one laughed.

"You seem troubled," said Pierre to Arthur. "Do those bits mean anything to you?"

"Almost," said Arthur. He rubbed his forehead. "But not quite. They remind me of something I've read somewhere, but I can't imagine what." He ran his eyes along the bookshelves, but didn't find whatever he was looking for.

"Considering all you've read," said Jonathan, "that's like looking for the proverbial needle."

"In the haystack of my mind," agreed Arthur. "It'll come to me eventually. It always does. And you, Pierre, what have you discovered, if anything?"

"Before I go into that," said our fearless leader, "Lads, I think we should fill our friend Arthur in on what we saw and heard last night."

I spoke my mind, for what it was worth: "He'll think we're crazy."

"He wouldn't be the first," said Pierre, dismissively. Then he proceeded to relate a lively summary of our adventures—or rather misadventures—taking care to minimize his own contribution to the camping disaster.

Arthur seemed intrigued by the floating lights over the fire pit. He, too, thought it might have been St. Elmo's fire, but had no suggestions when it came to the geometric shapes they made in the air, although he certainly looked pensive. He grimaced when Pierre came to the howl we heard by the lake, saying he was beginning to wonder if it had been a good idea after all bringing his sister into this. Jonathan assured him we would protect her— yeah, right. And of course Arthur rolled his eyes when Pierre got to the flying saucer. The more Pierre described it, the more blank Arthur's expression became. At first he made a gesture with his finger as if he had a hook in his mouth, but Pierre assured him it wasn't one of his yarns. In the end, all Arthur said was:

"Gents, I don't know what to say. The lake seemed a little choppy this morning, but otherwise normal. Beth even suggested we go for a sail when the weather clears."

"I would advise against it," said Pierre. "Whatever we saw, we certainly saw it. We've yet to determine if it means us any harm. Strange, though, that it should arrive when we're here."

"What do you mean?" I asked.

"Precisely that," said he. "Of all times that it or they might have chosen to come here—to Planet Earth, to Southern California, to Spirit Lake—why now? Why when *we* happen to be here?"

"You mean the odds are against it," said Jonathan.

"Like they are against winning the lottery," I pointed out. "But people do win it, from time to time. Maybe we just got lucky."

"Sounds like hubris to me," said Edward. "But what do I know?"

"Have you said anything about this to Dr. Horehound?" asked Arthur.

"About the lights, yes," said Pierre. "About the saucer, I guess we collectively figured that if he didn't see it, or did and didn't say anything about it, then it was best that we didn't, either."

"I guess that makes as much sense as anything around here," said Edward.

"So," said Arthur, seating himself in a chair facing the desk. He took a moment to consider the medallion in the glass case, then said to Pierre, "Okay, so what were you and Edward and Joel doing while Jonathan, Beth, and I were in the garden? I left them there because I very much wanted to inspect our host's collection. The word 'eclectic' comes to mind. Did you realize he has the complete works of Lewis Carroll? Robert Louis Stevenson? Aleister Crowley? First editions all, excellent condition— very expensive. But I digress. What were you about?"

"Exploring," said Pierre with enthusiasm. "First order of business, of course, was to inspect the wine cellar. I am happy to report that it is extensive and very thoughtfully stocked."

"How wine achieves splendor in such dank places has always puzzled me," said Edward. "It is impressive, the wine cellar I mean, as Pierre says, but it's only part of the basement. There's a maze down there as far and wide as the whole building. Lots of rooms, most of them dark and empty and riddled with cobwebs, several full of filing cabinets and cardboard boxes, and some stocked with household supplies."

"Lots of food," said Pierre. "Enough to last a world war. The boiler is huge and scary-looking. Couldn't help thinking of the beastie in *The Shining*."

"Stephen King," I agreed, proving that I, too, had read a book or two. "It gave me the creeps—all that gurgling and hissing. How it holds together is beyond me. And it leaks something fierce."

"But it does provide hot water for our sumptuous bathtubs," said Pierre, always quick to one-up me. "It can't be all bad."

"Ah, but tell him about the bugs," said Edward.

"Bugs?" inquired Arthur.

"Ah, yes," said Pierre, stuffing his hands into his pants pockets. "Our host, apparently, or someone on his staff, seems to dabble in entomology."

"Really," said Arthur.

"More than dabble," I assured him. "There's a room down there filled with aquariums—well, glass cases, anyway—rows of them."

"All under full-spectrum tube lights," added Edward. "Voltage regulators and timers. Top-of-the-line stuff."

"Crickets, beetles, ants, caterpillars," said Pierre.

"It's a regular bug emporium," I said, squirming my fingers.

"Everyone should have a hobby I suppose," said Pierre. "I asked Grayburn about it when we passed him on the stairway, and all he said was, 'The Master likes 'em.' Likes them? Strange pets, if you ask me."

"Yeah," I said. "Whatever happened to goldfish, turtles, and white mice?"

"Or," blurted Pierre, rolling his head sideways and making a crazed face, "boa constrictors, chuckwallas, and cockatoos?"

"Hmm," said Arthur. "Okay, what about upstairs? We've seen our own guestrooms in the north wing, of course. I was wondering what's in the other—" He paused to rub his forehead. "Say, that reminds me, I seem to have been assigned Madam Ouspenskaya's quarters."

"The medium who was murdered?" I asked.

"The same," said Arthur.

"Really," said Edward. "How do you know that?"

"I found her diary in the nightstand drawer," said Arthur. "I suppose I was expecting a Bible or something. I flipped through it before breakfast. She used a five-dollar bill, torn in half, as a

bookmark. Her handwriting was atrocious, but then, so is mine.
I'd like to give it some focused attention before dinner if there's
time. But I digress. You were exploring?"

"We counted sixteen guestrooms in all," said Pierre. "The
beds are stripped and the furniture covered with sheets in all but
ours. There are two rooms at the front that are the only ones
locked. I assume they belong to our host and one of his banshees. He said he saw us approach and drive on last night from
his upstairs window. Grayburn told me he and the cook have
quarters next to the kitchen where they expect never to be bothered by the likes of us."

"Two locked rooms, eh?" said Edward, pretending to carry a
one while doing a math problem. "Doc and two banshees, you
say? Maybe Miss Davenport and Dr. Horehound are—cover
your seminary ears, Joel—cohabiting?" (How I hated those endless jabs about my time at St. Joseph's!)

"Do not rush to judgment," cautioned Jonathan. "Beth and I
saw Madam Douceur enter a door at the far end of the boathouse. It wasn't a storeroom. There were lacy curtains in the
window. We heard music—a scratchy recording of 'You Only
Hurt the One You Love'—and then—"

"By the Mills Brothers?" asked Arthur.

Jonathan shrugged. "I wouldn't know. A minute later the music stopped abruptly, and she came out again wearing a different
hat and sweater. My guess is she lives out there."

"Away from the bustle and clatter of this noisy institution,"
said Pierre. "The lapping of waves against the pier for company.
Sure, why not?"

"Speaking of whom," said Jonathan, "what do you think of E.
I. D.?"

Pierre made a pensive face. "Madam Douceur? Hard to say,
since she hasn't said much."

"And Clarice Davenport?" asked Edward. "Did you get a load
of her?"

"If she's Horehound's confidential secretary," said Pierre, "I'm
William Powell, even if they do have separate rooms."

"You think she's just window-dressing?" asked Arthur.

"Could be," said Pierre. "She's good at dressing, if you like the 'working girl' look. Can't say I do, but she's been as talkative as Madam Douceur. Silent women: now there's an enigma for you. One might suspect that Dr. Horehound has some sort of hold on them."

"He pays their salary," suggested Arthur. "Maybe they're acting according to his direction."

"Maybe they're former patients," said Jonathan.

"A distinct possibility," said Pierre. "Oh, and here's a poser: unless there are extensions in the locked bedrooms upstairs, the only phone in this entire place is in the foyer."

"Odd," said Arthur. "I notice there isn't one in here. That would mean every time there's a call Dr. Horehound has to take it out there."

"Not very private," said Pierre.

"Maybe he uses a cell phone," I suggested.

"I tried mine," said Pierre. "No bars since we left Claw Junction. I used the house phone to call my editrix a short while ago to let her know we'd arrived safely. That Thorndale woman must have crossed the foyer three times in five minutes. The looks she gave me!"

"That raises another point," said Edward. "If there's no phones, there're no computers. I certainly haven't seen one anywhere."

"Right," said Pierre. "Kahlúa suggested I might e-mail her my first impressions of the place. I asked Grayburn and he cackled so hard I thought he was going to choke. 'The Master hates them corn-pooters,' he told me. Maybe so, but I still find it strange in this day and age."

"Dr. Horehound is retired," said Arthur. "Maybe he's chosen a quiet life uncluttered with high-speed communication."

"I suppose," said Pierre. "But didn't we get the impression he's working on a book or something, probably about these re-enactment sessions? Unless he uses a typewriter like Mr. Feeney, what's he writing with? A fountain pen?"

"Or a pencil," said Edward. "A holdover from his notepad days beside the psychoanalyst's couch. Did you notice there are also no televisions? Again, unless he's got one in his bedroom."

"Seems strange," I agreed.

"Maybe, maybe not," said Pierre, always contrary. "Father Baptist doesn't have one at the rectory. He doesn't strike me as being out of touch."

"Probably no reception," said Arthur.

"No cable or satellite dish," said Jonathan.

"Speaking of which," said Edward, "I asked Grayburn why there are no lines strung from the shore, phone or electrical. He said the Master thought they ruined the view so he had them routed under the bridge."

"Did you ask him about the scarcity of electric lights, too?" asked Pierre. "There's only this lamp in here, the chandelier in the foyer, a couple in the hallways—oh, and some of the bare, pull-string kind in the basement."

"He said there wasn't any 'lectricality' here at all until the Master brought it," said Edward. "And we should be darn grateful the Master is generous with candles."

"Right," said Arthur. "I've noticed a stash of them in just about every room I've been in." He smiled and mumbled the word "lectricality" to himself, then said, "What about the third story? Did you make it up there?"

"Ah," said Pierre. "It's not as big as the lower floors, and it's only comprised of three large connected rooms. One, believe it or not—the southernmost—is decked out like a ballroom."

"You don't say," said Arthur.

"Polished dance floor, albeit crusty from lack of use," said Pierre. "There's even a bandstand, and a very elegant bar—no booze, unfortunately. But it was made for grand occasions, I can tell you that."

"You'd think it would be on the ground floor," said Jonathan. "Why would Mr. Piaget make his guests climb all those stairs, all the way up there?"

"Maybe people didn't mind exercise back then," said Edward.

"Actually, I found a double door at the southeast corner," said Pierre. "I think it might be an elevator."

"Did they have elevators when this place was built?" I asked.

"Yes," said Edward, drawing on his extensive knowledge of everything to do with hardware. "The first electrical versions were built in the 1880s."

"But without 'lectricality' it would have been steam-driven," said Arthur, who reads a lot.

"I'll ask Grayburn," said Pierre. "He's such a warm, giving fountain of information."

I was trying to remember if there was an electrical generator at the Overlook Hotel in *The Shining*. There must have been, but it was the funky boiler that got all the attention.

"And what of the other two rooms?" asked Arthur.

"The north one seems to be an observatory," said Edward. "Not for watching the sky—the angle through the windows is all wrong. But there's an impressive telescope on an old-fashioned stand. Someone likes to keep an eye on the lake, as far as I can tell."

"I suppose it's worth watching," said Arthur. "You said there were three rooms?"

"Oh yes," said Edward. "You'd like the third, the one in the middle. It's an indoor pool."

"You're joking," said Arthur.

"Oh, not the swimming kind," said Edward. "It's more like the pond in that Boris Karloff movie you showed me once. The one where he's a resurrected mummy."

"Imhotep," said Arthur. "*The Mummy*, 1932. You mean the scrying pool in which he showed Zita Johann visions of their past lives in ancient Egypt."

"While his cat killed her dog," said Edward. "That's the one. There's even a statue of a goddess with a head shaped like a cat."

"Basket, the Cat Goddess," I said, having been at Arthur's the same night as Edward. I'd found the movie fascinating in a disturbing sort of way.

"Bastet," corrected Arthur, who always knew better.

"Bartholomew Piaget had some curious interests," said Pierre. "Or should I say his wife, Gabrielle."

"And the tower?" asked Arthur. "You said you saw flashing lights up there last night."

"Did you now?" said an unexpected voice. Dr. Horehound came into our midst. He was wearing a three-piece gray flannel suit with a wide black cravat. "You neglected to mention that detail last evening."

"We saw it just before—" I began, but the others stifled me with a look.

"That horrible howl," said Pierre, finishing my sentence for me. "Might we ask what's up there, Doctor?"

Dr. Horehound walked around the desk and took his usual seat. "Nothing, really. It's just a watchtower, apparently an architectural whim of Gabrielle Piaget to which Bartholomew capitulated. The surveillance turret is almost thirty feet above the highest part of the house. It is accessed from the observatory. I went up there once, when I first assumed ownership of the property. There's a rickety wrought-iron stairway that zigzags up to the top. It shook and rattled rather dangerously when I ascended it, and more so when I came back down. As a consequence, I keep the door to the tower locked for the protection of my guests."

"Ah," said Edward. "I assumed that was a closet."

Our host took a cigarette from the case on the desk, lit it, and eased back in his chair. "I can't say that it means anything, but the last few times I've been up on the third floor I thought I heard scratching sounds coming from the tower. I imagine some crows or even an eagle may be nesting up there. E. I. D. has suggested that the spirits are trying to enter the house through the surveillance turret. There is no glass, you see. She can be trying at times. But the tower is a trifling detail. Tell me, gentlemen, what do you think of the rest of Wolfram Lodge?"

"I could get used to it," said Pierre, seating himself. "It's like something out of a forgotten time. Tell me, have you ever used the ballroom?"

Dr. Horehound suppressed a laugh and shook his head. "The thought never occurred to me. I came up here for privacy, not to throw masquerade balls."

"If you ever change your mind be sure to call me," said Pierre.

"As the saying goes, don't hold your breath," said Dr. Horehound. "So, do you have any other questions?"

I was about to ask about the elevator, but Arthur spoke first. "I have one," he said, leaning forward in his chair to look closely at the display case on the desk. "This medallion. It intrigues me. Might I ask what it is?"

Dr. Horehound leaned forward, too, eagerly. "You're Mr. von Derschmidt, correct?"

Arthur nodded.

"Counting tonight, I have hosted forty-three reenactments," said the doctor. "You are the twenty-seventh guest to ask about that artifact. I shall issue you the same challenge I gave the others: if you can answer your own question, it's yours."

"Really," said Arthur.

"Unless Mr. Clubb here wishes to claim the honor," said Dr. Horehound. "He was number twenty-six last night, but it was late and I was tired. Mr. Clubb?"

"I haven't a clue," said Jonathan, scratching his head. "Go for it, Arthur, if you've a mind."

"Don't be too quick because you get but one chance," said Dr. Horehound. He smiled confidently. "I will only tell you that I found it among Mr. Piaget's effects."

"That's all?" asked Jonathan.

"It's just a medal with the letter X," I said doubtfully. "What could it be?"

"Mr. von Derschmidt has the dais," said Dr. Horehound. "It's his call."

"Hmm," said Arthur, stroking his beard. "Might I hold it, or at least see what is on the reverse?"

"Of course," said Dr. Horehound. "Open the case. It isn't locked."

Arthur did so. We crowded around as he gingerly lifted the medallion from its resting place. He hefted it in his palm. "Iron, I think," he said. "Nordic." He turned it over. "The image on the back is almost entirely obliterated by wear and corrosion. I see the faint suggestion of wings." He turned it over again and looked closely at the simple X on the front. After a few moments of consideration, he surprised us with his answer: "Dr. Horehound, I believe this belonged not to Mr. Piaget, but to his wife. It is a holy medal, a sacramental like a St. Christopher, but representing the Angel Gabriel."

"Heavens," said Pierre.

The rest of us remained silent for several long seconds.

"It's yours," said Dr. Horehound, easing himself back in his chair. He may have said it offhandedly, but his eyes were angry.

"Bravo!" said Pierre, slapping Arthur on the back. "How did you guess?"

"Yes," said Dr. Horehound. "That would interest me, too."

"It's obviously not a coin," said Arthur, sounding a bit like Basil Rathbone in one of those Sherlock Holmes movies he loves so much. "The Vikings minted lots of them, but they preferred copper for their coinage. It has a little ring extension at the top—see?—obviously to accommodate a chain or a string for hanging about the neck. The symbol on the front is not an X. Well, it is, but it's the Nordic rune that coincides with our letter G. It is largely forgotten that the Vikings converted to Catholicism, and the wings on the back suggest an angel. The Archangel Gabriel therefore comes to mind. They called him 'Engelen Gabriel.' And since Mr. Piaget's wife was named Gabrielle, it seemed likely that it belonged to her. Tell me, Dr. Horehound, was she a Catholic?"

"Nominally, I suppose," said the doctor. "She came from a devout family, but as she married Bartholomew Piaget, and considering her leanings, I doubt she was still—what's the colloquialism?—practicing."

"I thank you for this," said Arthur, slipping it carefully into his vest pocket. "I shall have it blessed at the earliest opportunity, though I imagine that was probably done centuries ago."

"You think the spell has worn off?" asked Dr. Horehound with a sniff.

"Just being thorough," said Arthur, patting his pocket.

"You impress me, Mr. von Derschmidt," said Dr. Horehound, though his voice sounded otherwise. He looked around at us. "You are an interesting bunch. Dare I ask, are there any other questions?"

"Will you put something else in that case?" I asked. "Now that it's empty?"

"I'm sure I'll find something," said Dr. Horehound, rotating his hand so his cigarette made smoke spirals that became rings in the air. "One out of twenty-seven isn't bad."

"I'm still wondering about the tower," said Pierre. "We were more than a mile away, but we definitely saw electrical activity up there. Maybe some wiring's gone bad. What would you say to one of us going up and taking a look for you? I suggest Joel."

"Me?" I said. I'm sure my jaw fell. "I'll pass."

"I'll go," offered Edward. "I know something about electrical systems."

"You sell hardware," said Pierre to him, then to me: "You're an electrician, and you're the lightest of our troop."

"And the least willing, thank-you."

"Joel," said Pierre, sternly.

"Pierre," said I, immovable.

"Gentlemen," said Dr. Horehound. "Need I point out that an electrical storm passed over us last night? The likely explanation is that the lightning rod atop the watchtower fulfilled the purpose for which it was intended."

That hit their pause button.

"I have a question, or rather an observation," said Dr. Horehound, apparently dismissing the tower idea. Whew! "You haven't asked me anything about the séance we'll be conducting this evening."

"I believe the word is 'reenacting,'" said Edward.

"As you prefer," said Dr. Horehound, still making those little smoke rings.

"I think we figured you'd tell us in your own good time," said Pierre.

"In that you are correct," said the doctor.

"Is now the time?" I asked.

"It is not," said he.

"Oh," said I.

"I have a tangential question, if I may," said Pierre.

"It depends on what you mean by tangential," said Dr. Horehound.

"Well, as I understand it, we'll be playing the parts of the guests that were here that evening in 1896, but you haven't pro-

vided us with information about them. I would have thought you
would have mailed us dossiers, *curricula vitae*, that sort of thing,
so we could familiarize ourselves ahead of time—"

"I'll answer that," said Dr. Horehound, pausing the hand-roll
thing, then starting it up again in the opposite direction. "You
see, when I first began conducting these sessions—sessions, yes,
that's how I think of them, my background as a psychologist you
understand. At the onset I did as you suggested. In exchange for
their deposit every guest received a profile of the individual they
were to represent. Many of them as a consequence arrived 'in
character,' 'living the part' as it were, believing they had truly
gotten 'under the skin' of the original guest—steadfast in their
preconceptions, confident in their second-guesses, obstinate in
their conclusions. The sessions degenerated into self-centered
theater-in-the-round which, though entertaining for them, spoiled
the result I was seeking."

"I would think that most people go to reenactments to be enter-
tained," said Edward.

"So I opted for a different approach," continued Dr. Horehound without pause. "It's called a Minimum Information Gambit. You'll find a book of that title by a retired anthropologist,
Beatrice Canard, on the shelf above Crowley. She conducts
similar but less lavish reenactments of the Alexis Grignion murders in New Orleans. I phoned her personally to tell her I concurred with everything about her hypothesis except for the title—
the reference to chess, so unoriginal—but that's neither here nor
there. The simple fact is that any portrayal of something as
complex and perplexing as another human being, even when the
role-player is a seasoned actor or trained psychologist, is essentially conjectured. Let's take your character, Mr. Bontemps, by
way of example, the role you will be assuming. He was an in-
dustrialist from New York with hereditary ties to not one but two
prominent families in Los Angeles. A successful businessman,
he somehow wound his way into the numinous monetary mire
that was Summerland and thereby lost his shirt. His wife of
eight years committed suicide when he sold off his holdings
there for a pittance. Do you really think you're capable of penetrating the mind of such a man as Eusebius T. Roundhead? In

truth, all you could possibly produce is an interpretation based on your own real or imagined experiences."

"Perhaps," said Pierre. "But even so—"

∞§[**Martin**]§∞

"Roundhead?" interrupted Edward. "Did he say Roundhead?"

"Eusebius T.," said Pierre with a knowing wink.

"Any connection with, you know, Roderick—?"

"Undoubtedly," said Pierre.

"But that's incredible," said Jonathan.

"Indeed," said Pierre. "But let's not get sidetracked."

∞§[*JOEL*]§∞

"Secondly," persisted Dr. Horehound, "even if the above were not the case, there is the problem of disparity of useful information regarding the original guests. We know much about the professional life of one Simon Nicholas Abraham, the celebrated barrister from England, whose career was shipwrecked when he came halfway around the world to tangle with Bartholomew Piaget—but we know virtually nothing of his personal relationships. He hindered, obstructed, and otherwise interfered in the lives of others, but didn't live enough of one himself to leave evidence of it behind. Contrarily, we know that the architect, Ian White Robinson, disinherited all eleven of his children from five failed marriages, that he sired four others between wedlocks whom he favored with posthumous gifts, and so on, but his professional file is a vacuity. Not a single building in this country stands with his signature on the blueprint. We know oodles about the scandalous affairs of Beverly Sarcenet from gossip columns and scandal sheets, including liaisons with two state senators, a city councilman, and, lo and behold, Bartholomew Piaget when he was conducting business in Los Angeles, circa 1894." He paused to turn and regard the not-so-blissful portrait of Bartholomew and Gabrielle, then resumed his authoritative posture and narrative. "We know nothing of Miss Sarcenet's immediate family, schooling, or upbringing. Her middle name, Maplewood, suggests a connection to Eusebius Roundhead, or at least to his extended family, but so distant as to be untraceable. Suddenly she arrived on the scene, wealthy and wanton like a movie queen, except Hollywood had not as yet become Tinseltown. She faded after the séance, to die in 1901 without heirs. We know even less about Roy Blackman Doyle, who produced and directed bawdy musicals at the Sweetwater Review, a theater he owned and operated in Sacramento. His legacy consists of a dozen naughty playbills preserved in a glass case in the Old California exhibit at the Huntington Library, along with a foreclosure notice signed by Piaget himself which shut the Sweetwater down in 1891. I could find no record of his theatric activities after the séance, although quite by accident I happened upon an article in a rural newspaper, *The Mountain View Chronicle*, which reported the discovery of an unidentified man—a man of Doyle's general build and description—who was found dead of unknown causes in a hotel in the town of Tehachapi, about ninety-five miles from here, a week after the authorities permitted the participants to leave the lodge. I could find no proof that the man was, in fact, Roy Blackman Doyle. I mention it only to show the extent of my research. Only one of the guests later published an account of the incidents surrounding the séance—the teacher, Louis Sartell—but his primary objective was to downplay his connection to a certain coastal town. That article contained practically all the information I could find about him, which was self-serving and defensive. He left no mark in academia that I could track down."

"Apparently everyone invited here that night had a grudge against Piaget," said Edward.

"Yet it was Madam Ouspenskaya who was murdered," mused Pierre.

"Therein lies the mystery," said Arthur. "And what about the other woman who was present at the séance, and the cook who was not?"

"Arianna Marigold, you mean," said our host, "and Natalie Currant. We'll start with Miss Marigold. She left no diary other than several filing cabinets worth of paperwork in her distinct script, all of which pertained to Piaget's business affairs. Piaget hired her at the suggestion of his barrister, Hawkeye McAllister. How McAllister knew of her, I do not know, but I found his letter of recommendation among Piaget's papers. She hailed from Boston and attended a high-class boarding school, which suggests that 'she came from good stock,' as McAllister put it. She must have been, shall we say, 'unfettered' and 'autonomous' for her day. She certainly proved to have a head for business. For a time she was the accountant for a company in Boston that manufactured and installed lightning rods. It was she who advised Piaget that a watchtower such as he had built here required such protection against electrical storms. After Boston she wound up as the accountant of a Japanese-owned import-export company in Stockton, although how she transitioned across the country is unknown. I do not know what inducements Piaget offered, but she left that lucrative job to work exclusively for him. Piaget mentioned her frequently in his diaries, but only in connection with business transactions."

"Doesn't sound like she had a grudge against Piaget or Madam Ouspenskaya," said Edward, "or anyone, for that matter."

"But she disappeared," said Pierre, "so maybe someone had a grudge against her."

"Maybe because she worked for Piaget," said Jonathan.

"And the cook?" asked Arthur.

"What was her name again?" I asked.

"Natalie Currant," said Dr. Horehound. "To refer to her as the cook is an oversimplification. Her family came to California via wagon train through Death Valley. They settled and grew olives where the Mojave Trail, the Old Spanish Trail, and El Camino Real intersected—"

"Present day Rancho Cucamonga," said Arthur.

"Bravo, Mr. von Derschmidt," said our host. "She was seventeen when Gabrielle Stonecraft took her on as a domestic assistant. That was about a year before Gabrielle married Bartholomew."

"Twenty years in her employ, all told," said Pierre. "She was practically family."

"She was certainly more than a servant," said our host. "More like a *demoiselle de compagnie*. In his written statement, Regis the butler referred to her as 'Mrs. Piaget's devotee.' Emilia Quinlan Blotter, editor of the *Summerland Sentinel*, described Miss Currant as 'poor ill-fated Gabby's disciple.'"

"Companion, devotee, disciple," said Arthur. "Was she perhaps Gabrielle's student? Or should I say apprentice?"

"In matters occult, you mean," said Dr. Horehound. "Yes, that is most likely."

Arthur sighed. "She must have been devastated when her mistress died."

"Indeed," said our host. "It is unclear to what extent her devotion to Gabrielle extended to Bartholomew, but we can surmise his lack of reciprocity by the fact that although she stayed on, her role in the household quickly diminished until she was, after all, introduced to guests merely as 'the cook.'"

"How sad," said Arthur. "The more I learn about Bartholomew Piaget, the less I like him."

"Elsewhere in Regis' statement," continued Dr. Horehound, "he described Miss Currant as having become 'wan and wraithlike.' Without Gabrielle, she faded physically and mentally. Although the purpose of the séance was to contact her dead mistress, Natalie did not attend because she hadn't been invited. As you know from the brochure, although the evidence overwhelmingly suggested that she met a violent end, her body was never found."

Everyone shook their heads, despondently.

"If I may backtrack somewhat," said Dr. Horehound, suddenly vivacious. "I'd like to finish answering your original question, Mr. Bontemps."

"And what question was that, Dr. Horehound?" asked Pierre.

"About dossiers, *curricula vitae*, and how we are going to proceed. I told you several of my reasons for resorting to the Minimum Information Gambit, among them were the deficiency of detailed information, and the unfeasibility of adopting personalities. There is one left to explain, and it is this: human beings rarely act predictably under stress. We all find ourselves behaving out of character in the midst of catastrophe. It is safe to say that none of those present in 1896 acted in accordance with their day-by-day disposition. No doubt they all surprised themselves. As shall we."

"So we're going at this blind," said Arthur.

"I prefer the term 'fresh,'" said Dr. Horehound. He stamped out his cigarette in a large pewter ashtray and immediately, albeit painfully slowly, lit another. "Gentlemen, I suggest that you all meet me at the séance room after dinner. I'll unlock the door at eight o'clock sharp. It would be helpful for you to examine the room, to satisfy yourselves that there will be no parlor tricks."

"Why?" asked Pierre. "Are books and vases going to start flying about?"

"Nothing so dramatic as that, I should hope," said Dr. Horehound, taking a long drag on his precious cigarette. "During previous reenactments there have been sounds—knocks, ticking clocks, chimes, other noises that were less discernable. The last group thought they heard voices. One distraught lady from the Bloomingdale Parapsychology Club swore she heard her Uncle Isaac taunting her. I want you to satisfy yourselves—and let's not forget Miss Hummingbird—that there are no hidden speakers or strings, or whatever devices dishonest mediums use to fool the gullible."

"Has Madam Douceur ever resorted to such contrivances?" asked Arthur.

"Not on my watch," said Dr. Horehound. "She is not allowed into the room prior to the séances—nor at any other time, for that matter."

"Never?" I asked.

"She's in my employ," said Dr. Horehound. "She does as she's told."

"In that regard," said Edward hesitantly, "I'm a little unclear about this séance business. Is this going to be a reenactment as promised, or is this lady going to conduct an actual séance?"

"Allow me to clarify," said Dr. Horehound, stamping out his half-spent cigarette. "E. I. D.'s job is to duplicate, move for move, word for word, precisely the actions described in Bartholomew Piaget's notes regarding that fateful night. I have extracted a script which she follows to the letter. You'll have copies, too, but not before the séance convenes."

Just then the window blazed with a blinding flash of lightning, followed immediately by a deafening clap of thunder. Timing is everything, as Mr. Feeney is fond of reminding us.

"The storm returns," said Arthur, rolling his shoulders.

"I wonder," said Pierre, picking his words carefully as rain started pelting the window. "I don't suppose her contract calls for her to be found mutilated tomorrow morning."

Dr. Horehound smiled and shook his head. "I would not want to ask a woman of Madam Douceur's stature, both professional and physical, to splatter herself with stage blood and recline on the muddy ground while we rummage and prattle around her. I commissioned a lifelike figure in wax. That will suffice."

"Good idea," said Pierre, "although by removing the element of surprise, you just dampened our possible reaction, if that is what you hope to observe."

"But you already know of the medium's demise," said Dr. Horehound, "and I hardly think any of you will be fooled by a mannequin. I suggest that you let me worry about what I hope to observe."

"Excuse me, Doctor," said Edward. "You were making a point of clarification."

"Was I?"

"About 'reenactment.'"

"Ah yes, Mr. Wyndham, I strayed again," said Dr. Horehound. "As I was saying, Madam Douceur's task is to follow the script I provide her to the letter. This she does very well. However, in fairness I must add that what she does mentally, within the canyons of her mind as it were, is entirely outside my control."

"So you're saying she may actually be performing a séance," said Edward.

Dr. Horehound shrugged.

"Then without her explicit assurance to the contrary," said Edward, his voice solemn, "I will have to withdraw my participation."

What!? I silently glared. After all the rigmarole we've been through—?

"I beg your pardon?" asked the doctor.

"I will not involve myself in a genuine séance."

"You're not serious."

"Always about my soul."

Pierre bubbled and sputtered a bit, sighed, and then said, "Dr. Horehound, I'm afraid I must concur with Mr. Wyndham. So must we all."

Speak for yourself! I almost retorted. What the heck did we come here for?

"But, but this is unheard of," said Dr. Horehound, sputtering a bit himself. It was obvious he wasn't used to being contradicted. "Not once, not once I say, have any guests made such a demand."

"What can I tell you?" said Pierre, almost flippantly. "It's a Catholic thing."

"But several of the attendees have been priests," said Dr. Horehound, shifting in his chair. "They were all, all—"

"Complacent," said Edward, disgusted. "I'm not surprised. The fruits of that conundrum you mentioned this morning: Vatican II. I can't take responsibility for the likes of them. But I can and do for myself. You said at breakfast that our religion is about fear of death. You're wrong. We're a lot more concerned about Hell."

"Attempting to contact the dead is called necromancy," said Arthur.

"It's what we fearful Catholics call a mortal sin," explained Pierre. "The willful commission of which is punishable by eternal banishment to the fires of Hell."

"You don't really believe that," said Dr. Horehound. "Good God, no one really believes that."

"Saint Ignatius Loyola certainly did," said Arthur. "It's his feast day today, you know. We'll not besmirch his memory, nor our immortal souls, for the sake of one of your sessions."

Nooooo! I almost groaned aloud. Condescending rhetoric, dispersions against Vatican II, appeals to moral theology, convoluted conclusions—once again we were descending into the inexorable vortex of Tumblar lunacy! Why should I be surprised? But in fact, I was so flabbergasted I didn't know what to say. Were my loony companions really considering packing up and going home? And Dr. Horehound wasn't making any more sense than the rest of them. Hadn't he, the master skeptic, just called upon God?

"You have me at a loss," said Dr. Horehound, sinking back in his chair. "I have never in all my days as a psychologist encountered anything like this. You're intelligent men, obviously well read, educated. How can you subscribe to the tales of long-dead shamans contrived to control unknowledgeable peasants?"

"We call those long-dead shamans the Church Fathers," said Pierre. "We take them very seriously. It's called 'Embracing the Faith.' Your insults regarding our religion are not appreciated, but we understand. You're a skeptic. Fine. You want material for your next book? Also fine. Consider us willing subjects, but only if Madam Douceur accedes to our demand. Otherwise we'll take our leave and quit the premises immediately."

Who elected you our spokesman? I seethed. *Of all the —*

"What about Miss Hummingbird?" asked Dr. Horehound.

"She would agree," said Pierre.

"She's a Catholic, too," explained Arthur.

"This is too much," said Dr. Horehound. He folded his hands. Then unfolded them. Then folded them again. Finally, he pounded both of them palms down on the desk. "All right, gentlemen. I'll talk to Madam Douceur. She will deliver her promise to you over dinner. But I warn you: don't cross me."

"How can we possibly do that?" asked Pierre. "We'll sit through the reenactment tonight and in the coming days. We'll follow your script to the letter — as actors, not participants. We'll react to your scenario according to our proclivities. You'll take notes or whatever you do. Your book will have an interesting chapter. Miss Hummingbird publishes a three-part article. Everyone wins."

The doctor didn't look convinced.

Neither was I. But again, I kept it to myself. I felt very much alone.

"Very well," said Dr. Horehound, rising mightily to his feet. He headed for the door. "We'll finalize this development over dinner."

"We'll be there," said Pierre. "Six, you say."

Dr. Horehound gave us all a blistering look and slammed the French door as he exited the room.

"Well," said Jonathan rubbing his chin as the rattling panes settled down. "I don't know about you guys, but I'm about due for my afternoon shave."

∞§[Martin]§∞

"That's tellin' him," said Millie as Joel meandered back to his seat with downcast eyes.

"And how," agreed Kahlúa. "Whoopie zing zowie!"

"You shave twice a day?" asked Beth, tapping Jonathan's left shoulder. "I mean, obviously not anymore, but before?"

"It's a genetic thing," explained Edward, resting his hand on Jonathan's other shoulder sympathetically. "He went on this tour of a nuclear reactor one day—"

"Actually, it was one of Millie's hangover cures," said Arthur. "They'll make hair grow where it never dared before."

"And how," agreed Millie proudly.

"Essentially," said Jonathan, his ears glowing like Christmas tree lights, "it goes back to when I was—"

"Well done, Gentlemen," intruded Father, replacing the book in its niche on the shelf. "Edward, Pierre, all of you held your ground. Dare I say I'm proud of you?"

Joel looked disheartened, like he wished he could shrivel up and slip though the cracks in the floor. His discomfiture was noticed, but not noted, by the others.

"I'd say 'Ah shucks,'" said Arthur, "but except for an occasional transitory flicker, I still don't remember any of this."

"It will come," said Pierre. "As sure as I'm standing here, it will come."

"What about that medallion, Arthur?" asked Kahlúa, dabbing yellow froth from her lips. "Do you still have it?"

"Not that I'm aware of," said he. "'Engelen Gabriel.' Heavens, if I possessed such a precious thing I'd surely cherish it. Chances are I'd be wearing it." He felt his chest. "Nope, just my trusty five-fold."

"Can't wear medals myself," said Millie, not bothering to wipe away the eggnog coating her upper lip. "Turn 'em green."

"Imagine wearing something made of iron," said Beth. She poked her brother. "Hey, Sherlock, wouldn't it get all rusty?"

"I wouldn't know," said Arthur. "That's the problem. I wish I remembered, and I wonder what became of it."

"So what happened over dinner?" asked Beth. "Was I pretty?"

"Let's find out," said Pierre, scooping up the next set of pages. "Edward, front and center."

"I'd rather drink my eggnog in peace," said Edward, but he got up to do his duty all the same.

∞§[†]§∞

10. Better Than Steak

∞§[Edward]§∞

"I THINK IT'S DOWNRIGHT MANIPULATIVE," said Madam Douceur, snapping her cloth napkin and tucking it under her chins to shield her ample—*ahem!*—from splatter. "Mortimer, I'm appalled that you're cowed by these, these ... religious fanatics!"

"Well, I think it's charming," said Clarice Davenport. She fluttered her eyelashes at Pierre while slowly inserting a big green garlic-stuffed olive into her mouth. She chewed it a while thoughtfully, working her glistening shocking-pink lips. Swallowing provocatively, she added, "I like men with *chutzpah.*"

Beth bristled but held her peace.

Apparently the boss had given his banshees permission to speak, and they intended to run with the privilege.

"We're simply insisting that words mean what they say," said Pierre, apparently oblivious to Miss Davenport's attentions and, I suspect, enjoying the doctor's employees' about-face in the silence department. "We've come all the way up here to Spirit Lake in good faith anticipating a *reenactment* of a séance as promised in your brochure."

"I phoned my attorney, E. I. D.," said Dr. Horehound, seated at the head of the table. "Mr. McAllister says they've got a point."

"Two of them," said Madam Douceur, indicating their position on her own forehead with her index fingers. "They want to control my thoughts. My thoughts, do you hear?"

"As I understand it, they want you to turn them off," countered Clarice, still playing to Pierre. "That shouldn't be too hard, should it?"

"Clarice," said Dr, Horehound sternly.

She puckered her lips at her boss, and then turned her radar upon Jonathan, but he was looking steadily at Beth. Smirking at the implications, Clarice focused instead on Arthur.

"Ah say, ah say, wah cain't we awl jeeyust gyit alowng?" drawled Pierre, resorting to his famous impression of a certain wide-eyed televangelist he enjoyed parodying. Famous to us, that is—lost upon them.

"Oh, let's," whispered Clarice, but Arthur was distracted by the cook backing into the room through the swinging door with a large canapé tray in her hands.

"McAllister," I said. "Haven't I heard that name recently?"

"My attorney?" asked our host. "I cannot see in what possible connection."

"You mentioned him, Doctor," said Pierre. "You said he wrote a letter of recommendation for Arianna Marigold, which of course, would be impossible."

"Ah," said Horehound. "That was Hawkeye 'Fine Print' McAllister. His great-nephew, Geronimo, happens to be my attorney. Something they share in addition to their bloodline and colorful first names is the nickname 'Fine Print' on their business cards."

"Geronimo 'Fine Print' McAllister," I mused. "Sounds formidable."

"Persnicketyness must run in their family," said Beth.

"You have no idea," said Clarice.

"Ah, Thorndale, at last," said Dr. Horehound, clasping his hands in anticipation. "Mr. Wyndham, Mr. Bontemps: since you hold to the precision of words, you will appreciate this. You insist on reenactment, and as your host I have decided to provide it, as completely and accurately as I am able. It has been our custom here at Wolfram Lodge to serve prime rib the first night—a hearty, filling meal appealing to all but an occasional vegan guest. But for you—yes, just for you—well, the Piagets were gourmets, true pioneers in the realm of world cuisine. Gabrielle left behind drawers of index cards on which she had penned her favorite exotic recipes. Bartholomew cherished and preserved her memory, and shared her culinary preferences. Tonight we are going to partake of the very dishes Natalie Currant cooked and served to his guests on that fateful night in 1896. I must commend Thorndale, who responded graciously to the last-minute change of menu, even though it meant a dizzying amount of extra work for her."

While Dr. Horehound said all this, Thorndale was making several trips to the kitchen and back, each time returning with another covered dish, bowl, or tureen. She smiled inscrutably at our nods of appreciation as she set them down on the dinner table. Unfamiliar smells emanated from these vessels—pungent and spicy, with a hint of vinegar in there somewhere.

"Allow me," said Dr. Horehound, lifting the polished silver lid from the canapé tray. "We'll start with a little *amuse bouche*."

"Are those what I think they are?" asked Beth, incredulously.

"I wouldn't know what you're thinking," said Dr. Horehound. "I only know that they are delectable." With that he pinched one of the crispy fritters between thumb and forefinger and inserted it whole into his mouth. A couple of appendages needed an extra push to get them all tucked in. His eyes rolled up inside his head ecstatically as he sucked, then slowly ground, then swallowed the grisly *hors d'oeuvre* with the passion of a gourmand. His vacuum pump sucking made me queasy; the crunch, crrrunch, crrrrrrrunching made the room tilt; and the prolonged gritty swallow caused my stomach to lurch. To our mounting horror, Madam Douceur and Clarice Davenport reached and did likewise, although they didn't turn the act of eating into quite so protracted an epicurean crawl.

Simply put, the canapés were *beetles*—great big deep-fried bugs in a crusty citrus glaze. They lay there on their backs with their legs sticking up. Dr. Horehound feigned surprise when, having returned content from his trip to Planet Gastro, he opened his eyes and beheld our faces.

"Well, come on, everyone," he beckoned grandly. "As the townspeople would say, 'Dig in!'"

∞§[Martin]§∞

I'm not going to try to reiterate here all the sounds and comments that punctuated Edward's description of this unsavory culinary episode. Suffice it to say that, by the end, everyone shared a strained facial expression of utter distaste.

∞§[Edward]§∞

With that same unfathomable smile, Thorndale lifted the lids off the other vessels and proudly named the results of her culinary labors. "The Master is enjoying the *Scarab L'Orange*. Egyptian dung beetles, you know—only the best. This here is grasshopper soup with lemongrass stock; honey-baked mole crickets from Puerto Rico; and Madam's favorite: curried green weaver ants all the way from India. The salad is a Siamese delicacy tossed with raw red ant eggs and plum sauce. I apologize that it is served on this myrtle wood platter—I can't seem to find my Stoke-on-Trent salad bowl, which would match the rest of the tableware."

"We'll suffer through," said Dr. Horehound, winking encouragingly.

"Dee-lish!" warbled Madam Douceur, grabbing a spoon and helping herself.

"Do try me—I mean *it*," said the flirtatious Clarice, still vying for Arthur's attention, but he couldn't take his eyes off the dark shapes floating in the soup. With a peculiar lopsided roll of her shoulders, she turned her big blue eyes toward me. "As my mother always told me: it's good to try new things."

"I believe Hannibal Lecter's mother gave him the same advice," muttered Arthur under his breath.

"This is all very nutritious," said our host, gleefully. "Mr. Piaget was big on high-protein foods, and insects are an excellent source—better than steak."

"This explains the bugs downstairs," said Joel, his eyes wide and disbelieving.

"His guests ate this?" said Beth, cupping her hand over her mouth.

"Of course," said Dr. Horehound, dabbing a bit of leakage from his lips with a napkin. "They came to fawn, not to offend their host."

I almost said something like if this is what Natalie Currant served the original guests, her bloody end was no longer a mystery. Knowing that would be in poorer taste than the meal set before us, I held my peace.

"Oh well, what ho," said Pierre, taking up one of the glassy beetles and inserting it into his mouth. He was big on trying new things, and fastidious about the rules of etiquette between guest and host. He made a convincing series of yummy sounds while grinding the horrid thing into gritty sludge, but when he swallowed his eyes gave his revulsion away. He turned a little limey as the masticated critter chittered down his esophagus to nest in his stomach. Pierre's attempt at a gracious smile was marred by dark bits of exoskeleton between his teeth. I turned away and found Clarice Davenport drilling me with her eyes. I so wanted to leap up, grab my keys, get in the van, and head for Howler's Café.

"This is horrible," said Beth.

"No," said Dr. Horehound. "This is authenticity."

"It's payback and you know it," said she, slapping her napkin down on her empty plate. "And it's petty."

"Wrong again," said Dr. Horehound, regarding her with appreciative eyes. "In point of fact, this is our usual fare here at Wolfram Lodge. You all want things your way, and now you have them. Clarice, pass the curry."

∞§[Martin]§∞

"And I thought chit'lin's was gross," said Kahlúa as Edward resumed his seat. "Pierre, Baby, your poor tummy!"

"Upstaged by bugs," sighed Beth playfully, her chin in her palms. "No mention of what I was wearing."

"Actually, I've had worse," said Pierre. "As it turned out, Joel saved the day by sharing his stash of candy bars with us after we quitted the dining room."

"The ones I said I bought at Claw Junction?" asked Joel.

"From the greasy-fingered lady at 'Hal's Grocery,'" said Pierre, rubbing his thumbs and forefingers together for effect. "Are your synapses perhaps making connections?"

"I wish they were," said Joel. "On the other hand, I'm kind of glad they're not. This is not a fun story, Pierre."

"No indeed," said Pierre seriously.

"And you've been keeping this to your lonesome all this time," said Millie.

"It hasn't been easy," agreed Pierre. "But what could I do? What concerns me at present is that, even while reading your accounts in your own handwriting, it's still not coming back to any of you. Perhaps this will help." Out of the chest he pulled a small white card with gilded edges and handed it to Edward in the front row. "A copy of this was provided for each of us. It was apparently a standard form. You can see that our names were entered by Clarice Davenport in blue ink."

"She misspelled my name," said Jonathan as he handed it over his shoulder to Beth.

"You rejected her advances," said Beth. "What do you expect?"

"She ate bugs, according to Edward," said Jonathan. "What was I to do?"

It took a while, but eventually the exhibit made its way back to Father's and my corner:

OUR CAST
— + —

Historical personage:	To be played by:

Bartholomew W. Piaget (Host)	Dr. Mortimer Horehound, Ph.D.
Cassandra Ouspenskaya (Medium)	Madam Elaineileen Douceur
Arianna Marigold (Secretary to Mr. Piaget)	Clarice Davenport

-+-

Eusebius T. Roundhead (Industrialist)	*Pierre Bontemps*
Ian White Robinson (Architect)	*Jonathan Clubs*
Louis Sartell (Educator)	*Joel Maruppa*
Beverly Maplewood Sarcenet (Socialite)	*Elizabeth von Derschmidt*
Simon Nicholas Abraham (Barrister)	*Arthur von Derschmidt*
Roy Blackman Doyle (Theatrical producer)	*Edward Strypes Wyndham*

"So what happened next?" asked Edward.

"The opening of the séance room," said Pierre. "Arthur, will you do the honors?"

∞§[†]§∞

∞§†§∞

11. The Thing about Parlor Tricks

∞§[Arthur]§∞

I DON'T KNOW WHAT I EXPECTED to find when Dr. Horehound ceremoniously produced a skeleton-shaped key from his vest pocket and inserted it into the mouth of the skull-shaped lock. I was still reeling from a sugar rush, thanks to Joel's candy bars, as we entered the forbidden chamber.

∞§[Martin]§∞

"Excuse me for interrupting so soon," said Joel, "but is there no account of me actually bringing out my candy bars and sharing them?"

"Interesting that you ask," said Pierre. "Everyone mentioned it in passing like Arthur just did, but no one—not even you—described the scene in detail. Sorry."

"But you claim to remember it," said Joel.

"Claim to and do so," said Pierre, tapping his temple. "But it isn't my memory that needs a jumpstart. It was agreed that reading your memoirs would supply the necessary jolt. Trust me, larger things are looming."

Joel grunted his annoyance.

"Sorry I didn't write more about it, Joel," said Beth sympathetically.

"Me, too," said Arthur. "However, in the immediate ..."

∞§[A**RTHUR**]§∞

The door was at the end of a long, narrow corridor that commenced at the foyer next to the staircase and plunged straight, level, and deep into the heart of the lodge. There were no rooms, no other doors, along this hallway, for it had but one purpose, one destination. Interestingly, the Master's "lectricality" had penetrated this part of the mansion, for this hardwood course was illuminated by five small evenly-spaced chandeliers, each with five flame-shaped light bulbs with piercingly bright filaments.

As for the room at the end, it was dodecagonal and rosewood paneled, dominated by a round table of deeply polished mahogany. A large Tiffany chandelier provided mellow light from above, and heat was the province of a river rock fireplace in the farthest wall, which of course had lain cold and dark since the last reenactment.

There was an ornate metallic coat of arms bolted to the panel above the hearth. Except for a wolf, a pair of dragons, and a red raguly line, I did not recognize the heraldic symbols emblazoned upon it. Looking down upon us from the other panels around the room were large oil paintings of Tarot characters, just as Grayburn had described. In addition to his favorite, the Queen of Cups, there was the Fool striding merrily and obliviously towards the edge of a precipice, the Magician wielding the mystical tools of his craft, the Hierophant ruling from his throne, the brooding Hermit hefting a lantern in which a six-pointed star blazed, the Hanged Man dangling by one foot from a T-shaped cross, the Emperor on his magisterial throne, the Empress on hers, golden-crowned Justice brandishing her decisive sword, and a foreboding armored skeleton riding a white steed while bearing a black banner displaying a white rose—Death. I turned around to see what image might adorn the twelfth panel above the door through which we had just entered. It was different from the rest in that it didn't depict a person. The Ace of Cups was a reverential representation of the Holy Ghost as a Dove with the Blessed Sacrament in its beak descending upon the Holy Grail.

Nine high-backed matching chairs sat brooding around the perimeter of the table, with faded hand-printed place cards indicating where the original attendees had seated themselves. The crystal ball I had expected to find in the middle was absent—no, rather, it resided on the mantelpiece above the fireplace. In the center of the table, in its stead, rested a deck of cards, face down. Their yellowed, tarnished edges indicated considerable age. On the back of the top card I noticed a swirled design which I recognized. When I casually reached for the deck, I was brought up short by an alarmed retort from Dr. Horehound:

"Don't touch that!"

"Pardon me," I said, withdrawing my hand. "I thought we were here to examine the room."

"The room, yes," he said, "but not the cards. Arianna Marigold, Mr. Piaget's personal secretary, painstakingly gathered them in the order in which they had been dealt immediately at the conclusion of the fateful séance in 1896. The following morning, shortly after Madam Ouspenskaya's body was found in the garden, Miss Marigold placed the deck in Mr. Piaget's safe. When I assumed possession of the estate, I took pains to preserve the deck in its historical order. During our reenactments Madam Douceur deals the cards one by one, and at the end of each session they are returned to their proper sequence."

"That's interesting, if true," said my sister, whose dislike for Dr. Horehound was escalating by the hour.

"You doubt my word?" asked the doctor, not amused, but clearly interested.

"I find it hard to believe that the cards have remained untouched for more than a century," said Beth. "Mr. Piaget's lawyers and relatives must have gone through his effects when he died. Just because those cards were in the safe—"

"Mr. Piaget disappeared two days after the séance," interrupted Dr. Horehound. "No one knows when or how he died. The safe was sealed by his solicitors at the direction of the police at the conclusion of their investigation. It was finally opened seven years later—"

"All the same," insisted Beth. "Just because—"

"Sometime during the day after the séance," persisted Dr. Horehound, "Mr. Piaget meticulously listed the order of the entire deck in his diary. It was he who shuffled the deck before the reading, you see, and he believed his fate was somehow concealed within them."

"You're saying he memorized the whole deck?"

"He had a head for lists, apparently."

"So we'll just have to take your word for his word for it," said Beth, heaving her shoulders in frustration.

"Yes, we will," said Dr. Horehound with finality. "The only cards that really matter are the six that were dealt, after all, and police reports indicate that their order was confirmed by the testimony of those in attendance."

Just then Grayburn came bustling in with a vase crammed to bursting with red roses. Grumbling to himself, he set the vessel on a white marble pillar at the right side of the fireplace. Then, with a perfunctory bow toward his boss, he elbowed his way out of the room again.

"So only six cards were used?" I asked.

"Yes," said Dr. Horehound.

"That's a fairly lean spread," I observed. "While I realize there are arrays as small as three, most of the arrangements take at least ten, some as many as twenty-two."

"You know the Tarot?" asked Dr. Horehound.

"Somewhat," I said with a shrug.

"Books," said Beth pointedly.

"Madam Ouspenskaya was of the Kedakesh Clan," explained Dr. Horehound with an academic air, "descended from an ancient line of Hungarian gypsies who traced their lineage to the Pannonian Plains before the coming of the Magyars. She called her peculiar ancestral card arrangement the Revealing Star. Madam Douceur will explain when she herself deals them shortly."

I considered commenting that the earliest recorded use of cards for divination was in the early 1400s, long after the arrival of the Magyars. There was also a legend that the original inhabitants of Pannonia were a race of shape-shifting cat people. Finally, I knew something of the life of the actress Maria Ouspenskaya, who played Maleva, the gypsy fortuneteller in *The Wolfman*, 1932. She came from Russia, not Hungary. Of course, all that meant was that Cassandra's father was Russian. Those Hungarian gypsies could still be on her mother's side. But regarding these matters I opted to hold my tongue.

"Sounds contrived to me," said Beth. "How can a deck of randomly shuffled cards predict the future? And how can a man of your background believe in such things?"

"I never said I believe it," said Dr. Horehound. "While I admit I find the concept interesting, I am more intrigued by people who actually do place their faith in arbitrarily-derived divination."

"You, the detached observer," said Beth crossly, "looking down on everyone, preying on their hopes and fears, figuring them out like a—"

"As they say, it's a living," said Dr. Horehound, flippantly. "Find anything?"

That last was directed to Pierre, Edward, and Jonathan, who had busied themselves tapping the walls, examining the chairs, and peering under the table. Joel had remained standing in the doorway, his eyes sour and distrusting.

Just then Grayburn returned, squeezing by Joel with another vase of flowers. Grumbling all the while, he placed it on a black marble pillar at the left of the fireplace. Then he noisily addressed the issue of making a fire.

"The thing about parlor tricks," said Pierre, wincing at the obnoxious clank and clatter of Grayburn's metal implements, "is that the adroit magician does something while drawing his mark's attention elsewhere while he does it, leaving the decoyed observer wondering how the thing was done. Not being an adept of sleight-of-hand, I don't know what to look for."

"These walls sound hollow," said Jonathan, thumping the panel beneath the Hermit. "If there's a catch to open one of them, it might be anywhere in the room."

"Did you examine the area around Madam Ouspenskaya's chair?" asked Dr. Horehound, indicating the one with its back to the fireplace. "That's where Madam Douceur will be sitting."

"Yes," said Edward. "But like Pierre said, it's a matter of drawing one's attention. If there's a switch or a pull-string, it might be at someone else's seat. Yours, for example, Dr. Horehound."

"An excellent point," agreed the doctor.

"And Grayburn could be in the room above," said Pierre. "From there he could make all sorts of things happen."

"Equally excellent," said Dr. Horehound.

"Not on yer life," protested Grayburn, swatting soot from his pants as he regarded the growing, fluttering results of his noisy labors. "I'll be hidin' in my room while y'all is doin' what you does. I'll have no part of it."

"Grayburn is a believer," explained the doctor with a knowing smile.

"Yet you stay here," said Beth. "At Wolfram Lodge, I mean."

"It's a livin', Missie," said the old coot, bowing to his employer on his way out. "At my age you take whatcha get and keep whatcha got."

"Is this the original table?" asked Edward, who was running his fingers around the smooth edge.

"Almost everything in this room is as it was," said Dr. Horehound, "the main exception being the carpet, which had become moth-eaten. In his account, Louis Sartell described it as being 'a deep crimson red inclining to purple.' What you are walking upon is Miss Marigold's interpretation. I trusted her opinion more than my own because I'm slightly colorblind in the lower frequencies. The crystal ball on the mantel belonged to Gabrielle Piaget. The distinctive stand on which it rests is made of genuine Hepatizon bronze. She purchased the set in Moldova from a mineralogist of some renown by the name of Dragos Banulesco, who was also a meteoriticist. It is not, in fact, made of polished quartz, but of pyrogenic compounds that defied analysis at the time. A tornado-shaped defect in its center is described in the bill of sale—but I digress. It doesn't play a part in our story. These are the original table and chairs, although I had them refinished along with the wall panels. Sections of the hardwood floor in the corridor had to be replaced, but I'm confident Bartholomew Piaget would find these surroundings familiar. I beg your pardon if my answer has exceeded the scope of your question. I admit I'm proud of my restoration efforts."

Edward, who seemed to have lost interest halfway through Dr. Horehound's reply, nodded vaguely as he ran his hands up and down the black marble pillar beside the fireplace.

"By the way," said I to our host. "You sometimes call Madam Douceur by the initials E. I. D. Might I ask why?"

"A triviality, but I'll explain," said he. "As you surely read from the cast list, her parents graced her with a first name that combines Elaine and Eileen—her mother's favorite aunts, so she tells me. E is for Elaine. I is the phonetic for Eileen."

"And D is for Douceur," I deduced.

"E. I. D.," said Dr. Horehound. "It's my *homage*, of a sort, to the notorious theosophist, Madam Helena Petrovna Blavatsky who preferred to be called by her initials: H. P. B."

"You, a fan of a woman like that?"

"Anyone who could write such utter bilge and get away with it—nay, make a career out of it—deserves some modicum of appreciation," said Dr. Horehound. "Gentlemen, Miss von Derschmidt, if you will excuse me, I'd like to change into something more comfortable. You are free to remain in here if you like. Otherwise I'll see you out and lock the door—"

"I'd like to stay," said Pierre. "This room interests me."

"You mentioned the hollow sound of the panels," said Dr. Horehound, pausing beside Joel in the doorway. "I've examined the blueprints, and also the rooms adjacent to this one. Obviously, this is a twelve-sided compartment built within a larger square space. Mr. Piaget had the gap between these and the real walls filled with asbestos as a way of isolating this space. No, do not worry, I've made thorough tests. The asbestos is hermetically sealed within. There is no danger to us while we're in here."

"So you say," said Beth.

"So I do," responded Dr. Horehound. "Oh, I almost forgot." From the seat of the chair reserved for Ian White Robinson (Architect) he produced an ornate crystal bowl. This he placed rim-down over the precious Tarot deck. "As Madam Ouspenskaya instructed him, Mr. Piaget shuffled the cards before she entered the room. For the sake of our reenactment, we'll protect them thusly." He started to leave but paused again. "It's not that I don't trust you; it's that I defer to human nature. If that has been touched or moved, I will know."

With that he left us.

"The blowhard," said Beth when he was out of earshot.

∞§[Martin]§∞

"I'm with you, Betsy Babe," said Kahlúa as Arthur paused for a sip of eggnog.

"He sounds simply awful," agreed Beth. "Imagine serving insects to paying guests. And the way he talks down to everyone."

"It was his way of regaining control," said Pierre.

"Just ask Millie," I said, waving playfully at her around Monsignor Havermeyer.

"You just wait," said she.

"Can't," I assured her.

"I've got a bit more to go," said Arthur, setting his mug on the mantel.

∞§[Arthur]§∞

Although we were deep within the heart of Wolfram Lodge, vibrations from repeated thunderclaps penetrated all the way to the séance room, rattling Grayburn's rose-filled vases on both sides of the fireplace. Occasional raindrops made their way down the chimney chute to thud and hiss among the dancing flames. It was a mightier storm than the night before.

"I wish Dr. Horehound would let us review the script," said Edward, gazing up intently at Death on horseback. "We really have no idea what to expect."

"That's the way he wants it," said Pierre.

"He's just mad because we have principles," said Beth. "With all his wealth and psychology, he's really a trifling little man."

"You said it," said Jonathan, trying to catch her eyes with his. "If you don't mind my saying, I don't like the way he looks at you."

"What?" retorted Beth. "No way. Not a chance!"

"Of course not," said Pierre. "But I've noticed it, too. You interest him."

"So do glazed dung beetles," said my sister, fuming.

"I'd—we'd better keep our guard up," said Jonathan.

That slip caught Beth's attention. She smiled.

"Whoa, what's that?" said Edward.

"What?" several of us asked.

"There!" he hissed, pointing to the air above the table. "I thought—"

"You thought what?" asked Pierre.

"There it is again."

"Yikes!" exclaimed Joel, still hovering by the open doorway.

For a brief moment, a light appeared about three feet above the center of the table. I thought at first it might be a reflection of the fire off the overturned bowl. But no, it wasn't that. It seemed to blossom into existence like a flower, though it was much simpler. No petals, no definite shape at all, really. It was perfectly round without specific form, circular without rim, bright but not blinding, there but not really there. It was white, and yet there were suggestions of blues and greens around the edges—and the hues were rich in their way: not just blue, but tranquil sky blue; not just green, but tropical lagoon green. As I marveled at it, wishing not to touch but just to appreciate its beauty, it collapsed back into nothingness.

"Like at the campground," said Jonathan.

"Indeed," said Pierre. "Like what we saw there."

"What else haven't you told me?" insisted Beth, poking me in the gut.

"I wasn't there, remember?" I retorted, rubbing the hole she had bored into my stomach. "Ask *them!*"

∞§[Martin]§∞

"How do you like that?" interrupted Kahlúa. "Betsy Pie, imagine them not filling you in! Men and their secrets!"

"They can't keep 'em from us, though," said Millie. "Not for long."

"You said it, Sugar Plum."

"'Specially when their secrets reveal themselves on their own."

"They don't stand a chance."

∞§[Arthur]§∞

"There it is again!" said Joel, less than a minute later.

This time it appeared at eye level in the air between the table and the door. It's hard to say, but I had the impression it had trouble materializing this time. There was a faint snap as it popped into being, its edges undulating as though it had poked though some invisible membrane and was wobblingly regaining its equilibrium. The blues and greens seemed to flare slightly, as if its energies had momentarily exceeded their bounds in its effort to punch through into our world.

"I don't like this," said Joel. "This is—this is really—"

As if attracted by Joel's voice, the orb moved toward him. It maneuvered smoothly, with apparent purpose.

"Oo-o-ooh no-oo-ooo," stammered Joel, his knees pumping but his feet not responding. His hands twitched helplessly at his sides. "Guys! Do something!"

In an instant of uncertainty, I thought to reach for it—perhaps swat at it—I'm not sure. I had no sense of it having ill intent, but Joel was terrified, and he was my friend. There was also the element of risk. If it was electrical, was it hazardous to touch? The others teetered in a moment of indecision as well, and, in that brief span of time, the orb traversed the distance directly, deliberately, and inexorably toward him.

In the nick of time, Joel lurched away, arms flailing as he fell backward into the hallway. The sphere halted at the place where he had been standing a moment before. It wiggled a bit, then vanished—imploding with a rubbery snap.

"Did you see that?" yelled Joel, heaving himself off the floor. "It tried to get me!"

"I honestly don't know what it was doing," said Pierre, rushing to help Joel to his feet.

Joel shook him off. "The Hell you don't!"

"Dear Chap—" said Pierre, but our young friend was already running spasmodically down the hall.

"I'll go after him," said Edward, giving Pierre an assuring glance before he dashed out the door.

∞§[Martin]§∞

GARDENING TIPS: I considered making this next

section a separate chapter entitled "Father

Baptist Waxes Prolix" or "The Slap-Happy Bappy

Tarot Primer." However, upon further contem-

plation, I decided it functions comfortably as

a continuation of "The Thing about Parlor

Tricks." No less editorial authority than

Kahlu/a Hummingbird concurred. Multiple-

choice quiz to follow.

                                        --M.F.

"That was unexpected," said Jonathan. "I wonder what it was, and why it went for Joel."

"Flowers lure bees," said Kahlúa. "Joel draws light bulbs!"

"Balls," corrected Millie. "Light balls."

"It's a wonder we didn't all scram out of there," said Edward. "If that light already appeared twice, it could certainly appear again."

"Who knows who it would go after next?" imposed Jonathan.

"Did I really behave like that?" asked Joel, rubbing the back of his neck fretfully.

"We were all dealing with things we didn't understand," said Pierre. "What were we to do?"

"What do you think, Father?" asked Jonathan.

"Forgive me," said Father after a long moment, blinking distractedly. "I've no theory as yet about the appearances of these mysterious lights. My mind is on another track entirely. Arthur, two things puzzle me. The first is your comfortable familiarity with the Tarot. You've never mentioned it before."

"It surprises me, too," said Arthur, scratching his head as he handed Pierre his pages. "I don't remember ever studying it, yet I wrote as though I were fluent in its terminology and practice. Such knowledge would have to have been acquired before our excursion to Spirit Lake, and over a considerable period of time."

"Have you ever read *The Secret Doctrine* or *Isis Unveiled?*"

"Not that I know of."

"Yet you knew about Madam Blavatsky."

"Apparently, although I can't say that I do now."

"What do you say to that, Pierre?" asked Father.

"I suppose," said Pierre, choosing his words with care, "that some recollections of things pertaining to the events at Spirit Lake, but which happened previously, may have had to be erased lest they prematurely trigger memories that needed to remain forgotten."

Everyone stared silently at him for a minute.

"If I understand what you just said," I ventured, "it borders on terrifying."

"It's certainly unsettling," said Arthur, "to think that my memory has been expunged without my realizing it. More so that whole subjects I have studied are now lost to me."

"I should think you'd only realize it if it had been improperly purged," said Edward. "At least whoever did it demonstrated competence and proficiency."

"That makes me feel so much better," said Arthur sardonically.

"What can I tell you?" said Pierre with a shrug. "What else puzzles you, Father?"

"That was a dodge," said Joel.

"Nonetheless," maintained Pierre, adjusting his monocle. "Father?"

"I'm wondering what version of the Tarot deck Mr. Piaget shuffled all the way back in 1896," said Father Baptist. "My guess would have been the Marseilles deck, which was used extensively in the nineteenth century, but the pictorial specifics don't match."

"Excuse me?" asked Arthur, seating himself sideways on his chair so as to face Father. "*What* doesn't match?"

"Details in the artwork," explained Father. "The Marseilles deck depicts Death as a skeletal figure brandishing a scythe, complete with severed hands, feet, and heads scattered at his feet."

"Ew!" scowled Beth.

"Sounds like the cardinal pitching one of his archdiocesan fund drives," said Jonathan.

Chuckles ensued.

"Whereas in your description of the painting on the wall," said Father to Arthur, "which I assume was rendered from the card in the deck on the table, Death is personified as a knight on horseback holding an unfurled banner of a white rose. These details are peculiar to the Tarot deck designed by A. E. Waite. Grayburn described the Queen of Cups holding an impressive goblet, but the stream he mentioned at her feet was absent from the Marseilles version. The Marseilles Ace of Cups was so garish it wasn't recognizable as a chalice at all—it looked more like a castle on a pedestal—whereas the Holy Ghost descending with the Blessed Sacrament in its beak is only to be found in Waite. The Marseilles Hermit was holding a lantern, but only in the Waite is a six-pointed start glowing within—a symbol known as the *Mogen Dovid*, the Star of David. Oh, and Waite, in what was perhaps a gesture of religious universalism, called the fifth card of the Greater Arcana 'The Hierophant.' In the Marseilles deck, which was formulated in Catholic France, it was designated *'Le Pape.'"*

"So obviously this Waite deck is probably the one Mr. Piaget used," said Jonathan.

"Not possible," said Father. "It wasn't published by the Rider Company until 1909, some thirteen years after Cassandra Ouspenskaya's death at Spirit Lake."

"Mr. Piaget apparently fraternized with a lot of occultists," said Arthur. "Perhaps he wiggled an advance copy out of Mr. Waite."

"The actual artwork was executed by a woman named Pamela Coleman Smith," said Father. "She drew them according to Waite's specifications. Their collaboration occurred in the months just prior to publication. Incidentally, the imagery was based on the research of Eliphas Lévi, the influential occultist who gratefully died a Catholic in 1875."

"I thought he wrote bartending guides," said Pierre.

"Hah!" retorted Kahlúa.

"You have one of his books on your 'To be forewarned' shelf," said Monsignor Havermeyer.

"A. E. Waite?" asked Father with an academic nod. "Three, actually."

"Eliphas Lévi," said our grimacing monsignor. "I remember reading his *The History of Magic* last All Saint's Day during the aftermath of, well, the events of the previous night."

"Halloween?" said Joel. "Oh, right."

"Three of his also," said Father. "I might add, for no reason other than the way my mind works, that two of the paintings in the séance room did not belong: the Queen of Cups that Grayburn liked so much, and the Ace of Cups above the only door. These two, beautiful though they are—and specifically Catholic in meaning as the Ace of Cups obviously is—belong to the Lesser Trumps, whereas all the rest are part of the Greater Arcana. The difference being—"

"Father Baptist!" exclaimed Beth. "First my brother, now you!"

"I've read books, too," said Father. "Unlike your brother, I remember them. Don't forget that, back in my days in Homicide, I earned a reputation for solving murders involving the occult. It was my job. I had to study the Tarot and witchcraft and all manner of occult practices in order to ferret out criminals who employed them. What can I say? I have the knowledge." He tapped his forehead. "It's up here, and on a number of occasions in the past few months it has proved useful, even providential."

"You can say that again," agreed Edward.

"The Farnsworth affair," recounted Pierre. "And our encounter with the malevolent Monsieur Portifoy."

"Even so," said Beth, "you can't believe a stack of cards can tell the future!"

"The Tarot is, as you say, but a deck of cards," said Father. "Some occultists believe that the seeker, by some subliminal, unconscious process, determines the order of the cards as he shuffles the deck, even though he doesn't see the faces of the cards as he does so. Others go so far as to say the cards have the power to arrange themselves in the shuffling process."

"Do you believe that?" asked Beth.

"That the cards can arrange themselves?" Father stroked his chin. "Under normal circumstances, of course not. Once shuffled, the order of the cards is randomized. Nonetheless, once placed in a spread on a table, however they may land, inferences and interpretations may be drawn from their positions."

"What about under not-so-normal circumstances?" asked Jonathan.

Father chose his words carefully. "I suppose there is always the possibility that unseen forces may be called into play by an adept. I have never witnessed such a thing, but I am open to the possibility. But, as I said, normally this would not be the case."

"This interpretation of the spread," said Beth. "That's what a 'reading' is. I suppose that's obvious. And the cards are supposed to predict the future?"

"My sense of the Tarot," said Father, "drawn from considerable experience, is not that it predicts the future, but that it can be used somewhat reliably as a means for exploring the human psyche in its *present* circumstance. A successful card reader has to be a good judge of character. He observes subtle cues in the seeker's behavior and capitalizes on them as he explains the meaning of the cards."

"Gypsy parlor psychology," said Jonathan.

"Probably more accurate than the clinical kind," said Father. "Carl Jung certainly believed the Tarot was useful for psychoanalysis. He, by the way, refused to treat Catholics. I understand he kept a list of able confessors in his desk as referrals. Though not a Catholic himself, he recognized the efficacy of the Sacrament of Penance."

"Come again?" said Millie. "The Tarot is Satanic. If you touch a blessed object like a Rosary, you gain Grace; but if you come in contact with something evil, what do you expect you'll get? The moment I heard the word *séance* in connection with this business, I knew something wicked was in the works."

"Let's not mix apples with oranges," said Father. "Séances are evil because they delve into the realm of necromancy, that is, attempting to communicate with the spirits of the dead. From Old Testament times the practice was condemned, not because the dead are necessarily evil, but because we humans are limited in our ability to discern whether they are evil or not, or genuine or not. Some spirits may be wicked, others quite the opposite. We know that certain Saints were actually spurred to holiness by conversations with Souls in Purgatory. These Saints did not seek them out, but were nonetheless visited by them. You'll remember, Gentlemen—and Martin in particular—that such visitations must be tested. Saint John of the Cross warned that visions and inner locutions should be shunned until their origin could be ascertained, and even then he was cautious because he understood his own frailty in this regard. Spiritualists try to contact the spirits of the dead without testing them, naively assuming they are telling the truth. This stems from pride—pride, and a perverse misconception that they, the spiritualists, are inherently good and that the spirits they contact are likewise honest. It doesn't occur to them that their own human nature is, in fact, fallen and that evil spirits will pretend to be the souls they seek, telling them precisely what they want to hear. 'Summerland,' for example, was the name such contacted spirits gave for the place people go when they die—not Heaven, not Hell, but Summerland: a meadow of eternal serenity. We Catholics know that this is contrary to Revelation, but spiritualists deny the rectitude of our religion; hence they are so easily misled. But who of us—even devout Catholics—can tell, by merely looking and conversing, whether an entity has our ultimate good in mind? We cannot, for we haven't the perception or the experience, hence the Church forbids the attempt in the first place. This, Gentlemen, is why I applauded your standing firm with respect to attending the séance."

"How is the Tarot any different?" persisted Beth.

"I disagree that the Tarot is intrinsically Satanic," said Father. "It can certainly be put to evil purpose—foretelling the future being the obvious example—but not necessarily."

"Guns don't kill people," said Jonathan, helpfully. "People kill people."

"Forgive me for being circuitous," said Father, "but few people today would object to a psychiatrist presenting a patient with indiscriminate blotches of ink on a piece of paper and recording their reactions."

"The Rorschach test," said Arthur, "exploring the personality though inkblots."

"Right," said Father. "But otherwise informed churchmen will furiously object to an introspective man holding a card in his hand depicting the Holy Grail, or people rising from their tombs at the Last Judgment as a great Angel blows a trumpet, or another Angel pouring the Water of Life between two chalices, the Devil as tempter of animal passions, or the Pope ruling the Church from his throne. These representations are all in the Tarot. Arthur Waite himself wrote that the images were to be interpreted according to the Law of Grace rather than by the pretexts and intuitions of that which passes for divination. That's close to an exact quote, but not quite."

"In other words, if I understand your meaning," said Arthur, "Mr. Waite did not intend his cards as talismans for telling the future, but as prods to the imagination? The point being—what? Enlightenment? Self-understanding?"

"That's not a bad way to put it," said Father after a moment's consideration.

"So what are you saying?" insisted Beth.

"The first time I saw any Tarot image, believe it or not," said Father, "was in the office of the official exorcist of Los Angeles. His name was Father Johann Piasecky. I went to see him at my wife Christine's insistence when I was first assigned a case that involved a murderous fortuneteller. When she saw the unopened Tarot deck I brought home to study, she got out the archdiocesan directory and made the appointment herself. I wish she had been with me when I entered his office. Father Piasecky, as it turned out, had a penchant for Grail Lore. On his wall were more than a dozen renderings of the Cup of Christ, from medieval woodcuts to a stunning photograph of the Holy Chalice of Valencia. There, in a place of prominence above his desk, was a reproduction of the Ace of Cups from the Waite deck. I might add that in addition to the details Arthur described, the Grail is held in the palm of a hand emerging from a cloud, with four rivulets of life-giving water pouring from the base of the cup into a body of water below—from which Father Piasecky construed the symbolism of Baptism. As I was there in my official capacity, seeking information, he gave me several books to read; and because I was a Catholic, he firmly pounded into me the teaching of the Church regarding the occult. First: we are forbidden to seek contact or information from spirits, this for all the reasons I've already explained. Second: Free Will remains paramount and immutable. Saint Thomas Aquinas said it best with regards to astrology, a practice with which he was intimately familiar: 'The stars impel, they do not compel.' The same is true of the Tarot: as a tool for exploring the human psyche, it can be marvelously insightful and therefore useful. But the moment someone believes that the cards are controlling his destiny, he has crossed the line. The step is all too brief, I fear, which is why I don't recommend its use. As I said, it was my job to learn thoroughly everything I could about many occult practices. I can appreciate them without employing them."

"Methinks we's a'walkin' on quicksand," said Kahlúa seriously, then she perked up. "My Aunt Gayleen used to tell fortunes. She had a little shop and everything!"

"Did she ever read yours?" asked Millie.

"Did she ever!" said Kahlúa. "She swore I'd be governor of California one day; but just betwixt you and me and the Boogie Man, I think she reshuffled the cards when I weren't lookin'."

"Excuse my ignorance, Father," said Edward. "If you could return to an earlier point. Greater Arcana, Lesser Trumps—?"

"'It sounds like a lot of supernatural baloney to me,'" said Jonathan, giving Arthur a friendly nudge.

"'Supernatural, perhaps,'" said Pierre, adopting his unconvincing impression of Bela Lugosi.

"'Baloney, perhaps not!'" said all the Lads together.

GARDENING TIPS: They were quoting a cele-

brated exchange between Peter Alison and Dr.

Vitus Werdegast (played by David Manners and

Bela Lugosi respectively), in the 1934 movie,

The Black Cat. Arthur threw a party the day

Universal Pictures released it in some digi-

tal whirly-thingie format.

                                    --M.F.

"The Tarot is neither," said Father. "It is divided into the Greater and Lesser Arcana or Trumps. The Lesser Trumps are four sets of fourteen cards—Ace, Duce, Three and so on up to the King—very much like what you'll find in a standard deck of playing cards today except there's a Page and a Knight instead of the single Jack. Instead of the four Suits we're familiar with in

poker decks—Clubs, Hearts, Diamonds, and Spades—in the
Tarot we find Cups, Wands, Swords, and Pentangles."

"Pentangles?" asked Edward.

"Sometimes called Coins," said Father. "Golden disks emblazoned with a five-pointed star. Now, over and above the Lesser
Trumps, the Greater Arcana consists of twenty-two cards, each
with a stylized picture representing a universal concept: Justice,
Temperance, Strength, the World, the Pope, Death, and so on."

"I heard somewhere," said Jonathan, "that modern playing
cards descended from the Tarot deck. Is that true?"

"It depends on which authority you read," said Father. "Although some occultists have claimed what you say, and more—
that the Tarot originated in ancient Egypt, for instance—decks of
fifty-two cards, consisting of the four Suits without the Greater
Arcana, date back to the fourteenth century. It is unclear when
the Greater Trumps were formulated, let alone added to, or even
whether they preceded the Lesser Trumps. Some historians who
lack the occult agenda have surmised—who knows with what
accuracy?—that playing cards first came from China, where paper was invented, and made their way into Europe through contact with the Islamic Empire. In other words, the origin of cards
used for divination as well as games of chance and skill is unknown."

"I love it when that happens," said Jonathan.

"The Marseilles Tarot I just mentioned," said Father, "consisting of seventy-eight cards including the Greater Arcana, was
probably designed in France by Jean Noblet around 1650. In
answer to your question, Jonathan, the one contribution the Tarot
made to the modern poker deck is probably the Fool transformed
into the Joker."

"Food for thought," said Pierre, "the next time we resort to a
game of five-card stud."

"But we've never played poker," said Arthur.

"'To be forewarned,'" said Pierre.

"'Is to be forearmed,'" said the Lads.

"Two final points," said Father. "First, the Waite deck was the
first Tarot with detailed pictorial representations in the Lesser
Trumps. I'll give you a random example. The Five of Pentan-

gles is a card of destitution—destitution probably in the financial
sense, but it could also mean emotional, marital, or otherwise. In
the Marseilles deck, the Five of Coins shows precisely that: five
golden Coins, much like a Five of Clubs in a modern deck shows
five Clubs, or a Five of Spades shows five Spades. In the Waite
deck, however, we find five Pentangles arranged artistically in a
stained-glass window. The window is set is a wall—"

"The wall of a church?" asked Edward.

"The implication is there," said Father, "but there are no religious symbols on the window or the wall. It could be the wall of
a bank or a wealthy manor. But you demonstrate how the imagery kindles speculative thoughts in the mind. Consider this:
beneath the wall we see a man on crude crutches and a woman
wrapped in a shawl, both in rags, trudging their way through ankle-deep snow."

"Destitution," said Arthur thoughtfully. "in the shadow of opu-
lence."

"The scene is riveting and thought-provoking," agreed Father.
"Now, imagine your reaction if that card is placed in the position
in the spread representing your current condition, or your distant
past. Naturally, you will consider in what ways you are or have
been impoverished, damaged, perhaps cheated."

"Who hasn't been?" said Jonathan. "Cheated, I mean, or
slighted or whatever?"

"The cards present concepts we all share," agreed Father.
"Now, take the same card, and place it in a position of future
outcome. You will likely be spurred to reflect upon what ele-
ments of your current circumstance might lead to such an unwanted, unfortunate result. I stress *might* lead. The danger lies
in assuming that things *must* turn out that way."

"That's how fortunetellers make their living," said Edward.

"Exactly," said Father.

"Your other point, Father?" asked Pierre, glancing at his
pocket watch.

"A. E. Waite fervently believed that the Tarot had been handed
down from antediluvian times," said Father. "That esoteric principles, universal truths if you will, had been deftly woven into its

fabric by the ancients so as to be preserved through the ages; that those with the eyes to see could discern these arcane secrets."

"Do you believe that?" asked Beth.

"I believe I'm on the verge of derailing your meeting," said Father, leaning back in his chair, "and Martin is about to utter the word 'prolix' in the guise of a cough at any moment."

Mind reader, I disguised behind a yawn.

"Shhh!" shushed Millie.

"So I will cease and desist for the nonce," said Father, "and defer to our Master of Ceremonies, Pierre Bontemps."

"Thank-you, Father," said Pierre. "We'll likely rely on your expertise from time to time as we proceed."

"So where are we?" asked Jonathan. "I guess we've come to the séance, or its reenactment, or whatever."

"Right you are," said Pierre, relieved to be back on track. "Things are about to take a turn. I think Beth should be the one to guide us around the bend."

"I'm not sure I want to go on with this," said Beth, rubbing her arms. "I'm getting all creeped out."

"And well you should," said Father. "I shudder to think where this is leading."

"If I may paraphrase Bram Stoker," said Pierre. "We will have to pass through the bitter water before we reach the sweet."

"Then there *is* a happy ending," said Beth, rising to the occasion and accepting her next installment.

"I believe your own term, Sis," said Arthur, "was 'wildly right—well, mostly.'"

"Don't forget 'except for ... Oh dear!'" warned Kahlúa.

"We are all here, alive and kicking," said Pierre. "That much you know. I'll leave the interpretation of the denouement to you when the time comes."

"Pardon my candor," I whispered to Father as he settled himself. "It seems to me that if you hadn't been so distracted last summer, you might have given the Lads the same crash course in the Tarot before they departed for Spirit Lake."

"I dropped the ball, you mean," said he, pensively. "Had I given them my full attention I might have forbidden them from going in the first place."

"I doubt it," I said. "Not on the basis of that silly brochure. *'Come and relive the ghostly events of that fateful night.'* A séance reenactment with a murder on the side, of all things. It didn't exactly beg to be taken seriously. For all you know, you would have sent them on their way with your blessing."

"That we will never know," he sighed. "Ah well, let's let Beth have her say."

∞§[†]§∞

∞§✝§∞

12. Spirits of the Light

∞§[*Beth*]§∞

"THAT'S THE LAST OF IT," said my brother, screwing the cap back onto his holy water flask. It was the clear glass bottle Mom gave him at his Confirmation, shaped like a Cross. He had just completed three rounds of the séance room, sprinkling everything.

"Hope it helps," said Edward.

"I think it should," said Pierre. "Everyone have their scapulars on?"

"Absolutely," said Jonathan.

Edward looked carefully at Joel whom he had just led back from the library. "You okay?"

"No," said he, sullenly. "I really don't want to be here." It had taken the persuasive power of five snifters of brandy to get him back—plus Edward's promise to drive him into Claw Junction in the morning for a hamburger, onion rings, and a chocolate shake. For breakfast, yet! "I can't believe I let you talk me into this," said Joel, tugging fretfully on his ear.

"Chin up," said Pierre. "The session, as the doctor prefers to call it, will be over soon."

"If that light shows up again," said Joel, "the blur you see will be me."

"Steady," said Edward. "We're with you."

"We'll be right behind you," said Jonathan, "flying on your fumes."

Uneasy chuckles drifted around the table as we seated ourselves.

"Next time we take a vacation together, I pick the place," I whispered to Arthur as we heard the Master and his girl Fridays approaching from the foyer end of the corridor. "Get me?"

"No argument," said he, protecting his paunch with his hands.

I leaned closer. "And when were you going to tell me about the thing that landed in the lake?"

"How—?" His eyes went wide, then his eyebrows did that endearing scrunchy thing they do when he's figuring something out. They relaxed as he said, "Jonathan."

You can't, Beth! You just can't! You don't realize ... What's out there ... What we saw ... It's ... It's ... You just can't!

I fluttered my eyelashes at my brother. "He felt obliged to dissuade me from joyriding in one of the sailboats tomorrow."

It was HUGE!

"So that's what you two were whispering about in the hallway."

"He's cute."

"If you say so."

The footsteps in the corridor were getting closer.

"So I'm all caught up?" I insisted.

"Far as I know," said Big Bro, still protecting his gut. "Did you learn that finger thing from Mom?"

∞§[Martin]§∞

Beth paused.

"Something wrong, Sis?" asked Arthur. "Something you wrote?"

"More like the way I wrote it," she answered thoughtfully. "These sentences— 'You can't, Beth! You just can't,' and 'It was HUGE!'—they're highlighted and bracketed before and after with double asterisks."

"I assumed they were things Jonathan said to you," said Edward.

"Like flashes of memory," agreed Jonathan. "You know, woven into your train of thought."

"That is so," said Pierre, eyeing Beth closely. "Those are quotes from a conversation you had with Jonathan shortly before. Since you alluded to it here, I thought it unnecessary to present it twice."

"It's just ... I don't know," said Beth. "Why would I stick them in here, and this way?"

"Maybe it's a stylistic touch," said Jonathan helpfully. "You know, like Stephen King. He does that sort of thing."

"Flashes of memory within a forgotten memory," said Monsignor Havermeyer thoughtfully.

"Artsy," said Kahlúa appreciatively. "It works for me."

"Well, I think it's cute," said Millie.

Father and I both glanced quizzically at her, surprised that the word was in her vocabulary.

Arthur looked as though he were about to say something, but changed his mind.

"Well," said Pierre, as if he had something to add, too, but was unsure whether to proffer it just yet, "let's proceed and see what happens. Beth?"

"Of course," she said, still a bit perplexed. "Let me see ..."

∞§[*Beth*]§∞

"Gentlemen, Elizabeth," said Dr. Horehound as he sauntered into the room like he was somebody special, his two female toadies close behind. I couldn't believe he was wearing a puffy, stuffy, silky smoking jacket. He probably thought it made him look elegant, but it struck me as pompously casual compared to the guys in their spiffy tuxedos. The dress code obviously didn't apply to him—the snot. He also had one of those overturned buckets on his head with a tassel like I've seen in some of Arthur's old movies—a fez, I believe it's called. It was made of maroon-colored felt, and the yellow tassel flopped around with every movement of his head. I found it distracting. Maybe that was a good thing, all things considered.

Madam Douceur was dressed in a black hand-knitted gypsy shawl over an electric brown blouse—shimmering silk that adhered to her folds, poor dear, someone should tell her—also a purple turban with a green jewel in front and a red feather sticking straight up. Pearls the size of golf balls elongated her earlobes, and a matching string of them rattled around her neck. Clarice Davenport, on the other hand, must have slimed herself with liquid dishwashing detergent in order to slip into that red satin surgical glove she was wearing. Even I couldn't take my eyes off all the low-this and barely-that. I felt like clamping my hand over Big Brudder's lonely bachelor eyes and urging him to do the same to Jonathan.

"Gentlemen," prompted Pierre as he rose to his feet. All the guys got up with him—yes, even for the likes of Alien-Eileen and Clare-Grease! Madam Douceur clearly was unaccustomed to men climbing to attention as she entered a room. She got all flustered, then plied them with one of her gooey smiles. Clarice Davenport, on the other hand, acted as though it was all perfectly normal—although she probably preferred men on all fours with their tongues hanging out.

Dr. Horehound stood beside the fireplace, looking amused. He had some black folders tucked under his arm, the kind my brother used to present his term papers in when he was attending Ohio State. "The time has come," he said as the ladies parked themselves and the fellows settled back into their chairs. He handed Madam Douceur one of the folders. "Your script, E. I. D."

She closed her eyes and clutched the thing as though she were reading it through the cover, her hands, and her eyelids.

"And ours?" asked Pierre.

"Of course," said Dr. Horehound, passing them out as he circled around and finally pulled out the chair next to mine. I knew that was his place—or rather, Bartholomew Piaget's—from the card on the table, and, even though I shimmied myself closer to Arthur, he managed to press his knee against mine as he adjusted his chair. I wished I had a fork to stick in his erudite thigh as he handed me the last folder with a smile he probably thought was charming. It was not.

Nervously, we all opened our folders and examined our scripts. I was a little surprised to find typewritten onionskins within, hammered into the paper with a heavy, uneven hand, rather than slick laser-printed sheets. I counted four typos on the first page. Those term papers I mentioned—Arthur's—he never would have made his deadlines if not for the secretarial skills of his sweet, efficient Li'l Sis. Of course, that had been in the days before personal computers. His spell-checker is probably digital these days.

"I will ask that you keep your paper shuffling to a minimum," said Madam Douceur, her eyes remaining closed. "Noise upsets the spirits."

"So what?" snipped Pierre, riffling his pages purposefully. "It's a reenactment, right?" Rudeness was uncharacteristic for him, but he had a point to make.

"As you say," said Madam, her sightless smile sliding down her face and into her—oh, never mind. "My word is my bond," she assured us coldly.

"So," said the doc, that darn tassel flipping and flopping. "Shall we begin?"

∞§[Martin]§∞

Beth paused again, squinted at the page, and said, "Okay, I drew a seating chart here, but how am I going to explain it to you? Ah, I know." She started pointing as if to an invisible blackboard between her and us, referring repeatedly to her drawing. "Let's see. D. U. I. is up there, Dr. Whoremonger down here, and Caprice Any-Old-Port over there—like 12 and about 8 and 4 on a Salvador Dali coo-coo clock. Joel and Pierre are between Doc and Doozie, Edward and Jonathan are between Doozie and Slut. That leaves me next to Mort the Hound and Arthur next to Capeesh Pop-the-Cork, and Li'l Sis and Big Bro neck and neck down here. Everybody got that?"

Everybody didn't, but she went on anyway.

<u>GARDENING</u> <u>TIPS</u>: Time for me to step in with a
convenient visual aid. And I bet you thought
I was asleep on my tricycle!

                    Madam Douceur

          Pierre   Edward

     Joel   Jonathan

     Dr. Horehound   Clarice D.

            Beth   Arthur

                                        --M.F.

∞§[*Beth*]§∞

"Spirits of the Great Beyond," began Madam Douceur without
opening her folder or her eyes, proving she knew her lines by
heart. She set it aside and continued, "We gather here to reach
out to the light of Gabrielle Piaget. Can you help us? Will you
guide us?"

There really wasn't much for the rest of us to do at this point.
Cassandra Ouspenskaya had clearly hogged the show, so Madam
Douceur was in her element.

"Wish we do to pierce the veil," she crooned tremulously.
"Eclipsing the light so pale. We know that you will not us fail.
Spirits of the light."

We know that you will not us fail???? Talk about bilge! It
wasn't even decent poetry! Did I mention Jonathan had tried

some on me in the hallway? Poetry, I mean. Good stuff. Gerald
Manley Hopkins, yet. His delivery was so— No, never mind.
"Please turn down the lights," said Madam Douceur, her eyes
still shut.

"Of course," said Dr. Horehound, reaching for a knob behind
him on the wall. That was actually in the script, though back in
those days Mr. Piaget probably turned down the gas. This provided our host with another opportunity to press his knee against
mine, and for me to wish for a longer, sharper piece of silver-
ware. The room grew dark with just a slight amber shimmer
from the bulbs overhead and the undulating glow of the fireplace
behind Madam Douceur.

"That is good," said she, inhaling deeply and letting it out
forcefully. "O Spirits who are all around us, come and hear our
plea. Favor us with your kindly presence. We open up our
hearts to thee." She blinked several times, as if waking, and
said, "Let us all hold hands."

Eeew! Dr. Horehound wrapped his sweaty fingers around
mine. Boy, was he damp! And icky warm, too! Three trickles
of perspiration meandered down the side of his face. The fire
under the coat of arms may have been a little on the too-close-to-
the-barbecue side, but Madam Douceur's girth was blocking
most of its radiance, and we were seated a table's diameter beyond her. Even so, the man was moist and feverish. I wiggled
closer to Arthur. He squeezed my right hand reassuringly. He's
a good Big Brudder.

Closing her eyes again, Madam Douceur began rolling her
head around, like a top losing its spin. Meanwhile, I noticed
Clarice Davenport's index finger gently tapping Arthur's other
hand. Darn if that vamp wasn't doing the same to Jonathan's.
Stereo sluttery! Pierre was watching from across the table. His
smile did not convey amusement. Edward looked on somberly,
his jaw muscles tight. Joel looked like he was going to be sick.

"Ooooh, ooooh," moaned Madam Douceur, as if she was—
never mind. She heaved and billowed a bit, then suddenly sat up
straight. "I am Ram-Ankh-*Hop*-Sut-Sput," she said in a deep,
almost manly voice. I'm spelling phonetically. "High priest of

Karnak, mystic seer of his divine highness Pharaoh *Bath*-Nah-Ket-Mop-*Ho*-Sop-Tep the Second."

I nudged Arthur and gave him a quizzical look which I hoped conveyed, "Hey, Big-Bro-Art-Ho-Tep, are those goofy monikers historical or made-up?" He shrugged and rolled his eyes in reply. Pierre's smile turned humorous, and Edward smirked. Jonathan was looking across Clarice and Arthur at me. I flashed him a double wink. Joel was turning green.

Everyone had to let go of one hand to turn the page. I tried to use my left hand but Dr. Horehound wouldn't let go. I released Arthur's hand for the task, then grabbed it again quickly for moral support—and because it was nice and dry. Good hand, nice hand.

"What is it that you want?" asked Ram-Ankh-Whatever supposedly manipulating the larynx of Elaineileen Douceur. Who did she think she was kidding?

We were looking around at each other, wondering that very thing, when Pierre realized he had a line to deliver.

"Ah," he said, finding his place. He delivered his part stiffly, with a touch of purposeful amateurishness. "Great mystic seer of ancient Egypt, we wish to speak with Gabrielle Piaget who has recently passed over."

"She is near," said Ram-Boy earnestly. "But she is shrouded in darkness. She cannot find the light. You must call to her."

"Gentlemen," said Dr. Horehound. His voice caught on the last syllable. He swallowed hard, making a *goink!* sound, then grunted, "Your cue."

The guys glanced around sheepishly, then commenced intoning more or less together: "Gabrielle ... Gabrielle ... Gabrielle." All except Joel. He wanted no part of this. "Gabrielle," they kept chanting, over and over. Presently one of them, probably Pierre, stomped his foot lightly on the floor. The others took it up. "Gabrielle ... (thump!) ... Gabrielle ... (thump!) ... Gabrielle ... (thump!)"

Dr. Horehound cleared his throat again, this time conveying professional disapproval. The guys stopped their chanting and thumping, but the air was charged with a silent, barely-held-in outburst of laughter all around. Madam Douceur's lips quivered.

Even Clarice was having trouble holding it in, so much so that her baby blues almost popped out of their mascara-encrusted sockets.

Just then the dim lights in the Tiffany chandelier flickered. Then they went out for a moment, and came back on.

"Whoa ho," said Pierre, his eyes darting around playfully and curious.

I felt Dr. Horehound shift in his chair ever so slightly. Maybe there was a button or something on the floor he was pressing with his foot. Maybe not. He was probably just experiencing a cramp, although I preferred my momentary fantasy of him realizing a giant tarantula was crawling up his leg. The one thing I was sure of was that his clammy hand was leaking all over mine. I flexed my fingers but he didn't let go. Then he started trembling.

"She's trying to reach you," said Ram-Ankh-Hop-Go-Figure of Karnak. Darn if Madam Douceur's channeled voice wasn't becoming disconcertingly convincing. Maybe she'd had a sex change along the way—who knows? "Gabrielle wishes to speak to Bartholomew through the cards."

"Ah, here it comes," said Arthur. That was impromptu. It wasn't in the script.

"Mr. Bontemps, would you mind?" asked Dr. Horehound, who by now was quivering all over. Great. Either touching my hand was giving him palpitations or, more likely, he was coming down with something contagious! Clearly he was deviating from the script, too. It was Bartholomew W. Piaget who was supposed to lift the glass bowl from the cards, not Eusebius T. Roundhead. What kind of a name is Roundhead? In any case, so much for authenticity.

"No problem," said Pierre, reaching over and removing the bowl and setting it down on the floor beside his chair. As he did so, the lights blinked off and on again. Arthur gave my hand in his an assuring squeeze. I gave him one back.

"Bartholomew Piaget," said Madam Douceur, now herself again, though her eyes remained closed. She, at least, was following the script. Her next line was there in mistyped black and white—

```
You hve shurffled the dcek, yes?
```

—although she pronounced the words correctly.

"I have," rasped Dr. Horehound. The man was definitely not well. He let loose with a deep-throated belch. The scent of putrefying bugs wafted by. So gross! I tugged my fingers out of his sopping grip. He didn't try to gather them back. "I have indeed, Madam Ouspenskaya," he said, suppressing another poison gas expulsion, "before we began, as you requested."

"Very well," said Madam Douceur. She opened her eyes and ladled honey all over us. "Ladies and Gentlemen, you may release your hands, but let us agree that you won't leave your seats for any reason. Do relax, but attend." A sigh fizzled around the table.

Arthur and I relaxed our grip but kept our pinkies touching, for courage. My left hand, meanwhile, having been slimed by Dr. Horehound, slipped under the rim of the table and huddled quivering in my lap, traumatized. A moment later the lights blinked off and on again. Arthur gathered my right hand in his again, protectively. Sweet Big Bro.

"Now," said Madam Douceur, her voice gentle but imposing, "the spread, or card arrangement I use, which my grandmother taught me, and hers her, is called *A Nyilatkozo Csillag:* the Revealing Star. It is extremely accurate, but difficult to control. It is tried and true. It never lies."

Unlike you, I thought to myself.

∞§[Martin]§∞

```
GARDENING TIPS: Beth's spelling was incorrect

because Hungarian doesn't share many phonemes

with English.  I took the liberty of making

adjustments after consulting Father Stephen
```

```
Nicanor at Saint Basil's.  Hungarian being one

of the eleven languages in which he is fluent,

he informed me that there is no direct equiva-

lent of "The Revealing Star."  A Nyilatkozo

Csillag comes close while sharing certain con-

sonants with Beth's courageous attempt.  Nei-

ther my Underwood nor the highfalutin comput-

ers at the L. A. Artsy have the necessary dia-

criticals.  We do what we can.

                                        --M.F.
```

∞§[*Beth*]§∞

She drew the deck to herself.

"Man is a star," she said loftily. "A five-pointed star. Picture his head as the topmost point, his spread feet the lowermost points, his outstretched hands the left and right points. He is facing us, so his right hand is opposite our left." Madam Douceur paused for emphasis: "Yes, Man indeed is a five-pointed star—"

∞§[Martin]§∞

"So how many points does a *woman* have?" asked Millie, resting her chin in her upturned palms.

"Countin' all of 'em?" asked Kahlúa, regarding various sections of herself. "Or just our good 'uns?"

"At my age I'll take what I can get."

"Don't sell yourself short," said Monsignor Havermeyer. "I've been a priest a long time, and you're the finest cook and housekeeper I've ever known." He was laying it on a little thick—but what the hey? It was Christmas Eve!

"If we were having something special tomorrow," said Millie with a satisfied smile, "you'd get an extra helping."

"The thought is enough, my good woman."

"It will likely have to do."

"Oh, brother," said I, thinking of the family-size cans of corned beef hash I'd noticed on the shelf in the pantry.

Pierre cleared his throat. "If Beth may be allowed to continue."

"Go on, Dearie," said Millie, lifting her chin from her palms. "Point the way."

"Twelve, I think," said Kahlúa as she finished her self-guided self-assessment. "Maybe thirteen."

∞§[†]§∞

∞§ † §∞

13. The Revealing Star

∞§[*Beth*]§∞

MADAM DOUCEUR PAUSED FOR EMPHASIS: "Yes, Man indeed is a five-pointed star. Watch closely and you will see his light unfold."

Gingerly, she drew the top card from the deck, turned it over, and set it down on the table. "This first card we call the Identifier. Its position is the head, the topmost point of the star. Bartholomew, this is the man you see yourself to be."

"The High Priestess," said Arthur, naming the card. It wasn't in the script, but he couldn't help himself.

Well, phooey! I thought to myself. What a bunch of room-temp baloney! How can it be *him* if the card's a *her?*

She was the first Tarot female I'd seen so far who wasn't sitting on a throne. The thing she sat upon looked more like a block of cement between two pillars, the left black and the other white—hey, like Grayburn's flowerpot stands on each side of the fireplace. There seemed to be a crescent moon entangled in the hem of her sky-blue robe.

"The High Priestess is a card of power," explained Madam Douceur. "Overt power, not covert power. Some things are implied, while others are spoken. Her mystical name is *Shekinah*, the visible glory."

So, I thought, Mr. Bartholomew W. Piaget regarded himself as a blazing cross-dressing control freak!

"Now we proceed to your right foot, the realm of your Remote Past," said Madam Douceur, turning over the second card and setting it on the table about twelve inches from the first. "The Star," she announced.

There was a star on the card all right, a big yellow one with one, two, three ... eight points. Seven smaller white ones, also eight-pointed, cluttered the sky around it. There was a little bush in the background with a bird sitting upon it. In the foreground a naked woman—don't look, Arthur, you too, Jonathan! She was crouching by a pond with one knee on the ground. She had a pitcher of water in each hand. One she was pouring into the pond, the other onto the ground.

"This card suggests a solitary seeker of wisdom," said Madam Douceur. "Wisdom found primarily within oneself. This is a hopeful card, Bartholomew, an omen of good aspect. You started preparing yourself for greatness long ago."

How was this supposed to be Gabrielle communicating to her husband from the great beyond? I asked myself that question more than once as this charade went forward. I also began thinking of Howler's Café in Claw Junction—the sign in the window had said, "OPEN 24 HOURS!" Maybe we could make a break for it. Oh, my whimpering tummy!

Right then, Dr. Horehound may have been thinking of the pharmacy located at the rear of Hal's Groceries where lurked the lady who never wiped her hands. His face had grown taut, his eyes sunken. He let loose with another discharge of his gastric upset. If I'd had a bottle of antacid handy I would have shoved it down his throat. Served him right, serving us bugs instead of prime rib!

"Now we turn our attention to your right hand, the window to your Immediate Past," said Madam Douceur, lifting the next card and turning it over. The lights blinked off and on again, but she didn't miss a beat. "Ah, the Two of Swords."

Yes, I thought, there are two swords. No, the image looking up at us makes no sense.

There was a blindfolded gal in a white ankle-length garment sitting on what looked to be a stone bench. There was a body of water in the background. She held a sword in each hand. Her wrists were crossed in front of her, causing the swords to form a large letter V.

"Usually this card denotes courage," said Madam Douceur. "Also friendship, tenderness, intimacy."

My thought: I'd love to know a hoodwinked-gal-with-crossed-sword's outlook on the topic of intimacy!

"In this position," she continued, "it means you have recently made a decision, Bartholomew, a major decision of critical moment, the result of which will be seen in your left hand, your Immediate Future." She immediately turned over the next card and set it down without looking at it. "Justice."

I didn't have to squint at the card because the same lady in a royal red robe and golden crown was glaring down at us from the painting on the wall. In her left hand she held a set of scales, and in her right, a long sword. If you like girls that play with knives, the Tarot just may be your thing!

"There is moral justice," said Madam Douceur, "which deals with concepts of right and wrong. There is also spiritual election, which belongs to the order of providence. You are about to reap the fruit of your decision, Bartholomew, for good or ill. Justice, you will all note, is not blindfolded. Her eyes are wide open. But her action is based on the angle of the scale, not any compassion that she may feel."

A weird, leathery, twisting sound came from within Dr. Horehound's abdomen. Clearly the man needed a bicarb in the worst way. He drew in a deep breath of air, then expelled it abruptly. He brought his right hand up to his sternum and pressed his left against his forehead, tilting that stupid fez back. Fortunately for him—more so for poor me enduring the bitter, dog kennel smell that was pouring off of him—there were only two cards to go.

"All of which is flowing toward your left foot, Bartholomew," intoned Madam Douceur, turning over the next card. "In your Distant Future—what's this?—the Four of Swords, the card of repose." She was acting, don't forget. That "what's this?" was on page seven.

The lights blinked again.

"*Hngk!*" gulped Dr. Horehound. I thought he was suppressing hiccups, or maybe a cough. The fez teetered. The veins on his forehead were wiggling under his skin. "*Hngk! Hngk!*"

Amidst the distractions, this card surprised me. In all the others, someone was doing something. In this one, a noble fellow, perhaps a knight, was lying flat on his back, his hands clasped as if in prayer—or perhaps posed by the undertaker, for he seemed to be using a stone sarcophagus for a mattress. No, on closer inspection, I realized he was made of stone, too, like a sculpture on the lid representing the person interred within. One sword seemed to be an image in *bas relief* on the close side of the coffin, and three others were affixed to the wall above and behind the knight with their points down. In the background was a stained-glass window, so this was in some sort of chapel. Repose was right. This guy was out cold.

"Repose," said Madam Douceur again. "Whatever complications may arise, your decision will lead you to a place of eventual rest. It also suggests vigilance, retreat, or perhaps exile. Time will tell."

Helloooooo, I thought. Of course time will tell! What do you think we're all waiting for?

I sniffed. I sniffed again. Deodorant was invented because people, even us precious little ladies, smell when we perspire. Dr. Horehound didn't just smell, he *reeked!* His breathing had become a handsaw going up and down, up and down. Hang on, Doctor Green-Weaver-Ants-All-the-Way-from-India. Just one more bloody card to go.

The lights dimmed, then came back on gradually this time.

"Almost done," whispered Arthur, giving my right hand an assuring squeeze.

"And finally, Bartholomew," said Madam Douceur, "we come to the Significator. While this is the first card in most divination systems, chosen by the seer to represent the seeker, in the Revealing Star it is the last card, decided by your own shuffling of the deck. It represents who you will be when all is accomplished if you remain on your present path. Of course, you have a say in your destiny." Her fingertips gripped the top card. "You can make decisions that will alter this possible outcome, but if you stay the course, O Bartholomew, the final outcome will be ..."

Drum roll, please. (In my head—at that moment there wasn't a sound in the room.)

"Excuse me," blurted Dr. Horehound. As she turned the card over and set it down with finality, he rose unsteadily, almost knocking his chair onto its side. With shaking hands, he mopped his brow with a white silk handkerchief. His voice was hoarse and wispy as he said, "My deepest apologies, Ladies and Gentlemen. I am not well. I've tried to tough it out, but alas, I simply must excuse myself. Nothing like this has ever happened before." He placed a dripping hand on my shoulder. His volcanic sweat penetrated right through the fabric of my evening gown to my skin.

Ick! I groaned inside. My dress will have to be dry-cleaned, darn it! I really should dab myself with disinfectant! Am I fussy or what?

"Miss von Derschmidt," he said to me amidst a series of abdominal cramps, "no doubt the onslaught of my symptoms has been distracting for you. You were polite throughout, and for that I thank you. As for the rest, I realize that my behavior today has been unconscionable, and for that I apologize. You were right. You didn't deserve to be served a meal of insects. It was beneath me and abhorrent to your sensibilities. I will attempt to make it up to you tomorrow. But as for now, I really must bid you goodnight."

With that he flung open the door and hustled down the hallway, likely in need of a bathroom. Poor man, the closest one was all the way at the end of the narrow corridor, through the foyer, past the drawing room, second door on the right. Or something like that.

"Well," said Edward. "There's a shocker for you."

Joel sat there nodding deliriously.

"Without turning to the last page," said Pierre after a moment's reflection, "I think it's safe to assume that didn't happen in 1896."

"It must have given Bartholomew Piaget quite a fright though, don't you think?" suggested Jonathan, indicating the Significator in the center of the Revealing Star:

DEATH.

"Actually, this *is* the last page," said Arthur, flipping his back and forth. "Madam Ouspenskaya reveals the card. *Finis.*"

"So we don't know how anyone sitting here reacted," said Jonathan.

"Precisely," said Arthur. "Dr. Horehound sets these sessions up to study *our* reactions."

"For his book, you mean."

"Or at least he would have, if he hadn't taken ill."

"The old Minimum Information Gambit ploy," mused Pierre. "Well, he can't blame us for a botched evening."

While the others stared at the card, I looked up at the painting. The skeleton in battle armor held no sword, only a banner. Under his horse lay a king sprawled face down in the dirt. Before him knelt a child and a woman, their hands clasped in supplication. Behind them stood a bishop, hands folded in prayer, bowing before the inevitable. Without raising a weapon, Death conquers all.

Thunder shook the lodge to its foundations.

∞§[Martin]§∞

GARDNING TIPS: I think it's time for another visual aid before we proceed. A roadmap is helpful when discussing the route to an unfamiliar destination. Presenting Cassandra Ouspenskaya's ancestral Tarot card spread, The Revealing Star, or as her spurious shapeshifting ancestors supposedly called it, A Nyilatkozo Csillag. Remember that the star symbolizes a man facing us. I have included the cards that Madams Cassandra Ouspenskaya and Elaineileen Douceur placed upon its blueprint more than a century apart. Warning: don't try this at home without parental supervision!

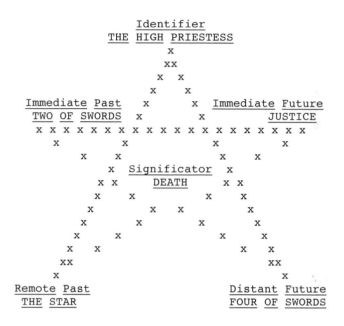

```
                    Identifier
              THE HIGH PRIESTESS
                      x
                     xx
                    x  x
                   x    x
  Immediate Past  x      x  Immediate Future
  TWO OF SWORDS   x      x          JUSTICE
  x x x x x x x x x x x x x x x x x x x x
      x          x          x          x
        x   x          x   x
         x  Significator  x
         x x    DEATH   x x
        x   x          x   x
       x       x  x          x
      x        x       x      x
     x    x          x    x
    x   x                  x   x
    xx                        xx
    x                          x
  Remote Past              Distant Future
  THE STAR                 FOUR OF SWORDS
```

My tricycle must have sprouted training
wheels!

--M.F.

∞§[†]§∞

∞§✝§∞

14. I Couldn't Have Meant It Like It Sounds

∞§[Martin]§∞

BETH FELL SILENT.

Just then a flash of lightning outside starkly outlined all the raindrops on the window. This was immediately applauded by a rip-roaring thunderclap that jiggled the star and wiggled the lights on the tree.

"Timing is everything," commented everyone more or less together. Well, maybe more on the less side. This was a lot to take in, don't forget.

"It doesn't get much creepier," said Beth, handing her pages to Pierre and then rubbing her arms against a chill.

"Whoo!" heaved Kahlúa as Beth settled sideways on her chair. "Aunt Gayleen never dealt me cards like that! If she had, I'd've ended my days in a convent!"

"That I'd like to see," chuckled Millie. She turned the thought over in her mind and came up with, "Sister Mary Lulu."

"Of the Blessed Sacrament Exposed," added Kahlúa, piously.

"Odd," said Arthur, pensively, but he didn't specify what.

"I'm curious, Father," said Monsignor Havermeyer. "Would you agree with this Douceur woman's interpretation of the cards?"

"You mean Madam Ouspenskaya's," said Father.

The monsignor thought that over and nodded.

"Good question," said Father, leaning forward in his chair. "I would say that her descriptions of the attributes of each card were fairly textbook. Not knowing much about Bartholomew Piaget, however, I can't really comment on her analysis."

"But if she's clever," said Beth, "she could make any card fit just about any circumstance, couldn't she?"

"The High Priestess was a bit of a stretch," agreed Father, "but she managed it."

"Nobody challenged her," said Havermeyer. "Not openly, anyway."

Father eased himself back in his chair. "Same thing."

"So Betsy Belle was makin' eyes at Jonathan," mused Kahlúa. "Hmm-HM!"

"He was reciting poetry, apparently," said Beth, patting Jonathan's left shoulder. "I could do worse."

"Jonathan, Jonathan," said Edward, patting him on his right. "At the risk of repeating myself: Jonathan!"

The pattee in question's cheeks were burning bright red.

"Hopkins, yet," said Kahlúa.

"Sounds serious," said Millie.

"That's it?" objected Arthur, snapping out of his reverie. "Horehound got sick and fled the séance just as the Death card was cast? That's the turn you said we were about to take?"

"Not quite, Old Chum," said Pierre. "Although his behavior will eventually prove significant, that was just the guardrail before the cliff. The evening was far from over."

"Like this one," said Jonathan, shaking off Beth and Edward's supportive, patting hands.

"Great," said Arthur. "So who's up next?"

"The celebrity of the moment," said Pierre with a bow. "Jonathan."

∞§[*Jonathan*]§∞

"I saw what I saw," I maintained as we got up from our chairs to mill nervously around the séance room.

"What are you talking about?" huffed Beth, perturbed and defensive. "I'm fine."

"You nodded off repeatedly during the séance," I explained. "I was worried."

"I couldn't have," she insisted. "I took my meds before dinner—such as it was." She paused, bewildered, then brightened. "I'll bet it was the lights. They kept blinking off and on. The shadows must've made me look asleep or something."

"Pierre?" I inquired. "How many times did the lights dim?"

"Hm?" he mumbled. He seemed reluctant to be drawn into the matter, but acquiesced. "Let me think. Once, right after the 'Gabrielle chant'—wasn't that a hoot?—and, let's see, again when the Two of Swords came up. I make the connection, of course, because of the blindfold—"

"That's it?" asked Beth with a perturbed gasp, her eyes wide. "Just two times? I thought—"

"I'm afraid they're right, Sis," said Arthur, who reluctantly quit his examination of Death up on the wall to come to his agitated sister's assistance. "You winked out several—well, quite a few times, I'm afraid. You know stress can bring it on."

"I wasn't that stressed," she insisted.

"Tense enough," said he, taking her hand gently in his. "That's why I kept squeezing your fingers."

"I thought you were just being kind."

"Well, that, too."

"I don't understand," Madam Douceur was saying, more to herself than to us. She alone had remained seated in her chair. "Dr. Horehound broke the circle. He knows that's never to be done. Never."

"He looked rather pekid," said Edward, who was tending the fire lest it go out. The room had grown chilly with the door open. "Maybe it was something he ate."

Several of us guffawed at that.

"It certainly wasn't the *Scarab L'Orange*," said Pierre, patting his stomach. "I'm fine."

"Sure, I'll bet you are," said Joel. He was slouching sullenly in the doorway, leaning against the frame, concentrating on his hands. For a second I thought he was whittling, of all things, because of the way he was gripping his camping knife in his right hand, the largest blade extended. Then I realized he was rubbing it against a black sharpening stone in his left hand. A peculiar thing to be doing at that particular moment, but there he was. He paused in his task to look up at Pierre and add, "You're quite the gourmand, aren't you?"

Pierre regarded Joel for a moment before he replied, "It was a bit sweet for my taste, but after all, in some parts of the world insects are standard fare."

"Right," said Joel resentfully. "Sure. You would know."

"He shouldn't have done it," muttered Madam Douceur almost inaudibly, but she wasn't talking about serving us insects. She shuddered and whispered, "The circle must never be broken."

"No, it mustn't," agreed Arthur, who had turned his attention to another painting on the wall. The Fool was portrayed as an effeminate lad in a girlish skirt with a bindlestiff slung over one shoulder and yellow boots on his feet, prancing happily toward the edge of a cliff. A card I'd definitely not want to turn up in a reading about me! Shaking his head, Arthur added under his breath, "Bad form; botched ritual; adverse outcome."

His comment seemed to snap Madam Douceur out of her reverie. Rousing herself, she cast her glance from person to person, fluttering her eyelashes and attempting unconvincing smiles of encouragement.

"How do these sessions usually wind up?" asked Edward, setting the wrought-iron poker in its stand beside the fireplace. "I mean, if he hadn't left, what would normally happen now?"

"The doctor would take everyone into the library for libations and penetrating conversation," said Clarice Davenport, who had maneuvered herself well within Arthur's personal bubble. "I, too, love to exchange ... ideas."

"I love to watch the mixing of peoples' auras," said Madam Douceur, hugging herself and heaving a squeaky sigh. "The interaction of *chakras*, the mingling of colors—"

"The popping of corks," said Clarice, squeegeeing closer to Arthur. "The unzipping of—"

"The clawing of eyes," interrupted Beth, shimmying in between them. "The hissing of cats."

"Careful," cautioned Clarice, flexing her claws.

"Don't mind Miss Davenport, my dear," said Madam Douceur, who was carefully retrieving the Tarot cards in reverse order from the table and replacing them reverently on the deck. She added loftily, "She can't help it if she has a superabundance of estrogen and a craving for testosterone."

Clamping her arms tight against her curvy sides, Clarice turned slowly until Elaineileen was squarely in her crosshairs. "Really, I. U. D., shall I give these lonely men a copy of your rates? She may not look like much, boys, but then the less attractive ones try harder."

"I think a spot of brandy would do nicely right about now," said Pierre, snapping to. "I say we retire to the library—"

"Yes, let's," said Clarice, "before Madam Dowser here starts begging."

"You all go ahead," said Madam Douceur, unperturbed, drawing the stack of cards longingly to herself. "Dr. Horehound never leaves me alone with these. Am I wicked? I so want to peruse them, to see for myself if Bartholomew's fate was indeed enfolded within them."

"We won't snitch," said Pierre.

"We owe our host that much," said Beth.

We all turned to leave except Arthur, who stood his ground beneath the portrait of the Magician. The fellow in the painting was wearing a red cloak, brandishing a white wand, and sporting an infinity symbol above his head like a halo. I had a weird, momentary premonition that Arthur would have been at home up in that picture frame. He stared down at the medium and said, "Excuse me, Madam. Something doesn't add up here."

She seemed lost in thought, running her fingers lovingly around the edges of the cards. I sensed we couldn't skidoo hastily enough as far as she was concerned.

"I believe the reading you reconstructed here this evening was misdirected," he persisted.

After that stunt he pulled with the medallion in the library, everyone stopped to listen to what Sherlock von Derschmidt had to say. All except Madam Douceur, who turned over the top card, the High Priestess, and examined its details. After a prolonged silence she asked vaguely, "Oh? How so?"

"Unaware as I was of Dr. Horehound's predilection for minimum information scenarios, I familiarized myself with newspaper and magazine accounts of the events of 1896 before coming here." Arthur smirked impishly as he added, "Also several blistering editorials in the *Summerland Sentinel*."

Madam Douceur placed the card face down on the deck and folded her hands on top. Summoning her patience, and perhaps a dose of courage, she closed her eyes and whispered, almost inaudibly, "Go on."

Arthur stepped forward, plunging his hands deep into his pockets. "A number of mystics and even some of Mr. Piaget's business acquaintances claimed the same thing."

"Mr. ... von Derschmidt, is it?" She opened her moist eyes and aimed them up at him. "Just what are you implying?"

"That it was Cassandra Ouspenskaya's fate that was displayed in the Revealing Star that night, not Bartholomew Piaget's."

A faint gasp of puzzlement flittered around the room.

"Dr. Horehound has hosted forty-two reenactments before this one," said Madam Douceur frostily. She lifted her hands from the deck and folded her arms within her shawl. Her jaws were clenched, giving her words a strained yet slightly slurred quality. "Do you really think that you're the first participant to have done a little research beforehand?"

"Of course not," said Arthur. "But I have eyes to see and ears to hear. I should think the discrepancy is obvious. Of the six cards in the spread, the first four depict women. I'd say that's gender-weighted, though not conclusively. It's the High Priestess as Identifier that clinches it. That's the key. The Identifier personifies the subject of the reading."

She pursed her lips smugly. "Oh?"

"The *female* aspect," he said intently. "'Overt power, not covert power.' That's what you said, wasn't it? 'Some things are implied, while others are spoken.' The rest of the cards in the spread proceed from her."

"And what would you know about that?"

"It is obvious," he answered. "The Star in the Remote Past reveals the subject of this spread, this overtly powerful woman, to be a 'solitary seeker' throughout her life. She is a loner in other words, and a deep thinker; and the Two of Swords in the Immediate Past suggests a decision begotten of a recent misguided intimacy."

Madam Douceur made an unintelligible sound, something between a grunt and a curse.

Arthur pulled his hands out of his pockets and pointed angrily
at the stack of cards. "The High Priestess corresponds to a powerful personality with an intensity of passion: someone not to be
crossed. Within such an individual, under such circumstances,
the desire for Justice in the Immediate Future would easily become a deep-seated craving for revenge. Clearly decisions,
likely of a dark nature, have been made in the secrecy of her
heart. And which card predicts her Distant Future? The Four of
Swords: the statue of a dead warrior, a heart imprisoned by its
grim nature within a sarcophagus of stone, for such is the bitter
end of vengeance. A card of repose? You could call it that. I
would call it an omen. Yes, when all is accomplished, what
could this woman's Significator be but Death?"

Needless to say, Arthur's soliloquy left us all—

∞§[Martin]§∞

—speechless, unlike the outburst of verbosity that erupted in
the study, about fifty percent of which was Arthur's name repeated and heralded enthusiastically. The rest was a mixture of
associated appreciation, interrogation, and a fair amount of flattery—but all peppered with a vague yet perceptible tang of trepidation.

"That was hardly textbook, was it, Father?" commented Monsignor Havermeyer as the hubbub subsided.

"There is a vast chasm between mere recitation and provocative insight," said Father Baptist appreciatively. "I would say
that Arthur definitely exhibited the latter."

Throughout this interruption, Arthur sat numbly—

∞§[*Jonathan*]§∞

—speechless. Beth mouthed the words, "Oh, Big Bro!" while placing her hand on his arm. Pierre hooked his thumbs in the armholes of his vest and rocked proudly on his heels. Joel, who had apparently stuffed his knife and sharpening stone into his pockets sometime during this exchange, looked from Arthur to Pierre, scowled, and shook his head.

"I suppose the reading could be open to that interpretation," said Madam Douceur, unraveling her arms and adjusting her shawl. "You are insightful, young man, but most certainly out of your depth." She paused, and then added knowingly, "The cards are hard to control, but they never lie."

"Watch out," whispered Clarice to Arthur. "Here's where she makes her play."

"I wouldn't doubt it," said Arthur. It took me a moment to realize he wasn't agreeing with Clarice. He was ignoring her. His comment and what followed was directed solely at Madam Douceur. "The odd thing is that it was Bartholomew Piaget who shuffled the cards. One might say that, even subconsciously, he arranged them. Ordinarily that would make him the 'owner' of the spread. But other factors were in play that night. Somehow, by some unseen mechanism or agency, when he handed them to Madam Ouspenskaya, the ownership passed to her. She read them, then she died."

"Harrumph," grunted Madam Douceur. "Are you implying that Bartholomew was somehow responsible for Cassandra's death?"

Arthur shook his head. "Not intentionally, no."

She scowled ferociously. "The very idea is utterly preposterous!"

"Madam," said Arthur, "I am willing to accept that when he saw the Death card, Mr. Piaget believed it was intended for himself. His preoccupation with the order of the cards afterwards seems to substantiate that. But that isn't what's bothering me."

"An excess of your own self-importance," said Madam Douceur, "that's your problem."

Arthur did not protest, but rather nodded. "Be that as it may, I noted your concern that Dr. Horehound broke the circle tonight. I can't help but wonder if Bartholomew Piaget may have done the same that night in 1896. It's not in the script, but it surely could have happened when Madam Ouspenskaya set the Death card in the middle of the spread. Faced with a threat, a man of his temperament would be roused to a fighting posture, thus pushing himself away from the table."

"Rubbish," she retorted.

"No, a valid inference." He shook his head and smiled. "I'll make another. You are a 'solitary seeker of wisdom' yourself, are you not? There is something of the High Priestess in you. 'Some things are implied, while others are spoken.' Despite your assurances to the contrary, I believe you went ahead and silently but surely conducted a séance this evening, didn't you?"

"Uh-oh," said Pierre and Edward.

"'Uh-oh' is right," said Clarice.

"Oh dear," said Beth.

"And what if I did?" she huffed, clenching her fists. "It's my business and my right if I want to learn what really happened to Bartholomew. And let us not forget the tragedy of his wife, Gabrielle, and the disappearances of Arianna and Natalie."

"You speak of them with such familiarity," said Arthur, "as if you have tried to contact them many times."

"What if I have? Don't you see? Their fates were entangled in mystery, and their spirits are not at peace." A tear trickled down her cheek. "I want to help them."

"Naughty, naughty," taunted Clarice.

"You mean she—?" I asked nervously.

"What does that mean for us?" asked Edward.

"I knew we shouldn't have gotten involved in this stuff," groaned Joel.

"Then the onus falls upon you," said Arthur significantly to Madam Douceur, after glancing around at the rest of us. "Don't you see? Contacting the spirits of the dead is necromancy, pure and simple. But worse, you involved us. You used us to form your Circle of Protection."

"Her circle of what?" I asked.

"Am I hearing you right?" demanded Edward.

"The Magick Circle is a mystical fortification," explained Arthur, "a defensive barrier, a bulwark against the penetration of evil forces."

"Arthur!" gasped Beth. "What are you talking about?"

Arthur glared at the medium. "You are right to be concerned for your employer, Madam. It is dangerous to break that barrier. Whether Bartholomew Piaget happened to or not, Mortimer Horehound certainly did."

Madam Douceur's face had become hard. "What do you, whoever you think you are, know of such things?"

"Arthur?" insisted Beth.

"Enough to leave well enough alone," said he, silencing his sister with a raised hand.

"Excuse me," I said, "if I remember correctly, by the time Dr. Horehound got to his feet, Madam Douceur had already told us we didn't have to hold hands any longer."

"The circle can be made of various things," said Arthur. "Chalk, stones, and copper wire among them. But when people are used, it is not joined hands that make the circle. Their united intent does. If you review the words of the script, we agree to stay seated. Ritually speaking, that sufficed."

"Oh," was all I could think to say.

"But I'm no necromancer," insisted Madam Douceur pretentiously. "There you're wrong. I don't talk to the dead. I commune with the living: those sweet, seeking souls who have passed on to dwell in the intermediary plane. They are as alive as you and I. Besides, it was Dr. Horehound who broke the circle. I should think the onus would fall upon him."

"Hold on," said Pierre. "Arthur, you said we're now involved. Would you care to elucidate?"

"You'd better!" said Beth, clasping Arthur's hand intently.

"Please, Sis," said Arthur, gently but firmly releasing himself from her grasp.

"You don't really think she's for real, do you?" demanded Edward, indicating Madam Douceur.

"Ninety-nine percent of spiritualists are fakes," said Arthur pointedly.

"No doubt," said Madam Douceur. "I am not one of them."

"Arthur?" insisted Edward.

"I'm not competent to judge," said he with a shrug. "But Madam Douceur has not been forthright, and I thought a cautionary note was in order."

"Well, I know what I'm doing," said Madam Douceur, stiffly. "Thank you very much."

"So tomorrow we're to find a wax body in the garden," said Edward, trying to change the subject without doing so. "That's what Dr. Horehound said. And what becomes of you in the meantime, Madam, if I may ask?"

"If you must know," she said, wrinkling her nose, "I'll spend the next few days out of sight listening to my favorite records in the boathouse."

"The red door with the white curtains," I said. "So that's your apartment."

"And it gets sooooo lonely out there," said Clarice.

"You wouldn't know, would you, my dear?" said Madam Douceur with a resounding sniff.

"So come Friday, Thorndale, being Natalie, also takes the last day off," said Edward. "Meaning we'll go hungry."

"Perish the thought," said Clarice.

"I'm still for brandy," said Pierre. "Who's with me?"

"I've had enough of this room," said Beth. "Let's go."

"Sure," I said. "Edward, Arthur, Joel? I say we leave Madam Douceur to ransack the deck. She's safe enough in here for the moment."

"Maybe one of us should escort her to the boathouse later, just to be sure," said Pierre. "There's still that howling creature about, you know."

"Yes," said Madam Douceur, sighing uneasily. "I would appreciate that. You all go to the library. I'll join you presently. Dr. Horehound would expect me to."

And so we took our leave.

"I say, Arthur, Old Bean," said Pierre as we sauntered down the corridor toward the foyer. "That was quite a performance back there."

"You worry me," said Beth.

"I told you," said Arthur, who looked like he had a lot on his mind. "I've read books."

"Many more than I realized," said Pierre.

"That worries me, too," said Beth.

"And what about Dr. Horehound's sudden change of heart?" I pointed out. "You know, just before he ducked out?"

"Making amends, you mean," said Pierre. "Didn't seem at all like him. Jonathan, Dear Chap, I haven't a clue."

"Remarkable," said Joel, shuffling behind us, brandy heavy on his breath. "Imagine. Pierre stumped. We must mark the calendar."

Pierre paused, so did we all, as we reached the foyer. It was dark, but we could see the firelight within the library playing on the curtained door to our left. An amber glow from the gas porch lights wavered through the narrow, frosted windows on either side of the front door. Rainwater flowed off the overhang outside, making a deep, rumbling, churning sound as it poured onto the gravel where our cars were parked.

"Why have we stopped?" drawled Joel. "Do I sense hesitation? Is Captain Pierre lost? Good Heavens! How will we survive the night?"

"What's with you?" scolded Beth.

"He's tanked," said Edward. "He'll get over it."

"Joel," said Pierre, adjusting his vest, "if I've said something—"

"You know," said Joel, reeling forward on unsteady feet, "you and Horehound could be brothers. Twin brothers. You're snots, that's what you are, and you're bug-eaters."

"That's not fair," said Beth.

"I guess it comes from overdoing being so British," said Joel.

"French, actually," said Pierre with a hint of panache. "My ancestry is decidedly French."

"So you say," said Joel.

"Hold on," said Arthur, placing his hand on Pierre's shoulder while beckoning diplomatically to Joel. "You both know it's the brandy talking."

"Is not!" blurted Joel, avoiding Arthur's reach. He glared at us all, the dim firelight from the library playing in his eyes. "You think you're all so smart, don't you? You'd follow him any-where, wouldn't you?"

"I say," said Edward.

"Oh, do let him rant," said Clarice, fascinated.

"Well? Wouldn't you?" snarled Joel, waving his arms around wildly. "Why are we here? Pierre. Who convinced us to drop everything and come traipsing up here to this godforsaken place? Pierre. Who made a mess of the tent? Our one and only resident Eagle Scout: Pierre. Who doesn't like to get his precious hands dirty? Who thinks he's above us all, so bloody pompous, when really he's just a lame-brained bumbling idiot? Who digs in when the Master says 'Eat bugs, they're better than steak!'? Who—"

"Joel," said Edward. "You've had enough for one night. Here, I'll help you—"

"Being sent to my room, am I?" said Joel, swaggering this way and that. He started pounding his chest for emphasis. "Me, Joel Maruppa. Poor little fallen Angel. Joel, the failed seminarian. Joel, the Slovak toady. The 'Slow Vock,' I've heard you call me. Embarrass you, do I? Well, to Hell with you! All of you! I am not—repeat, double not—going up to my bloody room!"

"How about mine?" suggested Clarice, rolling her hips.

"That's the ticket!" sniggered Joel, teetering toward her. "I'll show you—show you all! I'm tired of pretending! I'm not one of you! I've never really been—"

Suddenly we were stunned by a blinding flash of light accom-panied by a loud pop. For a second I assumed Grayburn was lurking in the foyer, camera in hand, taking a photograph of rat-tled guests at Dr. Horehound's behest for his upcoming book.

"Whoa!" exclaimed Edward, rubbing his eyes.

"What was that?" cried Beth, doing likewise.

"Grayburn," I growled. "What do you think you're—?"

But as the retinal trauma faded, we realized Grayburn wasn't there. Instead, in the center of the foyer, there hovered a glow-ing sphere. It was a ball of light, like before—yet somehow not at all like before. There were no hints of calming blues and greens this time. The flares around its rim were yellow and red—malicious yellow, and angry red. A streak of black, like malignant smoke, swirled over its insubstantial surface, reminiscent of the flying saucer when it settled into the lake. Then the orb turned a fiendish shade of crimson. It hovered for a moment, as if taking us in, then headed purposefully toward Joel.

"Oh ----!" he exclaimed, terrified. "Not again!"

"Lads!" said Pierre, instantly adopting a stance between the orb and our drunken comrade. We rushed to join him, but it swooped over our heads and bore down on poor Joel like a kamikaze pilot.

"No!" he screamed. "Guys! Help me! I didn't mean it! I didn't—" In his bewilderment he had backed into the hallway, the long narrow corridor with but one destination. Finding himself thus trapped, he spun around and broke into a clumsy run. "Keep it away!" he cried. "Don't let it get me!"

"After it!" ordered Pierre.

"Well, I'll be!" I heard Clarice gasp as we charged past her and headed down the hall.

The blazing sphere careened ahead of us, leaving flecks of yellow and red trailing behind. Beyond its eerie radiance, Joel was flailing, tripping, and stumbling in a blind panic. A strange humming sound filled the corridor. It seemed to emanate from the walls, reverberating ominously in that narrow space, mingling with the shuffle and rumble of our footfalls. The decorative chandeliers in the ceiling approached and receded over our heads as we hustled beneath, desperate to assist Joel while not knowing how. Five ... four ... I counted as we sprinted. The hum grew oppressive, deafening. Moaning and gasping, Joel scrambled toward the welcoming firelight in the séance room: an odd place to seek safety, but the only place to go. Fortunately we had left the door fully ajar. Three chandeliers ... two ... one ...

Then came another blinding flash, more fierce and brilliant than the one that had given birth to the vicious red sphere. It blazed malevolently in the doorway, buffeting us with waves of prickly heat and spears of blinding radiance. Then, with a crackling jolt as of electricity, it suddenly imploded, ferociously and instantly. The frightful humming ceased with equal abruptness, as did the electric lights in the hallway and in the séance room.

Grunting and puffing, we stumbled over each other as we piled through the doorway.

"What's going on?" squeaked Madam Douceur, still seated at the table, silhouetted against the amber glow of the fireplace.

"You tell us," I rasped, my lungs heaving.

"Joel," panted Edward. "Joel! Where are you?"

"Power's out," grumbled Arthur, bumping his way around the chairs. He retrieved a couple of thick, stumpy wax candles from the mantel and set them down hard on the table. "These will help."

"Allow me," wheezed Pierre, fetching a burning twig from the fireplace and touching it to the wicks.

As the candlelight permeated the room, Madam Douceur found herself surrounded by four very excited men in ruffled tuxedos, and of course, Beth. Clarice was still somewhere back down the darkened corridor, slowly clopping her way toward us.

"I heard screams," said Madam Douceur, fidgeting with the cards in her hands. "You all came running. What was that flash?"

"Where's Joel?" panted Pierre.

We looked frantically around the room.

Joel was not there.

∞§[Martin]§∞

"Good Lord," said Arthur, shifting in his chair. "You're not saying he vanished—*into thin air!*"

"I'm just reading what's here," said Jonathan, helplessly. "Heavens, if I'd have known—"

"It had to be a trick," said Beth. "Remember the discussion about magicians drawing attention away from what they're actually doing?"

"I remember reading my account of such a discussion," said Arthur, shaking his head, "but I can't remember the discussion itself."

"Where'd you go?" asked Edward, turning around in his chair to face Joel.

"How would I know?" he answered defensively.

"Got a bit lit on the way there," observed Millie.

"I'd say a weeeee tad more than a bit," said Kahlúa.

"What do you want me to say?" groaned Joel, embarrassed and angry. "I've only got his word for it."

"Joel, I'm sorry," said Jonathan, rattling his pages. "I couldn't have meant it like it sounds."

"Sounds pretty clear to me," said Millie.

"I can't imagine you behaving that way," said Beth, trying to be helpful. "Really, Joel, there must be more to it than that."

"Yeah," said Edward. "That didn't sound like you at all— well, not most of the time, anyway. You do have your sour side. But heck, we all do. Don't we, Fellows?"

"You most of all, Snarly," said Jonathan.

"I resemble that remark," said Edward, trying to be funny.

As conversation died down to an inarticulate mumble, Joel sank down in his chair, discouraged and unconvinced.

"Gentlemen and Ladies," said Pierre presently. "The only thing to do is continue."

As Jonathan did so, Pierre, visibly trembling, wiped his face with a handkerchief.

∞§[†]§∞

∞§✝§∞

15. This Is Too Much Like One of Arthur's Old Movies

∞§[*Jonathan*]§∞

"NO MORE GAMES!" SHOUTED PIERRE. "Where is our friend?" It was out of character for him to yell at a woman that way, which shows how upset he was. We all were.

"I tell you he didn't come in here," insisted Madam Douceur, flinching.

"He had to!" I said, pounding the wall panels. "I said before these sound hollow."

"But Dr. Horehound said the space behind is packed with asbestos," said Beth.

"Nice way to keep us from breaking through them," said Arthur, running his fingers along the molding beneath the Hanged Man. He stiffened and turned to face us. "His interest is fear, right?"

"Whose?" asked Edward.

"Horehound's."

"Of death in particular," said Pierre. "Why?"

"'A complete and irreversible severing,'" said Arthur. "Those were his words." He planted his fingertips on the table and leaned forward as he gazed around at us. The strain of this position on his vest caused it to ride up over his stomach. The effect would have invited comment if not for the circumstances. His tone of voice was anything but amusing as he said, "'The slicing of cosmic scissors separating what was from what is.' Now consider: isn't that what we're all feeling right now?"

"You mean about Joel," I said, thinking it over. "Yes, kind of."

"You think all this is part of an experiment?" said Pierre. "We're just mice in his labyrinth?"

Madam Douceur made a disparaging sound, but said nothing.

"Funny how he extricated himself from the situation just before the fireworks started," said Arthur, straightening and tugging his vest down over his paunch. "Best to observe from outside the maze."

"Twice, remember," I added. "Before the séance as well as after."

"And each time, shortly following his departure ..." Arthur left his sentence dangling.

"What fireworks?" asked Clarice, who had propped herself in the doorway where Joel had slouched before. "Oh, you mean that angry red whatever-it-was."

"It appeared in here earlier," said Beth, pointing to the air above the table. "It was different then, somehow. Light blue, not red. Or white with a touch of blue, maybe green. It went for Joel then, too. He was standing right where you are."

"Do tell," said Clarice, tracing the doorframe with her eyes. "Right here, you say? That *is* interesting."

"You work for Horehound," I said accusingly. "What's going on?"

"I haven't the slightest idea," said she, shaking her hair. "Nothing like this has ever happened before—the doctor leaving or the light show following, and certainly none of his guests ever vanished into thin air."

"Sure," said Edward derisively, tilting the chairs uselessly. "Guys, there's got to be a secret panel here somewhere."

"But there isn't!" insisted Madam Douceur. "I tell you there isn't!"

"There's a crowbar in my van," said Edward. "I can be back in five minutes."

"Don't!" pleaded Madam Douceur. "Dr. Horehound would be furious."

"And he'd send your editor the repair bill," said Clarice. "He only hires the best."

"Then help us!" shouted Pierre. "Tell us where Joel is!"

"I don't know!!" shrieked Madam Douceur. "He didn't come in here!"

"This is where he disappeared," said Arthur, pointing to the floor just inside the doorway. "Maybe there's a trapdoor."

"Joel!" yelled Edward, diving to his knees and pounding the floorboards. "Joel! Are you down there?"

We listened for a response. Nothing.

"He's got to be somewhere in the house," said Pierre. "Up, down, who knows? Edward, you and I will search the basement. We've been down there before. Arthur, Jonathan, check upstairs."

"What about me?" asked Beth. "I certainly don't want to stay here."

That brought us up short.

"We won't eat you," sneered Clarice. "Will we, E. I. D.?"

"I should say not, my dear," said Madam Douceur.

"Beth, you go with Arthur and Jonathan," decided Pierre.

"Candles will go out if we rush around," I said. "We'll need flashlights."

"Grayburn," said Pierre. "He'll have some."

"On my way!" I said, and charged past Clarice into the corridor. It was pitch black, but I knew the hallway to be straight. I ran with my hands outstretched, feeling for the walls. I burst into the foyer, grateful for the illumination of the gas porch lights through the frosted windows. The floorboards protested as I made a sharp turn and headed for the room that led to the room leading to the dining room. Once there, I felt my way around the dining table, then fumbled through the swinging doors and slinked into the kitchen. As I groped my way past the stove, a flash of lightning revealed a hallway I assumed led to the servants' quarters. I rattled the knob on the first door on the right. It was locked. I pounded the door, yelling for Grayburn.

"Who is it?" demanded Thorndale from within. My blood froze in my veins as I heard the distinctive sound of a pump-action shotgun within. I'd watched enough vintage westerns at Arthur's to recognize that sound anywhere. "Whoever you are," she warned, "you've got some nerve waking me at this hour!"

"Tuh-tuh-terribly sorry to disturb you, Ma'am," I answered. "It's an emergency! I must find Grayburn!"

"Harrumph! If you must, turn yourself around. His room is across the way."

I spun and threw myself at the opposite door. "Grayburn!" I yelled, slamming my hands against it.

After some grumbling and stumbling within, the doorknob creaked and the door opened a crack. "Whatcha want?" he croaked as he peered around the edge of the door.

"Joel!" I bellowed.

"Who?"

"Joel! One of us. He's disappeared."

"Uh-huh," he grunted drowsily.

"Disappeared! Vanished!"

"Well, whatcha want me to do about it?"

"We need to search the house!"

"Do you now?" he said, rubbing the stubble on his chin. "Well, ain't that somethin'."

"Flashlights!" I yelled. "Where?!"

"Hold yer horses," he said, allowing the door to open wider as he pulled his suspenders up over his shoulders. "I got mine here somewheres, and there's a couple in the kitchen drawer. Jus' wait a second—"

Frantically, I turned and charged into Thorndale's galley.

"She'll kill you," he called after me, "If you mess up her stuff!"

I saw the faint glint of drawer handles. I yanked the top one, felt around inside, and slammed it shut. I did the same to the next drawer with the addition of a yelp when my hand encountered Thorndale's trove of sharp knives. This process I repeated until I finally found a pair of flashlights rolling around in the bottom drawer. Cursing myself for starting at the top, I tried them. Both worked. Grayburn caught up to me as I stumbled through the dining room heading for the foyer where the others were gathered.

"Good man," said Pierre, accepting one of the torches. "Okay, everybody. Proceed with haste but take care. No one goes anywhere alone. Keep an eye on each other. Our comrade is in trouble, and we don't know what we're up against."

"What should *we* do?" asked Clarice, who was standing beside Madam Douceur.

"Keep out of our way," said Edward, savagely.

"Done," said Clarice, smiling.

"Hooligans," snarled Madam Douceur. Her violations against her employer were escalating. Earlier, she had perused Bartholomew Piaget's fate-enwrapped Tarot deck in the séance room without his supervision. Now, she had removed them from said room and was clutching them possessively to her bosom. In another minute, she would likely stuff them down her *décolletage* and head for Summerland.

"Meet back here in twenty minutes," said Pierre.

With that, we charged to our respective search areas.

∞§[Martin]§∞

"This is too much like one of Arthur's old movies," commented Edward.

"Or one hour before deadline at the *Artsy*," said Kahlúa.

"I wonder where you went," said Arthur, turning to Joel.

"Wish I knew," said he, setting down his empty mug.

"Time for a change of narrator?" asked Edward.

"I'd say Jonathan's on a roll," said Beth.

Indeed he was.

∞§[*Jonathan*]§∞

"We checked the basement," said Pierre as Beth, Arthur and I returned to the foyer.

"He wasn't there," said Edward, who was catching his breath beside him. "Any luck?"

"None," I assured them between pants, pointing my flashlight at the floor so as not to blind them. "We searched the second and third floors. Nothing."

"What about the tower?" asked Pierre, doing the same with his flashlight.

"Arthur and I shouldered the door open," I said. "Horehound was right, the metal stairway in there shakes something terrible."

"Hoodlums!" growled Madam Douceur, who had apparently remained in the foyer with Clarice Davenport during our search. "Destroying private property! And it's *Doctor* Horehound."

"Our apologies, Madam," said Arthur. "Emotions are running high. As for the door, the situation required—"

"They wouldn't let me climb it," fumed Beth, "even though I'm obviously the lightest."

"Sorry, Sis," said Arthur, turning his attention from Madam Douceur to Beth. "Wasn't going to happen. Remember the library scene in *The Haunting?*"

"I'm not Eleanor, and you're not Dr. Markway."

"I couldn't let you risk it, Liz."

"Oh, I know," she relented.

"Julie Harris would be proud," said Pierre impatiently. "But what happened?"

"Arthur pushed me aside and went up himself," I grumbled, still fuming a bit myself.

"So what's *up* there?" pressed Pierre.

"*Doctor* Horehound lied," said Arthur. "The tower's not empty. There's a big electrical apparatus up there: a bloody Tesla coil. It looks very old but well maintained. It's huge, too. The watchtower seems to have been built specifically to house it. It fills most of the stairwell, and the top six feet or so extend up into the surveillance turret, as he called it. He was right about there being no glass in the four lookout windows, but I saw no evidence of birds. They wouldn't nest up there if he turns that thing on with any frequency."

"How does one?" asked Pierre. "Turn it on, I mean."

"There's an elaborate control panel at the base of the stairway," said Arthur. "It's the first thing you see when you open the access door. "

"A Tesla coil," said Edward. "That explains the mad-scientist flashes we saw last night. But why would he have such a contraption up there?"

"It belonged to Bartholomew Piaget," said Arthur. "There's a plaque. Edward, you would appreciate this, and Joel as an electrician should see it: evidently he commissioned it from Nikola Tesla himself."

"It was Gabrielle's idea!" blurted Madam Douceur, who couldn't contain herself any longer. "Or rather Prof. Maxwell Axilla of Boston."

We looked at her with blank faces.

"Surely you've heard of Axilla's experiments with the effects of alternating electromagnetic fields upon ectoplasm?—upon psychic phenomena?—upon telekinetic manifestations?" Her outrage increased proportionately to our escalating lack of appreciation for whatever she was talking about.

"Enhancing them, you mean?" ventured Arthur tentatively.

"*Disrupting* them!" she retorted passionately, the green jewel in the front of her turban eerily reflecting the light of our flashlights.

"For what purpose?" asked Arthur, shaking his head. "I should think that in the study of psychic phenomena, amplification would be a welcome—"

"Young man," she said with the tone of a frustrated eighth grade teacher, "sensitives like Gabrielle can become psychic magnets, attracting unwanted forces as well as those desired, often without their conscious participation. It was conceivable that unmanageable forces could coalesce during one of her rituals; but, even in her day-to-day activities as the lady of the house, things happened. So it was necessary to have—"

"A kill switch!" said Arthur. "You're saying the high frequency alternating currents produced by a Tesla coil can—"

"Interrupt a psychical event," she said, "or nullify paranormal activity—at least, theoretically."

"I've never heard of such a thing," said Arthur.

"Again, you overestimate yourself."

"Don't be too impressed," said Clarice, heaving a sigh that made her skintight dress squeak. "The way I hear it, Prof. Axilla electrocuted himself during one of his experiments. I think it involved a Siamese cat."

"That was an unfortunate accident," said Madam Douceur. "As a result, his work was dismissed by the hoity-toity spiritualists of his day. But others of a more practical bent have carried on his work. When Dr. Horehound first purchased this property—"

"You should have heard E. I. D. here insisting that he contact some whacky organization in Philadelphia," said Clarice. "They actually sent a guy who looked like a cross between Einstein and Bullwinkle Moose to restore the contraption in the tower."

"It was the Mülheim Institute," said Madam Douceur proudly. "They are certified to do top secret work for the government. Their expert looked like Clark Gable, and he restored the coil to better than its original specifications. Dr. Horehound has a local electrician contracted to maintain it. He paid for the man to take night classes to better understand it."

"That's interesting," said Edward. "Horehound—the *doctor* said you had suggested that spirits were trying to invade the house through the surveillance turret."

"A private joke," Madam Douceur explained while Clarice twirled her finger beside her head and pointed to her companion. "In my enthusiasm, I did say that once, and he has teased me about it ever since."

"He thought she was bonkers," said Clarice.

"We disagreed," maintained Madam Douceur. "He doubted the usefulness of restoring the Tesla coil, but I held my ground. Who was to say what caliber of psychic might attend his reenactments? A 'subvection countermeasure,' as Prof. Axilla named it—what you call a 'kill switch'—seemed a prudent, practical precaution. Dr. Horehound conceded the point reluctantly—"

"The power of female persuasion," said Clarice, scraping an invisible chalkboard with her fingernails.

"The cost was considerable," explained Madam Douceur, "but he came to appreciate its efficacy. Just the other day, I'll have you know, he said to me over breakfast, 'E. I. D., maybe that contraption in the tower will prove to be useful after all.'"

"That's extraordinary," said Arthur, "considering his rather deeply-entrenched skepticism."

"Yes," said Edward. "Why would he have turned it on last night?"

"Running one of his tests, I suppose," said Madam Douceur. "He does that from time to time. But things have been happening here since the day we moved in. Odd things. Little inexplicable things. Nothing like tonight, of course. Maybe we should—"

"Excuse me for interrupting this fascinating discussion," said Clarice. "But speaking of Dr. Horehound, has anyone seen him?" She turned to me. "Did you knock on his bedroom door?"

"It was open," I told her. "So was yours. I assume your room is the one next to his. Both doors were ajar, and both suites were empty."

"I always keep my door closed," she said, a note of concern in her voice.

"Then someone looked in there before I did."

"How did you know whose room was whose?"

"From the kinds of things draped over the chairs, I suppose."

"Clever boy."

"For what it's worth," said Grayburn, who came trudging up just then, "I checked the north and south wings on the ground floor. Don't blame you if y'all don't trust me, but I was thorough, and I didn't find yer friend. I wanna see 'bout Thorndale and check out back. I'll be back atcha in two shakes."

"Appreciate it," said Pierre, rubbing his palms together. "Very much indeed." Throughout the above exchange, he had been growing increasingly restive. All this talk of Tesla coils and psychic countermeasures was a desultory waste of valuable time, or so his demeanor seemed to exude. The thrust of Joel's drunken outburst had been aimed at him, and I sensed he felt particularly keen to get to the bottom of the problem, to resolve the situation, and make amends if he could. Unfortunately, we were swiftly running out of avenues to explore.

Grayburn hadn't been gone more than a minute when the piano boomed in the recital room across the foyer from the library. It wasn't a pleasant chord, more like someone slamming down on the keys with their forearms. As we hustled to the curtained doors, we heard a similar clash of keys from the harpsichord, then someone running their fingers across the strings of the out-of-tune harp. Flinging them open, we swung our flashlights all around. The musical instruments cast wild shadows on the walls, but the room was eerily void of players.

"Arthur," said Beth, her voice thin with alarm. "What's happening?"

"Poltergeists," called Madam Douceur, who hadn't moved from where she had been standing.

"Or so we're supposed to think," said Arthur.

"It does seem a bit clichéd, doesn't it?" said Pierre.

"A cheap parlor trick," said Edward. "Has to be."

"Someone's toying with us," I said, turning off my flashlight. "I say, this is too much like one of Arthur's old movies!"

∞§[**Martin**]§∞

"Didn't I just say that?" interrupted Edward.

"Yes," said Jonathan, looking up from his pages. "But I said it first."

"I said it a couple of minutes ago."

"Aha. I said it five months ago."

"Supposedly."

"Boys," said Kahlúa, sternly.

"Ahem. Where was I?" said Jonathan. "Oh yes, at the risk of repeating myself ..."

∞§[*Jonathan*]§∞

"... this is too much like one of Arthur's old movies!"

"The library," said Pierre. "Did anyone look in there?"

We hustled back across the foyer. The French doors rattled and banged as we threw them open and shouldered our way inside. The fire had reduced itself to glowing cinders. Mr. and Mrs. Piaget glared dourly down at us from their gaudy frame. Except for the ghosts of the authors of all those silent books, the room was unoccupied. Madam Douceur produced some candles from a shelf and set them on a table. She struck a match and lit them.

"Interlopers," she mumbled to herself. "What do these amateurs know? They wouldn't recognize a restless spirit if it smacked them on the nose."

"I don't know what more we can do," said Pierre, running his hands through his hair as he collapsed into Dr. Horehound's chair. "The doctor ran out; Joel vanished before our eyes. We can't find either of them. I confess I'm out of ideas."

"We must keep our heads," said Arthur, seating himself wearily. "We know Joel didn't actually vanish. It has to be an illusion of some kind, something concocted by Dr. Horehound."

"Doing research for his book, you mean," said Edward. "We're his guinea pigs, aren't we?"

"The doctor doesn't do that sort of thing," said Madam Douceur. "He's a respectable psychologist."

"Yeah, well, I'd call him something else entirely," said Edward.

"Watch your tongue, young man," she said sternly. "I was as shocked as you were when he left so abruptly during the séance. He so looks forward to them. I tell you he's never acted like that before."

"Never?" asked Arthur.

"He has been unduly nervous of late," she admitted. "Something's been troubling him. I assumed he'd hit a snag with his writing, or with his research. But that wouldn't explain him breaking the circle, nor his disappearing like this."

"And he's never sequestered one of the participants?" asked Arthur. "You know, hid them away to shake things up?"

"He doesn't need to 'shake things up,'" she persisted. "People who come here are usually twitchy to begin with. He jokes about hidden buttons and strings, but he doesn't resort to fake noises and groans. He doesn't have to. People who want to hear and see such things usually do."

"If you're a genuine psychic," said Arthur, "why would you involve yourself in these shams?"

"They're not shams to me, young man. I approached Dr. Horehound years ago, when he was still in private practice, after reading his article about Cassandra Ouspenskaya and the Piagets in the *New Borderlands Quarterly*. My inner voice told me I could help them find peace. The poignancy of their story intrigued me, as did the use of the cards as a means of communication from the other side. At first, I thought it was mixing apples and oranges, using an instrument of divination as a way of ethereal contact. But upon further consideration, I realized the brilliance of it. What is communication but the exchange of ideas? What are ideas but pictures in the mind? And what are Arthur Waite's beautiful cards but a practical vocabulary of informative visualizations?"

∞§[Martin]§∞

"She claims to be genuine," huffed Beth, "and she sounds sincere, but she doesn't know about the cards. Like you were saying, Father, they couldn't have used Waite's deck in 1896."

"My, my," chuckled Kahlúa. "Look who's suddenly an expert on Tarot cards."

"And she doesn't even read books," added Millie.

"In my travels," said Father, "I've met many who were sincere in their beliefs about erroneous and egregious things."

"Many practitioners of our own religion don't know its history accurately, either," said Monsignor Havermeyer. "Like me, until recently."

"Are we going to get philosophical," said Joel, "or are we going to find out what happened to me?"

"What do you mean?" chided Edward. "You did fine. You're sitting right here, aren't you?"

"But I want to know how."

"So do I," said Jonathan, "if everybody doesn't mind. Ahem, as E. I. D. was saying ..."

∞§[*Jonathan*]§∞

"... what are Arthur Waite's beautiful cards but a practical vocabulary of informative visualizations?"

"I'll concede the point for the nonce," said Arthur.

"I shall never—"

∞§[Martin]§∞

"Apparently Big Bro didn't know either," said Kahlúa, "and he rode rings around Madam Douceur's Revealing Star."

"You mean Madam Oospin-skylight's," corrected Millie.

Kahlúa thought that over and nodded. "So sincerity doesn't equal competence, and neither equals knowledge."

"What about certainty?" asked Millie.

"Naw," laughed Kahlúa, "you only get that readin' chicken entrails."

"Ahem," said Jonathan, "as Madam Douceur was saying ..."

∞§[*Jonathan*]§∞

"I shall never forget our first conversation, sitting there in Dr. Horehound's office, sharing my thoughts and aspirations with him." She seated herself in a comfortable chair and gathered her shawl about her. "After I'd revealed what my inner voice was telling me about the cards, he went to his filing cabinet and returned with letters he had received from other mediums who claimed success with this method. He told me of his plans to retire the following year, to rebuild Wolfram Lodge, and to explore what happened here those many years ago, but all according to a new protocol he had developed—'empirical yet mystical' was how he described it. That very day he asked me to join him in his grand project. It meant severing long-standing relations with clients who depended on me for guidance and stability in their lives. I've had to make many adjustments and concessions, personal as well as dietary. Also professional: you see how he exerts control by restricting my access to the room and the cards. You have no doubt noted that I'm not on a first-name basis with him, although he has a nickname for me. He's not an easy man to work for or with. But he's no charlatan. He can be insufferable and condescending, but pulling pranks is outside his character."

"He's not above feeding bugs to his guests," said Beth.

"He really does love entomological cuisine," she countered. "I was aghast at first, but he made an enthusiast out of me."

"That may be," said Beth, "but it was sickening for us, not to mention nasty and insulting."

"You annoyed him," she admitted, "and me as well. It was mean of him, even childish I'll confess. But he's not been entirely himself lately. He did apologize."

"But these reenactments aren't about helping the Piagets find peace, as if that were possible," said Beth scornfully. "He just wants to watch people squirm with fear so he can write another book."

"Yeah," said Edward. "He as much as said so over breakfast this morning."

"He did seem to be goading you," said Madam Douceur. "I was surprised at that."

"Ah," I said, "he was just peeved because he lost that Viking medal. He underestimated Arthur here."

"No, that happened after breakfast," said Edward. "He was already mad at us before that; or rather, he was acting according to his true character. From what the sheriff said, upsetting people seems to be Dr. Horehound's thing."

"That isn't entirely fair," said Madam Douceur. "Most people who come here bring their own demons with them."

"And he's good at stoking the fire and stirring the soup," said Edward.

She shut her eyes as she said, "Whatever you may think of him, I solemnly assure you he does not seize guests and lock them away to worry their friends. As irritable and irascible as I've seen him in the worst of moods, he has never laid a hand on anyone."

"So we have your solemn assurance that Joel's disappearance is not some contrivance of your employer," said Arthur.

She opened her eyes. "You do."

"I'll accept your word for now, but the fact remains that he and Joel have to be somewhere. What about outside?"

"In that downpour?" sighed Edward, resting his hip against the desk. "Just listen to it. Where could they go out there?"

"There's the boathouse," said Madam Douceur, who was looking wistfully toward the window, although she couldn't see it from this side of the lodge. "My little home from home. Did your friend Joel know about it?"

"I don't know," I said, resting my hand on the mantle. "I think he was here when I mentioned it."

"Whether he was or he wasn't, he ain't," said Grayburn as he came lumbering into our midst. "After makin' sure Thorndale's safe and sound, I figgered I'd put on my rain slicks, go out the back, and check the boathouse. She's empty as my grave at the moment. The Master, I see, is still unaccounted for, and your friend is still hidin'."

"That was brave of you to go out there alone," I said.

"Just bein' thorough," he said with a wink. "I kept my shotgun dry underneath."

I folded my arms. "What makes you think Joel is hiding?"

"Accordin' to what I heard, he was last seen runnin' away."

"From that light thing," said Edward, "not from us."

"But if he's scared," said Beth, "and he's mad at you guys—"

"Whatever, he's gone," said Arthur. He slammed his hands down on his knees. "What in Heaven's name is going on?"

"Hold on," said Pierre. "Didn't our host say something about blueprints? Miss Davenport, where would they be?"

"In the safe," said she. "Want to see? He's shown them to participants before."

"Please," said Pierre.

"*Now* he's polite," said Clarice as she sauntered over to a wooden panel between two bookcases. Every movement she made was sexy. She pressed her hand against the right side and it swiveled out, revealing a large antique safe. Settling into a feline crouch, she twirled the combination dial. With a clink and a clank she pulled it open. Slowly and deliberately, she withdrew a heavy roll of architectural materials. "Here," she said, bringing it to Pierre. "Not that it will do much good."

"Why not?" said Pierre, untying the string and flattening the crackling layers of stiff paper on the desk. He settled into the Master's chair and examined the detailed plans before him.

"I was with Dr. Horehound when he bought this place," she said, looking over Pierre's shoulder. "He was sure the lodge was riddled with secret passages, but he never found any. E. I. D. will tell you. Grayburn and Thorndale, too."

"That's a fact," said Grayburn, sucking his teeth by the dead Tiffany lamp. "Darn near tore the place apart. Nothin'."

"We measured every wall, every closet, every hallway," said Clarice. "Except for the usual crawlspaces around the heating ducts and plumbing connections, there wasn't a single hidey-hole anywhere. Look, here's the séance room." She rolled the top sheet aside. "See what's directly under it? The boiler! If there was a trapdoor like you supposed, and your friend fell through, he would have landed right on top of it. He'd have fried like a strip of bacon on a skillet."

"What's this?" asked Edward, snatching something up from the floor. "I think it came out of the safe with that roll of blueprints."

"Appears to be quite old," said Arthur, reaching for it. "Hmm. Prof. Dragos Banulesco—something, something—Chisinau, Moldova. It's the receipt for the crystal ball Dr. Horehound mentioned. The letterhead is faded and the handwriting is barely legible, although it does appear to be written in English. I can't make out what Gabrielle Piaget paid for it."

"I'm sure Dr. Horehound would want that to remain in the safe," said Clarice.

"Of course," said Arthur, handing it to her.

"So where is he?" asked Pierre, lifting his frustrated face from the blueprints.

"Dr. Horehound?" said Clarice as she returned the receipt to its niche. "I have no idea."

"Where is he?" demanded Pierre again, pounding the desk.

"Listen, Buster, I said I don't know."

"I'm worried," said Madam Douceur. "Maybe it's time to contact Sheriff Brumus."

"Great," said Beth with a fretful sigh. "He's going to love this."

"There's no help for it," said Pierre, heaving himself from the chair. "I'll make the call."

"This time of night?" I cautioned.

"I didn't say it would be pleasant," said Pierre, striding toward the door. "Let's hope the phone is still working."

∞§[Martin]§∞

"Was it?" asked Edward as Jonathan came to the end of his chapter. "Working, I mean."

"Remarkably well, considering the storm," said Pierre, accepting Jonathan's pages gratefully. "Sheriff Brumus's roar came through loud and clear." He wiggled his ear with his pinkie, as if it was still ringing. "He said he'd be up first thing. I needn't repeat what he said would happen if this was some sort of prank."

"Not until morning, eh?" said Beth.

"Well, after all," said Pierre, retrieving the next set of pages from the chest, "I was reporting a disappearance, whatever that meant. If I'd said 'murder' or 'assault' he might have responded more quickly."

"What do you think about the Tesla coil as a paranormal dampening field, Father?" asked Monsignor Havermeyer. "'A subvection countermeasure,' I think the woman called it."

"It assumes that spiritual things are actually material," he answered, "that they are affected by electromagnetic fields. Measurement assumes materiality. There are devices that supposedly sample ectoplasm and quantify telekinetic forces. The literature on these matters is dubious and contradictory, as are the things themselves. But when it comes to real spirits—be they angelic, demonic, or departed human souls—they are essentially immaterial. I can't imagine them being affected at all by energy fields. There is no 'kill switch' for the Devil, in other words, although at times I wish there were."

We all considered that for a moment or two.

"So, Pierre," said Arthur. "Joel's disappearance, and I guess Horehound's. Is that the turn you promised?"

"The first of many," answered he.

"So who's going to drive us around the next bend?" asked Edward.

"You," said Pierre.

"Oh."

∞§[†]§∞

∞§✝§∞

16. If That's a Dummy
It's Sure Convincing

∞§[Edward]§∞

WITH THE EXCEPTION OF GRAYBURN, who insisted he couldn't sleep on furniture meant for sitting nor surrounded by strangers, and Thorndale, who never left her bedroom to see what was happening, we all decided to spend the night in the library. We'd seen enough of Arthur's movies to know that the surest way for another person to disappear in a haunted house was for each to go alone to their bedroom. The storm having grown steadily worse, no one volunteered to escort Madam Douceur to the boathouse. Arthur gallantly offered to escort her to the séance room to return the precious deck of cards to their place of rest. After that, she remained with us. Before returning to his bed, Grayburn brought in a substantial pile of wood which he piled unceremoniously by the fireplace. He also produced a two-gallon black-with-white-spatter enamelware cattle-drive percolator suitable for setting amidst the flames, along with a teetering stack of matching nesting cups. That was surprisingly thoughtful of him, in my opinion, considering how grouchily he managed it. Jonathan and Beth and I, accompanied by Arthur, went upstairs to fetch blankets. While we were up there Beth made a point of locating her prescription medication and taking two extra pills. Meanwhile Pierre worried over the blueprints, as if he had a clue as to what all those white-against-blue lines meant.

And so we eventually fell asleep, huddled in the library ...

... to be awakened by Sheriff Brumus when he came pounding into the room shortly after sunrise. The rain had ceased, and through the west-facing window we could see the renewing morning light playing on the timbers of the rain-soaked bridge.

"So," said the sheriff, regarding us coldly as we squirmed out of our blankets. "You couldn't keep out of trouble."

"It's not like we did something wrong," said Beth, fluffing her hair.

"As if I didn't have enough problems in town," he grumbled. "The front door was unlocked, did you know that? Slept in your fancy clothes, I see."

"Nothing like a tuxedo to keep you warm," said Pierre, whose starched collar was open and his tie hanging limply around his neck. "Seeing to the locks would be Grayburn's department, don't you think? I don't know where he is at the moment."

"We're sorry about your troubled town, Sheriff," said Arthur, staggering to the fireplace and hefting the unwieldy percolator. The fire had gone out but the hearth was still warm enough to produce a steaming cup of coffee. "We realize we're flatlanders from the city impinging upon your jurisdiction, but we didn't know where else to turn."

"So tell me what happened," said Brumus officiously. "From the beginning."

"It was just after the séance," said Pierre. "We came out into the foyer."

"Séance," said the sheriff, rubbing his chins.

"The reenactment thereof," said Arthur. "Or so we were led to believe. Dr. Horehound became ill and excused himself before it was over. We haven't seen him since."

"What time was this?"

"The séance began at nine," said Pierre. "So I'd say he excused himself about nine thirty, nine forty-five."

"Right," said Beth. "Then, when we came out, this ball of light appeared, right in the middle of the foyer."

"A ball of light," repeated the sheriff warily.

"You know, Sheriff," said Clarice, who could make anything sound seductive, even though her slinky red dress had lost much of its pizzazz during the night. "Like St. Elmo's fire. Ball lightning. Happens all the time during paranormal—er, electrical storms."

"Uh-huh," said Brumus. "It doesn't usually occur indoors."

"Well, this did," said Beth. "It was all red and nasty-looking."

"It chased Joel down the hallway to the séance room," said Arthur.

"Hold on," said the sheriff. "It *chased* him?"

"Like it was really ticked," said Jonathan.

"And then—poof!—he was gone," said Beth.

"Poof?" mouthed the sheriff.

"More like ... *zap!*" cooed Clarice.

"Strange as it may sound, Officer," said Pierre, "there was a blinding flash as Joel reached the threshold. We were right behind him. When we rushed inside, he wasn't there. Madam Douceur can tell you—"

"Who?" asked the sheriff. "Oh, Doc's fortuneteller."

"Where is she?" asked Beth.

"Apparently not here," said Clarice as we looked around. "Maybe she went to use the unmentionable."

"She took her blanket with her," said Arthur, indicating the loveseat where Madam Douceur had bedded down for the night.

"Maybe she went out to the boathouse when it stopped raining," said Jonathan.

"Why would she go there?" asked the sheriff.

"That's where she lives, apparently," said Beth.

"Okay, Madam Dowser aside," said Sheriff Brumus, rattling his head for a fresh start. "Mr. Bomtom, on the phone you said you searched the entire building? That must've taken a while."

"It's Bontemps, Officer," said Pierre, pronouncing his name through his sinuses as only the French can. "The lady's name, I believe, is Douceur. To answer your question, we split into groups. Edward and I checked the basement. Beth, Arthur, and Jonathan took the upper floors. Grayburn covered the ground floor."

"What about outside?"

"Grayburn said he went out back to check the boathouse," I said, "but other than that, we didn't see the point."

"Well, *somebody* came inside while it was still raining." The sheriff put his hands on his hips and looked heavenward for strength. "There's quite a puddle just inside the front door. Almost broke my neck. They left a trail of water across the foyer and moseyed on up the stairs."

"Joel!" said Pierre. "So maybe he went outside after all."

"If he's back—" said I, starting for the door.

"Hold on," said the sheriff. "Stay put a minute. You said Grayburn checked the ground floor. Is there anyone else here in the house?"

"Thorndale, the cook," said Jonathan. "She's still in her room by the kitchen, as far as we know."

"Excuse me, everyone," said Clarice. "Speaking of Grayburn—"

The old codger came stumbling into the room. His jaw was going up and down but he wasn't saying anything. His eyes were blinking, his hands were trembling, and his feet were stepping every which way but straight ahead. "The garden!" he finally managed to stammer. "Madam Douceur! Dead, she is! And your friend—"

"Joel?" asked several of us together.

"Steady there," said Sheriff Brumus, gripping Grayburn by the shoulders. "Old feller, are you sure?"

"She's covered with blood!" he replied, shivering. "So much blood!"

"Maybe it's the dummy," said Arthur.

"What?" barked the sheriff.

"Madam Douceur plays the part of the woman who was murdered," explained Arthur. "She told us she'd be hiding out in the boathouse today. Dr. Horehound said he'd had a wax figure made of her. We were supposed to discover it this morning in the garden."

"Yeah," said the sheriff, disgustedly, letting the old codger go. "I've heard something about the doc's shenanigans. One of the gals that came up here last May was really wigged out about it. Had to spend a night at Maggie's to settle her nerves before driving home."

"I've seen the fake dummy," said Grayburn, rubbing the dents left by Sheriff Brumus's heavy-duty hands. "What's out there ain't it."

"Of course it is," yawned Clarice Davenport. "What else could it be?"

"I sometimes helped carry the dummy," said Grayburn, glaring. "It ain't it. I knows Madam Douceur. It's her!"

"You said something about Joel," said Pierre.

"Not sure," agreed Grayburn. "Didn't see his face."

"Dead?" asked several of us together.

"Maybe," said Grayburn. "Prob'ly."

With that, over Sheriff Brumus's objections, we clambered out of the library, through the foyer, and out the front door. Whatever puddle the sheriff had slipped on was obliterated by the stampede. We marched around the perimeter of the lodge under the overhang until we came to the east side. The morning sun pierced our eyes as we looked down into the garden. The trees and shrubs glistened, and water was dripping and trickling everywhere. I noticed the walkways Arthur had described, smeared with fresh silt and mud.

"You say she's in there?" said the sheriff to Grayburn as we neared the entrance.

"Dead as dead," answered Grayburn. "Oh, the blood!"

"You all keep out," ordered the sheriff, trudging through the breach in the hedge and turning left on the circular walkway. His boots crunched on the muddy stones as he followed Grayburn's erratic tracks.

We all waited about twenty seconds, then followed him in.

"This way, this way," said Grayburn, pointing and stumbling ahead of us on the curved walkway. When he reached the first straight pathway, he veered right and followed it. About halfway down its length he stopped and turned right, facing the lawn in the center of the garden, and pointed.

"Stay back!" ordered the sheriff when he saw us gathering around Grayburn. "You've come this far, dang it, but not one step closer, any of you! There may be footprints—evidence!"

He was standing over a gruesome shape on the grass.

"If that's a dummy," said Jonathan, "it's sure convincing."

"I'll say," said Arthur.

"My God!" said Beth, turning away.

"Oh!" gasped Clarice, turning pale and sagging within her wilted dress. "No, it can't be!"

It wasn't a dummy. It was Madam Douceur, or what was left of her. She lay on her back, fingers extended in frozen clutches, glassy eyes staring at the cloudless sky. Her black shawl was splayed in shreds upon the grass, and her purple turban was a few feet further away, mangled.

But that wasn't all. Sprawled facedown beside her was none other than Joel! I'd recognize the back of that head and the way his hair curled over his crooked collar anywhere. He was formally attired, as when we'd last seen him. Sheriff Brumus nudged him with his boot, and he stirred. Suddenly he bolted up.

"Hold on, son," said the sheriff, helping him to his feet. "You hurt?"

"No," said Joel vaguely, his eyes wide and staring. He didn't look at the body, the sheriff, or at us. He didn't seem to be seeing anything. His face was soiled and flecked with blades of grass, and the front of his tuxedo was a mess of wrinkles, mud, and lots of blood.

"What happened here?" asked the sheriff, looking him over.

"No," said Joel, just looking.

"You all right?"

"No."

"Son?"

"No."

"Right," said the sheriff, guiding Joel in our direction. Leaving us to tend to him, he returned to the body, stood near the feet, and peered around. He was being careful to disturb the scene as little as possible. He ran the toe of his boot through the tousled grass, then crouched to get a close look at something. Straightening with a grunt, he ambled back toward us, his thumbs hooked on his gun belt.

"This can't be," Clarice was muttering, nibbling at the tips of her long red fingernails. "This wasn't supposed to happen."

"Poor woman," muttered Sheriff Brumus as he stepped onto the walkway. "Nasty business. Looks a lot like—" He shook his head. "How's your friend?"

"Badly shaken, obviously," said Pierre, planting his hand firmly on Joel's shoulder.

"I'd be, too," said Arthur, sighing shakily, "if I'd stumbled upon a sight like that."

"Uh-huh," said the sheriff, eyeing Joel up and down.

"You don't think—" said Beth, her trembling fingers playing on her cheeks.

"Got anything to say?" said the sheriff, but Joel just kept mumbling negatives.

"What're you going to do?" asked Jonathan.

"Gotta call the coroner," said the sheriff. "Need to get pictures taken before we touch anything. The Rangers will want to see this, too. Looks like whatever's been doing the killing around here finally got a taste of human blood. That's bad."

"So you don't think—" said Beth, nodding toward Joel.

"Let's all go back inside," said the sheriff. "I'll phone from there."

As we exited through the break in the hedge, the sheriff halted abruptly and cocked his head. We stalled behind him. "What's that?" he asked.

"What?" inquired several of us.

"That sound."

We all listened intently. In and around the slap of waves against the dock, there was a faint, continuous, swishing sort of scraping, like a carpenter rubbing sandpaper in a circular motion. It was coming from the boathouse.

"E. I. D.'s record player," whispered Clarice. "She must have left it going when she came out here to—"

"To what?" asked the sheriff.

"But she couldn't have moved the dummy by herself," said Clarice, more to herself than to him.

"You, Mister, uh—" said the sheriff.

"Wyndham," I answered.

"You come with me."

"Why me?"

"Why *not* you? And Mister, uh—"

"Bontemps," obliged Pierre.

"Yeah," said the sheriff. "You take everyone back up to the lodge. Wait for me in that room I found you in."

"I don't think I want to go back there," said Clarice, shivering all over. "Sheriff, can I get a ride with you into town?"

"We'll see," said he. "You go with them for now, Miss—?"

"Davenport."

"You'll be safe with them. This shouldn't take long."

"I'm not armed," I said uneasily, as I followed him along the graveled path toward the boathouse. I noticed white smoke oozing from the tin chimney jutting from the shingled roof.

"You've got eyes," he said. "I may need a witness."

"You're joking."

"Never about murder."

I would have called the door quaint under other circumstances. The boathouse was all white, but the door was painted bright red with yellow trim. There was a four-paned window set in elegant molding, with rose-trimmed white lace curtains pulled shut. The scratching sound pulsed within.

"Here goes nothing," said the sheriff, turning the knob and pushing his way inside.

"Good heavens!" said a woman's voice, startled but groggy with sleep. "What is the meaning—?"

"Sorry to intrude, Ma'am," said the sheriff. "Just who might you be, and what are you doing out here?"

"Thorndale," I said. "The cook."

She was bundled within a puffy pink and brown quilt, slumped in an old-fashioned rocking chair beside a potbelly stove. An antique phonograph with a hand crank—a genuine Victrola, I think—had reached the end of a record that was still turning, hence the scratching sound.

"I know you," she said to me, pulling the quilt up to her chin. "You're with them. And Sheriff Brumus—we haven't spoken, but I've seen you intimidating people when I've gone shopping in town."

"Oh," said he. "Is that what I do? I thought I was keeping the peace."

"Well you've certainly disturbed mine! You're here now. What do you want?"

Looking around the charming room, the sheriff halted abruptly at the sight of something on the bed. It looked eerily like a body with a sheet draped over it.

"I'll have you know that's Dr. Horehound's private property," snapped Thorndale as he lifted the corner.

"If that don't beat all," he said, regarding said property with cold eyes. He turned them toward me and asked, "What do you make of this?"

"I'd say it's the wax dummy we told you about," said I. "The one we were supposed to find in the garden this morning."

"This reenactment business," he said, dropping the sheet back into place. "I can see why people get so disturbed."

"What people?" asked Thorndale, squirming around under the quilt. The rocking chair creaked and croaked with her movements. "I suppose you have a warrant, or whatever you call it."

"Don't need one," said the sheriff. "Not at a crime scene."

"What crime? I haven't done anything."

"This isn't your room, is it?" he asked. "They tell me yours is just off the kitchen."

"These are Elaineileen's quarters," she huffed. "Madam Douceur to you. She gets lonely, you know, having to stay out of sight after the first night. I thought I'd keep her company, poor thing. Brought her a nice big plate of tidbits she likes to nibble. Leftovers, you know, from last night's dinner."

"That's thoughtful of you, I'm sure," said the sheriff, eyeing a tray on the dining table. I wondered what he'd have to say if he peeked under the checkered towel, but he didn't.

"She wasn't here," said Thorndale, rubbing her eyes. "So I made myself at home. Must've fallen asleep."

"Were you gonna help her move that dummy to the garden?" asked the sheriff.

"Not on your life, not that nasty thing. The Master—Dr. Horehound—usually helps with that, and Grayburn."

"Tell me," said the sheriff, facing her. "When did you last see Dr. Horehound?"

"At dinner, last night."

"And Mrs. Douceur?"

"Also at dinner—and she prefers to be called 'Madam.'"
Thorndale shifted under the quilt. "Why? There was a ruckus in
the house, around ten or so. Some ruffian came banging on my
door looking for Grayburn."

"Jonathan," I explained. "We needed flashlights."

"So you left your room right after that?" asked the sheriff.

"I did *not*," said Thorndale, clutching her blanket to her throat.
"Not with strangers pounding about the house."

"I understand," said Sheriff Brumus, glancing at me. "So
when did you decide to come out here with the goodies?"

"After the rain let up," she replied. "About four, I'd say. Why
are you asking me these things?"

The sheriff was rubbing his chin thoughtfully. "Weren't you
afraid of that critter that's been killing dogs and wildlife around
here?"

"I've got a gun here, Sheriff. It's aimed at you right now."

"I should have known," he sighed. "A Derringer, I suppose?"

"A Smith & Wesson Model 29," said she. Something clicked
under her wrappings.

Shaking his head, the sheriff meandered over to the stove,
opened the hatch, and thoughtfully inserted some chunks of
wood. The fire huffed within. "I'm sorry to be the one to tell
you, Ma'am, but apparently your friend didn't think to protect
herself when she went wandering in the garden early this morning."

"What are you saying?" Thorndale looked at the shrouded
thing on the bed, as if expecting it to sit up. "Is she—? She
can't be—!"

"'Fraid so," said the sheriff, somberly. "I need to ask you to
get yourself together and come up to the house."

The sheriff and I waited outside while she whimpered and
thumped about within. When she finally emerged, trails of mas-
cara running down her cheeks, she had wrapped herself in a thick
coat. Her rubbers squeaked and squawked as she preceded us up
the path to the back porch. Before following her into the kitchen
I stole a look back at the lake. There was a disturbance in the
water a hundred yards or so out. Several birds swooped and

shrieked, brushing the surface with extended talons. Some poor fish no doubt, I told myself.

The sheriff and I waited again outside Thorndale's bedroom as she scrubbed her face, ejected her raingear, and changed into something more presentable, mumbling and wailing to herself all the while. Pierre and Arthur were waiting somberly by the telephone when we entered the foyer. Clarice Davenport was pacing by herself near the front door. I could see the others milling around in the library.

The sheriff marched over to the antique phone, which was sitting on a wobbly table near the foot of the stairs. He snatched up the receiver, jiggled the cradle, glared at the earpiece for a moment, then slammed it down.

"Dead?" asked Pierre.

"As a doornail," said Sheriff Brumus. "We're in a valley here, so I can't radio from my car."

Suddenly an unexpected voice hailed from the stairway. Only one person pronounced the sheriff's name that way.

"Sheriff Brumus! What brings you up here? Don't tell me you've found my boat!"

"Dr. Horehound!" said Pierre, very much surprised.

Our host was standing on the twelfth step or so, big as you please, arrayed in bathrobe and slippers. For this dramatic appearance he sported a foot-long cigarette holder with a dark ciggie drooping from its end.

"I'm afraid not, Doc," said the sheriff, his neck cracking at that angle. "You always sleep this late?"

"Not usually, no," admitted Dr. Horehound, casually descending the steps. As he reached our level he ran his fingers through his tousled hair. "I was a bit under the weather last night. Something I ate, apparently. I suppose my digestive system required extra slumber to recuperate. Clarice! Is that you in the shadows? Where are you going?"

"Out for some air," she said, icily. "I'll be pacing on the porch if you need me, Sheriff."

"I'd rather you—" said he, but she was already shutting the door from the outside.

"Odd," commented Dr. Horehound.

"Harrumph," fumed Brumus. "Anyway, Doc, you just came from your bedroom?"

"Where else?" replied our host.

"You weren't up there last night," said Arthur.

"And how would you know that?" asked the doctor with a touch of annoyance.

"We searched everywhere," said I. "Joel disappeared after the séance. We looked all over for him."

"Indeed," said our host. "I do hope he turned up."

"He did indeed," said Pierre.

"Perhaps I was occupied in the lavatory when you checked my room," said Dr. Horehound, rubbing his abdomen to stress the point. "In any case, I awakened in my cozy bed just now. Hearing people about, I came down to offer my good mornings. I say, Sheriff, you look pale. Thorndale, where are your manners? Please be so kind as to bring the constable some coffee."

"No thanks," said the sheriff. "Doc, we need to talk. In the library, if you don't mind."

"Ordered about in my own house," said Dr. Horehound with a touch of melodrama. "Sounds ominous."

"Something like that," said the sheriff.

∞§[Martin]§∞

Monsignor Havermeyer mumbled something to himself.

"Pardon?" I asked.

"Ominous," he repeated for my benefit.

"Oh," I said, nodding.

"So what happened next?" asked Edward.

"A lengthy rehashing of events in the library which would be redundant for our purposes," said Pierre. "Ostensibly, the sheriff needed information for his report, but it was Dr. Horehound who exhibited an inordinate ravenousness for minutiae."

"For his book," said Edward, "or something else?"

"Yeah," said Jonathan. "Where the heck had he been?"

"Barfing bugs," said Beth. "Served him right!"

"Thorough chap that I am," said Jonathan, "I can't believe I wouldn't have checked his bathroom."

"And musical instruments played by unseen hands," said Arthur. "Spooky stuff."

"Oh dear," said Monsignor Havermeyer, who was rubbing his scarred lips with trembling fingers of his own.

"Something wrong, My Senior?" I asked him.

"Memories," he muttered. "Something ... long ago ... long, long ago."

"You ate bugs?"

"What? No, something else entirely. Don't mind me."

I was going to say, "After what you said in the kitchen?" but decided to let it slide. Besides, Pierre was itching to move on.

"In any case," said he, "Sheriff Brumus took Joel into town in his four-wheeler. He radioed the Forest Service when he was out of the valley. They were swamped with other matters after the storm, but a couple of men from Fish and Wildlife Services arrived an hour later."

"Sorry to repeat myself even though I don't remember saying it the first or second time," said Beth, "but that mean old sheriff didn't think Joel did it, did he?"

"No," said Pierre. "There was no question that Madam Douceur had been mauled by a wild animal. Fish and Wildlife looks into animal attacks, not murders. But there were questions that required answers, and the sheriff had a duty to dig them out—poor chap, if only he had known! In spite of his flair for imparting negative first impressions—"

"You can say that again," said Beth.

"Most cops is good at that," said Kahlúa. "Mmm-HM!"

"—there was a reason for his standoffish demeanor, as you will shortly see," concluded Pierre.

"So our story probably segues to Claw Junction," said Arthur.

"A brief sojourn," agreed Pierre. "One in which you took part. You're on, Herr von Derschmidt."

"Oh, joy," groaned Arthur.

∞§[†]§∞

∞§✝§∞

17. No Spoon Is Too Long When You're Supping with the Devil

∞§[ARTHUR]§∞

TWO AND A HALF HOURS after Sheriff Brumus left for Claw Junction with Joel stupefied and unshackled in the passenger seat, Pierre and I were arranging ourselves in my station wagon. We had decided to follow them into town to offer Joel our moral support. Pierre, ever debonair, had replaced his tuxedo with one of those tweed outfits with leather pads at the elbows and his favorite herringbone fedora hat. Preferring comfort to impressions, I had reverted to overalls. Meanwhile Jonathan was joining Edward in his van, which was belching dark smoke as the engine warmed for a very different task. Attired in jeans and sweatshirts, they had opted to make a run up the west shore to retrieve the tent from the campground. Deeming our stay at the lodge in danger of curtailment by police intervention, they judged it advisable to have the tent safely aboard and ready to roll. Whether they would be able to disentangle the mangled thing remained to be seen. Beth, in her casual denims and sunshine mood, had decided to join them. Nothing astonishing there, I supposed. Jonathan seemed pleased at the idea of her company.

As I turned my key in the ignition Edward suddenly jumped out of his vehicle and strode hurriedly toward mine. I rolled down the window as he dug a moth-eaten twenty out of his pocket and said, "If the opportunity arises, get Joel the works."

"Glad you remembered," I said, stuffing the bill into my pocket. "A hamburger, chocolate shake, and onion rings—right?"

"Make that a double bacon cheeseburger," said Edward. "He'll need it."

"No problem," I assured him as he headed back to his van.

Then, just as I put the gear into reverse, Clarice Davenport flung open the front door of the lodge, scampered across the porch, leapt down the stairs, and came charging toward us on the crunchy gravel—all hazardous maneuvers with two suitcases in high heels and tight skirt.

"That blasted sheriff left without me!" she panted by way of explanation as she tugged the back door open behind me and unceremoniously dove inside, her luggage thumping against the far door behind Pierre.

"The more the merrier," I commented as I backed the car with the steering wheel cramped to the left.

"Won't the good doctor miss you?" asked Pierre over his shoulder as I maneuvered around the officious green government vehicle which was parked at an odd angle, and eased the car across the bridge.

"Let him," she said, practically snarling. "My character is supposed to disappear today anyway."

"So where do you usually hide for the duration of these reenactments? Surely not with Madam Douceur in the boathouse."

"Only in my nightmares," she replied. "Meaning no offense to the dead, of course, but you saw how it was between us. No, I've got a guestroom prepared up on the east side second floor. I was all set this time around to read all seven volumes of *Harry Potter* while devouring four pounds of See's chocolates. But after this morning, heck, just get me the Hell away from here!"

"Kind of sudden," remarked Pierre, making a worrisome gesture with his hand. "I should think employers like Dr. Horehound won't take it kindly when the help skips without notice."

"He can write me a tear-stained letter when I send for my heavy things," said she, fastening her seatbelt. She was so upset it took three or four attempts to engage the buckle.

"Things get a little too close for comfort, eh?"

"This isn't funny!" she huffed. I could see her blow hair out of her face in the rearview mirror. I also noticed tears welling in her eyes. "Elaineileen's dead!" she wailed. It was the first time she had called the woman by name, at least in my presence, but it was hardly a sign of heretofore hidden affection. This was pure self-interest. "You saw how she looked!" she screeched. "Her eyes! All that blood! And her lying there, right in the middle of Gabrielle's garden, right about where—well—it's just a little too much like what happened to Madam Ouspenskaya!"

"And you don't want to disappear—really disappear—like Arianna Marigold," said Pierre calmly.

"You bet your—!" Suddenly discomfited by her hysteria, she reeled herself in and said coolly, "Right you are, Chum."

"Sounds like you've been giving this séance business some thought," I suggested.

"Arthur, dear boy," she said snidely. "Can't you pedal any faster?"

"My, but you've changed," said Pierre.

"Listen, Buster," she replied. "The doc paid me to act like I've been acting. From here on I'm acting like me!"

"For what it's worth," I explained over my shoulder as I proceeded down the muddy track toward town, "I'm going to offer to take Joel home to St. Philomena's. This trip hasn't been good for him. Surely he's made his statement by now. He could be placed in Fr. Baptist's custody in the event the investigators want to get in touch with him later. If the sheriff agrees, I'll be glad to give you a lift, too."

She lightened up at the idea. "Thanks, I may take you up on that. Who's Fr. Baptist?"

"Our pastor," said Pierre. "But I doubt the sheriff will let Joel go. The authorities are usually keen on keeping witnesses handy during an ongoing investigation."

"An animal attack isn't a crime," I said.

"But the circumstances are certainly suspicious, and he's the only witness."

I considered that for a moment and said, "We'll see after I make a phone call. The word of a former chief of Homicide to an overworked county sheriff who likely could use the help of a celebrated cop-turned-priest right about now might do the trick."

"You know a former police chief?" asked Clarice. "And what celebrated cop-turned-priest?"

"Fr. Baptist," we answered together.

The town seemed deserted when I eased the car into a diagonal slot near Howler's Café. The only person in sight was Sheriff Brumus leaning against a post in front of his office. Clarice said she had to see someone but she'd be back soon, and please don't leave without her. After assuring her I wouldn't forget and drive off with her luggage, Pierre and I jaywalked to greet the Law, a pensive harmonica theme from a 1932 western echoing poignantly in the canyons of my mind.

"Doc Langanhan gave your friend a clean bill of health," greeted the sheriff. "Physically, anyway. You probably passed him on your way down. Drives a big black van. He's our coroner as well, so he went up to do his doings about the body. Fish and Wildlife are on their way, too."

"Already up there," said Pierre. "They were taping off the garden as we left. One of them said you'd left instructions that we were free to come into town. I wouldn't have expected such high-speed efficiency up here."

"In this here backwoods, you mean," said the sheriff, spitting on the ground for effect. It got on his boot, so he wiped it against the back of his leg. "We're not exactly hillbillies, you know."

"I meant no offense," said Pierre.

"None taken," said the sheriff. "I used to be a cop in Los Angeles, you know. I understand the big-city perception of small towns."

"Come up here to escape the rat race?" I asked.

"Not exactly," he said, rubbing the back of his neck thoughtfully.

"So what about Joel?" asked Pierre. "Surely you're satisfied he didn't have anything to do with Madam Douceur's death."

"Not precisely," said the sheriff. "Whatever mauled Ma'am Douceur was one mean brute. Had to have nasty-ass claws and incredible strength to hack her up like that. Mr. Maruppa's no weightlifter, and he didn't even have blood under his fingernails. He certainly had something to do with it, though, seeing as how he's got the deceased's blood all over the rest of him."

"So what are you going to do?" asked Pierre.

"Here's the problem," said the sheriff. "Doc Langanhan could vouch for your friend's ticker, but not his tinker, if you get my drift. For a while all he kept saying was 'No, no, no' like a broken record. Then after a time he just sat and stared. Maybe the sight of that woman all tore up addled his brain, but then again, maybe he saw what did it. Till I know for sure, I've gotta keep him on a short leash. Maybe he should stay in town tonight."

"Perhaps Dr. Horehound could help," I suggested, albeit with reticence. "He's a clinical psychologist, after all."

"Whose story don't hold squat," said the sheriff. "I believe your friend, Mr. Clubb, when he said the doc's bedroom was empty when he checked, and somebody sure came tracking water in through the front door. I can't prove it, but I think Dr. Horehound knows more about what happened to that poor woman than he's willing to admit."

"But if an animal killed her," I asked, "what difference does it make?"

"There you've got me," he sighed. "There's just something cockeyed about the whole thing."

"I take it you don't like Dr. Horehound," said Pierre. "Or should I say you don't trust him?"

"I'd say both," said the sheriff, nodding. "Moving into that mansion was bad enough—that place should have been burned to the ground long ago—but I knew nothing good would come of his play-acting shenanigans. Who in their right mind would want to revive a century's old murder?"

"I'm surprised you're talking to us," said Pierre, "seeing as how we're here for that very purpose."

"That does seem strange, don't it?" he agreed, then smiled. "I had a nice chat with your boss, Mr. Bontom—"

"Bontemps," corrected Pierre.

"Sorry. She tells me you boys is all good Catholics."

"That surprises you?"

"It interests me, seeing as how I'm one, too. Catholic, anyway. How good ain't my call."

"Really," I said, my curiosity piqued.

"Just about the only one up here," he said, shifting his weight from one foot to the other. "Anglo, anyway. She told me about that occult mess you were involved in a few months ago, all those bishops getting killed by the witches. I read about that in the papers. So I guess you guys have some experience in these matters."

"That depends on what you mean by experience," said Pierre. "We were mostly just bystanders."

"But you hang with Jack Lombard," said the sheriff. "I'd heard he had a breakdown or something—left the force after some bizarre abracadabra case—but it sure floored me to learn he's now a priest!"

"Not to mention the 'cop-turned-priest-turned-cop,'" said Pierre, tossing me a wink.

"The best," said I, returning it. "You knew him back then?"

"Mostly just passed him at the courthouse," said the sheriff. "Spoke with him a couple of times. I doubt he'd remember me—my face, maybe, but not my name. Good man. I guess that's why I'm standing here talking with you."

∞§[Martin]§∞

"Small world," commented Beth.

"Do you remember him?" asked Jonathan, turning in his chair.

"Can't say I do," said Father. "I talked to a lot of police officers at the courthouse and all over town in those days."

"You'd think a name like Brumus would stick to the inside of your skull," said I.

"Any mention of his first name?" asked Father.

"Not yet," said Pierre.

"As he said, maybe I'd remember his face if I saw him."

"I never knew you'd had a nervous breakdown, Father," said Kahlúa. "Is it true?"

Father mulled that over, and finally shook his head no. "I knew there was such a rumor when I resigned, and in a way I encouraged it. People who think they know the answers don't ask questions. I just wanted to fade into obscurity."

"So much for that plan," grumbled Millie.

"When did they start calling you the 'cop-turned-priest-turned-cop,' Father?" asked Beth, forming a telescope with her hand and peering across the room.

"Jacco Babs of the *Times* coined it," he answered with a shrug. "My friends, unfortunately, perpetuate it."

"And the rest, as they say, is blistery," said Jonathan.

"Speaking of which," urged Pierre. "Arthur?"

"Sure," said he. "Let's see ..."

∞§[ᴀʀᴛʜᴜʀ]§∞

"Small world," I said.

"That it is," the sheriff agreed. "So Mr. Bon—uh, Pierre. I'm gonna ask a favor. Why don't you mosey on into my office and have a chat with your friend, Mr. Marrupa? Maybe he'll open up to you."

"Maybe Arthur should try," said Pierre. "Frankly, I seem to have been getting on Joel's nerves lately."

"Well," said the sheriff, "you give it a shot first. If it don't work, we'll send in Arthur, here. You know: good Tumblar, bad Tumblar."

"Kahlúa told you about that, too," I chuckled.

"I think she's a straight shooter," said the sheriff, "even if she was an exotic dancer."

"Whoa ho!" said Pierre, pretending to load a pistol and twirl the cylinder. "That I didn't know. Praise the Lord and pass the ammunition!"

"As for me," said the sheriff, "I could use some grub and high-test caffeine. I'll be over at Howler's Café. Mr. Von Dershudgit, why don't you join me? On me."

"Von Derschmidt," I corrected him.

The sheriff harrumphed. "Whatever happened to names like Smith?"

Pierre and I shared a mirthful glance.

"I'll be off then," said Pierre, striding purposely across the sidewalk and entering the sheriff's office.

"I'd be pleased to accept your invitation, Sheriff," I said as I accompanied him down his one-block town. "First, however, I wonder if you might tell me how far it is to the nearest Catholic Church?"

"About five hundred yards," he replied with a knowing smile.

"Really," I said, peering around. "I thought maybe the next town. I certainly don't see it, and there are no signs like you usually find for travelers."

"Probably the second-best kept secret in Claw Junction," said he, chuckling uneasily to himself. "City Council ordered the signs taken down. Most folks around here don't cater to—well, let's just say this ain't a homey God-fearing town."

"That must be difficult for you," I said seriously.

"You have no idea, son," he said, giving his gun belt an upward tug. "If it wasn't for me, Father Hobson would only have a handful of Mexicans for a congregation. A gaggle of maids, a couple of busboys, a half-a-dozen ditch diggers, and one mean sheriff: some flock, huh?"

I could have answered that from a dozen angles, but chose to say instead, "I take it you're not married."

His face went through several changes of expression before he answered, "Not anymore. The wife couldn't handle—oh, never mind. Mass was at seven, so you're out of luck there. I try to go most days, but this morning—well, you know about that."

"Second-best?" I asked.

"Excuse me?"

"You said it was the second-best kept secret in Claw Junction. What's the first?"

"Oh," he said, wiping his mouth with his hand. "That'd be Harley's Saloon. It's hidden around the backside of Hal's."

"Not visible from the main road?" I asked. "Can't be good for business."

"People here abouts get enough of tourists and passer-throughs. When time comes for drinkin' and thinkin', they don't like strangers gawkin' at them like critters in a zoo."

"That's a shame," I said. "One of the great things about traveling is talking to locals, at least for me—regional color, folklore, and all that."

"The last thing these folks want to do," said the sheriff forebodingly, "is chat with strangers about local history."

"Okay," was all I could think to respond, so I changed the subject. "Fr. Hobson, you said."

"Yeah, Oldwin Hobson, good man." He smiled approvingly. "Always available to hear Confessions. Real old-fashioned priest. Mean-spirited folks around here call him 'Old Hob.' Now that's backwoods irony for you."

"Hob being short for hobgoblin," I suggested.

"More likely the Devil," said the sheriff. "But he's nothing like. Got booted up here from Los Angeles way before me. I suppose we're kindred spirits that way. I understand he ticked off the archbishop."

"Not hard to do," I said, digging my new medallion out of my pocket. "Fr. Baptist—Jack Lombard's clerical name—has the same tendency. I just want to get some holy water, and have this medal blessed."

"Say, that's the one from Doc Horehound's desk." He leaned close and grimaced. "I thought it was some kind of witchery talisman thingamajigger."

"It's a medal commemorating the Archangel Gabriel," I assured him, hefting it in my palm. "I won it fair and square."

"Tell me about it over breakfast," he said, pointing beyond my shoulder. "You'll find St. Arnold's up that dirt trail beyond the bookstore. Don't be too long. I'm hungry, but not that hungry."

"Thank-you, I'll be swift," I said, pocketing the medal as I started on my way. "At least, for me."

As I strode past the bookstore I noticed that the CLOSED sign was tilted sideways. The lights were off within, but I beheld a pair of wide, forlorn eyes peering at me. When I paused in my stride, whoever it was withdrew, setting the sign rocking. The image of those dark, haunted eyes stayed with me as I pressed on.

The way to the ostracized church was steep, rutted, and muddy, but I kept to the edge as it wound its way up among the stately pine trees. In due course I came upon a rundown little hovel of a log chapel. Fr. Hobson was clipping flowers around a

weathered statue of Our Lady of Grace near the entrance. He
was wearing a tattered cassock and ratty gardening gloves.

"Fr. Hobson?" I ventured.

"Yes?" he said, removing his wire-rim spectacles so he could
wipe his brow.

"My name is Arthur von Derschmidt. Sheriff Brumus told me
where to find you. I wonder if I might replenish my holy water
bottle."

"The font's just inside," said he. "Passing through?"

"Not exactly. I'm staying at Wolfram Lodge."

That brought him up short. "Not one of those séances."

"Several of us came with a friend," I explained quickly, feeling
suddenly guilty. "He's a reporter on assignment for a newspaper. It's supposed to just be a reenactment—Dr. Horehound
gave us his word on that point—but the medium admitted afterwards that she wasn't playacting."

"No spoon is too long when you're supping with the Devil," he
said sternly.

"You can say that again, Father. I dowsed the room with holy
water before we began, for what it's worth, which is why I need
a refill. And now the medium—"

"Killed, I heard," he said glumly.

"Small town," I commented.

"No secrets," he agreed. Then he shook his head. "No, I take
that back. This town is one big, black, wicked secret."

"So I'm finding out," I said with a nod. "I was surprised to
find a Catholic Church in Claw Junction."

"Ha ha!" he chortled, waving his hands. "You and me both.
You may not like mine or me, I should warn you. I was relieved
of my parish duties in the Big City years ago when I refused to
say the New Mass."

"That's fine by us, Father," I said, happily relieved. "We're all
Trads in our group."

"Trads?" he repeated with a squint.

"Traditionalists."

He tisked a couple of times, shook his head, and said, "I suppose I shouldn't be surprised. We live in an abbreviated age."

"That we do," I agreed lamely. I considered telling him about Mr. Feeney's spiel about the notorious "Tradosaurus Rex," but decided it might throw us far afield. So instead I said, "Sheriff Brumus told me you were, uh, sent here from Los Angeles. If you don't mind my asking, I thought these mountains are part of Riverside County—Bishop Wigglesworth's diocese."

"You're right about that," he answered. "Morley Fulbright transferred troublesome me to the jurisdiction of his old friend, Jedadiah Wigglesworth, and Winkie banished me as far as his authority would reach."

I laughed. "Winkie?"

"A gibe that was beneath me," he said, frowning and shaking his head. "I apologize, to God as well as to you. No doubt this assignment was intended as a punishment. I reckon it was well-deserved. There's no collection up here to speak of, no money for repairs. I let them cut off the electricity long ago, but I keep the phone connected for sick calls."

"It must get dreadfully cold when it snows," I said, observing the cracks and splits in the walls of the rickety chapel.

"That's why God made trees, my son," he said cheerfully. "Firewood is one thing I have aplenty. I get no support from the Chancery, but a more devout group of parishioners I've never had the honor to serve." Then his smile sank into a concerned frown. "They're scared, that's what they are. They work for dreadful people—witches, some of them, and worse."

"And a Catholic sheriff to keep the peace," I said, shaking my head. "No wonder he complains of troubles in his town."

"The woman, the so-called seer at the lodge," he said, replacing his glasses and looking at me through them severely. "She was murdered, yes?"

I shrugged. "The sheriff says she was killed by whatever's been butchering animals around here."

"Mark my words—Arthur, is it? There's evil afoot in these mountains."

"We've certainly seen some strange things," I said. "Lights in the woods—glowing spheres, sort of—two inside the lodge."

"I've seen them around here, too, the last couple of days," he said, rubbing the back of his neck.

"Really?" I said, intrigued. "Balls of white light? Some with blue and green flecks? Some red?"

"Blue and green, yes," he said, thinking. "No red. I thought it was ball lightning at first. You know: from the storm. But yesterday at Mass, and again this morning, at the Consecration, one of them appeared above the tabernacle and, well, it just hovered there. I couldn't stop, of course—a priest never can once he's begun. It floated there in front of the Crucifix, through the Elevations and the Fracture, and then it blinked out—sort of sucked itself into nothingness—it's hard to explain. Sheriff Brumus saw it yesterday. He wasn't here today. Some of my flock thought it was an Angel, or maybe a ghost. I don't know what the heck it was."

I was considering Sheriff Brumus's reaction to Beth's description of the sphere that chased Joel, when Fr. Hobson said:

"If I were you, I'd collect my friends and get as far away from Spirit Lake as possible."

"I've considered it, Father, believe me," I said, shoving my hands into my pockets. "My sister, Beth, is with us, and I'm concerned for her. I doubt Pierre would leave, though. He's on assignment, and he's a stickler for seeing things through."

"I'd sure press for it, my son. I really would."

"The other problem is Sheriff Brumus. He will probably insist that we stay until his investigation is finished."

"That may be, unfortunately. Like your friend, he's the kind of man who sees things through."

"Oh, I mustn't forget," I said as my fingers encountered the medallion in my pocket. I held it out to him, the side with the suggestion of wings facing up in my palm. "I wonder if you would be so kind as to bless this medal for me."

"And what might it be?" he asked, looking closely.

"I believe it to be a Nordic medal honoring the Archangel Gabriel."

"Really," he said. "May I?"

"Of course," I said, handing it to him.

He turned it over and examined the other side.

"X was their runic equivalent of our G," I explained.

"Runes," he said thoughtfully. "It's been a long time since
I've read *The Lord of the Rings*."
I considered explaining to him that J. R. R. Tolkien created his
own runic alphabet in which G was represented by another symbol entirely, but then he asked:
"How did you come by this?"
"A dare from our host at the lodge, Dr. Horehound," I explained. "He said it was mine if I could tell him what it is. He
was a bit annoyed when I did."
Father Hobson fell silent, looking at me intently for several
long moments. Then he seemed to come to a decision. "I will
be glad to oblige you," he said. "Since, as you say, your departure may be delayed, I'm also going to see to it that you have
reinforcements. First, you will go to Confession—you need it, I
think—and then receive Holy Communion. Along with the holy
water, I will provide you with blessed salt, and maybe a little vial
of chrism. And as for this—" He snapped his fingers. "—Good
Heavens! I know just the thing!"
"I'm so glad I came here," I said gratefully.
"So am I, my son. So am I."

∞§[Martin]§∞

"Done," said Arthur, straightening his pages and handing them
to Pierre.
"Don't get too comfortable, Old Chap," said he. "You're just
pausing for station identification."
"Any port in a storm," said Arthur, addressing a well-deserved
mug of eggnog.
"Ladies and Gentlemen," announced Pierre. "I'll be reading
the next chapter myself. It has to do with my meeting with Joel
in the sheriff's office."
"What's wrong with my version?" asked Joel.
"There's a problem," said Pierre. "All you wrote was, 'Pierre
came to visit me in jail. He had little to say to me, and I to
him.'"
"That's all?"

"Afraid so. Whether you didn't remember the details, or didn't want to, I know not."

"I'm really not liking this," said Joel. "Pierre, I'm trying to be a good sport, but this is getting downright—I don't know."

"Chin up," said Pierre. "It's about to get worse."

∞§[†]§∞

∞§✝§∞

18. I Wouldn't Be So Quick To Burn My Bridges If I Were You

∞§[Pi℘rr℘]§∞

I HAD NO IDEA WHAT TO EXPECT. It was like something out of a low-budget movie. There was a roll-top desk up against the cinderblock wall to the right, a corkboard riddled with notices above, and a rack of rifles with boxes of ammunition opposite. There was an open doorway in the far wall, through which I could see the steel bars and crossbeams of holding cells. I found Joel slumped on the cot in one of them, the door widely ajar.

"I couldn't find a cake," I said after taking a deep breath and tucking my concerns behind a conspiratorial smile. "Not even a doughnut. The lady with the sticky fingers at Hal's Groceries ate them all. I managed to procure a file, but I see it isn't needed. Joel, my lad, you've already picked the lock!"

He looked up at me, not amused. He was fingering a coin in his right hand, slowly turning it over and over.

"Found something?" I asked.

"Yes," he said.

"Care to share?"

He looked down at the coin, then brusquely shoved it into his jacket pocket. I took that as a no.

"So what happens now?" he said accusingly after a long silence.

"The doc gave you a clean bill of health," I said good-naturedly. "Arthur's offered to drive you home, but Sheriff Brumus said he'd prefer you stay in town tonight. I assume he meant over at the motel, not this dreary place."

"I'd rather go back to the lodge," he said sullenly.

"You don't have to, you know," I said. "I realize you've had quite a fright."

"Pierre, you have no idea where I've been or what I've been through."

"True, and neither does the sheriff, and that's the point," I said, scratching my head for effect. "He knows you didn't kill Madam Douceur—"

"That's for sure!"

"Right, Joel, no problem. But he needs to know how you happened upon her, what you may have seen. That sort of thing. You gave us quite a scare, you know. One minute you were scrambling down the hall, that fiendish thingie hot on your heels. The next thing—*zap!*—you were gone. We searched the lodge from top to bottom but you were nowhere to be found. Where the heck were you?"

"You wouldn't believe me, Pierre."

"No, I mean it."

"I said you wouldn't believe me."

"Don't be like that. Of course I'll believe you."

He bore into me with angry pneumatic-drill eyes. "You think you know everything. You're so confident in your beliefs."

"I should hope so," I answered, undaunted. "Goes with the territory and all that."

"But you really don't know what you're talking about," he said derisively. "Any of you: Edward, Jonathan, Arthur, even Fr. Baptist. You think you know it all, but you don't know anything." He crimped his left thumb and forefinger in a gesture I recognized as an imitation of a mannerism of my own. "Not this much!"

That, I admit, took me by surprise. "What's gotten into you, Lad?"

"I'm not your lad. Don't pretend you're my friend."

"But Joel, what else am I if not your friend?"

"I joined you guys because I'd just been through a God-awful time at Bishop Brassorie's," he said irritably. "I was reconsidering my vocation. That's what they called it: 'reconsidering.' So they gave me a job to keep me busy. Told me I was to be his aide. Bootlicker's more like it. It was humiliating, and he was horrible. Small wonder I jumped at the chance to join your little men's club."

"Hmm," I replied. "There was also the matter of his being murdered, as I recall."

"Right, Pierre. He got murdered, and I got arrested. Just like now."

"I beg to differ, Joel. You were arrested, yes, and subsequently released, thanks to Fr. Baptist. Don't let that detail slip through the cracks. He swore he'd get you out, and he came through for you. As for the present, Sheriff Brumus hasn't arrested you. He brought you to town so the doctor could look you over. This cell door is wide open, and all jokes aside: you didn't pick it. You're free to go."

"But not very far," he said sullenly.

"Well," I said, "there is the matter of the investigation, my friend."

"Don't call me that!" he snapped.

"Okay. Okay. Have it your way." I was getting angry, and my voice betrayed the fact. "The sheriff needs your statement. It's his job, and you're his only witness. Satisfy him and you're on your way."

"Sure," he scowled. "Sure. Like with the Tumblars."

I mulled that over for a moment and said, "I fail to see the connection."

"How did you put it that first night in Father's study?" he hissed through clenched teeth. "You only accepted members you liked? What was there to like about me?"

"Hold on," I said sternly. "I believe what we said was that you had to be a practicing Catholic, that you must enjoy having a good time, and that we must take pleasure in your company. But I fail to see your point. We welcomed you into our midst, didn't we?"

"Sure," he said sourly. "The Slow Vock. Your little toady. Joel Maruppa: the littlest Tumblar."

"Dear fellow, you're putting a dreadful spin on things," I said, my own thoughts doing some frenetic twirling of their own. "We invited you into our fellowship because you passed all three challenges with flying colors, especially the last. You're a darn fine fellow—or were, if you've decided to change on us."

"Harrumph," he replied. "Well, I'm giving notice. I don't want to be part of your snobby little club anymore. I've got better things to do."

"Such as?"

He crossed his arms. "Something I have to do back at the lake."

"Such as?"

"You wouldn't believe me."

"Back to that, are we?"

He just sat there fuming.

"Joel," I said after a long silence. "Joel, if I've given you cause to doubt my intentions toward you—what can I say? 'Sorry' isn't adequate. Taking each other down a peg or two, that's our way: a manly form of affection, of keeping one another on our toes as we fight the Good Fight, as it were. If the Lads and I have ribbed you unfairly—I stress 'if' because none of us are exempt, myself included—it was never done with malice, but as a measure of our high regard for you, for one another. The word 'bonding' comes to mind, but you know how I dislike popular parlance. That's one thing, and I'm sure it can be worked out. On the other hand, when you attack our beliefs—ours and Fr. Baptist's—that's another matter entirely. What does he represent but the Catholic Faith, which we hold dear? To say we're limited in our understanding, that goes without saying. To say he doesn't know what he's talking about, that's beyond the pale. To say that you know better, what can that be but hubris? That is what you said, isn't it?"

"Once a bell is rung, you can't unring it," he replied. "I said what I said, and I meant it."

"That's your final word."

He said nothing.

I threw up my hands and let them fall against my sides. "Okay, Joel. You're your own man, and I'm certainly not going to beg. If you want out, that's your decision to make. If you had seen us tearing throughout Wolfram Lodge, searching frantically for you—but no matter. You've found something better? I bless you in it. I'll leave you to tell the others because I'm not competent to be your messenger. For the next few hours, at least, you're going to be stuck with us; and frankly I think you're behaving shabbily. I wouldn't be so quick to burn my bridges if I were you, but I sense you don't want my advice."

"Good," he said grimly.

"Now, as for me," I continued, "I'm going to go have breakfast with Sheriff Brumus. I'll tell him you want to return to the lodge, but the final say is his. You might do us the favor of joining us at Howler's Café, or you can stay here and sulk. Frankly, as of this moment, I don't care what you do."

With that I left him, and Heaven help me, I was glad to be away from him.

∞§[Martin]§∞

"That was rugged," said Edward after a profound silence.

"Not exactly a mistletoe moment," said Jonathan. "Wow, Joel, what was eating you?"

"I knew they forgot something," said Millie, looking around. "Mistletoe!"

"Joel," said Beth, reaching toward him across her brother. "You poor dear! You must be so embarrassed!"

"Beth is right," said Arthur as Pierre silently laid his pages atop the slowly growing stack on the kitchen chair beside the fireplace. "Pierre, I can't imagine what may have been going on in Joel's mind, but do you think it fair to air it out here, in front of us like this?"

"And how," said Edward. "That didn't sound like him at all. Good Heavens, Joel, I'd be chewing my socks if I were—"

"Yoohoo! Fellas!" called Kahlúa from her corner. "You guys is only makin' it worse!"

"Lulu," said Millie. "These guys are *kings* of makin' it worse."

"Oh dear," I heard Monsignor Havermeyer muttering to himself. "Oh dear, oh dear."

"Stop," said Joel, rising to his feet and holding up his hand.
"Everyone stop." He twisted around to gaze at Father Baptist
with fury and disbelief, as if he were somehow to blame, then he
turned and gave Pierre a withering glare.

Meanwhile, the hubbub sputtered to a halt.

"Pierre," said Joel, "I can't imagine why you're doing this to
me. It's mean—meaner than anything Dr. Horehound could
have served up. Not what I'd expect from a Friend. Even if I
did behave like that—which I doubt!—why are you parading it
out in front of everyone I care most about?"

"Hold on there, Joely Moley," said Kahlúa. "Don't go standin'
taller than you are. Just a short while ago you almost hit Good
Times with a chair!"

"You shush now," said Millie with an exaggerated wink.
"This is when we wimmins should keep our yaps shut!"

"Bosh," said Kahlúa. "God gave us yaps to use 'em."

"Please," said Beth, to no one in particular. "Please."

"If you want me to feel like the walls are closing in," said Joel,
his ears burning red, "you're succeeding. It's not fair, Pierre;
and it's not just you. It's everyone here. How can I defend myself against all this?"

Pierre looked wordlessly back at the youngest Tumblar.

"To hear you all tell it," said Joel, his spotlight eyes playing
about the room, "I'm a scoundrel through and through, self-
involved, self-absorbed, sullen, and paranoid to boot. In my
opening chapter I admit harboring a bit of antagonism toward
Pierre. He deserved it, and you all ran with it. Then came your
little digs and barbs, like with the Selwick book in Horehound's
library, Judas and all, none of which I remember from the seminary. Later, Beth says Edward got me tanked on brandy after
that first light thing came after me, which may or might not account for Jonathan's depiction of my behavior in the foyer after
the séance. Even he can't vouch for its accuracy, nor for his description of the thing appearing again and chasing me down the
hallway where I supposedly vanished into thin air. Setting aside
how all this sounds in the first place—the words 'insane' and
'utterly fantastic' come to mind—we're then led on a valiant,

desperate search throughout the lodge, while whatever supposedly happened to me happened, whatever and wherever it was."

"He's makin' it sound as though the whole story is about him," said Millie.

"Shhhh," said Kahlúa.

"Edward takes over," continued Joel, "describing how I was discovered at the scene of a gory crime, and I get hauled off to town by the sheriff. Then, next thing we know, Arthur and Pierre have become his pals, and eventually Pierre has me saying unforgivable things in a jail cell, making me out to be a traitor and an apostate. What a story you all tell; what a heel I am; so bitter and loathsome, so weak in character. Why, if not for your intervention, I would have wound up tangled in Clarice Davenport's ribbons."

"She wasn't wearing any ribbons," said Millie.

"Shhhh," said Kahlúa.

"But there's something glaringly missing," said Joel. "Something Pierre has overlooked."

"What's that?" asked Beth.

Joel stuck out his chin. "*My* account of what happened when I supposedly disappeared, that's what. I may not remember writing it, or the events I described when I did, but surely my side of things should be considered, don't you think?"

"There's nothing I'd like better," said Pierre, "but alas, it can't be done."

"Why not?"

Pierre reached into the chest and produced a thick stack of pages. They looked strangely dark from where I sat, and buckled somehow.

"What's that?" asked Joel.

"Your account," said Pierre. "You took considerably longer than the rest of us to consign your memories to foolscap. I didn't know why until later when it was too late. This evening I asked you to read the sections that I have, not only because they were rich in interest and detail, but because most of what happened to you, from your disappearance on, can't be read—not be me, not by you."

A murmur rumbled through the room.

"Why not?" demanded Joel.

Pierre fluttered the pages for all to see. "Because after you finished you went back and crossed most of it out. See? The beginning of your journal up to here, and this part at the end, you left intact. Everything between, except for a few brief sections, you obliterated. Wait a minute. Here. Here is the page where you wrote halfway down: 'Pierre came to visit me in jail. He had little to say to me, and I to him.' See? Everything above and below is scratched out. You were thorough. Every line, every word, every jot and tiddle crosshatched—scribbled over in black ink with a heavy hand. And here along the side of this page further on, you'll recognize the handwriting: 'Please, God! I don't want to remember!' I didn't go through these memoirs until weeks later, and by then you'd forgotten it all, at least consciously. What happened to you was painful—too painful to bear. You sought to thwart the process of remembering, to render the amnesia permanent, by annihilating your written recollections. But you were marked by these events—we all were—and at some deep level these memories are but sleeping, yearning to be awakened. I suspect this is why you still harbor the antagonism that you do, that infuriated edge that manifests itself now and again."

"Then I'll never know," said Joel, his face ashen.

"The truth will out," said Pierre. "As the medium said, 'Some things are implied, while others are spoken.' Your lone adventure will come to the surface through the revelations of the others."

"Covert power," said Father softly, "not overt power."

"Joel—Everyone," said Pierre, his face serious and his tone more so. "Believe me, if there were any other course, I would gladly have taken it. Indeed, if severing my arm would accomplish the same end, I would gladly lop it off and toast you all with my gushing blood. I thought to edit some of the details from our memoirs—Joel, I could have easily discarded these scratched-out pages—but I knew I could not spare you the painful knowledge of the heartbreak that smears them. *These— things—happened.*" Pierre rapped the antique chest thrice, angrily, almost as if it, more than anyone present, was accountable.

A pin dropped in that room would have been audible as Pierre took a moment to compose himself—and the floor was carpeted. Even the storm outside seemingly took a fifteen-second break until he was ready to continue:

"Father Baptist, Friends: we've all humiliated ourselves at times. No one in this room is exempt from failure, gross errors, horrible blunders, or the commission of deadly sins. We wish we could wipe away the stinging memory of such events, but they remain in our minds regardless. There are two courses we can take: we may walk away wagging our heads, feigning innocence that is not ours to claim; or we can face our mistakes, learn from them, ask God's precious Forgiveness, and move forward."

He wiped a burst of wetness from his cheek with the palm of his hand. "Joel, I love you like the brother I once had, the one who died years before I met any of you. His passing is a bitter memory, as is this one. I tell you I have carried the knowledge of these events every day since they happened. At times they have weighed so heavily upon me, I thought I would collapse. I've given myself to drunken oblivion more than once, but that was a waste of good booze. One terrible night, in a fit of weakness, I thought to end my life; but in the end I knew I could not. I had to seek out another confessor, other than Father Baptist, to rid my soul of the wrongs that I myself committed up at Spirit Lake and in dealing with my memories of Wolfram Lodge. I apologize to you now, Father Baptist, in front of everyone. Even my trust in you, my beloved Father Confessor, faltered: proof that I am not above reproach. Joel, my brother in arms, I swear on all that I hold sacred: if you will but stay with me a while longer, if you will endure the rankling that's eating at your heart and the bitterness that burns your very soul, you will see and understand, and I hope concur as to why I have done this to you and to my fellow Knights."

"You see?" said Kahlúa to Millie. "You done kept your mouth shut, now didn't you?"

"Ah," retorted she, "when Good Times gets a'yapping, there's no way to get a word in edgewise."

That broke the glacier, as it were. A couple of chuckles widened the cracks. They grew in hilarity, until the room resounded with hearty, relieved laughter. In the midst of it, Joel approached Pierre and said something into his ear that made Pierre guffaw with gusto. After some mutual back patting, Joel strode to Father's desk and poured himself another mug of eggnog. When he settled back in his chair, Father leaned forward and said something I did not catch. Joel nodded humbly, helped himself to a long, noisy sip, and clamored, "Well don't just stand there, Arthur. Be a good fellow and get on with it!"

As Arthur did so, Pierre, still trembling, wiped his face with a handkerchief.

∞§[†]§∞

∞§✝§∞

19. What Could Be Amiss At Wolfram Lodge?

∞§[ARTHUR]§∞

I FOUND PIERRE AND SHERIFF BRUMUS side-by-side in a booth way back in the farthest corner at Howler's Café. Pierre's face was flushed, and the sheriff didn't look happy. I slipped into the seat opposite, setting "Old Hob's" gift, a black leather case, beside me. The restaurant had that "back roads retro" feel without ever having been remodeled. It was the real thing, in other words, from the half-horsepower milkshake blenders to the Formica tabletops to the linoleum floors to the sky-blue Naugahyde upholstery to the neon Olympia Beer sign with the perpetual waterfall hanging in the window between red-and-white checkered curtains: "IT'S THE WATER."

"I've been suggesting that we build a communications tower up here for years," the sheriff was saying. "It would help me and the Forest Rangers and other services, but the locals won't have it. Say it'll wreck the scenery."

"Couldn't it be placed in an out-of-the-way spot?" asked Pierre.

"No," said the sheriff as a waitress suddenly appeared and slapped a laminated menu down in front of me. She was gone before he added, "Microwave communication is line-of-sight. It would have to be in plain view."

"Technology versus the scenery," I said, getting in my first word as I scanned the specials. "It's becoming quite a conundrum. Down in our fair city they had similar problems with the placement of cell phone transponders."

"That's right," said Pierre, "until it occurred to Archbishop Fulbright that money was to be made renting a few square yards

of all those Catholic schoolyards he technically owns to the tele-
communication companies. Alas, the only people who know
about it subscribe to the *Artsy*."

"Until those kids start coming down with brain cancer," said
Sheriff Brumus.

"What's yer pleasure?" asked the waitress who had just reap-
peared, scribbling on her pad before I answered.

"Well, on top of a grilled turkey-and-bacon sandwich, cole-
slaw, and a cherry Coke for me," I said hastily, mentally adding
Edward's contribution to what I had in my wallet and finding the
total satisfactory, "I'll want four of these he-man double bacon-
cheeseburger lunches with extra onion rings and chocolate
shakes to go. Don't worry, Sheriff, you aren't expected to cover
those."

"No problem," he said as the waitress snapped up the menu
and scurried on her way. "I kind of feel I owe you. I never
should have let you and your friends go up there. Those preen-
ing minks from the hoity-toity set—who cares? But you guys,
and especially your frisky sister—nope. I should've warned you
that Wolfram Lodge is a bad place."

"We wouldn't have listened," said Pierre and I together.

"Probably not," said the sheriff, turning that over in his mind.
"As it is, until we get things figured out, I'll have to ask you all
to stick around. I'll gladly pay for rooms at Maggie's, rusty water and all."

"Joel wants to go back to the lodge," said Pierre with a shrug.

"I take it your meeting with him didn't' go well," I deduced.

"That's the understatement of the year."

"So, should I go to bat as the good Tumblar?"

"In the mood he's in, I honestly think you'll strike out just as I
did."

"That's too bad," said Sheriff Brumus. "Somehow, I'm not
surprised, though. You friend has the look of someone who's
tangled with something that's beyond him."

"Whatever he's seen," said Pierre, "it's changed him, deep
down—beyond our reach."

"And he wants to go back to the lodge," said the sheriff, shaking his head.

"Well," I said, patting the leather case at my side, "aside from mischievous lights that kidnap your friends and howling creatures that murder fortunetellers, what could be amiss at Wolfram Lodge? Sorry, that wasn't funny."

"No, it wasn't," said the sheriff, folding his big hands on the edge of the table. He turned to Pierre. "You're a reporter, and you feel obliged to finish your story. I understand that. But nothing good will come of it. I don't know what Doc Horehound's up to, whether those lights at the campground, the lodge, and the church are his doing or something else entirely. More to the point, that murdering animal is on the loose, and it's had a taste of human blood."

"'Murder is an insidious thing, Watson,'" said Pierre. "'Once a man has dipped his fingers in blood, sooner or later he'll feel the urge to kill again.'"

I instantly recognized the tenet delivered by Basil Rathbone as Sherlock Holmes to Dr. Watson in *The House of Fear*, so I mimicked Nigel Bruce's erudite response: "'Good gracious me! Very unpleasant! Hmph!'"

"You guys sure like to kid around," said the sheriff.

"It relieves pressure lest we explode," explained Pierre.

"Well, cool it a minute, before *I* explode," said the sheriff.

"Right, sure," said Pierre. "Maybe it's the full moon."

"Unlikely," said the sheriff. "The moon won't be full for two weeks."

"Excuse me?" said Pierre, glancing at me. "I could swear it was full, or nearly so, the night the first of us arrived."

"No way," said the sheriff, shaking his head. "It was new. Folks around here call it a 'dark moon.'"

"You're sure," said Pierre.

"Sure as I'm sitting here," said the sheriff. "Obviously you don't know much about trout fishing. There are several lakes in the area, and these mountains are riddled with streams. Up here folks rely on the moon more than the sun. There's even a 'moon clock' above the tackle counter at Hal's. Check it yourself when we're done here if you don't believe me. Now, as I was about to say, the fact is I can't imagine what's doing these killings. There's nothing native to these mountains that rips and slashes like this thing does, and there isn't a single report of an escaped predator from any zoo or reserve for five hundred miles."

"What about Sasquatch?" asked Pierre. "Dr. Horehound told us that Lenore Poe believes there's a Bigfoot in the area."

"Oh, that," he said with a shrug. "Not as farfetched as it sounds, even from her. The locals say there's something hairy and manlike that's lived in these mountains as long as the town's been here."

"Really," said Pierre. "Not just a deranged hippie from the sixties."

"I thought something like that when I first came here," said the sheriff. "But you eat breakfast in this restaurant every morning and you hear a lot of tales. Many people claim to have seen whatever it is. After a while you begin to wonder. It's never bothered dogs or deer before, though. Some say they've found half-eaten squirrels along the hiking trails, but that could be the work of cats."

"Cats?" I asked.

"Bobcats, mountain lions," said the sheriff. "House cats stay in their houses up here if they want to survive. Come to think of it, some Sasquatch specialist from *National Geographic* came through once and left with a precious baggie of scat he was taking for analysis. Never heard back from him."

"You ever see it?" I asked.

"Naw," said the sheriff. "Not sure I believe it. There used to be an old Indian who lived near the cutoff to Spirit Lake. Died the year after I arrived. Called himself Black Owl. Claimed to be a hundred and fifty summers old. Said he was part Blackfoot and part Flathead, and that his parents fled the advance of the White Man up in Montana when he was a papoose and somehow ended up all the way down here. He swore on a prayer book he claimed once belonged to Fr. Pierre de Smet that 'Man with Hairy Heart' wasn't here when his family arrived, that he or it showed up after the gold rush, and that he or it was the protector of the 'Creatures in the Wilderness'—invisible beings who inhabit the valley to the north of Spirit Lake. You can pick anything out of that mess you want to believe with my blessing. Now, may I get back to the incident this morning?"

"Of course," said Pierre.

Actually, I wanted to pry more into the Sasquatch business, but saw that I was outvoted.

"I'll tell you something that's bugging the heck out of me," said the sheriff. "Your friend didn't just stumble his way onto the murder scene. He left no footprints in the soggy grass other than those he made when I led him away from the body. It was like he was dropped smack dab where we found him from above."

"From what?" I asked. "There weren't any tall trees in that part of the garden, no overhanging branches."

"No catapults that I could see," added Pierre.

"Who knows?" said the sheriff, rubbing his hands together. "Joe Bickers over in Devils Horns has a helicopter—flies tourists over Witches Cauldron, that sort of thing. But I know sure as I'm sitting here he'd never fly in stormy weather, not like we had last night. He's nuts, but he ain't crazy."

"And how would Joel have contacted him, let alone paid him?" I asked. "And why?"

"Excuse me," said Pierre, "but surely the rain washed Joel's footprints away."

"It had stopped raining for at least an hour when Madam Douceur was attacked there on the grass," said the sheriff. "I'm sure of it. Her footprints went out onto the lawn, and the predator's came from the right and knocked her sideways. Mauled her where she landed. Its prints—big, tangled depressions—went back the way it came after the deed was done. Joel came later. From the depth of the impressions, I'd say he landed on his knees and fell forward, unconscious."

"That doesn't make sense," said Pierre.

"No more than you guys going back up there," said the sheriff. Then he looked me in the eyes. "I'd think long and hard about your sister, if I was you. My advice is that you drive back up there for one and only one purpose: to get her the Hell away from there. Gather up your things, make your apologies to Doc Horehound, and hightail it back down here as fast as you can. I'll even go this far: I'll release Joel into your custody, and you can head for home. I'll take heat for it, but that's my problem. How does that sound to you?"

"Like running scared," said Pierre.

"Which we are," said I. "Pierre, if anything happened to Beth, I'd never forgive myself. I say we do what the sheriff suggests."

"I hate to agree," said Pierre, hanging his head low, "but I do."

"I can call your boss and explain the situation," offered the sheriff.

"Kahlúa!" said Pierre with a grimace. "She's got a lot riding on this venture, Sheriff, more than you know. She'll insist that I at least stick around to cover your investigation—"

"Hi, boys, mind if I join you?" interrupted Clarice Davenport, who had snuck up on us unnoticed. I say "snuck up" because we'd have heard her high heels otherwise.

"Sure," said I, picking up Fr. Hobson's black case and setting it on the table so I could slide over. "Hungry?"

"And how," said she. "I get this way when I'm angry."

"What's got you riled up, Miss?" asked the sheriff.

"Would you believe there're no vacancies?" she huffed, pointing in the direction of the motel.

"At Maggie's?" squawked the sheriff. "Unlikely on a Tuesday, with the bad weather besides. These guys are the only tourists in town. There ain't a single car parked in front of her place."

"My thoughts exactly," said Clarice. "But she insists she's all booked up through the weekend. I know Dr. Horehound isn't expecting any more guests this week, so who could it be?"

Pierre cleared his throat. "Has he ever made reservations there for guests who arrive early?"

"Sure, lots of times," said Clarice. "But the next group isn't due till September."

"What're you getting at?" asked the sheriff.

"I wouldn't put it past him," said Pierre. "Dr. Horehound exerting his influence, thwarting Miss Davenport's getaway."

"You know, you're right," said Clarice, slapping the table. "The creep! He knows Maggie from way back. He knows most of the people in Claw Junction."

"I thought he was a recluse," said I.

"Hardly," said she. "He was born here."

"In Claw Junction?" I asked, surprised.

"He didn't tell you?" asked Clarice, gracing us with a conspiratorial smile. "Once upon a time, Elmer and Annabelle Hammerhound ran a candle shop here in town. Their waxen wares were actually very popular hereabouts. Tourists bought them, too. But in the evenings, when the CLOSED sign went up in the window, the store became a sort of clandestine witching parlor. They were Wiccan, you see, and candles played a big part in their rituals. I don't know all the details, but their son, Mortimer, considered the whole thing rather embarrassing. When he came of age he upscaled his name and charged 'down to the flatlands' in search of fame and fortune."

"Out of the cauldron and into the fire," said Pierre. "From Hammerhound to Horehound. I can imagine him scrubbing invisible wax from under his fingernails every morning before whitening his teeth. This could account for his attitude toward religion."

"Condescension pickled with fascination," said I.

"Stir with curried green weaver ants, garnish with mole crickets," said Pierre, rubbing his palms together, "and you have the very recipe for obsession."

"Green weaver ants?" asked the sheriff.

"You don't want to know," said Pierre.

"Dr. Horehound's parents died in a cabin fire while he was writing his book on Navaho witches," said Clarice. "They're called 'skinwalkers,' among other things. I gather he didn't come back for the funeral. Didn't even make any inquiries. The candle shop sat there unattended while the inventory gradually 'disappeared.' The locals were surprised when he returned to Claw Junction some years later, rich and retired. They probably regarded his purchase of Wolfram Lodge as an omen—good or bad, you'll have to ask them."

"Strange," said the sheriff. "I'm not what you'd call an insider, but I hear things. Some families around here go back a hundred years. Their grandpas and grandmas worked for Bartholomew Piaget. Carpenters and craftsmen came to build the place, then stayed to maintain it. I've heard some of them practiced witchcraft."

"Dr. Horehound's great-grandfather was one of them," said Clarice. "Jasper Hammerhound. I think he was a plumber by day, and a warlock by night."

"You don't say," said Pierre. "You know, that's interesting. Piaget came here from Summerland, a seaside town built by mystics and psychics. They raised a ruckus when oil was discovered and derricks started cluttering the beaches, and there was Bartholomew Piaget with the mineral rights in his pocket. I wonder if the people who came to build the lodge were from Summerland, too."

"I'm pretty sure Jasper Hammerhound and his wife came from Massachusetts," said Clarice.

"Wouldn't know," said Sheriff Brumus. "Now Piaget's wife, the one who drowned in the lake: rumor has it she ran some sort of coven. Held rituals in that garden of hers—danced around bonfires, that sort of mumbo-jumbo."

"That I hadn't heard," said Clarice. "But I'm not surprised."

"Just how did you get mixed up with Dr. Horehound, Miss Davenport?" asked Pierre. "And where did he pick up characters like Grayburn and Thorndale?"

"And Madam Douceur," I added.

"Those three were entrenched in his innermost circle long before I came aboard," said Clarice. I was relieved that she had jettisoned her contrived, vampish behavior and adopted a more serious, businesslike tone. "I only know what they told me, and you've seen how open and sharing they can be. When I answered Dr. Horehound's ad for a personal secretary, he had just announced his retirement from his practice in Beverly Hills. He had books to write, and I was going to assist him in gathering data and collating his findings. The first order of business was the move to the lodge, and that was an exhaustive undertaking. It was only after the dust settled that he announced his strategy for the reenactments. It was Elaineileen's idea, actually, but he beefed it up and made it his own."

"Strange," said Pierre, "a man of Horehound's cynical predilections associating with a trance medium."

"Oh, it was more than a tangential relationship," said Clarice. "Not romantic—far from it—but they were tangled up somehow, deep beneath the surface—some sort of morbid codependence. Listen to me: I've been around him too long. But if there's a name for their syndrome, I'll bet Dr. Horehound made it up and registered it as soon as he'd diagnosed himself. In front of the guests, he treated her offhandedly, sometimes downright insultingly, and she took it like a diminutive toady—but only in front of the guests. Once they were alone, she became his equal—no, more than his equal. More like his tutor, or mentor, even. It was creepy to watch, let me tell you. Very creepy."

"Maybe she had something on him," said the sheriff. "Come to think of it, he didn't seem all that broken up when I told him she'd been mauled to death."

"It gets weirder," said Clarice, leaning forward on her elbows. "Last February, shortly after the January 31st reenactment, Dr. Horehound had a heart attack. It was mild, or so Dr. Langanhan assured him. It had been a really wild séance—freaky noises, ghostly sobbing emanating from under the table, even a terrifying howl when the Death card was revealed."

"You think maybe the guests had a hand in that?" asked the sheriff.

"Not likely," said Clarice. "They were just some little old ladies from Palm Springs. Called themselves 'The Blue Light Society.' They packed up and tore out of there the next morning. Elaineileen was very grim afterwards, and she and Dr. Horehound spent hours pondering the implications in the library. That's when he started getting chest pains. The pills Dr. Langanhan prescribed helped, but soon afterwards Dr. Horehound summoned Geronimo 'Fine Print' McAllister, his attorney, up to the lodge to draft a will."

"You don't say," said Pierre.

"I was called in to witness the documents," said Clarice.

"Documents, plural?" asked the sheriff.

"He appointed Madam Douceur executrix and primary beneficiary," explained Clarice. "He also gave her emergency and medical power of attorney should he become incapacitated."

"Tangled up indeed," said Pierre. "And not so deep beneath the surface."

"Doesn't he have any relatives?" asked the sheriff.

"Apparently not," said Clarice. "At least, none that he cared to leave anything to."

"But now Mrs. Douceur is out of the picture," said the sheriff.

"Yes," I said. "So who's next in line?"

"Thorndale," said Clarice, making a quizzical face.

"The housekeeper," said Sheriff Brumus, rolling his eyes. "Don't that beat all."

"Why not Grayburn?" asked Pierre.

"That I can't tell you," said Clarice. "After the will business, Dr. Horehound threw himself into his research with renewed vigor, ordering books from antiquarians, poring over them in the library, filling reams of paper with his handwritten notes late into the night. The strange thing is that there really hasn't been that much for me to do other than organize the guest lists and write my impressions after the séances. I haven't been asked to type or edit anything. Whatever he's working on, he's been keeping it secret—not just from me, but from Elaineileen as well."

"Forgive my candor," said Pierre, "but obviously you and Madam Douceur didn't get along. If he was under her influence, why did he keep you in the picture?"

"Influence, yes," said Clarice, "but not control. Dr. Horehound was always in charge. He holds the purse strings, don't forget, and he thrives on tension. Look at his household: Grayburn and Thorndale, a couple of grouches. Add me and Elaineileen and, with his constant goading, it's a veritable feeding frenzy of angst. The last six months have been especially awful, which is why I don't mind bailing. Big as Wolfram Lodge may be, it's become claustrophobic. Dr. Horehound's obsession permeates the place."

"Arthur," interrupted Pierre. "You look perturbed. Is something wrong?"

"I thought I remembered something," I said. "Something about those word fragments Beth found in the garden."

"Do tell," urged Pierre.

"Can't," I said, shaking my head. "Just a notion. When we get back to the lodge I'm going to check out something in the library."

"You're not going back up there!" said Clarice.

"Just to fetch our companions," said Pierre.

"Don't worry," I said. "We'll pick you up on our way back to Los Angeles."

"That'll take a while," said Clarice. "What'll I do till then?"

"You're welcome to stay in my office," said the sheriff. "It ain't much—just some empty cells and a broken coffeemaker— but no one will bother you there. Heck, no one ever drops by. You can lock the front door till these fellers come for you."

"What about you?" asked Clarice, reaching out to him. "Won't you be there? I don't want to be alone—not in this town, not now!"

"'Fraid I got work to do," said the sheriff.

"What about Fr. Hobson?" I suggested. "You could stay in the church."

"I'm not Catholic," said Clarice. "I'm not exactly—you know. Think he'd mind?"

"Can't speak for him," said the sheriff. "But he's a good man, and considering the circs, I'd say it's probably the safest place for miles."

"Speaking of Fr. Hobson," said Pierre, "what's that you got there, Arthur? It looks like a sick call kit."

"That it is," I said, taking up the black case. "You might call it a survival pack. Holy water, blessed salt, even some chrism. He didn't want me to return to the lodge unprotected."

"And the medallion?" asked Pierre. "Did he bless it?"

"Blessed it," I said, patting my shirt pocket. "Even exorcised it—twice—just to be sure, considering where it's been."

"You guys talk like Dr. Horehound," said Clarice, incredulously. "More so Madam Douceur."

"Exactly the opposite," said Pierre. "But sometimes you fight fire with fire."

"It gets better," I said, retrieving something from one of my overall pockets. "For reasons I can't fathom, Fr. Hobson gave me something utterly exquisite and precious. He came upon it at a parish swap meet in San Bernardino, of all places. He didn't know its story, but I suspect it dates back to the time of religious persecution in England under Henry VIII."

"It looks like a pocket watch," said the sheriff.

"It's supposed to," I said, savoring the moment.

"Beautiful craftsmanship," said the Pierre.

"More than you realize," I said, pressing the catch that opened the tarnished glass cover. "Now, notice it only has an hour hand. That's an indication of its age. It's how they made them back then. It's set at three o'clock."

"Does it still work?" asked Clarice.

"Not like you think," I said. "Now watch closely. Three o'clock is a significant time for all Christians, being the hour Christ died on the Cross. I'm turning it backwards, slowly, carefully, until we get to twelve noon when His Crucifixion commenced, at which point—"

The back of the watch popped open.

"A compartment inside," exclaimed Clarice. "So shiny. It looks like it's lined with gold."

"Precisely," I said. "Miss Davenport, this is actually a pyx."

"A what?"

"A vessel for transporting the Blessed Sacrament," said Pierre, eyes wide. "As when a priest visits the sick or infirm. Normally it would be gold outside as well as within, and it wouldn't be disguised as a timepiece, but in a time of persecution—"

"A priest could safely carry a Consecrated Host in this device without fear of discovery," I said. "Father Hobson, lacking the means to verify its origin, couldn't be sure if it was ever used for that purpose, although the function is obvious."

"But why would he give that to you?" asked the sheriff, his eyes also wide.

"For this," I said, digging the Nordic medallion out of my shirt pocket. I carefully placed it inside the gold-lined receptacle. "See? It fits exactly." I snapped the watch shut, the medal safe and snug within.

"Incredible," said Pierre.

"He gave an heirloom like that to you," said Clarice, "a perfect stranger?"

"He said he had no one to leave it to," I answered, resetting the hand to three o'clock before slipping it into my pocket. "And he had a strange feeling that it would soon prove useful to me. Go figure."

"Well, I'd say you're well-armed," said Pierre, giving me an appreciative look. "As soon as you're done feasting, let's run Miss Davenport up to St. Arnold's. I think I'd like a word with Fr. Hobson myself before we trot up to the lodge."

"Some quick questions, first, if I may," I said, tossing down my napkin. Somewhere in the midst of our conversation the waitress had delivered my sandwich and drink, and I had consumed them. But I didn't remember doing so. "Miss Davenport, does Dr. Horehound own a car? Ours have been the only vehicles parked in front of the lodge. Surely he must have some means of transportation. Thorndale mentioned coming to town to shop."

"He's got a Range Rover and a Hummer," she answered. "Keeps them in a garage around the back."

"I've seen no separate garage," said Pierre.

"That's because it's not separate," said Clarice. "It's built into the southeast corner of the building. Is it important?"

"No, probably not," I said. "Just wondering. I'm also curious about the elevator that goes up to the ballroom."

"You know about that?" she asked, smiling approvingly.

"Just that I couldn't get the doors to open up there," said Pierre.

"And I haven't seen how to access it from the lower floors," I said.

"I don't think it works," said Clarice. "On the ground floor you reach the elevator by going down a seemingly endless zig-zagging hallway off the dining room, opposite the kitchen. It goes behind the séance room, and ends up in the southeast corner. Imagine making guests trundle so far out of their way to get to an elevator, and it doesn't even stop on the second floor where their bedrooms are. It's one of the few things that wasn't well-thought-out in the design of the place."

"Does it go down to the basement?" asked Pierre.

She rolled her eyes and shrugged. "I really don't remember. It's never been high on my 'things I gotta do' list."

"How does it run?" I asked, nonetheless. "I mean, what kind of motor—do you know?"

"Now that you mention it," she answered, "there's some sort of enclosed engine in the corner of the garage. I think it has something to do with the lift. It was originally steam-powered, I think—wood-burning—but Dr. Horehound upgraded it to propane."

"An electrical generator?" I asked. "Apart from the electrical lines under the bridge?"

"Well, there's also that science project up in the tower," she said. "It takes more current—or maybe it's a different kind than the municipal lines deliver."

"You mean the Tesla coil," I said.

"The doctor's favorite toy, said Clarice.

"Old as it is," said Pierre, "it's certainly in working order from what I've seen."

"Like Madam Douceur told you," she replied, "Dr. Horehound brings up a repairman every six months to keep it running. Parts are impossible to find. The guy actually has to make them himself."

"It does make sense," I said as the pieces fell into place in my mind. "A dependable 'kill switch' would require its own power source in case a power line went down."

"All very interesting, Arthur," said Pierre. "Why are you asking about it?"

"One last thing and I'm done," I said, not sure myself why I'd brought these things up, but I was groping my way toward something I considered important. "Miss Davenport, those paintings in the séance room, the depictions of certain Tarot cards. They weren't part of the Piaget estate, were they?"

"How did you know?" she asked, smiling. "Dr. Horehound bought them from an esoteric art dealer in London—had them shipped here shortly after he moved in. Why?"

"Where's that waitress?" I said, glancing at my watch. "Sorry, but I'm anxious to get my sister away from that accursed lodge.

I'll explain when we pick you up on the way down to Los Angeles."

"Fair enough," said she. "Maybe I'll buy you a drink when we get to the Big Nowhere."

∞§[Martin]§∞

"So what do you suppose is so important about the paintings?" asked Edward.

"Yes, and those other details," said Jonathan. "Elevators, generators, and Tesla coils. What was Sherlock von Derschmidt on to?"

"I wish I knew," said Arthur, turning a page. "There's a little more here."

"Don't let us stop you," said Jonathan.

∞§[Arthur]§∞

Not long afterwards, having left Clarice Davenport in Fr. Hobson's care, I was maneuvering up the muddy road between the turnoff to Devils Horns and the lodge. Pierre was riding shotgun, humming an Irish folk tune, while Joel was slouched in the backseat, mumbling to himself. At one point I had to squeeze by a large black van coming in the opposite direction, likely the coroner transporting the body of Madam Douceur to town. All I could think of was getting Beth away from Spirit Lake as soon as possible.

About halfway there I saw a dark, indistinct figure up ahead. It was standing by the right side of the road where an unpaved driveway wandered off among the trees. As we drew closer it resolved into a woman all in black, with a diamond-stitched shawl wrapped tightly around her slender form. At first when she raised her hand I thought she was just waving to be polite, but then she stepped right in front of us so I had to stop. I rolled down my window as she came around to my side of the car. Her skin was pale, strikingly so, but not pallid or sickly—more like sweet cream or newly fallen snow. She looked at me with deep-set, forlorn eyes, and inquired without introduction:

"Did you find the diary?"

"Excuse me?" I asked.

"Madam Ouspenskaya's journal," she said. "I left it in the nightstand drawer."

"Why, yes," I said. "How did you—? Say, were you the woman in the bookstore?"

"Lenore Poe," she said, smiling surreptitiously. "My great-grandmother worked for Bartholomew Piaget. She was his housemaid."

"Was she there that night in 1896?" asked Pierre excitedly. "The séance? Did she know what happened to him?"

"Yes," she said, "but you wouldn't believe me."

"I'm beginning to think I have an incredulous face," said Pierre, glancing over his shoulder at Joel.

"Pardon me?" she asked.

"Never mind," said Pierre, settling back in his seat. "It's not worth explaining."

"The diary, sir," she said to me firmly. "Have you read it?"

"The first few pages," I said. "It looked intriguing, but there have been quite a few distractions—"

"Oh, but you must finish it!" she said, letting her shawl slip as she gripped the window frame. "It is important that you learn the truth!"

"Do you work for Dr. Horehound?" I asked, my suspicions piqued.

"No, not for him," she said, pulling back a little. "He orders books through my store. I deliver them. That is all." She let go of the door and gathered her shawl, shivering. "I know Wolfram Lodge well. My mother used to take me there when it was vacant. She let me play inside while she visited the garden."

"That's one heck of a playhouse," mused Pierre.

"The garden," I said warily, thinking of Gabriella Piaget's alleged activities there.

"But that is not important," she stammered, her eyes going wider still. "I am not like my mother, if that's what you're thinking."

"I'm not sure what I'm thinking," I said.

"I delivered a shipment to Dr. Horehound last week," she said. "Wicked tomes all the way from a dealer in Luxembourg. I should have burned them, told him they were lost in transit, but I knew you were coming."

"How did you know about us?" I asked.

"That isn't important," she said. "I needed an excuse to get inside the lodge. I left him gloating over those vile books in his library—yellowed pages stained with evil incantations. He says he is a skeptic, but he believes. More than my grandmother, he believes. I shudder to think what he intends to do with the knowledge they contain. Madam Douceur wasn't around, Grayburn was outside trimming hedges, and Thorndale was making noises in the kitchen. So I slipped upstairs and left the diary where you would find it."

"Me, personally?" I asked incredulously.

"I can't explain," she said. "The time of reckoning is coming. I sensed a different sort of guests were due to arrive—you men, and the young lady. You are unlike any who have come before, no?"

"I suppose," I said.

"It goes without saying," said Pierre, at the same time.

"The diary," she said, leaning close again. "Madam Ouspenskaya was evil, her heart more withered even than that crook, Piaget. She came to get revenge."

"But she was murdered," said Joel from the backseat. "Sounds like she botched it to me."

"It is the way with malevolent spells," said Lenore Poe. "Malice is hard to control. Once sent out on a vile purpose, it has a nasty way of coming back upon the sender. My mother and grandmother taught me this."

"But you're not like them," said Pierre flatly.

"They taught me too well," she said. "I've made my own choices."

"So Madam Ouspenskaya sought to harm Mr. Piaget?" I asked.

"She succeeded," said she. "More than she could have fore-seen, and the evil she loosed retaliated."

"Hold on, guys," said Joel, waving his hands derisively. "Lenore Poe. Dr. Horehound told us about her. She's the one who believes in Bigfoot, remember?"

"Ah," she said. "The doctor has poisoned you against me? I should have foreseen this."

"Got smudges on your crystal ball?" snorted Joel. "Window cleaner might help."

"Your companion," she said, nodding toward the backseat. "He is not like you."

"Apparently not," sighed Pierre. "Not anymore."

"Not at all," agreed Joel.

"Do you?" I asked. "Believe in Sasquatch?"

"Believe?" she said, shaking her head. "I have seen, so I know. But this isn't about Sasquatch. The Indians call him 'Beast Who Leaves No Trace.' He and his kin withdrew from this area when came 'Man with Hairy Heart.' It is he who has been stalking the valley around Spirit Lake since my great-grandmother's day."

"You're saying he's responsible for the recent killings?" asked Pierre. "This 'Man with Hairy Heart'?"

She shook her head vehemently, and then said, "I tried to warn Dr. Horehound when he first arrived. I did not realize the caliber of the man. I was foolish. Have I been also foolish with you?"

"I should hope not," I said. "Sheriff Brumus told us about your dogs. Do I understand correctly that you don't believe 'Man with Hairy Heart' is responsible?"

"'Man with Hairy Heart' does not maul and leave his prey for the scavengers," she said disgustedly. "He kills for food. When he brings down a deer, he breaks the neck, then hauls it up into a tree to feed."

"He must be awfully strong to do that," said Pierre.

"You've seen it do this," said Joel. It wasn't a question. It was a sarcastic remark.

"No," she said. "But I've seen eagles and crows tearing at pelts hanging in branches thirty feet up in the air. The thing that killed my dogs tore them to pieces and left them scattered on the ground. That was not 'Man with Hairy Heart.'"

"Then who or what killed your dogs?" I asked. "And the buck at the grocer's place?"

"If Black Owl was alive," she said, "I think he would have called him—"

"Don't tell me," said Joel, closing his eyes and pinching the bridge of his nose as if he was experiencing a moment of deep inspiration. "Ah, I have it: 'Dances with Wolves'!" When he opened his eyes he found that no one was amused.

"No," said Lenore Poe. "Black Owl would have called him 'Man with Wolf's Heart and No Soul.'" She turned her gaze to the stranger in the backseat and added, "Much like you."

"Sure, sure, sure," said Joel, taken aback but acting dismissive.

"You knew Black Owl?" asked Pierre.

"He was my godfather," said Lenore, returning her attention to Pierre and me. "My mother chose him because she thought he was a pagan shaman. She didn't realize his true heart."

"Of course," said Pierre. "The prayer book. Pierre de Smet was a Catholic missionary."

"You know this," said Lenore, smiling for the first time. "That is good."

"I'm confused," I said. "You're saying 'Man with Hairy Heart' is not a Sasquatch, and now something else, something worse, has come to Spirit Lake?"

"Read the diary," she said. "I will say no more."

"Please," I said. "You can't just leave it like that."

"If you are the ones," she said, "you will find out soon enough. If you're not, then bring the diary to me when you leave. Please, it is more important than words can convey."

"But if you'd only—" I began.

"Go!" she said, pulling back from the car. "I have said and done all I can!" With that, she ran gracefully across the road and up the driveway. A moment later we heard the start of a high-torque engine and the growl of deep-tread tires in the mud.

"What do you make of that?" I asked as I put my car in gear.

"A load of hooey," said Joel, slumping down in the back.

"I'm not so sure," said Pierre.

∞§[Martin]§∞

"Good Heavens," said Jonathan. "This just gets weirder and weirder."

"You've no idea," said Pierre, accepting Arthur's pages and setting them on the growing pile on the chair.

"I wonder if Sheriff Brumus wasn't the only Anglo to visit St. Arnold's," said Arthur. "Perhaps, fearing her neighbors, Lenore Poe kept her conversion secret."

"I don't know about this 'Man with Hairy Heart,'" said Monsignor Havermeyer. "He sure sounds a lot like Sasquatch, though, carrying his prey up into the trees."

"Oh no," said Edward. "Monsignor! Are you a Bigfoot authority?"

"I had a lot of time to read at St. Philip's," admitted our beloved monsignor sheepishly, "and I ministered to a lot of people who had way too much time on their hands."

"But so close to L.A.?" asked Jonathan. "I thought Bigfoot was more of an up-north phenomenon—if that's what you call it."

"As I understand it," said Havermeyer, "Sasquatch has been sighted all over the San Gabriel Mountains, from Santa Paula to Apple Valley. The Gabriellino Indians have a name for him, which I forget at the moment. But I suggest we not get sidetracked."

"Well said," said Pierre, lifting the next installment from the antique chest. "Edward, front and center."

"Just when I thought I was safe," said Edward, rising to the task. "But I'm beginning to see that the word didn't apply to any of us at Spirit Lake."

∞§[†]§∞

∞§ ✝ §∞

20. The Bolts, the Brackets, the Hoses, Even the Protruding Dipstick*

∞§[Edward]§∞

THE FISH AND WILDLIFE GUYS HAD LEFT while we were on our errand, and a fidgety coroner named Langanhan had driven off with Madam Douceur's body twenty minutes earlier. We were waiting on the front steps when Arthur pulled his station wagon to a gravel-scattering halt in front of the lodge. Dark clouds were rolling in for another tempest, and the air was humid and heavy. Beth was seated on the swinging bench, sewing kit at her side, deftly "letting out" her brother's vest—whatever that meant. Jonathan was reading a pocket New Testament he'd brought from home, and I was looking through a moldy book I'd borrowed from the library—I'm not entirely sure why. The title was in Latin, but the subtitle on the front and the text within were in English. It was a photoengraved edition of a manuscript in the British Museum, the original of which had been handwritten in the seventeenth century, according to the editor's preface. The print was cramped and almost illegible, the spelling and grammar archaic, but the diagrams were interesting in a morbid sort of way. (I'll get back to that in a minute.) We had all found diversions on the porch because none of us wanted to spend another minute inside the house. In fact, we were building our

---

* There was a heated argument over the title for this segment. The alternate suggestion was "Haven't Some Sort of Fundamental Laws of the Universe Been Violated or Something?" I voted to use both with the word "or" between them. That would have taken up half the page. Edward won because it's his chapter. —M.F.

courage to tell Pierre that we'd decided to pull up stakes and head for home.

"What ho!" said Pierre, emerging from the station wagon as the engine wheezed and sputtered and finally stalled. "Seems we're expected."

"Why the long faces?" asked Arthur, heaving himself from behind the wheel.

"The hours have been so empty without you," I joked, setting the book down as I got up from a wooden patio chair.

"Joel!" yelped Beth, dropping her sewing and leaping from the swing. It squeaked and groaned as she left it swaying behind her. "You're back!"

Joel didn't look happy as he extricated himself from the car. He rolled his eyes impatiently as Beth hugged him and hugged him again.

"Come and get it!" announced Arthur, retrieving a stack of Styrofoam containers from the trunk. "Hamburgers! Joel had his along the way. The rest are probably a bit on the cold and soggy side by now, but—"

"A feast nonetheless!" said I, thinking this was miles above yesterday's repast.

"Together again at last," said Jonathan, clumping down the stairs and clasping Pierre's hand. "We were beginning to wonder."

"Wonder no more," said Pierre, returning his grip. "Was your excursion to the campground successful? I assume no one stole the tent in our absence."

"Didn't get that far," I explained. "The road is washed out halfway there. Didn't want to risk getting the Wyndhamwagon stuck in the gully. I'll just have to pay for the damn thing, but it's a small price—well, not a small price—but what the hey, as Mr. Feeney would say."

"One for all and all for all that," said Pierre. "We'll all pitch in, of course. Maybe we'll throw a benefit to help cover the cost."

"Sure," I said. "Sure thing. Uh, Pierre—"

"Don't look so glum," said Pierre. "I've got good news. At the sheriff's suggestion, we're going to skip this joint."

"You mean we're leaving?" I asked, relieved and elated.

"You're joking," said Jonathan. "I would have thought, what with Kahlúa's expenses and all—"

"She'll understand," said Pierre. "She'll have to. And if not—again, what the hey—there are other subversive rags to write for!"

"I'm staying," said Joel, so quietly we almost didn't hear him.

"What's that?" asked Beth.

"I said I'm staying," said Joel sullenly. "You all go on. I'll be okay."

"You're not serious," said Jonathan. "What would you do up here?"

"Miss Davenport quit, apparently," said Joel. "Maybe Dr. Horehound will need a new assistant."

As if agreeing with our collective reaction to this, thunder rumbled across the lake.

"Listen," said Beth. "We took the liberty of packing your things. Your bags are just inside the front door."

"Aha," said Pierre. "I see the decision was already unanimous. Have you told our host?"

"He's fuming in the library," said Beth.

"Said it's not the first time," said Jonathan, "but he thought we, at least, would see the thing through. Shows you what he knows."

A bolt of lightning arced from cloud to cloud over our heads.

"Joel," said Arthur over the stack of grease-soaked he-man lunches in his arms. "I do wish you'd reconsider. If we're going to leave, we'd best do so quickly. The storm is upon us. I, for one, don't want to desert you, not after—you know—what happened to you last night, and out in the garden."

"I wasn't hurt, was I?" said Joel defiantly. "I'm in one piece, unlike the rest of you. I say be on your way."

"What's gotten into you?" said Beth, stomping her foot on the gravel. "We can't just go off without you. We're your—"

Her last word was cut off by a sudden flash of light—not lightning, this time. Another ball of crimson light suddenly appeared over our heads, buzzing and snapping like a bug zapper with the amperage turned all the way up.

"Oh no," I said, ducking.

We all crouched and clambered up the steps—all except Joel. He just stood there, considering the orb as rain started to pelt the gravel around his feet.

"Joel!" yelled Beth. "What are you doing?"

"I'll be all right," said Joel, calmly. "I'm not afraid—not this time."

"Look out!" cried Pierre as the orb started moving.

It began circling, spiraling down in widening arcs until it was buzzing around Joel in fast, crackling swoops. Around and around it went, quickening its pace, wisps of red fire trailing behind.

"What's it doing?" I asked.

"Don't move!" said Arthur to Joel, but he was slowly raising his hands, as if in welcome. It's the first time I'd seen him smile the whole trip. Joel wasn't just grinning, he was positively beaming!

"I don't like this," said Pierre. "But what can we—?"

Suddenly the sphere broke from its orbit and whizzed—not at Joel, not at us—but straight for the grill of Arthur's station wagon. It struck with a violent retort, splattering the hood and bumper with liquid fire.

"Hey!" said Arthur, dumping the lunches into a patio chair and charging down the steps. "Not my car!"

The flames sputtered out quickly, leaving dark, bubbled burns in the paint and chrome. We all rushed past Joel, who hadn't moved, and gathered around Arthur as he found the catch and heaved the hood open.

"Good Heavens!" said Pierre with a gasp.

"This can't be!" said Arthur, bewildered.

"I—I don't understand," said Beth.

"It—" was all I managed to say.

The engine was intact. I knew it well because I'd helped Arthur replace the fan belts and sparkplugs a couple of days before our trip up the mountain. I had suggested that he get it steam-cleaned one of these days soon. But now there wasn't a trace of grease or grime. There also wasn't a trace of metal in the engine compartment. The air filter, the engine block, the distributor with its curled cables, the radiator, the fan, even the belts we had lately installed—all had been changed, completely transformed—God knew how! I stared, speechless, my eyes tracing the swirls and spirals of the grain throughout the useless machinery. The bolts, the brackets, the hoses, even the protruding dipstick—every moving and unmoving part was now made of finely crafted, intricately detailed, deftly polished *pinewood!*

Wood, being porous unlike steel, was not suited for holding pressurized oil and hot water, which had remained unchanged within the transformed engine. The stuff began leaking between the seams and gaskets, hissing out the bottom of the radiator, dripping and slopping onto the gravel beneath the car.

Baffled, I glanced at Joel, who was still standing in the same spot. His smile had slipped somewhat. In fact, he was glaring, surprised at his empty hands, as though he had figured to catch something, but it had slipped past. He had the look of someone who had goofed, misunderstood, or clearly missed the boat. As our eyes met, he did a quick transformation of his own—from a lost child to an aloof, snobby snot—and glanced away.

"How?" said Jonathan. "The operating word here is *how?*"

"Haven't some sort of—you know—fundamental laws of the universe been—you know—violated or something?" asked Beth.

"As you say, Sis," said Arthur. "We are witnessing the impossible."

"I say, Arthur," said Pierre. "This puts something of a crimp in our plans to—"

But his sentence was hacked by another round of crackling buzzing and whooshing, this time culminating in a dreadful, viscous splat against the front of my van. I didn't have to turn to see the flames dripping away from the grill to know that my engine, too, had just been rendered useless. A moment later oil and boiling water began sputtering out the bottom and splattering underneath.

"That does it," I said, sighing dejectedly.

"Who would have thought?" said Jonathan, dazed. "Who will believe us?"

"Oh, Sis," said Arthur, engulfing her in his brotherly arms. "Oh, dear Sis."

"What are we going to do?" asked Beth, burying her face in his chest.

"I'd say we're going to unpack," said Joel with an air of maddening condescension.

∞§[Martin]§∞

"I say Edward, old Bean," said Jonathan, as Edward handed Pierre the pages in a daze. "There's bad, worse, worst, and then what?"

"I can't imagine," said Arthur, turning to look at Father Baptist. "What in Heaven's name were we up against?"

"Don't look at me," said Father. "But please, let's not waste time speculating. Pierre, who's up next?"

"Dear Beth," said Pierre. "Your description of what came next was the most complete."

"So sue me," she said, taking her pages begrudgingly. "Pierre, I'm really not sure I want to go on with this."

"Do you want me to read them for you?" asked Arthur.

"Not on your life," she said, clutching her pages close to her. "Whatever I wrote, I guess I'd better be the one to read it. But I'm not happy about it."

∞§[†]§∞

∞§✝§∞

21. Will Someone Please Help Me Screw My Head Back On?

∞§[*Beth*]§∞

"SO YOU WON'T BE FORSAKING my hospitality after all," said Dr. Horehound after a long, ponderous drag on his infernal black cigarette.

"It would be a nasty hike back to town even if we were properly rigged for it," said Edward, assessing the downpour through the window. He still had that book, with the bilingual title he'd been perusing, under his arm. He added unconvincingly, "I reckon it might be worth a try."

"I'd be up for it," said Jonathan, gripping the edge of the mantel, "but there's that creature to consider."

"Right," said Pierre around the pipe in his mouth. "We saw what it did to Madam Douceur."

She's covered with blood! So much blood!

Joel shifted in his chair but said nothing. He looked like someone confidently waiting ...

∞§[**Martin**]§∞

Beth crinkled her nose.

"What is it, Sis?" asked Arthur.

"Joel didn't say that," she answered, scrutinizing her words on the page. "Not if he said nothing."

"You mean about the blood?" asked Joel. "So much of it?"

Beth nodded.

"Double asterisks, Honey?" asked Kahlúa. "Like the time before?"

"*It was HUGE!*" quoted Millie, mysteriously with a touch of whimsy.

Beth nodded again.

"Another one of those memory flashes?" asked Jonathan.

"Memory of what?" asked Arthur, his tone conveying a sense of expectation.

"If I didn't say it, who did?" asked Joel.

"I'm not sure," said Beth. "I can almost ... No, I don't ... Oh, drat."

"That's okay, Sis," said Arthur gently. "Don't worry about it."

"Right, sure," said Pierre, exchanging a knowing glance with Arthur. "For the nonce, Beth, I suggest you continue."

Beth tilted her head at an odd angle, took a breath, and did.

∞§[*Beth*]§∞

Joel shifted in his chair but said nothing. He looked like someone confidently waiting in a station after the ticketer has assured him his train is on time. He was slowly rotating a shiny coin in the palm of his hand.

"If only the phone wasn't out, we could call Sheriff Brumus," I said, sitting by the Tiffany lamp, my brother's vest crumpled in my lap. "First the lights, then the phone."

"Now the cars," said Edward. "We're cut off."

"I can't believe this has happened," said Big Brudder Art, squeezing my shoulder as he hovered protectively over me. "Sis, we were so close to being away from here."

"What? Leave? I wouldn't hear of it," said Dr. Horehound, blinking and nodding as if he'd just become aware of us all over again. "It isn't unheard of for my guests to experience a temporary, shall we say, 'lapse of resolve' after the first night's activities, and more so upon the discovery of the body in the garden the following morning. I expected more of you people."

"What they usually find is a wax dummy, not Madam Douceur torn to shreds," said Jonathan, who had released the mantel in favor of hovering close by lest Arthur tire of overprotecting me and needed to be spelled.

"Or have one of their friends chased by some fiery sphere, only to disappear," said I, wringing Arthur's vest in my hands.

"Or have they?" asked Pierre, glaring at Joel, who did not return his stare.

"Excuse me, Monsieur Bontemps?" said Dr. Horehound drowsily.

"'The adroit magician distracts his mark's attention elsewhere,'" said Pierre, quoting himself—very convincingly, I might add. "Doctor, are those balls of light your doing?"

"Even if they were," said our patronizing host, "do you think I'd spoil everything by telling you?"

"Then they *are* some sort of trick!" said Edward, shifting the book from the crook of one arm to the other.

"I couldn't say," said Dr. Horehound.

"Couldn't or wouldn't?" demanded Arthur, gripping me tightly on the last word.

"It amounts to the same thing, doesn't it?" said Dr. Horehound offhandedly. "At least, as far as you're concerned."

"This is growing tedious," sighed Arthur, relaxing his hand.

"I will admit this," said Dr. Horehound, crushing out his spent cigarette in the ashtray. He must have jabbed that poor thing a dozen times before he let it topple over, expired. "If you think me capable of replacing two car engines with perfect wooden facsimiles, without pulleys or winches or whatever auto mechanics would use to hoist the originals out and the fakes in, this without disturbing the gasoline, oil, and water they contain, and all before your very eyes—let alone meticulously carving these veritable works of art in the first place—then I'd say you have an inflated notion of my talents. Maybe I should have pursued another career entirely."

"You seem pretty calm about the whole thing," said I, so wanting to stuff Arthur's vest down his condescending throat—except I'd hate to ruin the material.

"The residue of training and experience," explained Dr. Horehound, his leathery eyelids half-closed. "If you'd seen some of the whack jobs who once graced my couch in Beverly Hills—so unwholesomely rich and thoroughly depraved—very little would upset you, believe me."

"Still," said Jonathan, "you must admit it's mighty strange."

"If true," said Dr. Horehound. He planted his elbows on the edge of the desk and folded his hands. "I only have your collective word regarding these remarkable transmogrifications."

"You could have looked for yourself," I said.

"And risked catching a chill in the rain?" said the doctor, his voice strained with feigned distress. "With my compromised constitution? I think not. Perhaps in the morning I'll feel up to humoring you. Until then, I must rely on your—dare I say—questionable testimony."

"I like that," I said. "*You* questioning *our* reliability."

"Listen to yourself, Miss von Derschmidt," said Dr. Horehound. "Mysterious lights bombarding your vehicles. Car engines miraculously turning into wood sculptures. Does that sound reasonable to you? It certainly doesn't to me. I'll forego parallels in your Catholic rituals."

"Good," said Edward. "Don't go there."

"Maybe it's hypnosis," said Pierre, raising an index finger. "A drug in the coffee Thorndale dutifully provides in the dining room."

"An interesting theory," said Dr. Horehound, "but a rather overused melodramatic *deus ex machina*, don't you think?"

"Not for a mean man like you," I said, seething. "I don't care if you did apologize last night—you've wrecked it all now."

"I was not myself, I admit, during the séance," said Dr. Horehound. "I've spent most of the day recuperating here in my library while you all scurried about making plans to leave prematurely, thereby breaking our agreement. I fail to see how I've wrecked anything. In fact, I'd say I'm being extraordinarily patient, under the circumstances."

"Patient!" I exclaimed.

"Extraordinarily," he repeated. "I've listened to your wild stories, haven't I? I'm putting up with your insinuations, yes? In spite of which I'm offering you my hospitality, am I not? Beatrice Canard would have thrown you out on your ears by now, I assure you."

"Who?" I asked.

"An anthropologist who conducts similar reenactments in New Orleans," explained Arthur, bending over me to do so.

"I'll bet her assistants don't get found slaughtered in her backyard," I said.

"The infamous Alexis Grignion left his disemboweled victims sprawled along a levee," corrected our host, rising from his chair and strolling casually toward the door. "But that's neither here nor there. My point is that you might consider modifying your tone, Miss von Derschmidt. You are still a guest in my house."

We all looked at him, not knowing what to say.

As he reached the door he paused and snapped his fingers. "I've got it! Try this on for size: suppose Sheriff Brumus isn't the brutish but basically kind-hearted peace officer you think him to be. What if he's actually in my employ? You only have your assumptions to go on. I, on the other hand, wrote his script. He told you that Mrs. Piaget was involved with a witches' coven, didn't he? Now consider: none of you touched the body in the garden except Joel here. Don't forget he has subsequently sought employment with me, a proposition I'm seriously considering—or was it really 'subsequently'? I understand you've only known Mr. Maruppa for a handful of months. You think you can comprehend someone in so short a period of time? What if he and I in fact go back several years, to before he entered the seminary? For all you know he was once my patient, though hopefully not as depraved as the ones I just mentioned—or maybe more so. Consider further: how many of you have ever seen a dead body up close, let alone one with the throat and viscera torn out by a vicious animal? Perhaps Joel and Sheriff Brumus are excellent actors and you've all been taken in. In that case, the dummy the sheriff discovered in the boathouse was merely a decoy—a second, less artistically rendered version of Elaineileen Douceur than the one you saw in the garden; and at this very moment E. I. D. is munching chocolates and watching television at the motel with Clarice Davenport, my trusted per-

sonal secretary and confidant of many years. In hitching a ride
to town, Clarice was merely playing the part of Arianna Marigold, who disappeared the day after the séance. Give all that
some thought, if you can. It must be hard—thinking, I mean—
with the hallucinogen Thorndale administers via the coffee as
Monsieur Bontemps suggests. Or maybe it's Grayburn, a wayward over-aged child of the sixties who once made his living
pilfering illegal substances along Hollywood Boulevard. I
wouldn't put it past him to toss in a potent hypnotic with an am-
phetamine chaser. No wonder you've been seeing lights and
impossible transformations. What if nothing you've experienced
here at Wolfram Lodge ever really happened? It's all been
medication, suggestion, presumption, and an inordinate dose of
your own imagination. I repeat, give that some thought. When
you're done, I suggest you wash up, change into something suitable, and join me for dinner—last night's prime rib makes a delayed appearance—and then, with stomachs satisfied and minds
poised, let us gather again in the séance room at nine."

With that he left us.

∞§[Martin]§∞

"Will someone please help me screw my head back on?"
chuckled Jonathan.

"As soon as I can find mine," answered Edward. "It fell on the
floor here somewhere."

Beth blinked, smiled, and read the next few lines:

∞§[Beth]§∞

"Will someone please help me screw my head back on?" asked
Jonathan as the panes in the French doors stopped rattling.

"As soon as I can find mine," said Edward, setting his book down on a small table so he could massage his temples with both hands. "It fell on the floor here somewhere."

∞§[Martin]§∞

"Might misty memories be coming back?" asked Kahlúa expectantly.

"I wish," said Jonathan.

"Me, too," said Edward.

"We're just reacting the way we react," said Jonathan, making sure his head was, in fact, secure.

"And acting the way we act," said Edward, giving Jonathan's head an extra nudge, just to be sure.

"Oh poo," said Kahlúa.

"Shhhh," hissed Millie.

"What about you, Sis?" asked Arthur.

Beth shook her head and went on.

∞§[*Beth*]§∞

"Could he have been right about any of that?" I asked.

"About Sheriff Brumus, you mean," mused Pierre, hooking his thumbs in his vest pockets. "Madam Douceur and Clarice Davenport at the motel? What do you think, Arthur? Miss Davenport seemed mighty relieved when we left her at St. Arnold's."

"I don't trust my instincts when it comes to figuring out people," said Big Brudder Art, releasing his grip on my shoulders. He shoved his hands deep into his overall pockets and strolled slowly in the general direction of the window, deep in thought. He paused halfway there to regard Joel, who was absorbed in his coin. Arthur looked as though he was going to say something, but he shook it off and resumed his unhurried stride.

"Narcotics could explain a lot of what we've been seeing around here," said Edward.

"Individually, yes," said Pierre. "But would we all share the same hallucination, experience the same details?"

"If the drug in question was a powerful hypnotic," said Edward. "He might have put us all under at breakfast, yesterday. That was our first meal together with him. We all had coffee, didn't we? Or orange juice—whatever, it could have been in several things, just to be sure."

"He just nibbled, remember?" said I. "Such drama over the tiniest bit of food. Picky, too. Maybe he was avoiding all the tainted stuff."

"Once we were in a receptive state," said Edward, "he could have read us a script of detailed memories: the lights at the campground, the spaceship in the lake—which, frankly, has been the biggest befuddler as far as I'm concerned."

Well, certainly memory is a curious machine and strangely capricious.

"I'd say it's on par with Joel's disappearance," said Pierre.

Joel grunted, but made no comment.

"It's all one big par to me," said Jonathan, edging closer to fill the vacuum left by Arthur. He was so obvious, and he really was cute. But somehow I was beginning to grow wary of his attention. Things were complicated enough without, well, more complications.

It has no order, it has no system, it has no notion of values …

∞§[Martin]§∞

"There it is again!" groaned Beth.

"Those double-dealing asterisks?" asked Jonathan.

"Single ones this time, but yes," said Beth, gripping the pages as though threatening to throttle them.

"What's eatin' you, Honey?" asked Kahlúa.

"I don't get it," said Beth, scrutinizing her work. "'... *memory is a curious machine and strangely capricious ... It has no order, it has no system ...*'" She turned to Pierre. "That's not Jonathan again, is it? It doesn't sound like something he would say." Pierre shook his head no.

"Arthur, maybe?" she asked, almost pleadingly. "Big Bro?" Her brother shook his head and shrugged.

"And a minute ago it was '*She's covered with blood!*'" said Beth, her agitation mounting. "I don't remember who said that, either."

"I've been giving it some thought," said Edward, "and I believe it was me—or rather, something I read in my account. The blood, I mean. It was when Grayburn came into the library after finding the body—"

"That's right," said Millie. "He was fit to be tied."

"Grayburn." Beth shut her eyes and nodded stiffly. "Of course. '*So much blood!*' But I still don't understand why I interjected his outcry into my train of thought in this chapter, without any explanation."

"If I remember correctly," said Arthur, "we were discussing the possibility of walking to town, and the subject of the creature that mauled Madam Douceur came up. The likelihood is that your memory of Grayburn's distress was jarred by that."

"So it would seem," said Pierre. "And in the current instance, we were considering the notion that our host had tampered with our memories."

"Thus prompting this insight about the unreliability of memory," said Arthur. "So you see, Sis ... Sis? ... *Sis!*"

Beth had dropped her pages to the floor. Then, eyes clenched, she began to wince and flinch, as though bombarded by stinging insects. The pitch of her voice rose as she blurted, "'*You can't, Beth! ... it has no system ... What we saw ... It has no order ... Dead as dead ...*'" Then she practically screamed, "' *So much blood!*'"

"Honey!" exclaimed Kahlúa, now standing.

Beth opened her eyes wide and pressed her palms to her temples. Then, as if the mood in the room wasn't stretched tightly enough—Holy Moly!—she started speaking in tongues! No, that was just a first impression. Actually, I soon realized she was quoting a passage in Latin, but her voice had become so shrill and tremulous as to mangle her pronunciation: *"Transibo ergo et istam naturae meae, gradibus ascendens ad eum, qui fecit me, et venio in campos et lata praetoria memoriae ..."*

This catapulted Arthur to his feet, past Joel, around Edward, and to his sister's side. He stood at her left, wrapping a brotherly arm around her shoulders. "It's okay," he said encouragingly. "Sis, *you're* okay."

"Then what's happening?" she implored, gnawing on her knuckles. "It's like flashbulbs are going off inside my head, only instead of *taking* pictures, they *are* pictures! Pictures of words I must've read somewhere. But not just pictures. More like ... *events*. Like I'm reliving the moment I saw them, only with all my senses intensified somehow. And Jonathan's voice, Grayburn's, too—or rather Edward's—they're like gigantic mouths, and they're inside my head, behind my ears!"

"Now there's an intriguing image," said Edward. "Almost like—yeow!"

"You hush!" said Kahlúa, who, like Arthur, had also come to Beth's aide, but had taken longer to make her way past Millie and around Joel. She stomped on Edward's foot for good measure en route to Beth's right side, which she gained by knocking Pierre into the antique wooden chest. "Don't you worry, Sweetie," she said, enveloping her arm the other way around Beth, sort of on top of Arthur's. "Mama's here."

"You certainly are," remarked Pierre, clutching the chest lest it capsize.

"Lookie here, Puddin'," said Kahlúa soothingly. "Look at me. I don't know about the blood and the big huge or the gobbledygook you said a moment ago. But try this on for size: 'Well, certainly memory is a curious machine and strangely capricious. It has no order, it has no system, it has no notion of values ...'"

Beth was giving her a blazing look that seemed to shout, "I know! I know! I just said that!" until Kahlúa continued:

"'... it is always throwing away gold and hoarding rubbish. Out of that dim old time I have recalled that swarm of wholly trifling facts with ease and precision, yet to save my life I can't get back my mathematics ...'"

As if it were possible, Beth's eyes went wider as she gripped Kahlúa's hand excitedly. Together they recited: "'... It vexes me, yet I am aware that everybody's memory is like that, and that therefore I have no right to complain.'"

"Wow!" marveled Jonathan. "Asterisks in stereo!"

"What's going on?" asked several of us in surround sound.

"Mark Twain!" said Beth and Kahlúa together.

"'Three Thousand Years among the Microbes,'" said Kahlúa proudly, "although Twain actually wrote it—"

"As Samuel Clemens!" said Beth triumphantly, but the elation on her face was momentary. It gave way to a look of utter confusion. "I must have read that when I was twelve!"

"Thirteen, actually," said Arthur. "It was in an anthology you were assigned in the eighth grade."

"But I'm seeing it in my head as though I'm reading it now!" she cried.

"I know you're confused, frightened even," said Arthur. "But to tell you the truth, I've been hoping this would happen."

"You have?" retorted Beth, glaring at her brother. "What do you mean?"

"If you promise not to poke me in the stomach, I'll tell you."

"Okay, Buster, explain."

"Actually," said Arthur, meeting her look, "I think you're beginning to figure it out for yourself."

"I could have fooled me," she replied, bewildered.

"Well, while you're foolin' around," said Kahlúa, "what I'd like to know is what that gibberish was all about. Tell me you wasn't glossolaliating. Please! My Great-Aunt Lawanda used to drive me crazy."

Father Baptist cleared his throat as if he were about to object. I might have interjected something, too, but just then Beth's eyes did a loop-the-loop. Then she stared straight ahead as she exclaimed, "Doctor Shelly!"

"Who, Sweetie?" asked Kahlúa.

"Doctor Michelle Chodelka," said Beth. "My first neurologist. My favorite one, too. She specialized in memory disorders. She liked to be called Doctor Shelly. She always wore the most beautiful Byzantine Cross around her neck. On the wall of her office there was this page from an illuminated manuscript. It was preserved in a special glass frame this big." With her hands she indicated that it was two feet wide and more than three feet tall. "It was beautiful, the words executed with such attention to detail, and in the margins were miniature paintings of Saints and Angels and mythical animals, such stunning colors, all highlighted with swirls of gold. The first letter of the first word was a humongous T, with ivy growing all over. It formed a double archway over a bishop who was wearing his miter, his crook leaning against the T. He was sitting at a desk with a quill in his hand and an oil lamp at his elbow. He had the most interesting look on his face—unfathomable, yet kindly somehow. The words that followed obviously flowed from his mind through his hand onto the parchment. I can see them now, as clear as a bell: *'Transibo ergo et istam naturae meae ...'*"

"'... *gradibus ascendens ad eum,'*" quoted Father Baptist along with her, reading from a volume he had quietly retrieved from the bookshelf. "'... *qui fecit me, et venio in campos et lata praetoria memoriae ...'*"

Remarkably, the two of them continued to speak in Latin for two or three minutes. Father spoke with confidence, while Beth paused here and there, as if sounding out some of the syllables. Nonetheless, we all sat there, entranced by the sound of the mysterious words, until at long last they concluded:

"'... *nec ipsa sunt apud me, sed imagines eorum, et novi: quid ex quo sensu corporis impressum sit mihi.'*"

"Amazing," said Jonathan. "What was all that?"

"'I will soar, then,'" read Father Baptist, now without Beth, "'beyond this power of my nature also, still rising by degrees toward Him who made me, and I enter the fields and spacious halls of memory where are stored as treasures the countless images that have been brought into them from all manner of things by the senses.'"

"What's that from, Father?" asked Joel.

"Saint Augustine's *Confessions?*" suggested Monsignor Havermeyer.

"My interlinear edition," said Father with a nod. "Beth and I just recited all of Chapter Eight in Book Ten."

"A whole chapter," marveled Jonathan.

"And you understood it all?" asked Edward of Beth.

"No," said Beth. "I don't speak Latin. I mean, I follow it in my missal at Mass, but that's about it."

"Yet you remembered all that?" asked Kahlúa. "How often did you see this Doctor Shelly?"

"Oh, lots of times," said Beth. "But I only met with her in her private office once. After that I only saw her at the clinic. She retired five or six years ago."

"You just saw that passage once?" gawked Jonathan.

"Bravo, Sis," said Arthur with a satisfied smile. "Bravo. I've often said that what would be considered extraordinary in others is commonplace for you."

"My episodes!" she exclaimed, turning to him. "Arthur! I'm having eidetic episodes!"

"I've missed them," sighed he, gratefully.

"What're you talking about?" asked Jonathan, as did, well, everyone.

"I'm complicated," said Beth, hesitantly. "Didn't you know?"

"Doctor Chodelka believed Beth has a rare form of hyperthymesia," said Arthur. "That's from the Greek for 'excessive remembering.' It means she can recall personal experiences and events with stunning clarity, as though she were physically there again. Most people with this condition spend abnormally large amounts of time dwelling in their past. In Beth's case, however, she just gets flashes of events, some recent, some remote. Usually it's something somebody said aloud, but now and then she'll quote from a book, or even, as you've just witnessed, a lengthy passage that she merely perused, sometimes in a language unfamiliar to her. These incidents are erratic, unpredictable, and involuntary. Often, after they occur, the words or gestures that triggered them may seem obvious; but despite all efforts to bring them on, to actuate the process, they defy all intentional coaxing. They remain illusive and mystifying."

"Doctor Shelly said she had to call them something,'" said Beth, "so she came up with the term 'eidetic episodes.'"

"Might this be connected with your narcolepsy?" asked Monsignor Havermeyer.

"Good question," said Beth. "Bro? You're better at explaining me than I am."

"I doubt that," said Arthur. "But as to your question, Monsignor, it's hard to say. Beth's eidetic experiences preceded the onset of her sleeping disorder by almost a year."

"That's why Doctor Shelly was my *first* neurologist," said Beth. "After that came 'the gaggle.'"

"Beth's pejorative for her other specialists," said Arthur.

"All they do is preen their feathers and squawk," said Beth. "The lot of them."

"Yes, well," said Arthur. "They seem to suspect that the stray wires from her first disorder are somehow entangled with the second. However, they have only been able to medicate the narcolepsy, not the hyperthymesia—so, I repeat, it's hard to say. She had to learn to live with it, and in a sense, so did I. We agreed not to joke about it, broadcast it, or even to allude to it between ourselves, except when it occurred on its own in the course of daily life." He paused to cast an intent look that effectively conveyed that we were all now drawn into this pact. Then he continued, "As with all things, we regard it as a gift from God, and therefore an Occasion of Grace. At times it has proved to be informative, even insightful. She came up with the asterisks as a way of conveying these episodes in her letters to me when I moved to California."

"So," said Monsignor Havermeyer, "all that being said, is it like having a photographic memory?"

"I wish," said Beth. "A photographic memory is constant, consistent, and reliable. You look at a page of a book of your choosing, your brain stores a detailed image, and you can read it from memory later at your leisure—great for preparing for a midterm. What I have is entirely different. My high school exam experience was riddled with startling flashes of Sister Mary Theophilus bawling me out in the first grade, family squabbles during TV commercials, Dad's wrinkled road maps in the glove compartment, or passages from Arthur's copy of *Caesar's Gallic Wars*."

The crisis having been resolved, or at least diffused, Kahlúa gave Beth a kiss and a hug, and quietly made her way back to her seat.

"I gather you haven't been experiencing these episodes lately," said Jonathan.

"I guess I haven't," said Beth.

"Not on the phone or in her letters since last summer," said Arthur, also heading back to his chair. "Nor during our adventure back in November. It is strange that I noticed, considering all I've forgotten. But I have been aware of it, and I've been wondering how and when to say something without upsetting her."

"He thinks I'm sensitive about my hyperthymesia," explained Li'l Sis.

"You *are* sensitive about your hyperthymesia," said Big Bro as he seated himself with finality. "Far more than your narcolepsy."

"Yes, well," said Pierre, retrieving Beth's pages from the floor and handing them to her. "I'm sensitive about the time, and more so its inexorable passage, so with this bit of fascinating but incomplete understanding of your extraordinary condition—"

"Condition!" objected Beth.

"Right, sure," said Pierre, bumping against the antique chest again. "With compassionate acceptance of your unique *syndrome* tucked away in the backs of our non-photographic, non-eidetic minds, and with our promise not to joke, harp, or babble about it except when it intrudes again—which it will—would you be so good as to continue?"

"I suppose," she said, regarding the pages in her hands and backing up a bit.

∞§[*Beth*]§∞

"Narcotics could explain a lot of what we've been seeing around here," said Edward.

"Individually, yes," said Pierre. "But would we all share the same hallucination, experience the same details?"

"If the drug in question was a powerful hypnotic," said Edward. "He might have put us all under at breakfast, yesterday. That was our first meal together with him. We all had coffee, didn't we? Or orange juice—whatever, it could have been in several things, just to be sure."

"He just nibbled, remember?" said I. "Such drama over the tiniest bit of food. Picky, too. Maybe he was avoiding all the tainted stuff."

"Once we were in a receptive state," said Edward, "he could have read us a script of detailed memories: the lights at the campground, the spaceship in the lake—which, frankly, has been the biggest befuddler as far as I'm concerned."

Well, certainly memory is a curious machine and strangely capricious.

∞§[Martin]§∞

"Pardon my interruption," said Arthur, "but as you can see, it is as we surmised. The notion that Doctor Horehound had tampered with our memories, and likely Edward's specific use of the word, spontaneously triggered Beth's eidetic recollection of Mark Twain's thoughts on the subject. Nonetheless, I can guarantee that if we purposely tried to induce the same response, we could talk about memory, microbes, and Mark Twain all day long without success."

"Like I said," remarked Beth. "I'm complicated."

"Pardon my extension of your brother's interruption," said Edward. "But if this is going to keep coming up, there's something I don't understand. Since we're on the subject, let's take this quotation from 'Three Thousand Years among the Microbes.' You bracketed it with asterisks. So did it come to you then and there, during our exchange in Doctor Horehound's library, or did it strike you later, while you were committing the conversation to paper?"

"Good question," said Beth. "I can't say positively because I don't remember either the discussion or writing about it."

"Well, what about in your correspondence with Arthur? Do you have any way of differentiating the two?"

Beth regarded the ceiling, then the floor, and finally said, "I'm afraid I'm still a bit fuzzy about all that."

"Very astute, Edward," said Arthur. "As a matter of fact, it was confusing at first. I had to phone her several times to ask the same question. For the most part, she uses the double asterisks to indicate an episode intruding itself during the course of events, whereas the single asterisks represent a memory that occurs while she's writing about it later. I say 'for the most part' because, as I have come to realize, a vivid recollection of a stunning memory can easily get entangled with it."

"So," said Kahlúa, "appropriating lingo from the so-called Revealing Star: single star, immediate past; double star, remote past."

"Clever, Lulu," said Millie.

"I see," said Edward thoughtfully. "So Beth, a couple of minutes ago, it seemed as though a bunch of these memory flashes caught up with you all at once."

"I guess that's one way of putting it," said she.

"Did you have any sense of where they were coming from?"

She shrugged. "Augustine and Twain were from my childhood, of course, if that's what you're asking. Jonathan and Grayburn were from our readings here."

"That's what I thought," said Edward.

"Your point?" asked Jonathan.

"Oh," said Edward, still addressing Beth. "It's just that the one thing you're not remembering, vividly or otherwise, is anything specifically from our supposed sojourn at Spirit Lake."

"I guess not," agreed Beth, a mite defensively.

"At least, not yet," added Jonathan.

"Right," said Edward with a heavy sprinkle of skepticism.

"Right," said Pierre, consulting his watch.

"Yes, well," said Arthur. "Better press on, Sis, before Pierre blows a gasket."

"We wouldn't want that," said Beth, backing up again, but not as far.

∞§[Beth]§∞

"Once we were in a receptive state," said Edward, "he could have read us a script of detailed memories: the lights at the campground, the spaceship in the lake—which frankly, has been the biggest befuddler as far as I'm concerned."

Well, certainly memory is a curious machine and strangely capricious.

"I'd say it's on par with Joel's disappearance," said Pierre.

Joel grunted, but made no comment.

"It's still all one big par to me," said Jonathan, edging closer to fill the vacuum left by Arthur. He was so obvious, and he really was cute. But somehow I was beginning to grow wary of his attention. Things were complicated enough without, well, more complications.

It has no order, it has no system, it has no notion of values ...

"And the howling you heard the other night," I found myself saying. "Are you thinking now that it wasn't real?"

"Like the doctor suggested," said Pierre, "maybe none of what we've experienced here has been real. Joel's disappearance, Madam Douceur's murder, the car engines turning into wood—that's *my* bugaboo, folks—maybe all these events were just seeds he planted in our heads, experiences triggered by key words or anticipated events. Mystery literature abounds with ploys of this nature."

"Speaking of literature," said Arthur as he joined Edward at the window, "what about Lenore Poe?"

"Who?" I asked.

"She runs the bookstore in town," he explained, peering out at the storm.

"Oh, The Raven," I said. "I saw it when we stopped for gas. What about her?"

"Didn't the sheriff say her dogs were killed yesterday?" asked Edward.

"That's right," said Arthur. "She met us on the road from town; told us some confusing things about Sasquatch and a man with a hairy heart."

"A what?" asked Edward.

"Some beastie she says has been stalking this valley for a hundred years," said Pierre. "And now there's yet another one with a wolf's heart and no soul."

"Huh?" huffed Jonathan.

"Not important right now," said Arthur. "But something she said is germane to our perplexing situation: she's the one who planted Madam Ouspenskaya's diary in my nightstand. Her great-grandmother worked for Mr. Piaget."

"As did lots of ancestors of people around here," said Pierre. "Sheriff Brumus told us that. I wonder what other mementos from the infamous séance have survived as family heirlooms in and around Claw Junction."

"Oh yes, the diary," said Edward. "Does it shed any light on, well, anything?"

"So much has been going on," said Arthur, "I plumb forgot about it. Maybe, now that we're not going anywhere, I should give it some attention."

"You do that," said Jonathan. "Meanwhile, this business of being drugged is really bothering me."

"It rankles," agreed Pierre, "the thought of us sitting there hypnotized at his table, drool trickling from the corners of our mouths." He illustrated the point by running his pinky down his chin.

"Ewww!" I groaned.

"Him and all his talk of the duties of hosts and guests!" said Edward, stomping angrily from the window to the fireplace.

"Would drugs really account for everything?" I asked, hoping someone would come up with a better solution.

"The alternative is far more ominous, in my opinion," said Arthur, for once no help at all.

"You mean everything happened just, uh, like it happened," said Jonathan. "Great."

"What do you think, Joel?" asked Pierre. I'd noticed him eye-ing Joel throughout the conversation, as if expecting him to im-part something significant.

Joel just sat there, slouched in his chair, absorbed in his silver coin.

"I don't suppose you knew Dr. Horehound back when," said Jonathan, perhaps expecting Joel to smirk and deny any previous acquaintance with our host. When Joel didn't react at all, Jona-than rubbed the side of his nose vigorously and mumbled, "No, of course not."

"So what's that you've got there?" I asked Joel.

He said nothing.

"Joel," said Pierre. "The lady asked you a question."

"Oh," said Joel. Written, it's but a small word consisting of two letters, but the way he uttered it, extending the vowel with a rise and fall in pitch, I half-expected him to add, "So, if a *lady* asks a question the whole world screeches to a full and complete stop?" He moved to slip the coin into his pocket.

"Please don't put it away," I said, not expecting the world to do any such thing. "I'm interested. Really. I am. May I see it?"

He hesitated.

"Joel," said Pierre. "The lady asked—"

With a sudden thrust of his arm, Joel granted my request. Rather than hand it to me, or lay it flat in his palm, he leaned forward, gripping the rim of his precious coin with all five fin-gertips, and held it inches from my face. "There, look at it if you must," his eyes conveyed, "but you aren't gonna touch it 'cause it's mine, mine, *mine!*" From that angle it looked like a flower with five oddly shaped pinkish petals around a shiny silver cen-ter. I got a glimpse of the profile of a pupil-deprived Franco-Grecian woman—Lady Liberty, I supposed—with the words *"E Pluribus Unum"* above and the year "1896" below.

"So it's a silver dollar," I commented.

"Uh-huh," he said, pulling it away.

"May I?" asked Arthur, who was approaching Joel's chair from behind.

Joel grimaced, curled his hand back over his shoulder, and snidely allowed my brother to view his precious bauble upside down.

"Ah, as I thought," said Big Bro, smiling assuredly. "A 'cartwheel.'"

"Come again?" asked Pierre.

"Also known as a Morgan silver dollar," said Arthur. "They were minted of silver from the Comstock Lode between the 1870s and the early 1920s."

"You tell 'em," I said, proud of my big brother. He knows things.

"When Jesse James was robbing banks," he added, "these were what he was after. I'm no numismatist, Joel, but that is sure to be worth considerably more than its face value."

"It looks new," I said.

"It is," said Joel.

"Hardly," I said, smiling. "It's over a hundred years old if it's a day."

"It is a day," said he.

"What do you mean?" I asked.

"Yes, what are you saying?" asked Arthur.

"You think the medallion you won is so special," sneered Joel.

"It certainly is to me," said Arthur, patting his coat pocket.

"It's nothing compared to this," said Joel.

"Really?" said Arthur, genuinely amused. "How so?"

"You wouldn't understand," said Joel, shoving the coin deep into his pocket. "None of you would. Not unless you saw—" He caught himself, glancing around suspiciously.

"Saw what?" pressed Pierre.

"Nothing," said Joel, gulping and twitching and wiping his nose with the back of his hand.

"Joel, what did you see?" demanded Jonathan.

Joel clamped his lips tightly.

"Nothing worth mentioning," sighed Arthur. "Apparently."

There followed a protracted moment of aggravated silence.

"Should we go to the séance, you think?" I asked, desperate to change the subject.

"That is the question," said Arthur. "I'm curious as to our host's ..." He left his sentence hanging as he happened upon the book Edward had set down on the small table. "Hello, what's this?"

"I found it over there," said Edward, pointing in the general direction of a bookcase set against the opposite wall. "The Latin title with English beneath caught my attention."

"Good Heavens," said Arthur, examining the spine. "Do you have any idea what this is?"

"Couldn't make out very much," said Edward. "The words inside are all squished together—handwritten, you know, at least the original was. It's what's called a photoengraving."

"Do tell," said Pierre, stepping closer.

"'Lemegeton: Clavicula Salomonis,'" read Arthur, running his fingers over the bas-relief letters on the front. "'The Complete Lesser Key of Solomon the King.' I'm surprised I missed this."

"Solomon," said Jonathan. "You mean like in the Old Testament?"

"It's attributed to him," said Arthur, slowly lifting the cover, "but in actuality it was written in 1641 by a pair of scribes who were copying sources less than a century old."

"What's it about?" asked Edward. "It's full of squiggles and insignias, and there're pages of circles with cramped writing all around, but I couldn't figure out what any of it meant."

"'The Lesser Key of Solomon,'" read Arthur audibly from the first page, squinting as he did so, "'which contains all the names, orders, and offices of all the Spirits that ever he had converse with; with their Soals or Characters belonging to each Spirit, and the manner of calling them forth—'"

"Wait a minute," said Edward. "Spirits? What spirits?"

"Calling who forth?" asked Jonathan.

"'The first part,'" read Arthur, further down, "'is a Book of Evil Spirits called *Goetia* ... the second part is a Book of Spirits partly good and partly evil—'"

"You mean I've been carrying around—?" moaned Edward.

"These squiggles you found so interesting," said Arthur, pointing to several on the next page. "They are 'Soals,' or 'Sigils'—

basically, insignias that represent specific spirits, symbols which are used when invoking them."

"*Invoking* them!" exclaimed Edward.

"If I remember correctly," said Arthur calmly, rapt in his academic cloud, "there's a diagram a few pages further on—yes, here it is. Not all the editions include it." He peered closer. "Yes, this is legible once your eyes grow accustomed to the style."

"Arthur, Old Bean," said Pierre, puzzled.

"'A Figure of the Circle of Solomon,'" Big Bro read aloud, tracing the drawing with his index finger, "'that he made to preserve himself from the malice of those Evil Spirits.'" He looked up but not at us. He was conversing completely with himself. "As I admonished Madam Douceur last night, but too late: she effectively committed necromancy in the open, the protection of her circle having been thwarted by Dr. Horehound's sudden departure." He bent to look closely at the page. "And this diagram here: 'The Triangle that Solomon commanded the disobedient Spirits into ...'" Suddenly my scholarly brother slammed his hand down on the page and looked around, this time seeing us. It was good to have him back. I was worried there for a minute.

"*That's* what I was trying to remember!" he announced. "Oh, the haystack of my mind and the needles I find therein!"

"What is it?" asked Edward.

"Sis! Jonathan!" exclaimed Big Bro. "The word fragments we found on the walkways in the garden! We saw 'G—A—B—R' just inside the western entrance, and assumed it was a segment of the name of Mr. Piaget's wife, Gabrielle."

"It wasn't?" asked Jonathan. "What else could it be?"

"*Gabriel*," said Arthur. "Think of the garden as a compass, a huge navigational compass. Gabriel is the Archangel of the West. Along the eastern rim we found 'P—H—A—E'—letters which are to be found within the name of *Raphael*."

"Seems to fit," said Edward. "But what does that have to do with anything?"

"In Ceremonial Magick," explained Arthur, "the celebrant of a ritual is called the Magus. He stands within a circle—his Magick Circle—protected by the names of the four elemental

Archangels inscribed around it: Raphael in the East, Michael to the South, Gabriel in the West, and Uriel to the North. I haven't a doubt that, when Grayburn gets around to hosing off the walkways, these are the names that will be revealed."

"I suppose we could just ask him," said Edward.

"We did," I said. "He refused until the storm has passed."

"Well, one of us could do it then," said Edward. He then grinned and added, "But I suppose that would be too simple."

"Excuse me," I asked, "protected from what?"

"The demons the Magus orders to appear in the Triangle of the Art," said Arthur. He stabbed at the page again. "Like his Magick Circle, it, too, is bordered by names. Along its sides are written three Greek or Greek-like words, supposedly ancient names of God: *Tetragrammaton*, *Primeumaton*, and *Anephezaton*. Obviously, our other fragments, 'T—R—A—G—R—A' and 'E—P—H—E—Z,' which we found along the straight paths, are contained in two of them."

"The first I recognize," said Pierre. "*Tetragrammaton*: the unpronounceable, untranslatable 'Four-Lettered Name' of God from the Old Testament."

"The other two are problematic," said Arthur, "hence my use of the words 'supposedly,' and 'Greek-like.' I've seen *Primeumaton* translated as everything from 'The First Thought' to 'Thou Who art the First and the Last.' *Anephezaton* gets even more complicated because it's spelled variously in different editions. In any case, the three divine names are supposed to imprison the demon within the Triangle so it can't harm the Magus. What's odd about Mrs. Piaget's setup is that she placed the Triangle of the Art *within* the Circle of Protection rather than *outside*, where the diagram in the *Lemegeton* clearly places it."

"What's so odd about that?" asked Jonathan.

"If I'm getting this," said Pierre, "it's like grounding your house electrically for the sake of safety, then sticking your tongue into a light socket in the comfort of your living room."

"I suppose that's one way of putting it," said Arthur, smiling quizzically.

"Or rather," said Edward, "like installing screens all around your patio, and then bringing a hornets' nest inside with you."

"That's another," agreed Arthur. Then he frowned as he added, "and it raises the question of just how and why—perhaps even if—Gabrielle Piaget was killed by lightning."

"And that book is supposed to be King Solomon's instruction book?" asked Jonathan.

"Although of questionable origin," said Arthur, "it bolsters an esoteric tradition that King Solomon, in addition to building temples to false gods in order to please his pagan wives, also practiced Ceremonial Magick. For many a sorcerer's apprentice, the *Lemegeton* is their first handbook."

"Um, excuse me again," I ventured. "Demons are evil, yes? So why would anyone want to summon them in the first place?"

"To access their power and knowledge," said Arthur. "To learn things from them, perhaps gain wealth and influence through them."

"And the demon obeys this Magus guy," I said, snapping my fingers. "Just like that?"

"In theory," said Arthur. "I've never witnessed an Invocation, nor would I want to. You know a tree by its fruit, and I'd much rather gain wisdom through Our Blessed Mother, whom I trust, than a Fallen Angel, whom I could not. Besides, there's a lot more involved than just drawing geometric figures on the ground and scribbling unpronounceable names within them. There are all sorts of lengthy preparations, ritual cleansings, incensings, then the incantations themselves which can go on for hours, and of course—"

"Hang on, Merlin," I said. "Whoa, unicorns! Back up a second. So why would this *wicked* celebrant summoning an *evil* demon call upon the *holy* names of God and His Angels for protection? Wouldn't he prefer the help of—I don't know—let's say Lucifer and Beelzebub? I should think they'd be on his side."

"At a recent Knights' meeting," said Arthur, "Mr. Feeney recounted a riotous conversation he had with a witch and a Satanist in an occult shop."

"Oh, yeah," said Edward. "That was a real side-splitter."

"My kingdom for a short answer," I groaned softly.

"In the midst of the exchange," said Arthur, "Mr. Feeney proposed the notion—and the Satanist agreed—that in order to be a practicing Satanist one had to believe in what the Catholic Church teaches more than most Catholics do these days. Well, the same applies to Ceremonial Magick. It is thoroughly infused with Catholic terminology and concepts, prayers lifted right out of the *Rituale Romanum*, the 'Book of Roman Rituals'—in fact, some aficionados concede that the first practitioners may well have been Catholic priests testing spiritual hypotheses much as scientists conduct experiments to prove their theories."

"Fr. Baptist said practically the same thing about alchemists," said Jonathan.

"I'm still waiting," I said, "for why the evil guy uses holy names for protection."

"Because demons are dangerous," said Arthur, "and divine names are efficacious. They really do provide protection against them."

"Whatevah woiks, Toots! Nyuck! Nyuck! Nyuck!" said Pierre, imitating one of the Three Stooges—Curley, I think.

"I'm getting a headache," I said, though I really just wanted to change the subject.

"But here's the point," said Arthur. "Sheriff Brumus mentioned—and darn if Dr. Horehound didn't, too—that Mrs. Piaget was a witch. The layout of her garden proves that she was much more than that, much more. Witches deny Christianity and call upon natural deities that mostly inhabit only their imagination. Ceremonial Magicians fastidiously believe in and regularly summon demons. Real demons."

"You should have spoken up more last June," said Jonathan, shaking his head. "You could have helped Fr. Baptist solve the Farnsworth Case."

"It was because of our involvement with that dire business," said Arthur, "that my bygone interest in the occult was rekindled."

"In demonology?" I asked.

"Not precisely, no," said Arthur. "Pierre, Edward, Jonathan, Joel. Remember the day we charged to the Del Agua Mission in the Wyndhamwagon to save Archbishop Fulbright from certain death? On the way there, while Edward was dodging motorists on the freeway, we were discussing astrology, alchemy, and the like in the back with Fr. Baptist. I'll never forget his words, as they were very much what I needed to hear at the time: 'The danger of these medieval practices lies not in the magickal system itself, but in the tendency of the uninformed and the intelligence-challenged to fall into the trap of denying Free Will.'"

"'The stars do not compel, they impel,'" said Pierre.

"Exactly," said Arthur. "He further said, 'To the medievals and ancients, these topics were regarded as fields of lifelong research, not ha'penny solutions for lonely hearts and feeble minds. Today they have become watered down to a degree of dilution beyond uselessness. But many Saints studied them within their proper contexts, with the guidance of holy teachers, and suffered no ill effects.' I repeat that he was speaking of alchemy and astrology, not Ceremonial Magick. Nonetheless, a day doesn't go by without someone coming into the bookstore in search of information in this area. Many of them are lapsed Catholics. If I am to help them, truly help them—warn them of the dangers, I mean—I need to be able to converse with them on their level, from a position of knowledge rather than ignorance."

(I just want to add here that I have no doubt that Arthur was quoting Fr. Baptist verbatim. He really does have an astounding haystack behind those thoughtful eyes of his. Me, being his argumentative little sister with erratic flashes of eidetic memory, I have to be a little contrary, just to keep him on his toes.)

∞§[Martin]§∞

Beth hesitated, but before another discussion could ensue, Arthur waved his hands and huffed, "Enough said!" so she continued.

∞§[Beth]§∞

"Isn't there something about forbidden books?" I asked. "A list or something?"

"You mean the *Index Librorum Prohibitorum*," said Arthur.

"Pope Paul VI abolished it in 1966," said Pierre, "along with most of Catholicism."

"Even when it was in force," said Arthur, "scholars were routinely granted permission to study works listed in the *Index*."

"But still," I said. "If you're going to sup with the Devil—"

"Hold on, my dear Sister," said Arthur. "I've no intention of cavorting with demons, preferring as I do the company of Saints and Angels. But even back in Ohio, those hours I spent in the stacks at the university, I often came upon books about esoteric things. I never brought them home, of course. Mom and Dad would have flipped! You, too, Sis. But I must admit that there, in the quiet and solitude of the library, I sometimes lost myself pondering the imponderable—and I did so love to daydream about the images on the Tarot cards."

"Like those paintings in the séance room?" I asked, injecting a few CCs of skepticism into my voice for good measure.

Big Bro smiled. "An man named Arthur Waite once described the Tarot as 'fragments of a secret tradition under the veil of divination.' It was obvious to me, looking at the Pope and the Grail and all, that the secret tradition he was so afraid to name was Catholicism. Throughout all my forays into occult literature, in fact, amidst all those writers who claimed to have access to secrets hidden throughout the ages, I came to recognize the collective, ubiquitous irony: the Catholic Church remained the proverbial elephant in the room."

"I like that," said Pierre. "By George, that's wonderful."

"Okay," I said to Arthur. "So you liked the pretty pictures—no doubt better than what most guys your age were ogling—but there's quite a leap from that to demons appearing in triangles and such."

"The kind of witchery Father uncovered last June," said my Big Brudder, who in my imagination was wearing a star-studded pointed hat on his head. "The casting quilt and all. In the end it was about power—raw, self-serving power—and we know ultimately the source of such power. I figured if these things were hitting so close to home, it was better to know more than less about them. Folks with little knowledge tend to panic, jump to unsupportable conclusions, attack and destroy the wrong people, and usually resort to flight in the end, rather than standing firm to face the enemy head on: knowledgeable, resolute, and unyielding—or so it seems to me."

"I suppose," I said doubtfully. "Okay, so you know about circles and triangles and stuff. What does all this icky knowledge do for us here and now?"

"If I may," said Pierre, nodding to Arthur.

"Certainly," said Arthur, nodding back.

"It tells us that we're walking on unholy ground," said Pierre. "I mean that literally as well as allegorically. In spite of the head-turning spin Dr. Horehound gave us just before leaving the room, the fact remains that something virulently wicked and hostile is lurking at Spirit Lake—something that was invited here more than a hundred years ago by Gabrielle Piaget, and redoubled by the efforts of her iniquitous husband, Bartholomew."

"And stirred up afresh and anew by Dr. Mortimer Horehound," said Edward.

"I'm afraid so," said Arthur. "He's the dyed-in-the-wool skeptic, or so his writings indicate, but a man doesn't have to believe in dynamite to set off a landmine. Lenore Poe said she recently delivered books of spells to him. Disparager he may be, but he is fascinated by the occult nonetheless. She went so far as to call him a believer. I would say he is a consummate naysayer. My study of the history of Magick convinces me that cynics can be just as dangerous as zealots."

"Ah, nuts," said Joel, getting up from his chair and heading for the French doors with his hands in his pockets. "All this chatter convinces me that you guys don't know what the heck you're talking about." He slammed the door on his way out.

"What's gotten into him?" I asked when the glass panels stopped rattling. "He was sulking almost from the first moment I met him, and he's been going downhill ever since."

"I'm worried about him," said Pierre. "Coming up to Spirit Lake has been bad for him somehow. He's always been a bit moody, but it's as if termites are eating away at his soul. I haven't a clue what to do for him."

"Other than to pray," said Arthur.

"Maybe we should," I said. "Pray, I mean."

"Bravo, Beth," said Pierre. "We've been missing the *Angelus* with all these distractions. Let us correct that oversight. 'In the name of the Father—'"

"—and of the Son," we said together. "And of the Holy Ghost. Amen."

"The Angel of the Lord declared unto Mary," said Pierre.

"And She conceived by the Holy Ghost," answered the rest of us ...

∞§[†]§∞

∞§✝§∞

22. A Large Mound of Meat and Bones In a Pool of Juice

∞§[Martin]§∞

"THANK GOD THAT'S OVER," said Beth, handing Pierre her pages and landing solidly sideways in her chair so she could roast her brother with a penetrating stare. Arthur seemed too immersed in his thoughts to notice. Indeed, the temperature in the room had risen a couple of degrees from the friction of all our brains spinning in our skulls.

"For you, Beth, certainly," said Edward, whose noggin decelerated first. "But the jig is up for the next poor lug."

"Strange as it may seem," said Pierre, "after crossing out so much, Joel did leave us a concise summation of Tuesday night's dinner."

"Great," said Joel, lowering his eyes as he rose to the occasion.

"I know this is going to sting," said Pierre, as he handed Joel his pages. "Please remember that it gives you and us an insight into your state of mind at the time. I ask the rest of you to bear in mind that Joel was, in a very real sense, under the influence of a spell."

"You think so?" asked Joel. There was a tinge of desperation in his voice.

"Without a doubt, dear Chap," said Pierre.

"And Joel, don't you forget," said Arthur, "that no matter what, we are your fast Friends."

"Hear, hear!" agreed Edward and Jonathan.

"I'll do my best," said Joel. "Oh God, I'll be glad when this night is over."

∞§[*JOEL*]§∞

It was a complete waste of time, but I got through to dinner somehow. Everyone had treated me shabbily all day, and I had no desire for their company whatsoever. Even Dr. Horehound, who wouldn't give me a straight answer about the job. It was a good thing I had no intention of working for him anyway. He thought he was above it all—certainly above *us* all—but he was merely dust in the corner that Thorndale had missed, as far as I was concerned. Pierre, of course, had been the worst, coming to my jail cell earlier and acting so chummy, suggesting I hadn't been arrested—hah!—when all he really wanted to do was to kiss up to that fathead sheriff—why, I don't know. Arthur was so proud of that Viking doohickey he diddled away from Dr. Horehound, but it was trivial compared to the awesome significance of my silver dollar. Little did he know! He was subtle, Old von Der-sleep, the Eldest Tumblar, him and his big vocabulary and erudite phraseology. He kept his prize in his pocket, patting it every now and then just to remind us that he was Sherlock Holmes' older brother. Seeing him and Edward swallow their shoes when they lifted the hood, just when they thought they were making their getaway—such moments were priceless. I hadn't expected that amazing intervention, and I must say it was brilliant. Be sure your engines get plenty of water and sunlight, boys, but don't overdo the fertilizer! I could have told them about the P. D. R., but they would find out soon enough, and oh, so too late, and by then I'd be on my way, away from them and all this idiocy! Edward might have appreciated the theory more than the others, but then he, like them, would have to deal with the *reality*. As for Jonathan and Beth, why didn't they just get on with it? Why all this waltzing around, as if everyone didn't know they had the hots for each other? Or at least Jonathan did. (Beth, being female, was acting kind of standoffish while giving no clue as to what her real intentions were.) To think I had so looked up to these guys, only to find that they didn't know squat. They had placed all their hopes at the foot of a great big nothing. I suppose I could've tried to warn them, to ease the shock, but why should I? They wouldn't have listened to me. Boy, were they going to be surprised!! But I'm getting ahead of myself.

It was raining again. Not a ferocious downpour this time, but a steady patter against the windowpane. The others had just finished saying grace—recited aloud, this time, like a bunch of first graders.

"You can all relax," said Dr. Horehound as Thorndale brought in a large covered platter and set it on the dinner table. "The donor of this repast had horns, not antennae, and four legs, not six, and all of them hoofed."

"Ah," said ever-clever Pierre. "Roast centaur."

"Somehow I'm still not very hungry," said Beth, all delicate and flustered.

"You need to keep up your strength," said Jonathan, looking as though he'd gladly scamper around the table to spoon-feed his frail, helpless darling.

"Standing rib roast," said Thorndale, lifting the lid without a trace of enthusiasm. As the steam cleared we saw a large mound of meat and bones in a pool of juice. "I'll be back," she said blankly, "with the salad and mashed potatoes."

"It's the way of things," said Dr. Horehound, unfolding his napkin. I bet he wished it was a platter of tarantula tempura. "Higher life forms invariably feed on the lower, just as owls eat squirrels and cats eat mice, and the hierarchy of your Church sucks the life out of its parishioners."

"If you're trying to bait us," said Edward, crushing his napkin in his mighty fist, "you're succeeding."

"Surely you know, sir, considering your penchant for things that crawl," said Pierre, daintily polishing water spots off his fork with his handkerchief, "ultimately it is the lowest forms that feed on the highest. As St. Bernard reminds us, in the end we are all food for worms."

"An interesting point," said Dr. Horehound. "I would add that worms, ultimately, are food for ants, and bacteria always have the final say."

"The way of things," said Beth accusingly. "Is this how you deal with the death of a loved one?"

"If you mean E. I. D.," said the doctor loftily, "I would hardly call her a close acquaintance, let alone a loved one."

"Close enough to cite in your will," said Pierre. "Executrix, no less."

Now that tidbit surprised me.

"And how would you know that?" asked our host without the slightest facial reaction. "Let me guess. The jealousy of my former personal secretary strikes in the night, indicative of Miss Davenport's venomous nature."

"Actually, it was in the light of day," said Pierre.

Dr. Horehound considered that for a moment. "Not that it's any of your business, Mr. Bontemps, but it was a matter of mine. My literary legacy, so to speak. I wanted someone to attend to the copyrights of my books, to delay their relegation into the public domain after my demise. Call it professional vanity if you must, or even— Excuse me, Mr. von Derschmidt. It is considered indecorous to read a book at the dinner table."

"Normally I would agree," said Arthur, absently as he turned a page. "But I'm doing so at the behest of my comrades."

"And how," said Jonathan.

"He's preparing for the séance," said Edward.

"This is my dinner table," said Dr. Horehound sharply.

"This is Cassandra Ouspenskaya's diary," said Arthur, equally pointed.

Aha! Dr. Horehound hesitated for two and a half thousandths of a half second. This information genuinely startled him, but he was one cold oyster. "I know of no such diary," he said with exaggerated disinterest.

"I'm surprised," said Arthur, likewise imperturbable. "I found it in my nightstand."

"Perhaps Thorndale is having a joke," said Dr. Horehound.

"Doubtful," said Jonathan. "That would require a sense of humor."

"E. I. D. then, or even Clarice."

"Really, Doctor, a hoax this elaborate and detailed?" countered Arthur, unhurriedly turning another page. "I should think not."

"Strange, the chasms represented by vacant chairs," said Pierre, tipping his wineglass toward the empty place settings. "I wonder how they're enjoying the chocolates."

"I beg your pardon?" asked Dr. Horehound, blinking away his momentary derailment.

"In their motel room," explained Pierre. "You said they were eating chocolates and watching TV."

"Oh that," said our host, his composure fully regained. "'Twas merely a projection, a possible outcome I offered by way of explaining the strange things you've been experiencing in and about my home. I never meant to imply that it was true."

"You also suggested that Sheriff Brumus is your lackey," said Edward. "That you and Joel here are old pals."

"Oh, that rain were beer, or pigs had wings," said Dr. Horehound, twirling his hands in the air. He then brought them down abruptly on the edge of the table. "Mr. von Derschmidt, I must insist."

"If you must," said Arthur, examining another page closely before turning it. "My, but Madam Ouspenskaya had a cramped and angry hand. She certainly despised Bartholomew Piaget, although she hasn't revealed why as yet. It's a wonder she came to Wolfram Lodge at all, considering how much she loathed the man."

"A nod from him would have rekindled her career," said Dr. Horehound.

"It had to be more than that," said Arthur. "From what I've read so far, she was already well-established as a trance-channeling medium. The *pied-à-terre* she lost in Summerland was but one of seven little getaways she had tucked away around the world, including a bungalow on the French Riviera and an Ionian island all to herself. She owned a palatial mansion in up-state New York and a horse ranch in Santa Barbara. No, he must have had something on her, some powerful magnet he used to draw her here in spite of herself."

"Like the one you must've had trained on Madam Douceur," said Edward.

"Hm," said Dr. Horehound, wiping his mouth with his napkin.

"I suspect she had her reasons," said Arthur absently. "She will explicate them in her own good time. A woman who revels in self-expression and expository clarity to the extent that she did would not be able to contain herself."

Throughout this conversation, Arthur kept his attention on the diary, while Pierre's was riveted on Dr. Horehound. No doubt they were playing what they considered to be a "deep game," but it was a shallow ploy. Neither of them glanced at me, even though I had been with them when "Woman with Bigfoot on Brain" claimed to have planted the diary, authentic or bogus, in Arthur's bedroom. Obviously they were baiting Dr. Horehound to see if he knew the reason why "Medium with Loquacious Pen" came seeking revenge on "Crook with Deep Pockets and Spooky Wife." Much as I would have liked to derail their objective, I was enjoying Dr. Horehound's discomfiture even more. Indeed, the doctor looked as though he was about to say something snidely profound, but let it go when Arthur, eyes darting over the page before him, remarked:

"Speaking of magnets, I wanted to compliment you on the Tesla coil up in the watchtower."

Another tidbit that was news to me.

The doctor dropped his napkin.

"Didn't Miss Davenport tell you?" asked Pierre.

"The door to the tower, it is locked," said Dr. Horehound.

"But Joel, he was missing," explained Jonathan.

"As were you at the time, Herr Doctor," said Arthur, his eyes never leaving the diary, "or I would have asked for the key. Looking to bolster my burgeoning reputation as an ill-mannered guest, I shouldered my way in and climbed that rickety staircase you described."

"You'll be glad to know that your loutish reputation is indeed growing by leaps and bounds, Mr. von Dershmidt," said our host indignantly. "You and Miss Hummingbird will receive the bill for all repairs."

"I could take care of that," interposed Edward. "The parts, anyway, seeing as how it's in my line of work."

"I doubt that very much, Mr. Wyndham," said our host. "I'll have you know that when I restored this house I had all the hardware and fixtures custom-made in Germany to match the photographs of the Piaget's original appurtenances."

"A. J. Fenstermacher, Ltd.," said Edward with an assured nod. "I recognize their work."

"I spared no expense," said the doctor, literally swelling at the thought, "and so neither will you, I can assure you."

"And I can assure you," said Edward, likewise expanding, "that Fenstermacher outsources all their custom work to the Nanyan-Hejian Machining Company in JungSu, Peoples' Republic of China. My employer, Thomas Brackmore, doesn't carry their products because they skimp on the copper-to-tin ratio in their bronze. But I'm sure he could make an exception in your case."

Dr. Horehound's eyes narrowed a wee bit and his Adam's apple went up and down twice, but otherwise his facial expression remained unchanged.

"It's a museum piece, really," said Arthur, squinting at something in the diary.

"What is?" asked Beth.

"Why, the Tesla coil," he replied, undaunted by the conversation around him. "Bartholomew Piaget commissioned it from the inventor himself, as the monogram beside the on/off switch indicates. Nikola Tesla was an inspired genius. That being said, Dr. Horehound, my friends told you they saw flashing lights up there, so I can't help but wonder why you weren't forthcoming regarding their source."

"I believe you are recounting our exchange in the library Monday afternoon," said Dr. Horehound. "If memory serves, I interrupted your conversation as I entered and pointed out that your friends had overlooked that very detail in their account of their unsettling experiences the previous evening. I then acknowledged my one and only visit to the tower when I first came to Wolfram Lodge, after which I locked the door in the interest of safety. I also told you that I'd heard noises, that I believed birds might be nesting up there, and that Madam Douceur believed spirits were trying to enter the lodge through the paneless windows in the surveillance turret. In summation, you left out a detail; I left out a detail. Are we all prevaricators at this table, or merely imperfect storytellers?"

"You are one slippery man," said Beth.

"I like that," said Dr. Horehound, leaning forward in his chair. "In your own holy book—Matthew chapter ten, I believe—your spiritual founder admonishes you: 'Be ye therefore wise as serpents and simple as doves.' Wise as serpents, are you? Selfish, I'd say! Sounds to me like you want to keep all the deviousness for yourselves!"

"You are slanting the meaning by quoting out of context," said Arthur. "If my memory serves, Jesus began by saying, 'Behold I send you as sheep in the midst of wolves.' The world into which we carry our Faith is full of devious men."

"I repeat," said Beth.

"And I with her," said Jonathan.

"Big surprise there," said Dr. Horehound, deflecting the conversation by pointing at Beth and Jonathan with his index fingers, then drawing a big heart in the air. Then he frowned. "So, Mr. von Derschmidt. You are not going to set that book aside."

"Whatever I may have said by way of conversation or jest," said Arthur, "I believe it is imperative that I explore Cassandra Ouspenskaya's mind. Our safety may depend on it. If it really bothers you so much, I will withdraw to the library."

"And have you miss this repast?" mused Dr. Horehound. "Read if you must. It is your loss if you divide your attention while tasting the palette of flavors being set before you. Tell me, is my safety included with yours?"

"I suppose that's up to you," said Pierre. "By the way, you didn't happen to go outside and look under the hoods, did you?"

"Hoods?" asked Dr. Horehound. "Oh, you mean the vehicles. No. Why?"

"Just interested," said Pierre. "Strange that you're not. You tell us things; we check them out for ourselves. We tell you things; you already have your answers."

"And from this you deduce ...?"

Pierre shrugged. "As per St. Matthew chapter ten, that we're wise not to trust you, for one thing."

"Touché. And for another?"

"That you're either pulling the strings," said Arthur, turning yet another page, "making impossible things happen, which is iniquitous; or you're not, and yet you don't care, which is worse."

"Sounds ominous," said Dr. Horehound. "I can see we're at odds."

"And that excites you," said Beth. "All this tension and angst, and you at the helm looking down on us all, gathering juicy tidbits for your book."

"Miss von Derschmidt," said Dr. Horehound, regarding her over his glass of merlot. "You haven't a *clue* as to what excites me."

"Thank heavens," said Beth, setting down her napkin on her clean plate. As she got up from her chair, the guys jumped like jack-in-the-boxes, but she waved them down. Then she made a circular motion with her hand in front of her tum-tum. "Arthur, that greasy hamburger—yummy as it was—is sitting in here like a big old cannonball. I'm sure the prime rib is excellent, Dr. Horehound, but I'm simply not hungry."

"Same with me," said Jonathan, as transparent as a picture window, getting up to leave with her. "Please give Thorndale our apologies."

"You're sure it's not the conversation—?" posed Dr. Horehound as they pushed in their chairs. "Perhaps a change of topic would help?"

"Burgers, fries, banter, lies," said Edward, patting his own gut as Jonathan and Beth made their exit. "Nothing's going to keep me from prime rib."

"That's the spirit," said our host.

Just then Thorndale came in from the kitchen with a large stainless steel salad bowl brimming with several kinds of lettuce. Her necklace, which seemed to be made of silver marbles, rattled noisily against the rim as she set it down next to the rib roast. She started to say something about her Stoke-on-Trent salad bowl still being missing, but then caught sight of the empty chairs—their number having doubled in her brief absence. Glaring questioningly, she left the room without another word.

"I missed out on the cannonballs with cheese," said Pierre, helping himself to a hefty slab of meat. "Tell me, Doctor, do you really prefer beetles to beef?"

"Once you get past the revulsion factor," said Dr. Horehound, doing likewise, "insects really are quite tasty, and so much more economical. You know, Thorndale makes a marvelous dessert confection that you would swear is caramel-covered corn, but in actuality it's fried caterpillars. They pop, you know, when dropped onto a hot skillet—"

"I'm afraid I'm not feeling well," I said, getting up from my chair. "Maybe it was the onion rings."

"Sorry about that, Joel," said Arthur, still absorbed in that medium's diary. "I didn't know we were going to be having prime rib—"

"Yeah," I said. "Wish I'd known."

"Keep track of the time," reminded Pierre like a persnickety schoolmaster. "The séance, or should I say the reenactment, commences at nine."

"I'll be there," I said. As if I cared, either way.

"Mr. Bontemps," Dr. Horehound was saying as I left, "since you are the only one of your party who has shown any interest in alternative protein sources—"

I didn't want to know. Since my unexpected sojourn the night before, there was little I needed to know. They said they'd be back for me this night to show me more, and best of all, to take me with them. They said they had sensed that, of all our group, I had the greatest capacity, proclivity, and potential to make the transition. Imagine that. Me, the littlest Tumblar.

Pierre and Dr. Horehound could stuff themselves with bugs, for all I cared.

∞§[Martin]§∞

Monsignor Havermeyer stiffened beside me, so much so that the overturned wastebasket on which he was sitting creaked against the hardwood floor. I turned to look at him, cracking my neck as I did so. He didn't return my look, so I guessed the moment had passed. Still, I wondered what had pricked him—Pierre and Dr. Horehound on bugs, or Joel's capacity, proclivity, and potential for something-or-other.

"Who're *they?*" asked Jonathan and Edward together.

"And where were they going to take you?" asked Beth.

Shrugging, Joel continued.

∞§[*Joel*]§∞

Actually, there was something I did want to know. Not that I'm nosy or anything, but I was curious about Jonathan and Beth. At practically every Knights' meeting, Jonathan always asked us to pray that he meet the proverbial "good woman." The same hormones that fired up those amazing rampant facial hair follicles of his were also driving him in a desperate quest for the ravenous maws of matrimony. (Hate to admit it, but I got that line from Pierre.) Or, as St. Paul wrote in his epistle to the somebody-or-others: "It is better to marry than to burn."

∞§[Martin]§∞

Now that set me off, at least somewhat. Misquotations from the *King James Diversion* always do. But much as I wanted to interject, "'Than to be *burnt*,' you mutilator of Sacred Scripture," I wasn't about to interrupt the flow just then.

Jonathan appeared to be thoroughly mortified.

Beth didn't look pleased, either.

The others resorted to knowing grimaces and rolled eyeballs. Of course, it wasn't the translation that troubled them.

∞§[*Joel*]§∞

I found them sitting on the swinging bench on the front porch. They had left the door slightly ajar—I assumed to make a hasty dash inside if the local bloodthirsty monster made a sudden appearance. Not wanting to intrude, I stood just inside.

"Full moon tonight," said he.

"Mm-hmm," said she.

"Odd time to bring this up, I know."

"Hmmm?"

I peeked around the edge of the door to see if he had put his arm around her shoulder and she had snuggled up against him, but neither had gotten that far. They were just sitting side by side, not even touching. What were they waiting for?

∞§[Martin]§∞

Beth reacted to that. I think she wanted to reach over and pull Joel's face off for eavesdropping. I think Jonathan wanted to do something similar. Pierre cast them a reminding glare that Joel had been under some sort of spell, whatever that meant. In a strange way, it seemed to me that this little bit of clandestine snoopery on Joel's part, being such a personal intrusion, struck a deeper nerve than his other objectionable behaviors thus far.

I felt genuinely sorry for Joel. It's one thing to admit your sins to a priest in the confessional, but this communal outpouring was downright demeaning—though I had to admit it was a fair comeuppance.

∞§[Joel]§∞

"Do you know what a Rosary Novena is?" asked Jonathan. Of all the things he could have said at that moment, he just had to bring up religion!

And she was just as screwy: "Is that the one where you say twenty-seven rosaries, one a day, petitioning Our Lady for something; and then twenty-seven more in thanksgiving, regardless of the answer?"

"That's the one," he said. "Would it interest you to know that I just finished day number fifty-four on Sunday? I said my last rosary silently, squeezing my Hail Marys in between the verses of Pierre's songs on the way up here."

"An exercise in concentration if ever there was one," she said. "And what were you praying for?"

There was a long pause. Then he said, "I think that I would meet you."

There was another long pause. "Me?"

"Well, someone," he said clumsily. "I was praying to meet someone, and there you were—are."

"Someone," she said, thoughtfully. "That's a tall order. I don't know what to say."

He cleared his throat—twice—then said, "Just so you don't tell me to get lost."

She inhaled slowly, then sighed quickly. "Of course not, Jonathan. I assume you prefer Jonathan to Jonnie or Jon?"

"Yes."

"Jonathan, then," she said, as if something important had been settled before tackling the lesser problem. "It's just that I'm not—you know—looking just now. Don't know what I want to do, you know? If I did, and if I were—looking, I mean—I'd certainly give you more than a glance." There was another long silence. Then she said, "I'm sorry. I can see that I'm disappointing you."

"Funny how it never works both ways," he said in a low, wounded whimper.

"Don't be too sure," she said. "Sometimes it does. I'm almost twenty-eight, you know."

"I'm twenty-six," he said.

"Does that bother you?" she asked.

"No, should it?" he answered and asked.

"I don't know," she answered. There was another pause. Then she said, "Here, I'll tell you what: Let's you and me begin a Rosary Novena together. We can start tonight before we go to sleep. I'll be leaving at the end of the week, but we can still continue saying it parallelly—is that a word?—together, you know, from afar. Not necessarily reciting it at the same time—like on the phone or something—but knowing that we're both doing it each day."

"What would we pray for?" he asked.

"Guidance, I should think."

"Good idea, Beth. Whatever I may think I want, what I really want is to do God's Will. That's all that really matters in the end."

"I'm with you, Jonathan."

What jerks, I thought. Prayer partners! By this time tomorrow—oh, what the heck. They'd find out, and boy would they be surprised!

∞§[Martin]§∞

"Beth, Jonathan," said Joel, gripping the pages as though to crumple them into a ball. "I'm not going to even try to say how embarrassed and sorry I am."

"Well," said Beth, pressing her index finger to her chin. "It's not as though I never eavesdropped on anyone."

"It's not good form," said Jonathan, "but it's human nature. To tell you the truth, Joel, I'm kind of glad you did. I was beginning to wonder if—if—"

"If what?" asked Beth pointedly.

"Uh, you know," said Jonathan to her. "Whether you and I would ever, um, you know. Aren't you the least bit curious?"

"Uh-HMM!" said Kahlúa.

"Oh, go wash your mind out," said Millie. "Of course she is if they would."

"As I was saying," said Beth, turning her attention to Joel, "I've overheard a few conversations I shouldn't have. I could have slipped away, or distracted myself somehow, but didn't."

"I second that," I said a little louder than I'd intended. As all eyes turned toward me I decided that an admission, once begun, must be blurted out *in toto:* "Surely you fellows remember that night in the Champlain Room when you scared the cocktail waitress so thoroughly she ran right out of the bar."

"You what?" insisted Beth, eyes wide.

"Ah, we just set her up," said Edward. "It was the bartender, Barlow, who delivered the punch line."

"Barlow?" said Millie, perking up. "Did you say Barlow?"

"I don't remember you being there, Mr. Feeney," said Jonathan.

"Yes, well," I answered. "That's my point. I was observing from behind a fishing net."

"A what?" asked Beth.

"Part of the nautical décor," I explained. "I confess I had been listening in on the conversation for some time."

"You don't say," said Jonathan.

I shifted uneasily in my chair. "I heard my name mentioned, you see, just as I entered the bar, and well, I just sort of slipped into a niche where I could listen for a bit. You were talking about my manuscript, you see, and I wanted to hear your honest opinions."

"Uh-huh," said Edward and Jonathan together.

"So what did you guys do to this poor waitress?" insisted Beth.

"I'll tell you later, Honey," said Kahlúa. "It was kind of mean, but it was a riot."

"My point being," I said, "that you're not alone, Joel."

"It's hardly the same thing," he said as he handed his pages to Pierre.

"Snooping is snooping," I assured him. "At least you were man enough to admit it. Look how long it's taken me."

"Certainly food for thought," said Pierre, "and fodder for future discussion, but we must press on."

"Gladly," said everyone gratefully.

∞§[†]§∞

∞§†§∞

23. So Your Claim of Authenticity Hits a Speed Bump

∞§[Martin]§∞

"OKAY," SAID PIERRE AS HE RUMMAGED around in that infernal wooden chest. "As it happens, Arthur had a little chat with Dr. Horehound after everyone left the dinner table. Arthur, my Friend, you are on your own."

"Why do you suppose I would have done that?" asked Arthur as he rose to the challenge.

"Only one way to find out," said Pierre, handing him his chapter.

∞§[Arthur]§∞

"Coming?" asked Pierre as he and Edward became upstanding.

I gave them a hand signal—a sideways wave with my palm downward—which meant nothing in particular. At that moment it occurred to me that it would indeed be handy if we Tumblars were to develop some communicative gestures for situations like this. "In a minute," I said to fill in the blank. "There's something I'd like to ask our host if he doesn't mind."

"But of course," said Dr. Horehound magnanimously, producing a cigarette and lighting it.

Pierre, always quick on the uptake, made a similar gesture in return. Edward blinked, shrugged, nodded, and left with Pierre.

"How may I be of service?" asked the doctor, tapping his ashes into a crystal ashtray. "And why did you wait until your friends excused themselves?"

"Conceivably, I'm trying to revamp my reputation as a boorish guest without being obvious about it," I said, closing Madam Ouspenskaya's diary and folding my hands upon it. "More so, I wanted to ask you something that wouldn't interest the others."

"Fair enough," said he, easing back in his chair. "First things first. How do you propose to redeem yourself?"

"An interesting way of putting it," I said, flexing my fingers but otherwise not moving my hands. "This journal. I'm less than a third of the way through, but I thought you might like to take a moment to examine it."

His eyes darted down at the book, then resumed their lofty angle down at me. "Why should I want to do that?"

"Because until this evening you weren't aware of its existence."

"Mr. von Derschmidt, I am something of an expert on the history of Wolfram Lodge. If Cassandra Ouspenskaya kept a diary, don't you think I would know about it?"

"Then you doubt its authenticity," I said evenly.

"I certainly do," he said, drawing circles with his cigarette. "Madam Ouspenskaya occupied the room recently vacated by Miss Davenport, so it's not as though she left it behind in your bedroom. I may not have personally gone through every drawer and closet in all the guestrooms when I assumed ownership of this property, but without a doubt Thorndale has. She would have brought it to my attention years ago."

"Unless it was only recently placed there," I suggested.

"Not by Thorndale. She's simple, dependable, and steadfast."

"Miss Davenport?"

"She was reliable until fear overcame her loyalty," he said coldly. "I confess her departure surprised me, but deception of this sort, it's hardly her style."

"You're sure of that?"

He chuckled. "As sure as I am of Grayburn."

"And you?"

"No, not me." His tone had become frigid. "That dispenses with my household. Who else might be responsible?"

"That depends upon whoever found it and kept it when the original party dispersed in 1896," I replied. "The police surely

went all through the place. One of them might have taken it.
Unscrupulous detectives have been known to help themselves to
the spoils of celebrated crime scenes. That's how murder muse-
ums get started. Six guests departed the premises, and there
were staff that suddenly found themselves out of work. Surely
amidst so much confusion the opportunity for looting—perhaps
'looting' is too harsh a word—let's say 'the understandable
temptation to abscond with a souvenir of a memorable weekend'
presented itself. Don't you agree that it should at least be considered?"

"I confess I like the way your mind works," he commented as
smoke dribbled from his nostrils.

Perhaps I should mention here that though I had decided to
protect Lenore Poe, I wasn't entirely sure that I trusted her, either. Perhaps her relationship with Dr. Horehound was limited
to the sale of the store property and his subsequent purchases
through her, but how could I be sure of that? Was her attempt to
warn him regarding "Man with Hairy Heart" a friendly gesture,
or perhaps an indication of something more? Among other
things, I wanted to ascertain what he knew of the alleged diary;
hence, my indirect tactic of peppering the conversation with co-
pious possibilities and irrelevant details.

"You said you investigated the subsequent activities of the
guests," I said, consciously blinking the thought of Lenore's eyes
out of my mind. "None of them ever produced any artifacts of
the event?"

"Not to my knowledge," he answered with a slight shake of his
head.

"Are you sure there was no mention of a diary in the police report?"

"I am."

I strummed the cover of the book with my fingertips. "And
none of the people who have participated in these reenactments
of yours has ever asked about it? Hinted about it? Made any
suggestion that they'd heard of it?"

"Not a one," he said flatly.

"None of them claimed to be descended from the original
party?"

"No. I don't see why you're harping on this."

I flexed my fingers again. "After all these years, this book appears in my bedroom and you're not curious?"

"Not really."

"I find that disconcerting, Dr. Horehound."

"How so?"

I leaned back in my chair. "It's as I said earlier: maybe you're responsible for the weird things that we've experienced up here; maybe not. Either way you exude an air of nonchalance, or did until you became ill last night. Something compelled you to make amends, but today you dismiss even that out of hand. Perchance your apologetic attitude was genuine at the time, maybe not. If you are indeed in control, that would account for your condescension. But I can't help wondering if you, in fact, are not."

"In control, you mean," he said, adjusting his legs under the table. "I have always found it amusing when my guests try to analyze me."

"One possibility is that this was left by whoever occupied the room last," I said, "and Thorndale simply neglected to check the drawer when she cleaned up afterward."

"Unlikely," said Dr. Horehound. "The woman in question was an unimaginative socialite who was so desperate for attention she tried to pick up Grayburn."

My jaw dropped. "You're joking."

"I wish I were," he chuckled. "Do go on."

I rippled my fingers on the book and continued. "If this is a fake, someone went to a lot of trouble fabricating it. I know something about books. These pages show signs of age, as do the faded ink and the frayed edges of the cover. Do you have any examples of Madam Ouspenskaya's handwriting? Letters she sent to Mr. Piaget?"

"I was wondering if you'd ask," he said, exhaling a robust plume of smoke. "The answer is no. She preferred to communicate by telegram, believe it or not. The nearest telegraph office was in Devils Horns in those days. I've no idea what arrangements were made for delivery."

"That is unfortunate," I said, shaking my head.

"And convenient for the perpetrator," said the doctor. "The historical museum in Summerland might have documents in her hand on file, but that doesn't help us in the immediate."

"No it doesn't," I conceded. Then I brightened. "There is a five-dollar bill in here—half of one, anyway—apparently used as a bookmark. Certain tangential interests have given me some background in American currency. There was a bit of controversy behind this particular bill when it was released in 1896. You see, on the front there's a depiction of a winged goddess holding an electric light bulb aloft to illuminate the nation. Electricity was a burgeoning national interest in those days, as the Tesla coil upstairs attests. Over to the left, we see Jupiter with a bolt of lightning in his hand, seemingly powering the lamp. At the light-bearer's side we find the buxom, deified Fame trumpeting the nation's technical achievements. Unfortunately, the bell of her trusty horn extends into the missing half of the bill."

"You said something about controversy?" asked Dr. Horehound disinterestedly.

"Oh, yes," I said. "A religious fundamentalist named Anthony Comstock, founder of the Watch and Ward Society, took issue with female nudity on the national currency. Personally, I'd take issue with the portrait of Gen. Philip Sheridan on the reverse side. He conducted the burning of Shenandoah Valley in 1864, a 'scorched earth' tactic that was encored by Maj. Gen. William T. Sherman in his infamous 'March to the Sea.' An odd choice of personage, seeing as how embers of the Civil War were still smoldering at the time this bill was printed. Silver Certificates issued in the 1890s featured dual portraits on the backsides. George and Martha Washington both graced the one-dollar bill, for example. I have forgotten whose picture is on the missing half of this fiver—something to look up later. Well, in any case, it goes to the authenticity of this diary, but if you're not interested, I'll not bother you further about it."

He seemed relieved. "You said there was something else you wanted to ask me."

"Ah, yes." I had rehearsed several approaches, but opted for the direct route. "I'd like to know what happened to the Tarot deck that Madam Ouspenskaya used that night in 1896."

That got him. "I don't know what you mean."

"Dr. Horehound," I said, leaning forward on my elbows, "even though it appears to be very old, the deck Madam Douceur used last night, the one sitting in the séance room as we speak, could not possibly be the one used by Madam Ouspenskaya."

"Oh?" he said, raising his eyebrows.

"I noticed something about the script you prepared for Madam Douceur," I explained. "At first I allowed it as a matter of style. Unlike most Tarot readers, Madam Ouspenskaya spoke only in divining vagaries. Strangely, with all the provocative imagery on each and every card, only once did she mention a specific pictorial detail—Justice without a blindfold."

∞§[Martin]§∞

"Excuse me," said Jonathan. "I distinctly remember lots of details about the cards: pillars, stars, pitchers of water, a sarcophagus, and the sword gal *with* a blindfold—to name a few."

"All features Beth provided," said Arthur. "I noticed it when she was reading her account. My sister described the visuals, while Madam Ouspenskaya's script, as read by Madam Douceur, addressed concepts. The only specific graphic detail she mentioned was indeed Justice without a blindfold."

"I believe Arthur's right," said Beth.

"Hmm," hummed Jonathan. "If you say so."

"She do," said Kahlúa.

"He do, too," confirmed Millie.

Arthur backed up half a sentence.

∞§[ARTHUR]§∞

"... only once did she mention a specific pictorial detail—Justice without a blindfold."

The doctor lowered his eyebrows. "And from this you infer?"

I gave him a smile that I hoped came across as perceptive. "It was one of the few visual details common to that card in both the Marseilles deck, which I suspect Madam Ouspenskaya used, and the one published by Arthur E. Waite in 1909, which is the deck under a glass bowl in the séance room."

A powerful emotion erupted behind the doctor's eyes, but nothing else on the landscape of his face betrayed it, making it impossible to interpret.

"When she drew the previous card, the Two of Swords," I continued, "she said it denoted courage, friendship, and so on, and that its position in the Revealing Star indicated that Mr. Piaget had recently made a decision. She made no mention of the girl holding the swords with her wrists crossed. She couldn't have, because the card before her would have only depicted two stylized swords."

The doctor swallowed audibly.

"The biggest giveaway, of course, is your choice of paintings," I added with finality. "I noticed them when I first entered the séance room. They match the cards on the table, and they're a nice touch. But they're all Waite's designs, and they postdated the séance we're reenacting by more than a decade."

Dr. Horehound looked frostily at me but said nothing.

∞§[Martin]§∞

"Aha!" said Jonathan. "So Arthur, you *did* know about the discrepancy."

"Much to my amazement now, yes," said Arthur, staring at his own handwriting on the pages. "Along with so much else I didn't know I knew."

"You're scary sometimes," said Beth. "Do you know that?"

"Don't stop now!" said Kahlúa. "The suspenders is killing me!"

Arthur wittily snapped one of his own at her, and continued.

∞§[ᴀʀᴛʜᴜʀ]§∞

"So your claim of authenticity hits a speed bump," I said. "As I suggested, this would not interest the others, but it does me."

"Very well," conceded Dr. Horehound, his jaws rigid and his lips barely moving. "The truth is that Madam Ouspenskaya's deck was hand-painted by one of her ancestral grandmothers. It was similar to the Marseilles deck, as you suggest, but was, in fact, a priceless family heirloom. Knowing this, Arianna Marigold placed it in Mr. Piaget's safe after Madam Ouspenskaya's body was found the next morning. None of her survivors ever came forward to claim it. I'm sorry to say it was lost in the shuffle of Piaget's relatives and probate litigation. I suppose I could have replaced it with an antique Marseilles set, but I so much prefer the Rider-Waite deck. Don't you?"

"Of course," I said, reluctant to agree with him about anything, but on this point I did. "Although the artwork is more simplistic in many ways, it overflows with details that earlier decks did not depict."

"Agreed," said the unsmiling doctor. "The imagery works so much better for my purposes. I came across the paintings in the catalog of an art dealer in London. Those eleven were all that was left of a complete set that was destroyed by a fire that decimated the ancestral home of a British lord who preferred that his name not be associated with them. They are unsigned, so the artist remains unknown, although the dealer believed they were painted around the time of the First World War."

"Considering your antireligious attitude," I said, "I'm surprised you included the Ace of Cups."

"I had considered installing it in one of the guest bathrooms," he said coldly, "but Miss Davenport liked it, for some reason. She suggested that it might provoke discussion amongst the more knowledgeable participants. As it turned out, you're the only one who has ever even taken notice of it. As I said a moment ago, Mr. von Derschmidt, I like the way your mind works. Nonetheless, all this granted and admitted, I can assure you that the order of the cards, which is the important thing, remains consistent with the list made by Bartholomew Piaget the day after the séance."

"But there we have a problem," said I, leaning back in my chair.

"How so?" he said, leaning forward in his.

"There is another list," I said, patting the diary.

"Hidden within that book you hold so dearly?" he asked derisively. "It couldn't have been. The list was only made after Madam Ouspenskaya was found murdered."

"Nonetheless, this book I hold so dearly contains a list." I allowed that to sink in before I continued. "I didn't realize what it was at first. Four columns of eighteen items equals seventy-two in all. They were rendered in pencil, not ink, and apparently erased and reworked several times. She used abbreviations." I began ticking them off from memory:

H.P.

STR

2—S

JST

4—S

DTH

"H.P. is the High Priestess," I explained. "S-T-R: the Star; 2—S: the Two of Swords; and so on. The first six match the cards Madam Douceur placed in the Revealing Star last night. I'd have to examine the deck to see if they coincide beyond that.

But even if she only predicted the first six, Madam Ouspenskaya was one Hell of a prophet."

"Not at all," said Dr. Horehound stiffly. "All it proves is the illegitimacy of that diary. The sworn accounts of everyone present agreed: Madam Ouspenskaya directed Bartholomew Piaget to shuffle the deck himself before she entered the room to conduct the séance. She was a clairvoyant of considerable renown, but even so I find it hard to believe that she could predict the order of a Tarot deck before it had been shuffled."

"As do I," I agreed with him again, darn it.

"Therefore that diary postdates the séance."

"Perhaps," I admitted, but then added, "or there was something hinky about the séance from the get-go."

"I think not, Mr. von Derschmidt, but as the saying goes, 'Let us agree to disagree.'"

"Dr. Horehound, I would prefer to say, 'Let us agree *that* we disagree.'"

"Oh?"

"Otherwise we're conceding that it's acceptable for one of us to be wrong. As an Ultra-realist, I find that untenable."

Dr. Horehound mulled that over before answering, "As you wish. I've never liked that saying, either."

I acknowledged his concession with a gracious nod before proceeding. "If I may trouble you further, there's another matter you can help me with. In all your research is there any mention of Madam Ouspenskaya having a penchant for roses?"

"Roses? Roses."

Dr. Horehound turned that over in his mind for a few moments. Then he got up from his chair and strode over to the sideboard. From a drawer he withdrew an eight-by-ten glass-covered picture frame. He handed it to me before resuming his seat. It was a group portrait, very old, the image rendered in that reddish-brown sepia tone characteristic of monochrome photographs of the late 19th century. Bartholomew Piaget I recognized from the painting in the library. He was posed on the front porch with two women and five men, all dressed in period clothing and huddled around a rotund woman with glaring eyes.

"Roses," I agreed. They protruded from Madam Ouspenskaya's ostentatious hat, and they were stitched into the pattern of her blouse and skirt.

"I used to have an enlargement mounted above the mantelpiece in the séance room," said the doctor. "But I soon realized all it did was emphasize how unlike the original party the participants inevitably were. So, in the spirit of the Minimum Information Gambit, I took it down and keep the original in the sideboard drawer while reenactments are in progress. The Wolfram family crest fills the space above the fireplace nicely, I think."

"She did seem to like roses," I said, setting the picture frame on the table next to the diary. "Many of the corners of these pages are decorated with them—the circled word, not drawings of the flower."

"Perhaps your forger wasn't an artist," said Dr. Horehound.

Thinking that most forgers, in fact, would be, I asked, "What about the roses in the center of the garden? Do you have any idea when they were planted?"

"During the renovation," he answered, crushing out his cigarette. "The landscapers were guided by receipts I found in the basement, mostly signed by Bartholomew Piaget, although it was likely Gabrielle who selected the plants. Mr. von Dershmidt, I appreciate your fervor regarding that diary, but as I said, it can't be genuine. The list is impossible, the rose references are coincidental at best, and while a torn bill printed in the specific year is a compelling touch, nothing connects it to the book. It could have been inserted between the pages at any time. If you wish to persist in your misdirected obsession, be my guest. I imagine you'll spend your afternoon getting a headache squinting at that cramped handwriting, but if you will excuse me, other matters demand my attention."

With that he left me to my questions, my thoughts, and my theories.

∞§[Martin]§∞

"So," said Beth as Arthur handed Pierre his pages. "You and Father Baptist should maybe go into business together."

"Sherlock von Dershmidt and Slap-Happy-Bappy," mused Jonathan. "It has a certain ring."

"Of what, I'm not sure," said Father Baptist.

"A cowbell, I'd say," said Arthur, seating himself.

"So what happened next?" asked Edward impatiently.

"Now we retire to the séance room," said Pierre. "Beth excels in descriptions of insidious Tarot readings."

"I'm not sure what that says about me," said Beth, rising to the occasion. "But I'm game."

∞§[†]§∞

∞§✝§∞

24. The Identifier This Time Around Is Death

∞§[*Beth*]§∞

"SO WHAT HAPPENS NOW?" asked Edward as we settled into our appointed chairs. "I mean, without Madam Douceur to deal the cards—?"

"We'll just have to wait and see what kind of script our host provides this evening," said Pierre.

"He's late," I said. "So unetiquettical—is that a word?"

"No comment," said Arthur. "I'm the indecorous lout." After a last furtive glance at one of the pages, he closed the diary and set it on the table near his right hand. With his left, he gave mine an encouraging squeeze.

"So did you finish it?" asked Jonathan, reaching across the void left by Clarice Davenport and tapping the cover.

"Unfortunately, no," sighed Arthur, pinching the bridge of his nose. "Such handwriting! But I've deciphered enough to know that the magnet that drew Cassandra Ouspenskaya to the home of Bartholomew Piaget was not a wish to bolster her career as a spiritualist. It was her seething desire for revenge."

"Revenge," said Edward. "That's a strong word. I wonder what he did to make her so furious."

"Miss Poe used it, too," said Pierre.

"Did Madam O specify what kind of revenge?" asked Jonathan.

"Not so far," said Arthur. "But considering the depth of her rancor, it would have been something fiendishly unpleasant."

"If that was indeed the point of her coming," said Pierre, "then her plan obviously backfired, whatever it was."

"Malice, once sent out, has a way of turning on the sender," said Arthur. "Lenore mentioned that, too."

"Oh, so it's 'Lenore' now, is it?" I kidded him.

"What do you think Madam O was trying to do?" asked Edward. "Hex him?"

"That would explain a lot," said Arthur. "Conceivably, she came here to lay a curse upon him, and her malevolence rebounded back upon her when Bartholomew Piaget broke the circle. Bad form, botched ritual, adverse outcome."

"So what do you suppose happened to him?" asked Jonathan.

"Why do you bother?" scoffed Joel, whose eyes had taken on an apprehensive furtiveness—like someone at a party who knows something super exciting is about to happen any second, but has been sworn to secrecy by the host. Only this wasn't that kind of party, and he seemed as put out with Dr. Horehound as he was with us. "I mean, really," he added derisively. "This is all going nowhere."

"To be forewarned is to be forearmed," said Arthur. He waved his hand, indicating the paintings looking down upon us. "And this is hardly nowhere."

"Darn near it," said Edward. "I tell you, I'm going bonkers wondering what we're going to do about our cars. How will we get them out of here? What are we going to say to the mechanic if and when we get a tow? And neither of us can afford new engines."

"That's for sure," agreed Arthur, tugging his lapels.

"It's quite a pickle," said Pierre. "I'm sure Kahlúa will feel obliged to help, if and when we get in touch with her. I wish now I'd thought to phone her while we were in town."

"And I got so distracted I neglected to call Fr. Baptist," said Arthur, rubbing his shoulder. "But as for Miss Hummingbird, she might not be so amenable if Dr. Horehound sends her a bill for the tower door before you get the chance to explain the circumstances to her. She may get the impression that we've been having a free-for-all at her expense."

"Well," said Pierre, stifling a yawn, "there is that."

"You're taking it all rather calmly," said Edward.

Pierre shrugged. "I strive not to fret about that over which I exercise no control."

"I envy you," said Arthur. "I'm fretting about just such a matter—the parallel between the events of 1896 and the present."

"You mean both mediums ending up dead," said Jonathan.

"And both personal secretaries disappearing," said Pierre, "although we had something to do with Clarice Davenport's getaway."

"So," said Edward, "you think Piaget's secretary—what was her name?"

"Arianna Marigold," said Pierre.

"You think Miss Marigold hitched a ride into town with someone?"

"I'm just noting the correspondence of events," said Arthur. "We'll come full circle if Dr. Horehound goes missing tomorrow."

"Yeah," said Jonathan. "Like last night, only permanent. Then what will we do?"

"The doctor has two vehicles in the garage," said Arthur. "Assuming we could find the keys—"

"And the engines haven't turned into wood," said Edward.

"—and we don't get arrested for car theft," added Arthur.

"Sheriff Brumus would understand," said Pierre. "Besides, he's bound to come up and see why we haven't returned to pick up Miss Davenport."

"Yeah," said Edward, "assuming his car engine doesn't sprout leaves along the way."

"Well," said Pierre with a shrug, "there is that."

"Good Heavens," was all I could think to say.

"Can I ask you something?" said Jonathan, regarding Arthur with furrowed brows. "I've known of your penchant for history, literature, and—shall we say—peculiar old movies, but I guess I'm a little surprised at your interest in the occult. You haven't said much about it till now."

"And for good reason," said Arthur. "In this arena, even among close friends, it is extremely easy to be misunderstood. If I were to admit that I find certain realms of the occult fascinating, it is a brief step to the assumption that I promote or encourage its pursuit. The fact is that I studied it years ago to fill a void during a time when I was thoroughly discouraged by what was going on in the Church, primarily in my parish and diocese, but also all over the world."

"The Vatican II blues," said Jonathan, settling back in his chair.

"Let me put it this way," said Arthur. "I'd found some occult practices that were redolent of incense, mysticism, and magickal imagery, concepts that had been leeched out of the revised rites of the Catholic Church—indeed, out of Catholic thinking altogether—to be replaced, to my horror, with Calvinism."

"I know about the changes, Big Bro," I said. "But I'm not following you. Calvinism?"

"You haven't met Fr. Baptist," said he to me with a smile reminiscent of the one he wore when he greeted me at the airport. "He calls Calvinism the 'Big Chopping Block.' Everything must be black or white—*chop!*—no grays allowed. Heaven and Hell, sure, but—*chop!*—no such transitory place as Purgatory. Jesus came to save us—*chop!*—no room for the Virgin Mary as Co-Redemptrix. Scripture alone. All that is needed to save one's soul is confined to a single book, so—*chop!*—goodbye less confinable Tradition."

"Uh, that last was Luther," I interjected.

"Same principle, same impulse," said Arthur. "Protestantism begins with a human innovation expressed as an assumption: faith alone, scripture alone, identification of the elect by material success, and so on. Once accepted as a premise, its adherents reject that which doesn't fit or conform to it. Luther says 'faith alone' so—*chop!*—so much for good works. What did St. James, a mere Apostle, know? There is only one mediator in Christ Jesus—*chop!*—so long Communion of the Saints. Jesus died once and for all, therefore—*chop!*—farewell redundant Holy Sacrifice of the Mass."

Jonathan wrinkled his brow. "What does that have to do—?"

"We've all grown up in a Protestant culture," said Arthur. "It percolates into our thinking without our realizing or wishing it. It's no secret that the *Novus Ordo* was a concession to the Protestants. A group of them helped write the darn thing at the

Vatican. We woke up one day—I did, anyway—to find myself
in a veritable desert, starving for a sense of the transcendent."

"I'm trying to understand," I said. "Really I am, but—"

"Let me tell you about the Latin Mass as I remember it from
my childhood," said Arthur. "I'm talking about growing up in
Ohio before you came along, Sis. Truly, it was the most
magickal thing I'd ever experienced, apart from fanciful tales
only found in books. It was a feast for all the senses. Our ears
were tantalized by the medieval modes of Gregorian chant, tonal
relationships not to be heard anywhere else in our daily lives.
The haunting aroma of smoldering frankincense, myrrh, and
other exotic resins titillated our nostrils, arousing brilliant and
unexpected images in our imaginations. Our eyes were drawn to
magnificent works of art all around us, statues of Saints, paintings of biblical scenes, architecture that uplifted our spirits.
Meanwhile, the priest practically ignored us, so intent was he on
performing every action perfectly. We all knelt there watching,
waiting, meditating, praying, worshipping because somehow we
knew that God was coming into our midst, signified by the
cheerful, endearing tintinnabulation of the altar bells."

"Oh, Arthur," I whispered.

"But then things changed. You had come along by then, Sis.
You grew up in the midst of the travesty. I well remember how
it affected Dad. Mom was a better sport about it, but he—he
took it hard. He went from being an enthused daily communi-
cant to a reluctant attendee just on Sundays. The reason was obvious. The profound was replaced with the trivial, the mystical
by the mundane. Even though St. Pius X had forbidden the intrusion of popular music into the liturgy, the organ and well-
rehearsed choir were supplanted by guitars and discordant ama-
teur singers with tambourines. Incense was deemed passé, and
kneelers were removed. Church buildings were gutted, Communion rails ripped out, statues of Saints relegated to the dumpsters. In short order we were subjected to folk Masses, rock
Masses, mariachi Masses, polka Masses, African drum Masses,
clown Masses, and kiddy Masses. The singing and handshaking
and participating consumed the whole liturgy, while every hint
of the transcendent, every scent of the magickal, every notion of

pure awe was leeched out, wrung out, and squeezed out. You may remember that for a while there, toward the end of high school, I stopped attending."

"Yes," I said, sadly recalling our parents' worried reaction to that. "Dad was upset, but he understood. Mom said you'd work your way back somehow."

"I did eventually," said Arthur, perking up, "although by a wildly circuitous path. Some of my chums looked into Oriental and Central American religions, but I already had my answers, I was just weary of seeing them trampled. One day at the university bookstore, I happened upon a book entitled *The Greater Trumps* by Charles Williams."

"I've heard of him," said Pierre. "Wasn't he one of the Inklings?"

"Inklings?" I asked.

"C. S. Lewis' literary club at Oxford," said Pierre. "J. R. R. Tolkien was a member. They used to read their rough drafts to one another at a pub or something."

"The Greater Trumps are part of the Tarot deck," said Arthur, pointing to the Hierophant, the Fool, and the Hermit on the walls. "I found Williams' story dark and implausible, yet the imagery was intriguing. Because of that book, I began researching the Tarot in the library. It was then that I began to rediscover that which I had lost."

"Williams died a Protestant, though, didn't he?" said Pierre. "As did C. S. Lewis."

"Ironically, yes," said Arthur, "in spite of Tolkien's staunch attempts to convert them. But even so, Williams was something of a renegade in Church of England circles."

"Now I'm thoroughly lost," said I. "Arthur, what are you saying? What did you rediscover?"

"Li'l Sis," he said, taking my hand. "Remember when Dad was transferred to the nightshift, and I took to reading to you before you went to sleep? The poems I taught you? You were only five or six, but—" He snapped his fingers and smiled conspiratorially. "Let's see if you remember this one." He puffed out his cheeks and rippled his brow, transforming himself into a Scottish minstrel:

> True Thomas lay on Huntlie bank;
> A ferlie he spied wi' his e'e;
> And there he saw a ladye bright
> Come riding down by the Eildon Tree.

Before I could express my total befuddlement, he reached out and ran his fingers through my hair. Then he splayed his fingers and waved them to indicate my dress:

> Her skirt was o' the grass-green silk,
> Her mantle o' the velvet fyne;
> At ilka tett o' her horse's mane,
> Hung fifty siller bells and nine.

For the third stanza he slipped off his chair and fell to one knee, just like he used to do at my bedside—only not nearly as graceful anymore. He pretended to remove a large feathered hat and bow deeply before me. I giggled then just as I invariably had all those years ago.

> True Thomas he pu'd aff his cap,
> And louted low down on his knee
> "Hail to thee Mary, Queen of Heaven!
> For thy peer on earth could never be!"

Then Arthur raised his head and looked at me with those mischievous eyes, expecting me to recite the next lines. I leapt into my part, shaking my locks and sitting up very straight, peering down at him over my right shoulder:

> "O no, O no, Thomas," she said,
> "That name does not belang to me;
> I'm but the Queen o' fair Elfland,
> That am hither come to visit thee."

"Splendid!" he said with an appreciative chuckle. "You haven't forgotten!" With that he heaved himself awkwardly back onto his chair. He took a moment to rearrange his jacket and waistcoat which had gone all cockeyed. I reached around and straightened his ponytail with a good yank. "You haven't forgotten," he said again, taking my hand in his and giving it a peck, "but the Catholic world certainly has."

"Good delivery, Beth," said Jonathan. "But Arthur, it's now I that don't follow you."

"'Thomas the Rhymer,'" explained Arthur, releasing my hand so he could address his friends. "An old poem about a Scottish laird in the thirteenth century. Don't you see? He's lazing there in the grass and this lovely lass comes riding up on a horse. What's the first thought that comes to his mind? A lady so beautiful surely must be the Blessed Virgin! Where do you hear that kind of thing today? We don't expect it on television, of course, but even in conversations with other Catholics? On the steps of St. Philomena's? What Catholic man, upon spotting a beautiful woman, thinks of the Queen of Heaven?"

"Granted," said Jonathan. "You've got a point."

"But Arthur," said Joel, almost sneering. "The lady in the poem—she's an *elf!*"

"Exactly!" exclaimed my brother. "What Catholic poem or song or story in living memory—barring Tolkien, our last great hope—talks about elves and dwarves and dragons?"

Joel scowled. "You're saying that Catholics should believe in elves and dwarves and dragons?"

"Not as an article of Faith, no," said Arthur. "But there's room in the Catholic worldview for such things. Indeed, some of the Saints wrote about them."

"Elves and dragons?" asked Joel, incredulously.

"Incubi and secubi, surely," said Pierre. "St. Augustine, yes? Or was it St. Jerome?"

"And satyrs and faeries," said Arthur, seriously. "I brought along a book I've been reading—thought it might come in handy 'round the fire at night."

"Little did you know," said Edward.

"I was sure I took it up to my room when we arrived yesterday," said Arthur, "but I can't seem to find it. Maybe it's in the car. Anyway, as I was saying, there used to be room in the Catholic mindset for inexplicable things. Theologians used to write copiously about beings that inhabit the mists between matter and spirit. In a Calvinist world there is only black and white, remember? Only that which can be pinned down is allowed. All else must go."

"Maybe it's because the things you've been going on about don't exist," said Joel. "Ever think of that? Grownups don't believe in magic."

"But grownup Catholics do," countered Arthur. "At every turn. Magick with a 'k.' Jesus turned water into wine and fed a crowd with a few loaves and fishes. He raised Himself from the dead, for Heaven's sake—and ours! What is the Consecration at Mass if not magick? Or Baptism, Penance, or Holy Orders? A formula is uttered, matter is manipulated, and things deeper than our senses can perceive are changed. If the God who made the universe chose to save us through such hilariously baffling, inexplicable means, should we not expect His creation to be spilling over with reflections of His mystifying nature?"

"Maybe I'm not comfortable calling those things *magical*," I said. "Jesus didn't say 'Abracadabra' over the water at Cana."

"No indeed," said Arthur. "That would be magical with a 'c.' Stage magic is illusion, trickery. Nothing really changes. *Jesus transformed substance.* He said 'Draw some and take it to the chief steward,' and thus water became wine: magickal with a 'k.' The priest at Mass says, *'Hoc est enim Corpus meum'*—"

"Which our detractors contracted to 'Hocus pocus,'" said Pierre.

"Because they saw it as magical with a 'c,'" said Arthur. "The Consecration is magickal in the classical medieval sense: High Magick with a 'k.' Again we see how Protestantism has muddled our concepts. I'll say it again: High Magick. Why are we afraid of the word?"

"I suppose because of those 'Maguses' you were talking about earlier," said Jonathan. "Summoning demons and all that."

"And where did they get the idea to do so?" said Arthur. "What gave the *'Magi,'* as they're properly called—yes, just like the Three Wise Men from the East, although they came centuries earlier—what gave ceremonial magicians the notion that they had the power to command demons in the first place? It's all in the ancient Rite of Exorcism of the Catholic Church! We cringe at the word 'magick' out of embarrassment, I fear—just like 'predestination'—because we don't take our own religion seriously anymore. Who among us really believes that we're surrounded by the clouds of witnesses St. Paul wrote about, the Angels and Devils vying for our souls every minute of every day? What Saint said that if we could see what's really going on in the ethereal world around us we'd faint dead away from fright?"

Pierre opened his mouth as if to answer, but just then another voice intruded into the conversation.

"Waxing eloquent are we, Mr. von Derschmidt?" said Dr. Horehound, quietly entering the room. The louse. He must have come creeping down the corridor, eavesdropping every step of the way. How long had he been standing just outside the door, that insufferable smile splitting his snooty grapefruit face in half?

"Dr. Horehound," said Arthur, settling back in his chair.

"Right," said Joel. "Sure."

∞§[Martin]§∞

GARDENING TIPS: Just thought I'd provide another chart of the seating arrangement to show
how symmetrical it was until Dr. Horehound
threw the whole thing off by sitting between
Joel and Beth:

Pierre   Edward

    Joel   Jonathan

      ---   ---

        Beth   Arthur

                                    --M.F.

∞§[*Beth*]§∞

"I've been observing, you know," said Dr. Horehound, not circling the table this time but going directly to his chair beside me and seating himself. He was wearing that puffy evening jacket again, and that infernal fez with the swinging tassel. "Old professional habits die hard and all that," he continued with an arrogant air. "By way of example: it's obvious from the deference you all pay him, that Mr. Bontemps is your leader, the head of your valiant troop. Leaders are not necessarily the smartest or the wisest, nor are they always the most manipulative. Still, they know when to defer to the expertise of their lieutenants, and, most importantly, they possess the courage—the spunk, the *chutzpah*, if you will—to make decisions on behalf of all. You, Mr. Bontemps, are quite the charmer, and you command because your instincts compel you. Thus you will always be alone, in a sense, even among your closest friends. But you, Mr. von Derschmidt, you are the heart—perhaps the soul—of your fellowship. You are the deep one, the mystic if I may be so candid. You live in a world of grays and mixed hues. I fear you will never know, therefore, what it is to be at peace, or to be truly happy. Mr. Wyndham, on the other hand, is your nuts-and-bolts man. He measures things in precise feet and inches, not nebulous leaps and bounds. It was he who first pointed to the letter of the law, insisting that Madam Douceur swear against performing a séance in your midst, and the rest of you followed his lead. The fact that he sought to retrieve the rented tent this morning, considering the commotion sparked by the discovery of Madam's corpse in the garden, shows that when the chips are down, he's the one who will see to the details everyone else overlooks. Boring, but dependable—and therefore indispensable. Mr. Clubb is a bit hard to read at the moment, other than that he's focused on Miss von Derschmidt, who, being more mature than he, is likely beyond his grasp. By the way, Beth—may I call you Beth? No? Well, in any case, I'm glad to see that increasing your medication has allayed your narcoleptic seizures. Would that some of your intrinsic postponement issues were so easily dispelled. With your permission we'll leave that for later, however, because the real delight of the hour is Mr. Maruppa, our Judas Iscariot. I rescind my suggestion that he ever met me before Sunday. He would have made a formidable patient, which is why he is not in my employ and never shall be. I couldn't trust him, and neither should you. He's no longer one of you, don't you know. He has moved on."

As much as each of us had some sort of retort to make by the end of our host's taunting soliloquy, this last drew all our suspicious looks at Joel, who glowered right back. His ears had turned crimson red.

"Thanks for the pocket psychoanalysis," said Pierre. "I suppose your bill will be waiting for us when we get home."

"I offer these insights gratis," said Dr. Horehound magnanimously. "Truly, you've been one of my most intriguing groups of participants."

"Speaking of which," said Edward, who had not been pleased by our host's analysis. "What are we going to do now? Without Madam Douceur to conduct another séance or read the cards—"

"There is the question," said Dr. Horehound vaguely. "The original guests did not disperse for several days."

"The police probably didn't let them leave," said Edward.

"That's right," said Pierre. "They didn't."

"So what did everyone do?" asked Jonathan.

"You didn't bring a script this evening," said Pierre. "Oh, I see—the Minimum Information Gambit."

"Precisely," said Dr. Horehound. "I'm curious to see what course you'll decide to pursue."

"I suggest we view the next six cards," said Arthur, indicating the deck nestled under the inverted crystal bowl. "I believe that is what Madam Ouspenskaya would have wanted. Perhaps Madam Douceur, also."

"An excellent idea," said Dr. Horehound. "However, the deck has been compromised since last we met."

"How so?" asked Pierre.

"Clarice Davenport should have secured them in my unexpected absence last night," said Dr. Horehound. "But I understand that she reneged, and while the rest of you were all tearing my home apart in search of Mr. Maruppa, Madam Douceur perused the deck in here, unattended. She went so far as to take it with her to another part of the house."

"Who told you that?" asked Edward.

"There are two obvious possibilities," said our host, smiling furtively. His eyes traced the contour of the ceiling as everyone turned their attention toward our Judas Iscariot. Then, just before Joel was about to blurt out an unconvincing denial, Dr. Horehound said, almost to himself, "You might say it was one of Miss Davenport's parting shots. A good one, too."

"Whatever Madam Douceur may or may not have done," said Arthur, placing his right hand upon the diary, "the cards are in their proper sequence. I checked."

"Really," said Dr. Horehound. "You mean the first six."

"No. All seventy-two."

"Did you now." The doctor gave Big Bro a penetrating, almost daring look. "And how would you know their proper sequence? Oh, the proffered diary."

"Precisely," said Arthur, taking up the book. "Madam Ouspensakya listed them beforehand, as I told you after dinner."

"Excuse me?" asked Pierre. "You said beforehand?"

"I did," said Big Bro as he opened the diary to a dog-eared page. Knowing his respect for books, I knew he had found it that way. His eyes widened and then narrowed as he examined something. Then, his memory of its contents refreshed, he closed the cover. "Yes, considering how many pages she filled afterwards, I would say months in advance."

"Incredible," said Pierre.

"Impossible," said Dr. Horehound.

Arthur shrugged. "I suggested to Madam Douceur last night that when Bartholomew handed the shuffled cards to Madam Ouspenskaya, his ownership passed to her. I am now convinced she owned the outcome long before that. She made a number of one-word glosses throughout her list. Beside the sixth entry, for example, she had scribbled the word, 'Risk."

"What card was that?" I asked.

"Death."

"Are you suggesting that she somehow manipulated the order of the deck?" asked Edward. "Why would she do that?"

"To control the outcome," said Arthur.

"Mr. von Derschmidt," said Dr. Horehound forcefully. "You insist on barking up errant trees. I told you: the accounts of those in attendance agree. At Madam Ouspenskaya's insistence, Bartholomew Piaget shuffled the deck before she entered the room. The deck remained in plain sight on the table throughout the séance. It would take time to organize seventy-two cards in hiding, let alone in view of eight witnesses."

"She was a resourceful woman," said Arthur, "and she clearly hated her host."

"Indeed," said Dr. Horehound. "I'll have to take your word for it, having never read or seen that diary before today."

"And I'll have to take your word for that," said Arthur. "Even so, you came in here before us and checked the deck yourself."

"Really," said Dr. Horehound. "Were you spying on me?"

"No," said Arthur. "Last evening, just before retiring, Madam Douceur felt obliged to return the deck to this room, and I accompanied her. With the greatest reluctance, before placing them under the crystal bowl, she allowed me to peruse the cards.

I did so again a few minutes ago. They had been handled in the interim, I assume by you."

"Indeed," said Dr. Horehound. "How could you tell?"

"With the exception of Madam Ouspenskaya's Revealing Star," explained Arthur, "every system I've studied emphasizes not just the position of the cards as they are placed in the spread, but also their orientation. When dealt upright they mean one thing, when inverted, the opposite. Call it force of habit, but I notice such things. Hence, I know that several of the cards in this deck, though still in the right order, have been inverted since last night."

"You are the bright one," said Dr. Horehound. "Okay, I'll admit it. I did inspect the deck. After Miss Davenport's assertion, I considered it mandatory. I confess I wasn't thinking of the orientation, so I may very well have replaced some of them upside down."

"No harm done," said Arthur. "If we were using the Celtic Cross or the Wheel of Life spreads, it would be critical. But since we're bound to Madam Ouspenskaya's system, it doesn't matter."

"In any case, you want to continue with the reading," said Dr. Horehound.

"Most assuredly," said Arthur.

"Excellent, excellent. During several previous reenactments, the same suggestion was made and seconded."

"But who will deal the cards?" asked Edward.

"Don't look at me," I said, folding my arms. "I don't want to touch them."

"Mr. Bontemps, then," said Dr. Horehound. "You are closest."

"With the caveat that I do not relinquish my Free Will to them," said Pierre, lifting the crystal bowl—for all the good it had done!—and setting it on the empty chair beside him, "I'll gladly oblige."

"Oh, caveat away," said Dr. Horehound. "I'll not interfere with your quaint superstitions."

"Quaint but true," said Pierre, gingerly picking up the deck. "Not being a medium, I'll skip the forced rhyme scheme; and, the transatlantic psychic lines being down, we'll dispense with the call to Karnak. Okay, so the first six cards were laid out thus." With the hands of an experienced dealer—poker, I assume, not divination—Pierre set out the first six cards in the order and pattern as before, the last card—the Significator, Death—set in the middle of the star. Setting down the deck, he spread his fingers and pressed them down upon the array and deftly slid them to his left, in front of Madam Douceur's empty place. "Okay," he said as he gathered the deck into his hands again, "I'll start the next spread here in front of me."

"A word," said Arthur as Pierre began to peel the next card from the top. "Humor me, please. Take the Significator from the first spread, and make it the Identifier of this one."

"Really," said Pierre and Dr. Horehound together.

"What are you up to?" I whispered to Arthur.

"It's never been done that way before," said Dr. Horehound. "All the cards will be offset from here on."

"I'm utilizing the minimum information at hand," said Arthur mysteriously as he rested his hand upon the diary, "also overlapping brackets, penciled so faintly alongside the column of abbreviations, I almost missed them. Whatever your guests have done in the past, I suggest we play it this way. You did say it was up to us."

"I did at that," said Dr. Horehound appreciatively. "Fine, have at it."

I couldn't help but notice sweat trickling down the side of our host's face again. He was trying very hard to steady himself, but I could see a slight tremor in his fingers. History repeats, I thought to myself, in more ways than one.

"I'd like to dispense with the handholding, if you don't mind," I blurted, failing to suppress the revulsion in my voice as the doctor's moist hand shifted toward mine. The thought of contact was a little too much just then.

"This won't be a séance," said Arthur. "Nor are our actions or intentions in any sense magickal. No Circle of Protection will be necessary."

The doctor's hand curled into a wet, pouting fist. Whew.

"Okay," said Pierre. "As we have agreed, the Identifier this time around is Death. I place it at the head of the Revealing Star.

The next card, the right foot, signifying the Remote Past, is ...
The Lovers." He placed it ceremoniously at the bottom left
point. I almost objected, but then remembered that the layout of
the Revealing Star represented a man facing us. His right foot
mirrored our left. Irksome.

It struck me as an earthy card, embarrassingly so. At the top
glowed the sun, the rays playing upon an elfish figure with
leaves for hair and flowing robes. Beneath him, to the left, stood
a naked woman—Eve, I supposed—because behind her grew a
fruit-bearing tree with a serpent entwined about it. Opposite her
stood a naked man, Adam, in front of a different tree with twelve
burning flames instead of apples in its branches.

"This is a card of entangled opposites," said Arthur. "Man and
woman, giver and taker, deceiver and believer, active and passive strength, active and passive weakness. It denotes the complexity that is affection, the peril that is trust, in other words, the
mystery that is love."

"All that in a single card," pondered Jonathan.

"Madam Ouspenskaya couldn't have said it better," said Dr.
Horehound.

"Actually, she did," said Arthur, patting the diary. "I, on the
other hand, would prefer to summarize it according to the specific imagery, thus: Adam stands at the Tree of Life; Eve
chooses the Tree of Knowledge. The Fall is at hand."

"Excuse me," said Jonathan. "Aside from being lost, I'm also
confused. Just who is represented by the Identifier? Is it still
Mr. Piaget?"

"Who else?" asked Dr. Horehound. "The reading was entirely
his."

"Not necessarily," said Edward. "There was a discussion after
you left us last evening. The first spread culminated in Death,
and it was Madam Ouspenskaya who died. Obviously she was
reading her own future."

"If she somehow manipulated the cards, as Mr. von Derschmidt maintains," said the doctor, "then it would follow that
she conceived and planned a horrible death for herself. Does
that make sense to you?"

"Again, not necessarily," said Arthur. "As you well know, the Death card is rarely taken literally. It usually denotes a consummation, a transformation, or perhaps an upheaval. She scribbled the word 'Risk' beside it in her list, which suggests that she was playing some sort of deep game. Her demise, I believe, was an unintentional outcome."

"In any case," said Edward with a touch of impatience, "the next person affected in some way was the secretary, Arianna Marigold. She disappeared the day the body was found."

"Therefore she wouldn't have been present at the second reading that night," said Dr. Horehound. "It couldn't have been intended for her."

"If the Revealing Star was in reality a cleverly disguised curse," said Arthur, "and if Bartholomew Piaget broke the circle, as I suspect he did, then a malignant force was released, more potent than Madam Ouspenskaya ever intended. Once unbound, it turned upon her that night, rendering her risk fatal. Freed from its instigator, it no longer needed the cards or the spreads to carry out its purpose. Thus liberated, it assumed a momentum all its own, overtaking Arianna Marigold prematurely. It did the same with Bartholomew Piaget the following day."

"A most interesting if convoluted possibility," said Dr. Horehound. "Nothing of the sort has ever been suggested before."

"We're suggesting it now," said Arthur, smiling appreciatively at Edward, our nuts-and-bolts man.

"You were concerned about Dr. Horehound breaking the circle last night," said Jonathan. "Arthur, do you think the same curse was unleashed again? Is that what killed Madam Douceur?"

"That could very well be," said Arthur solemnly.

"An *animal* killed Madam Douceur," said Dr. Horehound.

"For all we know an animal killed Madam Ouspenskaya," said Edward. "Was that ever suggested by anyone at the time?"

"Yes, as a matter of fact," said Dr. Horehound. "Several of the guests believed that to be the case, although the county sheriff remained skeptical."

"What does that prove?" demanded Jonathan. "Man or beast, a curse is a curse."

"So are we in danger?" I asked, horrified.

A rumble of outrage and concern spread around the table.

"Everyone, please," said Pierre. "As far as we know, none of the original guests were hurt or injured in any way, just Madam Ouspenskaya and members of the Piaget household."

"I feel so much better," said Jonathan.

"In any case," said Arthur, "we've come this far. For good or ill, the genie is out of the bottle. Shall I continue?"

His question provoked an uneasy pause.

"The maxim is *'Qui tacet consentire,'*" said Arthur, referencing, I suspected, Sir Thomas More in Robert Bolt's *A Man for All Seasons*, his favorite modern play. "'Silence gives consent.'"

"Oh, go ahead," said Edward and Jonathan.

"In for a penny," I added edgily, making a Sign of the Cross.

"Hmm," mumbled Dr. Horehound, his forehead furrowed in thought. "Ah well, it's your gambit. Let's see how it plays out."

Actually, there was a reason why I did want to continue. During the above exchange I had been studying the Lovers in the Garden of Eden. A thought had formed that I felt compelled to express. And so I did. "Excuse me," I said. "Could Arianna Marigold and Bartholomew Piaget have been lovers?"

"Another original, and I may say, intriguing possibility," said Dr. Horehound after a moment's consideration.

"You mean," said Jonathan waving his hands around, "Piaget was so devoted to his wife that he built all this, and then, then— you know—right under the same roof?"

"Hold on," said Arthur. "Sis, you may be on to something. Dr. Horehound, didn't you tell us that Piaget had had a fling with Beth's character, Beverly Sarcenet?"

"That is so," said our host.

"Here?" I asked.

"No," said Dr. Horehound. "While doing business in Los Angeles. In his youth he was quite a philanderer."

"When was that?" I asked.

"Hmm," he replied. "Two years prior to the séance."

"As recently as that," I said. "Not so young."

"That's interesting," said Pierre. "And how long had Miss Marigold been in his employ?"

"I don't know for certain," said Dr. Horehound. "If memory serves, Mr. McAllister's letter of recommendation was postmarked sometime in 1893."

"Three years," said Jonathan. "Plenty of time for the pot to boil."

"Bravo, Sis," said Arthur enthusiastically. "It would explain a lot of things."

"You may be right," said Dr. Horehound reluctantly. "You see, we've always presumed the Lovers card to be the Identifier of the second spread, and therefore assumed it referred to Dr. Piaget's passionate love for his deceased wife, Gabrielle, and proceeded from there. With the spin you're suggesting, Miss von Derschmidt, it was Arianna Marigold's persona that was represented by the Death card, perhaps indicating some tragedy in her past which still marked her in the present."

"Maybe she'd sought comfort in the cold arms of her employer," said Jonathan. "Maybe that was the real basis of their relationship."

"We mustn't forget," said Pierre, "that she was with him in the library at the time of Gabrielle's fatal accident on the lake."

"Bartholomew Wolfram Piaget," I said under my breath. "Two-timing scumbag."

"My dear," said Dr. Horehound, snatching my hand and squeezing it with his dripping, twitching paw, "you take the cards too seriously."

"And nobody else who's sat around this infernal table ever did?" I huffed, pulling my hand away and wiping it observably in my lap.

"Okay, okay," he said patronizingly. "I'll concede that per-haps—*perhaps*—we are getting a new glimpse into the soft white underbelly of the affairs at Wolfram Lodge. It is worth pursuing as a viable possibility."

"Why, thank you," I said stiffly.

"The next card, then," said Pierre, placing it at the upper left point. The sound of thunder came growling down the chimney as he said, "The Immediate Past: the Three of Swords."

A striking card: a large heart suspended in the clouds with raindrops trailing beneath them. Three swords were thrust downward through the heart, their hilts protruding above, their tips splayed below. An icy shiver rippled through me.

"Rupture, remorse, absence," translated Arthur. "Oh heck, it's obvious."

"Heartbreak at Spirit Lake," said Jonathan. "Arianna and Bartholomew had a falling out?"

For a second I thought I saw something hazy around Jonathan's jaw line, like angels' hair on a Christmas tree. I blinked several times to see if it was an effect of the lighting, but it didn't go away. Uh-oh, I thought, maybe I'm having another attack of the drowsies—but I had doubled my medication after last night.

"The Immediate Future," said Pierre, placing the next card at the upper right point. "Hm. The Four of Cups. Arthur?"

It was a strange depiction: a dispirited young man sitting under a tree regarding three goblets before him. A hand appeared out of a small white cloud offering a fourth, but he didn't seem to be taking notice.

"A card of weariness, even disgust," said Arthur. "Ignoring an offer of something better. Wallowing in one's ill fortune, perhaps. Refusing to get up and move on."

"Poor Arianna," I said. "Unlike Clarice, who definitely upped and went."

"But not far," said Dr. Horehound. "I understand the motel is full and there are no buses. She must be holed up somewhere in town."

Pierre looked at him knowingly, as did Arthur, but they said nothing. I glanced at Jonathan and back at our host, thinking that a rat like Horehound should be sprouting straggly facial hair, not the man I was going to say a Rosary Novena with. Shoot, I thought, maybe now I'm over-medicated!

"So what of Arianna's Distant Future?" asked Edward. "Hopefully she got a hold of herself and moved on."

"Let's see," said Pierre, placing the next card at the lower right point. "The Six of Swords."

It was a strangely tranquil card, and yet unsettling at the same time. A ferryman was pushing his boat in the water with a long pole. The boat was moving away from us. At the bow stood six swords in some sort of rack, as if he was transporting a stock of weapons. But in the middle of the boat, wrapped in a veil, sat a woman. Huddled against her, a child.

"A journey by water," said Arthur. "Her weapons stowed, the woman departs. Long, slow, unhurried, deliberate."

"So Arianna went away without causing trouble," said Jonathan. "Perhaps with Mr. Piaget's bastard child."

"Or harboring some hope of having a child by a better man," said Arthur.

"Did Arianna take one of the boats and head across the lake?" I asked.

"Funny you should mention it," said Dr. Horehound. "The police report did mention that one of the boats was missing from the dock that evening. They found it some distance away, though, halfway up the eastern shore. The mooring line was trailing in the water, so they assumed it had simply come undone and drifted there. They found no trace of her on the shore. They brought dogs and everything, but they picked up no scent in the woods beyond."

"I assume they searched the lake for a body," said Pierre.

"Of course," said Dr. Horehound. "They found nothing. She didn't turn up in town, in another city, or anywhere afterwards."

"Still, the boat," said Edward.

"What can I tell you?" huffed Dr. Horehound.

"So what's the Significator?" asked Jonathan. "What did Arianna become in the end?"

"Assuming she made no decisions which changed the course of events," added Arthur.

"The Moon," said Pierre thoughtfully placing the last card in the center of the star.

It was a card of clashing images. A large moon with a down-turned face hung in the sky, lots of large and small rays emanating from it. Below were two hounds—or perhaps a dog and a wolf?—apparently howling at it. In the foreground was a pool of water, with a lobster, of all things, crawling out onto the shore.

"Arthur?" I asked.

"The Moon," he said, almost dreamily. "Another card of entangled opposites, only unlike the Lovers, this struggle is entirely internal—the life of imagination apart from the life of the spirit.

Animal nature, rising from the murky depths, claws its way out onto the land, looking longingly up at the moon, a symbol of light, of dreams. Notice in the distance there are two simple towers, and beyond that a distant land, perhaps a land of promise. It is a card of tension, of indecision: to journey forward into the unknown, or to slip back down into the familiar."

∞§[Martin]§∞

GARDENING TIPS: A Nyilatkozo Csillag, Phase

Two:

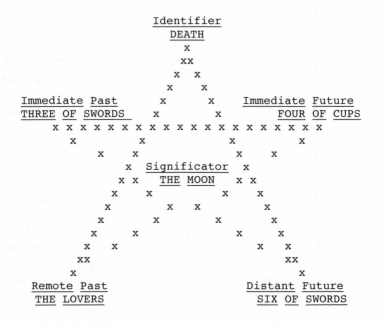

```
                        Identifier
                        DEATH
                          x
                         xx
                        x  x
                       x    x
Immediate Past         x     x      Immediate Future
THREE OF SWORDS        x     x              FOUR OF CUPS
  x x x x x x x x x x x x x x x x x x x x x
      x          x              x           x
        x    x                 x    x
          x  Significator  x
          x x  THE MOON  x x
         x    x        x    x
        x      x    x        x
        x      x    x        x
       x    x              x    x
      x  x                  x    x
      xx                        xx
     x                           x
    Remote Past              Distant Future
    THE LOVERS                SIX OF SWORDS
```

                                            --M.F.

∞§[ℬℯ𝓉𝒽]§∞

"And that's where we leave her?" I retorted. "Wondering whether to get the heck out of here?"

"Your sense of drama does you justice, my dear," said Dr. Horehound, dabbing his face with a silk handkerchief.

"Getting the queasies again?" I asked without a hint of sympathy.

"You noticed," he said, lifting his fez and mopping his brow. "I fear it's coming on again. I can't imagine what's effecting me this way."

"Prime rib this time," said Edward.

"I suppose I deserve that," said Dr. Horehound, securing his silly hat and tossing the tassel back out of the way. It fell forward again in front of his eyes. "But before I excuse myself, I want to say 'Bravo.' You've come up with something original and unique. Nowhere in Mr. Piaget's memoirs did he mention any such relationship with his secretary, and yet it seems to me that it was probably as the cards have revealed. You have achieved a breakthrough."

"What does that do to your skepticism?" asked Arthur, resting his hand confidently on the weathered diary.

Dr. Horehound clenched his teeth as a wave of discomfort engulfed him. "Oh," he rasped, "a skeptic can always fudge his way around hard evidence."

"You can't get around the list in this diary matching the one in Bartholomew Piaget's journal," said Big Bro.

"Unless the diary was a fabrication of one of Piaget's heirs," said Dr. Horehound, gulping down a surge of nausea. "The contents of his safe was in their possession for some decades."

Arthur, relentless, shook his head. "The perpetrator would have had to have done a tremendous amount of research into the minutiae of Cassandra Ouspenskaya's life."

"Piaget's heirs had plenty of cash to spend as they pleased," said Dr. Horehound, wiping his brow again. "Once they sorted out all the legalities, anyway. Who can predict the whims of the suddenly prosperous?"

"Can you squirrel your way around this?" asked Edward, tossing something onto the table. It clattered lightly and wobbled to stillness. Part of its length was darkly stained.

"What might that be?" asked Dr. Horehound, suppressing a burning burp. "I'm afraid I don't recognize it."

"I hardly do myself," said Edward. "It's the dipstick from my van."

"Turned to wood," said Dr. Horehound, his eyes widening slightly.

"Pine, I think," said Edward. "We're wondering how we're going to explain this to the local mechanic."

"You're serious, then," said our worsening host. "Your engines truly have—?"

"Turned to wood, as you say," said Arthur. "You wouldn't be up to a stroll outside with a flashlight, would you?"

"I think not," said Dr. Horehound, getting up from his chair. He clutched his stomach and grimaced. "I feel I'm frightfully ill. Do please avail yourselves of my hospitality in the library. You'll find an assortment of libations in the left-hand desk drawer."

"Holding out on us, were you?" said Pierre, also rising.

"Keeping them for the day of your departure," said Dr. Horehound. "No use sticking to protocol. Do please enjoy yourselves. Right or wrong, you have earned it."

With that he left us. His footsteps receded down the corridor, stumbling and hesitating, then hurrying on.

"I wonder what his problem is," said Joel. I suddenly realized it was the first thing he'd said since the reading began.

"I'm prepared to discuss it," said Pierre, "over something other than brandy in the library."

"Hear, hear!" said the Lads, except Joel. He glared long and hard at the cards before rising to his feet.

"Notice something?" I asked.

He looked up at me, startled. "No," he said. "Just thinking."

I lagged behind with Arthur as the rest headed down the hallway. Jonathan slowed to stay back with us.

"Horehound was okay back there yesterday," I said, "when we first inspected the séance room."

"Yes," said Arthur.

"But he became ill later, after you'd doused the room with holy water—and he got sick again tonight."

"You may be right," said Jonathan. "You think maybe he's a vampire or something?"

"Or something," I said. "Something that doesn't like holy water."

"He may just have the flu," said Jonathan.

"You said you got some more holy water in town," I said. "Do you have it on you?"

"No, I left it and the 'survival kit' Fr. Hobson gave me up in my room," said Arthur. "You think maybe I should get it?"

"I think you should," said I. "Before something else happens."

"I agree," said Jonathan. "I'll stay with Beth while you go get it."

"Any excuse," said Arthur, smiling. "I shall be swift, even for me."

∞§[Martin]§∞

"That was all very strange," said Jonathan as Beth handed Pierre her pages. "I'm not sure I followed everything. How do you suppose Madam Ouspenskaya arranged all the cards in the deck after Mr. Piaget shuffled them?"

"She fixed it somehow," said Edward.

"But the deck was in plain sight the whole time," insisted Jonathan.

"We've seen more amazing things than that at the 'House of Illusions,'" said Arthur.

"That's a very good point," said Pierre. "Remember our earlier discussion about distraction."

"Do you think she was maybe trying to embarrass Piaget by revealing his affair with his secretary right there in front of their guests?" asked Joel.

"Imagine if Arianna Marigold had been present," said Kahlúa. "More than sparks would have flown."

"A crystal ball and a few chairs for starters," agreed Millie.

"We'll never know," said Arthur distantly. "Some things we'll never know."

"You're thinking of Lenore Poe," kidded Beth as she seated herself, "and not just because she said malevolent spells are hard to control."

"You got me, Sis," he admitted. "For some strange reason, she does interest me."

"Then she probably did then as well," said Beth. "Don't you think?"

"So all this was just so Madam Ouspenskaya could hex Mr. Piaget," said Jonathan.

"There's the ticket!" said Kahlúa. "Madam O was gonna whammyize 'im."

"Whammyize?" asked Millie.

"I'm lost," said Joel. "How did spiking the cards achieve that?"

"Patience," said Pierre, gathering up the next set of pages. He paused to read the first couple of lines. His eyebrows went up high on his forehead as he announced, "Ladies and Gentlemen, hold onto your hats!"

"Uh-oh," said Millie. "What's going to happen now?"

"Our good Friend, Jonathan, is about to tell us," said Pierre.

∞§[†]§∞

∞§✝§∞

25. The Effects of Sub-Particular Teleportation Reassemblance

∞§[Martin]§∞

FOR REASONS THAT WILL BECOME readily apparent, Jonathan's recital of the next chapter was disrupted by frequent and vociferous outbursts of protest, incredulity, and indignation. It didn't get the highest interruption score for the evening, but ran a pretty good third place. To repeat here all the disruptions verbatim, in my opinion, would render the episode practically unreadable, as it nearly did that night. I considered shifting the lot or a hefty synopsis thereof to the end, but as you will see in the following chapter, other matters overruled that solution. Suffice it to say that it took about three times as long for Jonathan to read this chapter than it will you unless you're doing so while tending bar at Darby's Restaurant at lunchtime.

∞§[*Jonathan*]§∞

They way things turned out, Arthur didn't go up to his room for his "survival kit," as he called it. As we meandered out into the dark foyer from the dimly illuminated corridor, Pierre tried the phone and pronounced it *non compos mentis*. When I told him I didn't think that meant "out of order," he said I had misunderstood that he had intended it for the telephone. "It had to be working earlier," he grumbled. "How else could Dr. Horehound have arranged for the motel owner to turn on the NO VACANCY sign to thwart Clarice Davenport's escape? But now it's out of order again."

"So you think he has some way of switching it on and off?" I asked.

"I do," he scowled. "Him and his gambits, and at a time when communication may prove crucial."

Edward was striding toward the library, and Joel seemed to be veering to look out one of the windows beside the front door. I glanced up the stairway to see if I might glimpse the retreating heels of Dr. Horehound, but it was too dark or he was already out of sight. Arthur had just placed his hand on the post at the foot of the banister, when we heard and saw that now-familiar flashbulb-like pop and there, hovering and buzzing threateningly, was another orb of light in the middle of the foyer. We all froze, not certain what to do.

"There's your friend, Joel," said Edward, whom I sensed somehow considered Joel complicit in the transformation of his car engine.

I half expected Pierre to shout, "Lads!" at which point I was prepared to fling myself bodily between that thing and Joel, even if I half-agreed with Edward. But before any of us could do anything, the sphere swelled red and yellow, wobbled wildly, then popped out of existence again.

"What do you make of that?" asked Pierre.

"I guess it wasn't after you this time," said Beth to Joel.

"Beats me," said Joel, peering out the window. "Hey, it's stopped raining. I guess the storm has—"

Suddenly a deep rumbling surged under the floorboards. Creaking and straining sounds percolated throughout the woodwork on the walls and ceiling. The chandelier rocked and rattled. We teetered and staggered, flinging our arms about to maintain our balance. Then, as the ruckus subsided, the windows on both sides of the front door turned solid white. Sheets of blinding radiance poured into the foyer, silhouetting Joel and slamming our shadows against the wall behind us.

"Lightning?" I think I said.

"That's not lightning," said Edward.

Indeed it wasn't, because it didn't flicker and blink. It came on and held like a giant beacon.

"Stay here," said Pierre. "I'm going out to see—"

But we were all heading for the front door. Joel was the first, and the rest of us jumbled through behind him. It was like stumbling into the brightest day imaginable. The flames on the porch posts were overpowered by the glare.

"Where's it coming from?" asked Arthur.

"That way," said Edward, pointing to the right.

"The lake," said Joel.

"The lake!" exclaimed Pierre.

"The thing in the lake!" I yelled.

"Maybe we should go back inside," I heard Beth say, but she, like the rest of us, headed along the front of the building to the north side. As we rounded the corner, the sight that met us caused us to halt, bumping into one another.

"Is that what you guys saw the other night?" asked Arthur.

"Yup," said Edward.

"Good Heavens!" said several of us together.

The boats moored at the dock were tossing about as water surged beneath them. Waves heaved over the boardwalk, gushing around the vertical posts. The water itself was glowing white, as if illumined by floodlights under the surface. In fact, something big and furiously bright was burning in the depths of the lake. A hundred yards or so out, the surface was bulging upward, as if something huge was rising from below. Rivulets cascaded outward in all directions as a dome, like the top of a huge light bulb, emerged. The water all around boiled and churned, spurting wobbling globs of steam and foam.

"The spaceship!" I gasped.

"The flying saucer!" exclaimed Edward.

"It's rising out of the lake!" yelled Pierre.

"It's coming!" shouted Joel.

"What should we do?" wailed Beth.

Whatever thoughts of flight riveted our minds, we just stood there, our mouths and eyes wide open.

The sides of the dome swooped gently outward as the dazzling saucer rose out of the water. It was white, mostly, but curls of fiery red, Halloween orange, and India ink black swirled upward over its smooth contours. As the outermost rim of the saucer cleared the surface, water rushed in underneath with a ferocious

sucking noise. Plumes of sputtering steam erupted all around.
Within seconds the belly of the craft lifted out of the churning
water as runoff cascaded and splattered beneath. The thing hovered there silently, perfectly level, purposeful, as the lake seethed
and hissed and gradually stabilized.

"What do they want?" asked Edward.

"Me," said Joel, stepping forward toward the edge of the
floorboards.

"Hold on," we said, reaching out to stop him.

Then the strangest thing happened. The air began to sizzle and
sparkle, growing ominously luminous and dense. It pressed
against us from all sides. I was reminded of a moment from my
childhood when, moved by curiosity, I crept close to the television screen, pressed my forehead against the glass, and peered
deeply into the eerie cathode-ray blurs. But this was all around.
My skin tingled as waves of electrical activity meandered all
over my body. I found that I couldn't move. Not that I couldn't
squirm around inside myself—that I was definitely doing—but it
was as if I were suddenly trapped inside a stiff Styrofoam mold.
It wasn't hard, but it was unyielding. With considerable strain I
managed to turn my head just enough so I could see through it to
the others, who were likewise engulfed in solid light, frozen and
terrified—except for Joel who looked positively elated. All this
was accompanied by an uncanny humming sound, the same we
had heard in the corridor the previous night as we chased the
sphere that was after Joel. It grew louder and louder, and the
blurred haze around grew brighter and brighter until—

ZAP!

—I felt a jolt go through me, or me go through a jolt. It's hard to
describe. For a moment I couldn't breathe, and then my lungs
heaved. The air that came rushing in was cold with an acrid
tang, like in an air-conditioned hospital ward. The roar ceased
abruptly and the humming subsided slowly, as did the bright
blurriness around us. I realized with a start that we were no
longer on the porch looking at the saucer. We were standing on
a circular platform at one end of a larger, elliptical room. The
platform was perhaps a foot high and fifteen feet in diameter,
with a dozen or so metallic bull's-eyes evenly spaced all over it.

I say bull's-eyes because they seemed to be made of concentric rings of shiny metal with bands of purple glass between. Arcs of electricity seemed to be streaming through the glass, and overall the bull's-eyes were throbbing with diminishing pulses of light. We were each standing on one of these things, and above us was a suspended dome with matching circles of metal and glass, likewise pulsing and dimming. I had the sense of trails of sparks slithering along the edges of the dome and platform, like running lights around a disco floor. The air around us had lost its oppressive density, but still I couldn't seem to move beyond the limits of my skin.

In front of us, about twenty feet away, was some sort of control panel six feet wide atop a stout chrome pillar, behind which stood a tall, slender figure who appeared to be making adjustments. The floors and walls seemed to be made of a hard plastic material, deep red in color. Joel, who seemed to have shaken off his paralysis, was stepping clumsily off the platform and hailing the operator.

"Wait!" he exclaimed, waving his arms to indicate the rest of us. "What are you doing? This is all wrong!"

"A slight change in plans," said the figure. "Captain's orders."

"But you said it was just gonna be me!" insisted Joel.

"Patience," said the figure, but he was speaking around Joel to us mannequins on the platform. "Stand perfectly still as you are. The effects of sub-particular teleportation reassemblance will wear off sooner if you don't struggle. As you can see with your friend, Maruppa, the consequences are less severe with each successive transmission through the ethereal matrix."

"No!" screamed Joel. "This isn't the way it's supposed to be!"

"Calm yourself," said the figure. "All will be explained momentarily."

Bewildered, I looked around at Beth and Arthur and Pierre and Edward. They were all blinking and moving their mouths soundlessly, their arms hanging uselessly at their sides.

"The captain is on his way," said the figure, stepping into view from behind the control panel. I broke out in a prickly sweat. It was not human, although the form was roughly humanoid—two arms, two legs, and such. It was about six feet tall with a bulbous head atop a long, slender neck. The eyes were large and doll-like, glistening orbs of black glass without iris, pupil, or sclera. When it blinked, the eyelids came disconcertingly from the sides to meet in vertical lines in the middle. Instead of a nose, there were two little conical holes above a small V-shaped mouth with a tapered chin. Its ears, too, were just little holes behind its jaw. In fact, it seemed to have an ornate brass horn, like a miniature Victrola megaphone, wedged into its right auricle hole. Perhaps it was some sort of communication device. The skin was white and rubbery and hairless. The arms were elongated and thin, with delicate hands terminating in long, tubular fingers. I counted five digits, but the outer two were thumbs—opposable-opposing thumbs. The limbs had a stretched quality, like chewing gum pulled to nearly snapping. It was wearing a dark, glittery purple tunic secured with a golden cord around the neck, the material hanging down loosely to the enlarged, pulpy knees, with a second golden rope gathering the garment around the narrow waist. The legs seemed to be enveloped in some kind of translucent peppered hosiery, and the slender feet were engulfed in slick black shoes that reminded me of fresh-caught fish.

"Welcome aboard the *Flonkmorhorn Glor*," the creature said. "I am Commander Klargzguk, and I apologize if our mode of short-range ground-to-ship ingress has unsettled you." The pitch of the voice suggested masculinity, but that getup warranted a question mark. Whether it was due to the trumpet in the ear or cavities somewhere within the cranium, his vowels seemed to resonate hollowly, M's and L's sort of buzzed, while P's, T's, and S's tended to hiss. "We have traveled many light years, as you call them, through the vastness of space to harvest the seeds we have sown on this far-flung infinitesimal planet."

"You said I was the one you wanted," whined Joel.

"Patience, young human," said Commander Klargzguk. "Surely you wouldn't want to make the long journey alone."

"You could have asked me. You *should* have asked me."

"Joel!" I managed to say aloud. "You—disappeared—brought here? Why—you not—tell us?"

"Would you have believed me?" he answered, pouting.

"Might—have—tried us."

"As if any of you cared."

"Oh—Joel!" rasped Beth.

"Excuse—me," said Pierre, who was slowly flexing his hands at his sides. "What's this—about—seeds?"

"The product of a billion years of evolutionary refinement," said Klargzguk. "Our scientists found pools of random proteins and amino acids on this primitive, volcanic world, ripe for infusion with the double-helix, the spark of life. We left markers for you to find, and transmitters for when you were ready to contact us, but apparently you haven't discovered them. We figured it was about time, so we came to see. And here you are."

"This—can't—be," said Arthur. "Something—terribly—wrong."

"Oh," said Joel accusingly. "Arthur, the great wizard. This is a bit too much for you, huh?"

"Something—wrong," repeated Arthur. "Joel—don't—be—"

"Have no fear," said our abductor. "All will be explained. You have much to learn and we to teach you. You will all be indoctrinated—is that the right word? We will familiarize you with our advanced technology—"

Just then a door opened behind and to the right of the console. It slid open both ways from the middle with a swoosh and re-sealed with a chirp after someone entered. I caught a brief glimpse of a half-dozen aliens in black tunics slumped exhaustedly against the far wall of the corridor beyond. The walls and floor out there, in contrast to the room in which we found ourselves, were bright, seemingly luminous white. The being who had entered appeared to be human. In fact, it looked like a beautiful woman decked in strangely out-of-date apparel.

"Pho—to—graph!" gasped Arthur.

She wore a kind of bun-shaped hat that was tilted forward on her head with a black veil that obscured her eyes. Her blouse was golden and silky and covered with pink flowers with white frills around the neck and wrists. Her dark skirt went down to her ankles, and her shoes were laced. She was clutching something in her hand, something that looked strangely, ominously, like a *ray-gun*.

"Stop!" she yelled, pointing the weapon at Klargzguk. Her tone was shrill, desperate, and unsure. "Commander, you will return your prisoners! And me with them!"

"Put that weapon down," said Klargzguk slowly and evenly. "It's set to kill."

"I know," she said. "Long have I been watching, hoping, waiting for a chance to escape. Heaven help me, this is it!"

Joel took a step toward her, but she waved him back with the freaky weapon.

"This is not a prudent course of action," cautioned Klargzguk.

"Hear me, all of you," she called to us. "Ignore their promises; refuse their gifts. You do not want to remain among them! They will toy with your minds until you do not know what is real and what is not!"

"You don't realize what you're doing," said Klargzguk. "We have explained that you cannot go back. Time will catch up with you the minute you leave this ship."

"A chance I am willing to take," said she. "You stole my life from me, and so much more. I will reclaim what I can."

"You will die."

"You will join me if you refuse to do as I say. I am going to ascend that platform. You are going to return these people, and me along with them, to where we belong. Do you understand?"

"A hundred of your years," persisted Klargzguk. "They will overtake you like a predator its prey."

"Then let me be consumed," said she, anxiously approaching the platform. "Better to end my existence than to continue living as I have!"

"As you wish," sighed the alien commander, maneuvering himself back to the control panel.

"I'll stay," said Joel.

"Don't be a fool," she hissed.

"Go to blazes," said Joel. "I want to stay."

"Of course," said Klargzguk. "Mr. Maruppa, stand beside me." Then to us: "This is but a brief interruption. We will retrieve you shortly."

"No more gibbering," she threatened as she stepped gingerly up onto the platform. "Do as I say!"

"You can't take that field disruptor with you," said Klargzguk. "That technology must not fall into human hands. I shall nullify it during transmission."

"Do what you must," said she, positioning herself on one of the free bull's-eyes. "Just send me home."

"Very well."

That humming began again. This time it seemed to have a strangely reluctant, groaning quality about it, as if the machinery was exhausted yet being forced back into activity. Maybe it was my brain and body's instinctive aversion to going through the sieve of the ethereal matrix a second time. Nonetheless, the air grew dense and prickly, the blurry light engulfed us, and then—

ZAP!

—I experienced a momentary sensation of weightlessness, as if I were suspended in the air. Then gravity suddenly took over and I plummeted downward. My feet landed on something solid, but being unprepared I toppled over hard, sprawling facedown onto the ground. Only it wasn't *terra firma*. It was something hard and wet, with a little give to it. I heard and felt the others falling, landing, grunting and groaning around me. Stunned for a moment, my right cheek pressed against the wetness, I tested the surface with my fingers. Ouch—a splinter! Wood! Raising my head, I realized we had been dropped unceremoniously onto the dock. Through the cracks I could see glowing, foaming water slurping and sucking a few inches beneath the planks. The blinding light from the saucer bleached everything around us. As I struggled to my knees, I saw Beth curled into a tight ball a few feet away. I scrambled toward her and brushed the hair from her pained face.

"Beth!" I cried. "Are you okay?"

"No," she answered, grimacing. "So much for their advanced technology."

"Can you move?"

"Only parts that hurt."

"Blast!" said Pierre, somewhere behind me. "That loosened my teeth for sure!"

"Arthur!" I heard Edward say. "Get off me, will you?"

"I think it is you who are on top of me," retorted Big Bro.

"I say," said Pierre. "I think we should hightail it out of here."

"I'm with you," said I, helping Beth to her feet.

We stood there for a moment, looking each other over, rubbing the aches from our elbows and knees. All the while the blinding light from the saucer cut everything into stark clarity. A loud eruption of water made us turn to face the awesome thing, which was in the noisy process of settling back into the lake, eerie streaks of red and yellow swirling on its surface.

"Look out!" said Edward, as a wall of water rose and heaved itself onto the dock, knocking us over—all except Arthur who grabbed onto an upright post and held fast. The water was jarringly cold. The boats banged angrily against the pier, and the boards shuddered under our feet.

"I say to the lodge," said Pierre, scrambling to his feet.

"Maybe for starters," said Edward, pulling himself up hand-over-hand against a post. "We've got to get farther away than that."

"That way!" the rest of us agreed.

"Hold on," I said. "That woman! The one who saved us!"

"Zounds!" said Pierre. "Where is she?"

We looked around hurriedly, then peered over the edges of the planks into the water to be sure. She wasn't among us.

"That creepy space alien!" said Beth. "He didn't beam her after all!"

"He said she'd die," said Edward.

"Yeah, and you believed him," said I.

"Well," said Edward. "What the Hell am I supposed to think?"

"Thinking can wait," said Arthur. "Let's get out of here."

Shaken and wet, we clambered up the graveled path to the northern porch, then stumbled our way around to the front. The terrible truth was that none of us felt the least bit safer once the door was shut and locked behind us.

∞§[†]§∞

∞§✝§∞

26. Cold Sweats

∞§[Martin]§∞

MONSIGNOR HAVERMEYER LEAPT UP from the wastebasket. It toppled and banged noisily against one side of the doorframe, then rolled across to thwack the other upright for good measure. Before the second collision he was halfway down the hall to the kitchen.

"Land sakes!" exclaimed Millie, momentarily silencing the hubbub that Jonathan's story had instigated.

"What's with him?" asked Jonathan as he handed his pages to Pierre. "Is it something I read?"

"Your grammar," said Edward. "Atrocious."

"Not funny," said Beth.

"Monsignor!" I called, struggling to my feet with the aid of my cane and lumbering after him. "Monsignor, what's wrong?"

I saw the back of his cassock disappear through the doorway to the kitchen, heard his stocking feet pounding across the lino-leum, then the backdoor open and slam. Somewhere behind me Father was admonishing everyone to stay put, and Millie was insisting on doing anything but. My face hot with alarm, I hobbled through the kitchen, dodging the wet raingear, but skidding on the puddle the monsignor had left when he came in a lifetime before. Without pausing to grab my raincoat, I threw the door open, stepped outside onto the little porch, and lunged into the rain.

"My Senior!" I called as water poured down upon me as if from an open spigot.

Between the gentle glow of the stained-glass windows of the church and the soft yellow radiance of the porch light, I caught a glimpse of Havermeyer's hulking form receding through the

downpour. He was tromping down the path that led to the cemetery and his RV beyond. Wondering at myself, I sploshed after
him through pooled, icy water deeper than my shoes. Oh joy! It
was unnerving, plodding through curtains of blinding rain,
guided by the splutter and plopping in the surrounding bushes
and the tumultuous splatter on the flooded path before me. Using my cane as a prod, I managed to avoid most of the deepest
sections—but not all. More than once I almost lost a shoe to the
spongy, sucking mud beneath. Funny how unfamiliar a habitual
trail could become under these conditions.

He slowed to a halt at the entrance to the cemetery. Turning
toward the tombstones, he buried his face in his hands. Fortunately the ground rose out of the lake to form an island where he
stood, though it would have been nicer if it had been under a
tree. I came spattering up to him and stopped a few feet away.
Rain pattered and tinkled all around us. I felt kind of stupid
shivering there in my squishy shoes and sodden corduroys, not
having a clue what was troubling him or what I could possibly
do to help.

It had better be better than what I'm missing back inside, I
thought malevolently. The last thing I need is a winter cold!

"Martin," he said at last, lifting his face from his fingers but
not turning to look at me. Of course, he knew who had followed
him. Who else would make sounds like a three-footed hippo-
potamus in a swamp? "You're a faithful friend," he said, "following me out here like this."

"Call me Fido," I said, patting my chest through my sopping
wool sweater. "And boy am I going to smell like a dog when I
get back inside. Could you, um, maybe explain to me why we're
out here sans raingear?"

"What can I tell you?" he said, gazing off into the watery
gloom of the graveyard. "Just when you think your skeletons
have been laid to rest, something like this comes along and sets
the bones rattling again."

"Cemeteries are good for that," I said lamely.

"Munda cor meum," he moaned desperately.

"Um," I said, uselessly swiping water from my eyes,
"wouldn't the faucet in Millie's sink have sufficed?"

He shook his dripping head and held out his hands, palms upward. "Not even all this."

I drew closer, moving around to face him with my back to the cemetery. I dread graveyards more than fish sticks on Friday, but this way I was facing the one-and-only door to my little apartment. I'd left a reading lamp on and the window curtain parted so it looked warm and inviting. Hoping to nudge his attention in that direction, I asked, "Want to tell me about it?"

"I guess I owe you that much," he said. "It's just that—"

"You think maybe you'd like to get out of the storm?" I asked, pointing. "My place is just over—"

Suddenly something came between us and the rain. The incessant globules were no longer pelting us, but were instead pattering the top of an umbrella over us.

"Father Baptist," I said, as he moved into our midst. I could barely see his outline against the distant porch light, let alone the glimmer in his eyes. He seemed to be wearing something thick and furry over his cassock. I indicated the umbrella he was holding and said, "I see you opened Lieutenant Taper's present after all."

"No," he said. "This is Millie's."

"Leave it to you," I said, grateful that I could only dimly see the extra-large yellow canopy with pink polka dots that had become our little home from home. I didn't have to look down to confirm that he'd taken the time to put on some waterproof boots. At least someone around here showed a modicum of common sense.

"Now that we're all here," said Father, gathering his overcoat tightly around his neck with his free hand. "Monsignor—?"

"I suppose an explanation is in order," said Havermeyer.

"I suppose so," agreed Father.

I suppose we could hear it better inside! I thought, but held my peace.

"It's all so embarrassing," said Monsignor. "Father Baptist, if it weren't for those young people in there bravely telling their incredible story, I could never bring myself to recount what happened to me so many years ago."

"Perhaps you'd prefer if I left," I said hopefully. "You know, priest to priest—"

"Oh no, Martin," said Monsignor Havermeyer. "After coming out here like this, surely you deserve to hear."

"Really," I assured him. "I wouldn't mind—"

"Do stay," he said. "I insist."

"As you wish," I mumbled through cold, trembling lips.

"Do please begin," said Father.

The sooner to make an end! whimpered the gardener silently.

"Very well," said Havermeyer. But he still didn't say anything.

"Monsignor?" prodded Father.

MONSIGNOR! squealed that swollen sponge of self-pity, me.

"It happened three months after my Ordination," said Havermeyer in the tone of voice usually reserved for horror stories from high school days. "I had been assigned to the assistantship at Our Lady of Knock in Sylmar. Father Hourahee, the pastor, had sent me up to Bakersfield in his station wagon to fetch a television from an old college chum of his who had offered to donate it to our rectory. I was on my way home. This was back in the days before Interstate 5 was constructed through the mountain pass between Los Angeles and the San Joquin Valley. There was just a twisting, turning, two-lane highway they used to call 'The Grapevine.'"

"I remember it," said Father. "My dad used to take me camping up in the Los Padres National Forest—a place where Pyramid Lake now sits. Highway 99—it was quite a sidewinder."

Like our garden where Lake Philomena now sits, I thought to myself. I wonder how often Highway 99 got washed out by torrential rains?

"It was a Thursday evening," said Havermeyer. "Clear as crystal, stars aplenty—like Southern California nights used to be. Few cars on the road. Only saw an oncoming vehicle every ten minutes or so. Still, I didn't like driving at night, and I found the incessant curves and cutbacks frustrating and wearying. But it was an emergency: Fr. Hourahee's set had self-destructed and he couldn't survive without *Perry Mason*."

Della! I thought. Get me a dry pair of shoes, will you? That's right, Paul, a hot toddy would hit the spot just about now!

"So there I was," said Havermeyer, "gritting my teeth, listening as the radio drifted in and out. It was approaching ten o'clock—Joe Pyne was about to come on. I remember seeing headlights looming in the rearview mirror. There were four of them—high off the pavement—so I thought it must be a big truck. They were so bright I assumed the driver had his high beams on. I began hoping for a passing lane so he'd go around me. I remember gripping the steering wheel extra hard with my left hand so I could reach up to tilt the rearview mirror with my right—you know, to get the glare out of my eyes. And then— suddenly my hands were empty. I found myself sitting in the backseat, parked on a turnout, the ignition and lights off. I didn't remember pulling off the road. I had no idea what happened to the truck. And another thing—the television in the back was gone."

"Did you feel groggy?" asked Father. "As though you had just awakened?"

"No," said the monsignor, rubbing the back of his neck. "I was wide awake. It was as if I'd just blinked and—poof!— everything changed. There was something else. As I climbed out to move to the front seat, I realized that my wrists, my abdomen—someplace else I'd rather not mention—different parts of my body felt sore. Once behind the steering wheel, I turned on the dome light, pulled up my sleeves, and saw fading red marks on my forearms, as though I'd been gripped tightly. I checked my watch. It was ten minutes past midnight. I had lost more than two hours."

"So what did you do?" asked Father.

T-t-t-turned on the heater? I thought.

Monsignor Havermeyer shrugged. "What could I do but continue on my way? Father Hourahee was anxious when I arrived. His friend had phoned him when I left Bakersfield and I was long overdue. I had no excuse other than the truth, so I told him what happened."

"And what did he say?" asked Father.

Come over by the fire, my wayward son, I thought. Warm yourself!

"Douglas Hourahee was an intense but kindly man," said Havermeyer. "He had studied psychiatry before pursuing the priesthood. At first he chalked it up to a fit of drowsiness and thanked my Guardian Angel that I had managed to pull over safely and sleep it off—though he couldn't account for my waking in the backseat. The marks on my arms had faded completely away, so I had no evidence to present to the contrary. The missing television, well, someone must have happened by and taken advantage of the situation. But my sleep that night, and the following nights, was shattered by nightmares. I jolted awake in cold sweats, with dim memories of rubbery hands touching me, prodding me all over. And something about a face, a woman's—so sad, frightened—yet fiercely wary." He wrapped his arms around himself and shuddered—not from the cold, but from the recollection. "After a week or so of getting no sleep himself, Father Hourahee offered to hypnotize me, and being desperate for answers, I allowed him to try."

"And?" asked Father.

"When he snapped his fingers and I came out of it, he looked perplexed," said Havermeyer. "He told me he had given me the suggestion that I would remember everything when I awoke, but I didn't. All he could tell me was that the car had been enveloped by a bright light, that I had described a metallic room with a domed ceiling filled with menacing-looking contraptions, and me being surrounded by peering, impassive, glassy eyes."

"He could offer no explanation?" asked Father.

No long ones, please! I shivered silently.

"Hardly," said the monsignor. "Not wanting to sully my record by sending me to a specialist, he suggested that we just let things be and hope the nightmares would subside. But they didn't. And then the noises began."

"Noises?" asked Father.

The hiss of gas, I wished. The strike of a match, the puff of flame in the fireplace—

"Rapping in my bedroom, pounding on the walls," said Havermeyer. "Clawing sounds like talons scraping all over the

ceiling. It wasn't my imagination, and I held no delusions that
my sanctity rivaled that of the Curé of Ars."

GARDENING TIPS: Saint Jean-Baptiste-Marie Vi-

anney, Patron Saint of Parish Priests and

known in his life as the "Cure/ d'Ars," was

pestered for years by pounding noises, moving

furniture, spontaneous fires, and worse. He

called his demonic tormentor the "Grappen."

Famed as a confessor, the good priest noted

that the commotion grew worse whenever a sin-

ner was approaching Ars to repent of his evil

ways.

                                    --M.F.

"Father Hourahee heard it from his quarters," continued
Havermeyer. "Then the noises spread throughout the rectory.
Dishes would fall from the cupboards and shatter on the floor.
The upright piano in the sitting room started playing spontaneously. It sounded like someone was pounding the keys with their
fists. We'd run in there and find the room empty. Needing a
good night's sleep himself, Father Hourahee finally called someone he knew at the Chancery, an administrator who had something to do with placing priests in their respective parishes. As
far as I know, he just told him I might be better suited to a low-
pressure situation. That's how I found myself on a career track
as confessor to the rich, famous, and utterly bored—go figure."

"Did the noises follow you to your next parish?" asked Father.

Did your new parish have central heating? I wondered.

"No, thank God," said Havermeyer. "A few weeks later, my replacement back at Our Lady of Knock called to inform me that he had found a nest of raccoons in the attic. He wanted to know why hadn't I done something about it. So Father Hourahee had been discreet, thank Heaven."

"And the nightmares?' asked Father.

"They went on for several years," said Havermeyer, "gradually subsiding and disappearing amidst the tedium of parish life among the affluent."

"Until this evening," said Father.

"Until tonight," agreed Havermeyer, slowly running his fingers through his limp hair. "First, when Joel described the spaceship landing in the lake, while the others expressed disbelief, I was filled with apprehension and dread—and worst of all, an underlying sense of profound doubt. I remembered when I'd felt it before: those months of nightmares and grisly sounds in my room—those were no raccoons! The instruments playing themselves in the recital room struck a chord, if you'll forgive the pun. Then, when Jonathan related their teleportation experience, and that poor woman so wanting to get away from her captors, I started getting glimpses, vivid scenes, jolting flashes—memories of being snatched aboard an alien spaceship. It happened!" He wiped his hands over his face. "And my captors told me the same kind of thing: that they planted the seed of life on this planet eons ago and had returned to see how their little research project was doing. I remember shaking my head no, no, no!" He looked down at his gnarled hands. "I'd forgotten until tonight, but I realize I've been marked by the experience all along. Perhaps that's why I was quick to embrace modernist ideas as my priestly career progressed." He shuddered all over. "We're supposed to be made in God's image, not just the random byproduct of some ancient experiment by glass-eyed aliens."

"And you doubted your beliefs because—?" asked Father.

"Why, the evidence of my senses," the monsignor answered, his voice tight and cracking. "I was helpless in their power. Their technology—it was overwhelming. How can I dismiss what I saw with my own two eyes, and felt all over my body?" He put his left hand on my right shoulder, and his right on father's left. "Father, Martin: God is Love, and I suppose Jesus would even come to save such irrelevant flotsam and jetsam on some alien Petri dish, but why would He lie to us about our origins?"

"I imagine someone would say, as many have," said Father, assuming a scholarly tone not foreign to him when he presented views not his own, "that the primitive Hebrews weren't ready to hear the Truth at that stage of their cultural and spiritual development."

"That's absurd," said Havermeyer. "Is the story of the creation of Adam and Eve in Genesis any less fantastic? If He had said we grew from seeds planted here by beings from another world, they would have accepted it—as would we. But He said He made us in His image—direct, pure, and simple. He said our First Parents disobeyed him, and their Original Sin explains the miserable condition in which we find ourselves. Looking back on it, I realize this seed of doubt took root deep within me, and has defined my priestly existence ever since—until last June. All those thousands of volts of electricity, which left me so humiliatingly disfigured, weren't enough to shake these memories loose from their moorings, but they did cause a mixed-up old fool to reconsider his priorities."

We stood there in a silent huddle for several long, tremulous seconds.

"You've said it yourself, Monsignor, more than once," said Father. "Transferring to Saint Philomena's was the most significant decision of your life. It seems you have some unfinished business that needs finishing, and though I have no idea how those courageous young people back in the rectory resolved these issues, I'm confident they did so and rightly, or they wouldn't be here today. I'm certain their solution will be of benefit to you."

"You think so?" asked Havermeyer.

"I'd wager the deed to this parish," said Father.

"You have that much faith in them?" asked Havermeyer.

"I have that much confidence in God's ability to transform the appearance of failure into the surety of success," said Father. "Case in point: the Crucifixion and the Resurrection."

"Then what are we waiting for?" said Monsignor Havermeyer, turning Father and me toward the distant kitchen door beyond the flooded swamp. "Let's get back in there and hear the rest of their story."

"Certainly," said Father.

"I want to thank you, Martin," said the monsignor over his shoulder as we trudged and splashed our way toward a promise of warmth and dryness.

"S-s-s-s-sure thing," I agreed. "Any t-t-t-t-time."

∞§[†]§∞

∞§✝§∞

27. There's a Third Reason

∞§[Martin]§∞

TO SAY THAT MILLIE THREW A FIT when she beheld Monsignor's muddy socks and my swollen shoes defiling her precious kitchen floor, would be an understatement. I won't repeat here what she called Monsignor Havemeyer's lapse of good sense, because I'd be obliged to quote her assessment of me for following in his socksteps. Although Jonathan and Edward poked their heads into the castigation zone, offering to fetch some dry clothes from our respective living quarters, it was decided by our housekeeptrix that Monsignor and I, having shed our waterlogged clothes, would learn our lesson in a couple of Father Baptist's threadbare bathrobes, these wrapped within a couple of moth-holed blankets from her emergency shelf in the linen closet. Father also having provided us with two pairs of scruffy woolen socks, we were set to go.

Father's study had undergone another transformation during our absence. Instead of three rows facing the fireplace, the mismatched chairs had been rearranged into a dented ellipse facing the center of the room. The indentation was due to Father's desk in the corner as before, upon which the Christmas tree still twinkled and blinked merrily. Details of our ill-equipped adventure outside having apparently made their way to the study, my favorite chair had been considerably moved over near the hearth so I'd be close to the crackling fire. This new position I readily accepted, approved, and occupied—embarrassing though it was to hobble through the room in bathrobe, blanket, and stocking feet with half my toes sticking out. I fended off their snide remarks with my trusty cane.

"Where have you been?" asked Jonathan, as if he didn't know.

"Bah!" said I, swinging the aforementioned walking implement.

"Tell 'em, Ebenezer!" laughed Kahlúa.

"Who you callin' Ebenezer, Lulu?" asked Millie.

"Mister Marty," said Kahlúa as Havermeyer lumbered over to the fire. "Who else? And how's by you, Monsignor, Honey?"

"Much better, thank-you," said he as Pierre directed him to my favorite chair's twin. I knew for a fact it was as comfortable as my favorite chair, and much more comfy than an overturned wastebasket.

"Monsignor *Honey?*" asked Jonathan. "Are you all right, Madam Hummingbird?"

"I certainly is," said she. "I was asking Mon Zinger how's by he is."

"I should think the question is 'why'," said Edward, "as in outside, in the rain, and everything."

"In the interest of time, if you wouldn't mind," said the monsignor, wiping his damp hair back from his scarred face, "I'd rather explain later. Suffice it to say that your experiences impinged upon mine, and I was momentarily disconcerted by the similarity."

"You mean you—?" gaped Jonathan.

"Ladies and Gentlemen," said Father, easing his dry self into his own squeaking office chair, "I suggest we be seated and pick up where we left off."

"Dem three men done hab dem a meetin'," crooned Kahlúa to a melody vaguely reminiscent of "It Ain't Necessarily So." She pressed her palms against the sides of her face as she continued: " 'Twas pitch dark, an' dah rain it was beatin'. They's bein' discreet, dey won't dare repeat. Dem three men done hab dem a meetin'."

So now my back was to the fire (or rather my left shoulder), and Father Baptist's chair had been left in its corner by the bookcase, diagonally across from me, so we could look each other in the eyes when Edward didn't get in the way. Joel had more or less taken my place under the light switch, though he opted to partially block the doorway to the hall. On the other side of the room's only entrance (moving clockwise), sat Millie with her muscular arms folded, and then Kahlúa in her original corner although in a less comfortable chair. Kahlúa had relinquished my favorite chair's twin so it could be placed to the left of mine—to be occupied by Monsignor Havermeyer so that he, too, could benefit from proximity to the fire. She, in turn, had been given the kitchen chair upon which Pierre had been placing delivered pages face down. This pile had been relegated to the floor at his feet, and he had been consigned to the overturned wastebasket—though he wisely shanghaied a copy of *Webster's International Dictionary, Second Edition* for a cushion. He was seated between the monsignor and myself, with the mysterious antique chest at his right elbow, next to me. Edward and Jonathan sat with their backs to Father's desk. Beth and Arthur sat opposite them, between Kahlúa and me.

GARDENING TIPS: Feeneyite visual aids again:

the proportions and positions are approximate.

This chart is oriented as before, while my

verbal description is from my new point-of-

view.

--M.F.

Apparently, it had been decided among themselves that things would move along more efficiently if everyone was in plain sight of everybody else and thus could remain seated as they read their memoirs. This made things less formal and more intimate, which, as I look back on it, was not only suitable and expedient, but necessary. Tempers and nerves were about to be tested further than before.

"So we escaped from the alien spaceship," said Arthur, "though not by virtue of our own wits."

"Don't forget me," said Joel, grimacing. "I'm still happily aboard—or perhaps not so happily. I'm still at a loss to explain my behavior."

"I'm still at a loss as to what the heck this is all about," mumbled Edward.

"What in Heaven's name did we do after that?" asked Arthur.

"Thank Heaven your sister was with us," said Pierre. "She was present during a difficult and significant discussion—an exchange which proved to be pivotal not only to the outcome of events at Spirit Lake, but to our Friendship and Fellowship."

I wished I could look into the chest as he dug down inside it, but it was situated such that all I could see was the back of the open lid, upon which a bas-relief dragon with a twice-curled tongue glared at me with sinister eyes. Around this he handed me a sizable clutch of pages, which I entrusted to Beth.

"Oh dear," said she, riffling through her handiwork. "Sit back, everyone. I'm going to be prattling on for a while."

∞§[*Beth*]§∞

"So far so good," I gasped, as we groped our way through the foyer. My sweater hung wetly from my shoulders, and my dress clung to my legs. My muscles were all tight and jittery, as though I'd been working out or something. I would have likely stumbled if Jonathan hadn't been gripping my arm, although I could feel his fingers trembling. "You think we'll be safe in here?" I managed to add without conviction.

"They can probably zap us anywhere," said Edward, pushing ahead through the French doors and making for the desk. Strands of wet hair dangled in his eyes. He was shaking all over, too, and his larynx wavered noticeably as he tried to say jovially, "But I could use a shot of something before they do!"

"Invitation is the sincerest form of flattery," said Pierre, going around the desk in the opposite direction. He was shivering so hard I half expected to see wisps of condensation puffing from his mouth, but fortunately the air in the room was not that cold. "I say, we've certainly got the twitchies, haven't we?" he said with a failed snap of his fingers. "We've done it. We've been aboard a flying saucer. We're now official members of Abductees Anonymous. It's not often you get your atoms smashed into subatomic particles and reassembled aboard an alien space vessel."

"Funny thing about that," said Edward as they met at the promised desk drawer, almost butting heads. "Mr. Brackmore, my boss, gets this newsletter from a think tank in Europe somewhere—I forget the acronym. Their five-year mission: to nudge the futuristic technology on *Star Trek* into our present reality. Last month they reported their conclusion—an apology, really— that to reduce the human body to subatomic particles would take a great deal of energy, the kind we find at the center of our sun. Actually, it would take a much bigger sun."

"No space alien is worth his ammonia-based bloodstream if he can't defy the laws of physics," said Pierre, motioning for Edward to go first with respect to opening the drawer.

"The sheriff was right," said Arthur, who had sauntered over to the window, his ponytail drooping dejectedly. His pants were drenched up to his knees, but his pockets were apparently dry. He shoved his hands down inside them and began jingling his car keys and loose change. "Joel didn't wander into the garden and stumble over Madam Douceur's body. He was dropped there from above, as we were, onto the dock. We're lucky none of us broke or sprained something. You'd think with all their technology they could get a simple thing like beaming us safely to the ground worked out."

"Better six feet above than below, I always say," said Pierre, who was still crouching before the desk drawer eye-to-eye with Edward. "After you, my dear Fellow."

"One for all and both whatever," said Edward. "I say together."

"I second it," said Pierre. They were quivering so hard it was likely the only way the task would get accomplished. "One ... two ... *three!*"

Smiling, they pulled the drawer handle together, then cheered spasmodically at what they found within.

"This will settle the nerves," said Edward, unsteadily holding up a bottle of Bombay Blue Sapphire.

"Here, there!" croaked the voice of a toad of a figure who was squatting by the fireplace poking the logs. "Did the Master say y'all could pinch his private stock?"

"Grayburn!" acknowledged Pierre, clumsily hefting a bottle of Tillamore Dew, the tawny liquid wiggling furiously within. "He did indeed."

"I'll hafta take yer word for it," said Grayburn with a careless shrug. "Where've y'all been? Why're you all wet?"

"Didn't you see the light?" I struggled to say as Jonathan eased me into the chair by the Tiffany lamp. "The flying saucer?"

"Can't say as I did," said Grayburn, resting the implement by his feet. "Just woke up a coupla minutes ago. Found the place deserted, 'ceptin' Thorndale who was sawin' logs in her room. Noticed it stopped rainin', but couldn't imagine why you'd've gone outside. Anyways, I reckoned y'all could use a fire when you came in. Haven't seen the Master, have you? What's that yer sayin' 'bout a flyin' saucer? Saw one myself up near Witches Punchbowl once."

"Did you, now?" said Pierre, as he picked ineffectually at the paper seal around the cap with his fingernail.

"Gave me the heebie-jeebies for a week," said Grayburn. "Guess that makes us whatcha call simpatical."

"That may well be," said Arthur, "but I have a question for you. When you came upon Madam Douceur's body this morning, Joel was with her, is that correct?"

"Yup," said Grayburn. "That's a fact. Why?"

"I'm just ordering events in my mind," said Arthur, turning his attention out the window. "The sheriff said it had stopped raining for an hour when Madam Douceur was attacked, and Joel was deposited there sometime later. It's almost as though the aliens wanted to implicate him in her death."

Though I was safely seated, Jonathan crouched beside me, still holding my arm. I knew he was trying to be manly and reassuring and protective and a host of gallant things—including possessive—but speaking of six feet above and below, I wanted just about that much room all the way around me just then. The quaking of his hand only intensified the chills that were seizing me all over. For a nasty second, I suspected that it was he, the terrified child, who was desperately seeking comfort from me, the maternal substitute men are always really looking for, and I resented him for it. I'd like to think I'm open to the complexities of mature male-female relationships, but just then I was filled with distaste, dread, and the wish to be left alone.

"I'm okay," I told him.

His fingers remained clamped on my arm.

"Really I am," I said, patting his hand. "You can let go now."

"Are you sure?" he said, peering at me with fretful eyes.

"Yup," I tried to say good-naturedly, but I suspect a hint of my mounting annoyance slipped out. "Very sure."

But his hand remained, and his face just seemed to loom. There, close up, with the lamplight playing on his features, I noticed it again: the straggly hairs all over his jaw and chin, and handfuls of strays up around his cheekbones. Having a father and a brother, I knew about five o'clock shadow, but this was like a radiation-induced mutation from one of Arthur's bizarre monster movies. These hairs grew every-which-way—some straight, some zigzagged, most of them corkscrewed. I was reminded of the platter of beetles Thorndale had served the previous evening, those revolting legs and antennae sticking up at all angles. I was as repulsed now as then—selfishly so, with no thought of Jonathan's feelings in the matter.

"I said let go!" I snapped, swatting his hand. "Get away, would you?"

Dear me, not only did he still not release me; his big, infatu-
ated eyes slopped apprehension, alarm and trepidation all over
me. I'm sorry to say that I then blurted: "They sure botched your
face when they beamed you back!"

He let go, pulling away as though I'd slapped him. Anger
flared in his eyes, but he blinked it back. His hands went to his
jaw, then his cheeks, searching his features with shaky fingers.
"What do you mean?" he gasped. Then realization dawned. He
pressed his hands against his face attempting to hide his weird
follicle eruption.

Part of me wanted to apologize for being so mean, but more of
me reveled in recapturing my personal space. Jonathan had presumed, after all. He'd made his overtures out on the porch after
dinner, and I'd hosed him down to douse his fires somewhat, but
here he was, coming on like a fireman.

∞§[Martin]§∞

"Ewwwww—hosed!" groaned the Lads severally.
Kahlúa and Millie tittered gleefully.
Jonathan buried his face in his hands.
Undaunted, Beth continued.

∞§[Beth]§∞

"He just missed his afternoon shave," said Edward, who was
frantically clawing at the seal that was obstinately keeping him
from his gin. "It's a genetic echo, a vestigial throwback to his
australopithecine ancestors."

"Roll over Zinjanthropus, and tell Pithecanthropus the news!"
rock-and-rolled Pierre, who had finally conquered his own stub-
born seal and was now erratically unscrewing the cap. His confidence enhanced, he adopted a pedagogical tone as he added,
"Make room for the next evolutionary step: *Jonathanthropus
Hairyectus.*"

"What did you say?" demanded Authur, whirling from the window to stare at Pierre.

"Oh drat!" said Jonathan behind his hands as he turned away from me. "Oh double drat!"

"If Jonathan grew hair on the top of his head at the rate he grows it on his face," said Pierre, oblivious to Arthur's concern, triumphantly pouring whiskey into a glass, "he could open his own toupee boutique. As it is, there isn't much call for chin rugs these days."

"Don't panic, Beth," said Edward, pouring gin into his own glass, spilling most of it on the desktop. "It's not all that bad. He can be rid of it in five minutes. How many deformed men can say that about their—you know—unsightly abnormalities?" He tilted back his head and tossed the liquor down his throat. About half gushed over his cheeks and trickled down his chin. He wiped the overflow with the back of his sleeve. "But that can wait. I say let's grab our things and get the Hell out of here."

"And go where?" asked Pierre, who was having similar trouble getting his whiskey into himself.

I thought to mention how uncharacteristically impolite Pierre and Edward were behaving, helping themselves without first offering some to their friends, especially the lady present—even though I didn't want any. I hesitated because of my own callousness toward Jonathan, which I didn't know how to begin to take back.

"Over the bridge and down the road," said Edward, who was pouring himself another glassful. "The rain has stopped. The full moon's out. We can see enough to find our way by it. I say let's head for town."

"Hold on," said Arthur, still standing with his back to the window and his hands in his pockets. I knew he disliked it when others jingled their change, so I thought it odd that he would still be doing so. "Sheriff Brumus said the moon wouldn't be full for a couple of weeks."

"That's absurd," said Edward, wincing after downing his second round. "It was full the night we arrived. That flying saucer came out of it, remember?"

"I wasn't with you," said Arthur. "Just the same—"

"Pierre, Jonathan," said Edward, slamming his glass down on the desk. "You were there."

Jonathan mumbled something behind his hands that sounded vaguely affirmative, but Pierre paused mid-sip to reflect. "Arthur's right," he said, setting down his glass half-finished. "The sheriff did say the moon is currently new, or dark, or whatever."

"It's out there now!" said Edward, pointing vaguely toward the window.

"Whatever's out there, it's not the full moon," said Arthur. "I checked the doctor's desk calendar earlier. Look for yourself."

Edward snatched up the spiral-bound convenience and glared at it. "New moon tonight?" he sputtered incredulously. "Full moon: August fourteenth?" He tossed it onto the desk. "It's got to be one of Horehound's tricks."

"I don't think so," said Arthur seriously. "Not this time."

"Grayburn," said Edward. "You said you saw the full moon the night we first arrived. Remember?"

"If you say so," said Grayburn, scratching his whiskers. "I don't rightly recall."

"You're a big help."

"I tries to be," said Grayburn. "At my age, things sorta run together. Come to think of it, though, the Master was sayin' this mornin' that he was lookin' forward to night fishin' later in the month. Claims they get hypnotized lookin' up through the ripples at the Man in the Moon. Snap at anythin'."

"This is crazy," said Edward, brushing back his hair. "Okay, whatever. Moon or no moon, we can take the flashlights."

"Better stick in some fresh batteries," said Grayburn. "Y'all used them mostly up last night, I'll bet. They mightn't get you very far as they is."

"Would you get them then?" asked Edward. "Batteries, kerosene, whatever. Please. Time's a wasting."

"Hold on," said Pierre. "We can't go."

"Why not?" asked Edward. "Give me one good reason why not."

"Gladly, I'll give you several," said Pierre, trying but failing to control the quaver in this voice. "First, picture us in our tuxedos plodding down that muddy track in patent leather shoes. Even if we changed into street clothes we'd be no match for that space-ship. Any distance we could cover in two hours, they'd overtake us in a matter of moments. For another thing, there's that crea-ture out there, the one that killed Madam Douceur. It is vicious and cunning—"

∞§[Martin]§∞

"She's covered with blood!" cried Jonathan, making five-finger asterisks on both sides of his face. *"So much blood!"*

No one laughed.

Beth looked at him coolly.

"Come on," he said, lowering his hands. "Your hyperthermia. You haven't had an idyllic episode for a while, and Pierre's men-tion of the creature is just the kind of thing that triggered it be-fore."

"First off," said Arthur, "the term is hyperthymesia—"

"Yes, of course," said Jonathan. "I was just—"

"—second, it's eidetic, not idyllic—"

"Actually, I know that," sputtered Jonathan defensively. "Hey, I was—"

"—furthermore, it is unpredictable, you never know what is going to trigger it—"

"—just making—"

"—and finally," said Arthur, "as I thought I made clear, it's not something we joke about."

"—a fool of myself," said Jonathan softly. "Sorry."

"It's okay," said Beth. "Arthur's making more of it than he should, and that's my fault. I kind of freaked out about it when I was a kid, all the more when the narcolepsy developed on top of it. I'm older now. I shouldn't be offended, and I'm not, really. Still, between all my fits and attacks, I must seem peculiar."

"No weirder than Beard Boy here," said Edward, trying to give Jonathan's facial growth a good-natured tug.

"Or Dipstick Dude here," said Jonathan, pushing him away.

"No stranger than any of us, Honey," said Kahlúa.

"You should know, Lulu," said Millie.

I peered across Pierre at Monsignor Havermeyer with his interior secrets and the external Occasion of Grace that was his face. I could only imagine how peculiar he thought himself to be. For me, weird is just the fabric of my life.

"Anyway," said Beth, without further ado, "as Pierre was saying ..."

∞§[*Beth*]§∞

"For another thing, there's that creature out there, the one that killed Madam Douceur. It is vicious and cunning, and we have no weapons, no way to defend ourselves against it."

"The Master's got huntin' rifles," said Grayburn, "but if y'all don't knows how to use 'em, you'd likely just hurt yerselves."

"I'm willing to take my chances," said Edward, "besides—"

"There's a third reason," interrupted Arthur, who had been mulling over something ever since Pierre's "Roll over Zinjanthropus" quip. He stopped jingling his change, pulled his hands from his pockets, and said, "I must say, the fact that it wasn't first, I find disturbing."

"I'm finding a lot of things disturbing," retorted Edward.

"That crazed woman warned us they'd toy with our minds," said Jonathan. "Maybe they're in the doctor's pay, or vice versa."

"We're all rattled, to be sure," said Arthur, "but we're hardly acting like ourselves. Pierre, Edward, look at you: glugging away without offering any to the rest of us. Beth, that callous discourtesy toward Jonathan was hardly like you. And Jonathan, you're overreacting, behaving as though she threw sulfuric acid in your face. I'm standing here dazed and wounded, as if run through like the heart on the Three of Swords. We're all bogged down, paralyzed, like the lad on the Four of Cups. We have decisions to make—decisions with consequences we'll have to live with for a long time to come—but we're acting as though we've all scurried down our private holes like frightened rabbits."

Edward opened and closed his mouth several times, but said nothing. Grayburn harrumphed, took up the poker, and jabbed at the fire. Jonathan lowered his hands from his face just enough to expose his bewildered eyes. I shrank down in my chair, ashamed.

"Arthur's right again," said Pierre, tugging on the hem of his vest. "Ever since I hit the dock I've felt this terrible dread gnawing at my insides. I could call it fear of the unknown—or just plain fear—but it's more than that. Good Heavens, we've been aboard a flying saucer! Lots of people would be congratulating themselves and packing their belongings for the next beam-up. But I'm not drinking to celebrate. I'm not elated at all. If anything I feel empty, as though somehow during that second transmission part of me didn't rematerialize—as though I've lost my very self in the process. I don't know how to verbalize it, but I've never felt so pointless in all my life."

"I second that," said Jonathan, letting his fingers slip from his face and dropping his hands to his sides, "though I could never put it into so many words. It's like part of me is still on that spaceship, and only half of me is standing here now."

"Y'all was on the insides," marveled Grayburn, seating himself on the edge of the hearth with his back hunched to the flames and his ankles crossed. I don't know what crackled more, the logs or his joints. "The insides," he muttered to himself. "I was nowhere near the insides. And so close to home—my home, anyways."

"I'm like a clock spring," I admitted, "tightened till the key can't be turned the tiniest bit more, and so distracted by the tension I can't think of anything or anyone else. I just want to cut myself off, to hide and hope it all goes away somehow. Jonathan, I'm sorry, that's why I lashed out at you."

Jonathan had turned to face the portrait of the Piagets, his back to me. Oh drat, I thought. Oh double drat!

"Call it what you like," said Edward, shoving his hands into his back hip pockets. "Unless you're keen on going to Andromeda or the Pleiades Cluster, or wherever that ship is from, we've got no choice but to flee."

"It makes no sense to run if it's impossible to get away," said Pierre.

"So we should just sit here twiddling our thumbs until they rise up again and snatch us?" said Edward, appalled. "That's absurd!"

"Maybe so," said Arthur, " but the most important reason for not going remains unsaid."

"What's that?" asked Jonathan.

"Joel!" said Pierre, his eyes widening at the realization. He slapped his forehead for emphasis. "We can't leave him behind!"

"Precisely," said Arthur.

"What are you talking about?" groaned Edward. *"He* left *us* behind! He's been acting weird since we got here. He'd been aboard that saucer on his own and said nothing. He made it plain while we were aboard that he doesn't want us with him. He's not a prisoner. He refused to beam back. There's no way we could sneak aboard and get to him even if he wanted us to— which he doesn't. I say leave him!"

"Let's say we do precisely that," said Arthur. "Let's suppose we make it to town, and somehow hitch a ride home. What are we going to say to his family, to Father Baptist, to God in the confessional?"

"How should I know?" said Edward. "His grandfather and his parents, they weren't here! Father Baptist, with all his knowledge and acumen, what could he have done differently? And as for God, I'm not hearing Him giving us any advice."

"We haven't asked Him," I said meekly. "I mean, all this talking and fretting, but we haven't asked Him, have we?"

"Father Baptist?" asked Edward.

"God," I answered with a shrug.

"You're right, Beth," said Pierre. "I'm ashamed to admit we haven't."

"You're saying we should pray?" scoffed Edward, pulling his hands out of his pockets. "That's all good and well, but what if we don't have time? What if they decide to come back for us while we're—?"

"That is beyond our control," said Pierre, his voice growing noticeably calmer. "But even if they should, I would rather we be praying than fleeing when the moment comes. Wouldn't you?"

Edward made a face as though he was going to explode, but then let his breath out uselessly.

"It was St. Pius V," added Arthur intently, "who said that more works are achieved in this world by two joined hands than by any means of warfare. Europe was coming apart at the seams when he said that."

Shaking his head slowly from side to side, Edward set his knuckles on the desk and leaned his weight against them. "I don't know. I just don't know."

"Gentlemen, Lady Elizabeth," said Pierre firmly, suddenly standing straight and rolling his shoulders back. "I'm calling a council."

"That's the spirit!" cackled Grayburn. "Whatever it is."

"A what?" asked Edward, pushing himself up from the desk. "A council of what?"

"A council of the Knights Tumblar," said Pierre. "Clearly we have important decisions to make, but we're at an impasse. I say we convene with a prayer, as Jesus Christ instructed: 'For where there are two or three gathered together in My Name, there am I in the midst of them.' I say we act like the Knights we pretend to be, that we aspire to be. We will take Our Lord and Redeemer at His Word. We will ask His guidance, and then worry the problem out together. We will be honest before God and each other. If any of you has something to say, you will be welcome to say it."

We all looked around at one another—except Jonathan, who still didn't look at me. Edward folded his arms, unconvinced, and Arthur stood expectantly with his arms at his sides.

"What about me?" I asked. "I'm sure not a Knight."

"You are involved, Beth," said Arthur. "You have a voice."

"I like that," said Edward. "I say a voice without a vote."

"You would," I said, offended yet determined. "But I'll concede that you are right, Edward. I am not and cannot be one of you. It's not my desire, place, or station. But I do hope you will let me speak my mind just the same."

"The mind of a woman," said Edward derisively. "Go figure."

"Enough of that," said Jonathan, much to my surprise. "Beth has paid her dues up here. If she has something to say, let her say it."

"I can see she already has her foot planted on the back of your neck," said Edward. "Why don't you and she just—"

"This isn't the time for petty squabbles," said Pierre determinedly. "I have called a council. Comrade Knights, let us come to order."

"Where's Eroll Flynn when you needs him?" mumbled Grayburn, wrapping his arms around his bony knees and rocking himself. "Or was it Douglas Fairbanks, Jr. Or was it Senior?"

"No offense, Pierre," said Edward. "But who put you in charge?"

"He did," said Arthur, indicating Pierre. Then he waved his arm in an arc. "We all have. Dr. Horehound pointed out the way we defer to Pierre."

"And you defer to Dr. Horehound?" scoffed Edward.

"He only stated the obvious," said Arthur. "I have no problem with it. Jonathan?"

"Pierre's the boss," said Jonathan, finally turning to look at me. He smiled meekly. "Who else could be?"

"Don't look at me," said Edward, surrendering. "I'm just the boring nuts-and-bolts man."

"Dependable and therefore indispensable," I said to Edward, but my relieved smile was for Jonathan.

"What 'bout me?" asked Grayburn. "I don't know what y'all're talkin' 'bout, and I'm not whatcha'd call a prayin' man—Maw an' Paw was Cath'lic, though I ain't given it any more thought than they did—but I guess I'm here nonetheless."

"You live here," said Arthur, "and we are guests in your Master's house."

"I suppose you can stay if you like," said Jonathan. "We're going about this blind. It's not as though we have a list of rules."

"Then let us call upon God and the Queen of Heaven," said Pierre, dropping purposefully to his knees. "In the name of the Father, and of the Son, and of the Holy Ghost."

"Amen," said we all likewise kneeling, except Grayburn, who silently bowed his head.

We solemnly recited the Our Father, three Hail Marys, a Glory Be, the *Salve Regina*, and the prayer to St. Michael the Archangel. Ending with the Sign of the Cross, Pierre rose and took command.

"Stand or sit as you like," he said. "But speak your minds — sharp and true. I shall go first, but join in as seems fitting. My fellow Knights, we have banded together as men of Faith. We have presumed to call ourselves Knights — somewhat in jest, more so in hope I should think — but the time has come when we must act the part. As you know, Fr. Baptist has been so involved with the mess at the Chancery that he's cancelled our last two Thursday night meetings at the rectory. But in Arthur's apartment we spoke of approaching Father, when time and opportunity permit, to investigate the possibility of taking the next step: becoming genuine Knights. We know that this will require the involvement of a Catholic king — no doubt in exile, or a bishop — surely not from this neck of the woods, or a duly sworn and dubbed Knight — surely they're out there, but how to find one? All of that is relegated to the future, but I say that if we're to pursue the matter, if we're to have any hope of our wish coming to fruition, we must act as True Knights now, at the moment of need. Can we agree on this?"

"It depends on where you're going with it," said Edward, folding his arms again.

"Jonathan," said Arthur. "Do you have that pocket New Testament with you?"

"Sure," said Jonathan, digging it out of his jacket and handing it to my Big Brother, in whom my respect was growing with leaps and bounds.

"Here it is," said he, finding the page immediately. "Luke chapter sixteen, verse ten: 'He that is faithful in that which is least, is faithful also in that which is greater.'" He flipped two pages. "And in chapter nineteen, verse seventeen: 'Well done, thou good servant, because thou hast been faithful in a little, thou shalt have power over ten cities.'"

"Thank you," said Pierre, slipping his hand into his jacket. "I have here in my pocket something I brought along for a fireside discussion at the campground. Yes, we know how that turned out, but this is a much more fitting setting, surrounded as we are by all these ponderous books—and, thanks to Grayburn, a heartening fire. Jonathan has said we don't have a list of rules, but on this page I have copied down a set from a work by the French literary historian, Émile Théodore Léon Gautier, that I propose we make our own:

THE TEN COMMANDMENTS OF CHIVALRY

i. Thou shalt believe all that the Church teaches, and shalt observe all Her directions.

ii. Thou shalt defend the Church.

iii. Thou shalt respect all weaknesses, and shalt constitute thyself the defender of them.

iv. Thou shalt love the country in which thou wast born.

v. Thou shalt not recoil before thine enemy.

vi. Thou shalt make war against the Infidel without cessation, and without mercy.

vii. Thou shalt perform scrupulously thy feudal duties, if they be not contrary to the Laws of God.

viii. Thou shalt never lie, and shalt remain faithful to thy pledged word.

    ix. Thou shalt be generous, and give largesse to everyone.

    x. Thou shalt be everywhere and always the champion of the Right and the Good against Injustice and Evil.

"That's quite a mouthful," said Edward. "What are we going to do, discuss them one by one?"

"Not necessary right now," said Pierre. "But I do think we need to look very carefully at Number Three: Respect those who are weak, and be prepared to defend them."

"You mean Joel," said Jonathan.

"I do," said Pierre. "Edward, you said a moment ago that he's been acting strangely since he got here. I wonder if that is true, or whether he's been feeling left out for some time and it just came to the fore when we left the distractions of the city behind. I confess I was shocked this morning to learn how deeply he resents us. Me especially. I have since asked myself: if I am so forthright in virtue, how did he come to feel this way toward me? If Joel despises me so much—believe me, I saw it in his eyes— surely I must have fueled the fires of his animosity."

"Maybe you're just annoying," said Edward with a smirk. "You are sometimes, you know."

"It's not like you've bullied him," said Jonathan to Pierre. "At least, no more than the rest of us."

"We all have," said Arthur. "How long was the 'Froo-Froo Squad' pickling his brain at the archdiocesan seminary? Their addling techniques didn't quite take with him, so he left and circuitously came blundering into our midst. Sure, we took him in, but did we treat him as an equal? Did we not swat him mercilessly whenever he spouted the drivel he'd learned at St. Joseph's?"

"If you'll permit a lady's perspective," I said, "or rather a woman quoting a man's. St. Vincent de Paul once said something that stuck with me: 'I have never, never in my life, succeeded when I spoke with the faintest of harshness. I have al-

ways noted that if one wishes to move another's mind one must
be ever so careful not to embitter the person's heart.'"

"Well said," said Pierre. "I fear we've left our mark on our
Joel."

"The old Tumblar branding iron, I'd say," said Jonathan. "I've
felt it from time to time myself. But we've always agreed it's
our way."

"It is the way of fighting men to toughen each other," said Pierre. "It serves a useful purpose. Maybe Joel didn't understand.
Surely none of his experiences at the seminary prepared him for
camaraderie with the likes of us. Perhaps, on our part, we resented his past affiliation with that heresy mill. Maybe we de-
lighted in knocking him down a bit too much as a result."

"And he took it personally," I said.

"You've got to admit he's said some truly stupid things," said
Edward.

"And you and I haven't?" noted Arthur. "We've thickened our
skins on each others' barbs because of the dimwitted things we
all say. We don't take correction from each other personally.
We're used to it. You might say we revel in it. I hate to think
that Joel didn't understand. We can be a cruel bunch."

"So what's to be done?" said Edward. "It's not like we can
ring him up, bring over a pizza, and apologize. If we're to be of
any real use, I still say we should hit the road, get to town, and
call for help."

"Call whom for help?" I asked. "Who would believe us?"

"Well, there's Brumus," said Edward. "He's the sheriff."

"In a town full of witches," said Pierre.

"He's been sympathetic," said Arthur. "But asking him to believe we've escaped from a flying saucer is a bit much."

"What's he going to do?" asked Pierre. "Shoot it?"

"Fr. Baptist, then," said Edward.

"Perhaps," said Arthur. "But even if he believed us, what
could he do?"

"Okay, okay," said Edward. "If not for help, then to save ourselves. I'm sorry about Joel, but I for one don't want to be abducted by spacemen and never heard from again. We had a

close call. I say let's get as far away from here as fast as possible."

"Joel suggested that very thing our first night here," said Jonathan. "We didn't listen to him."

"In the spirit of fellowship we can follow his advice now," said Edward. "What else can we do?"

"I don't knows what you guys is talkin' 'bout," said Grayburn. "But where I comes from, y'all don't leaves a friend behind."

All eyes turned to him.

"Commandment Number Five," said Pierre meaningfully. "'Thou shalt not recoil before thine enemy.'"

"You're not serious," said Edward. "Do you realize what we're up against?"

"I was aboard their spaceship," said Pierre, sarcastically. "Where were you?"

"Didn't someone say 'He who fights and runs away—'?" countered Edward.

"We haven't fought yet," said Arthur, "and whoever coined that maxim certainly wasn't a Knight."

"So we just stand and wave at them when they rise out of the lake again?" exclaimed Edward. "This isn't the Del Agua Mission, you know. We can't storm the place. There's no front or back as far as we know. We've only seen the transporter room. There must be dozens of other compartments. Some 'Minimum Information Gambit'! If there's any other way inside, we don't know of it, and we've no idea of the layout of the ship,"

"Knights do not run away," insisted Pierre.

"Even if the enemy is huge, powerful, technically advanced, and not even human?" demanded Edward.

"Even so," said Pierre.

"Still," said Arthur, "with all their superiority and sophistication, they hide their magnificent craft in the depths of a remote lake. Why do you suppose they do that? Why not land openly in a population center and announce themselves?"

"They certainly aren't shy," I said. "Or are they?"

"Maybe they don't think the human race is ready to deal with them," said Edward.

"But *we* are?" asked Jonathan. "Come on. And Joel most of all? I mean, not to put him down as we've been saying, Pierre, but just being honest: he's the least mature of our gang of castaways."

"The least rooted, I think you mean," said Pierre, putting it more charitably. "Therefore the most susceptible."

"Or gullible," said Jonathan, just being honest.

"They lied to him," said Arthur, significantly. "They're duplicitous."

"Maybe he misunderstood them," said Edward. "You know, cross-species miscommunication."

"The lady said they play with our minds," said Jonathan.

"The lady had apparently been abducted a long time ago," said Edward. "Maybe they didn't let her go because she's whacked."

"Or maybe they're evil," said Arthur.

"As in deceitful and devious?" asked Jonathan.

"As in wicked, malevolent, 'Serpent in the Garden' evil," said Arthur.

"Are you suggesting Satan is a space alien?" asked Edward.

"Funny you should put it that way," said Arthur. "Frankly, I don't have any idea what they are or whence they come. All I know for certain is that our brief contact with them produced in us a profound sense of loss, self-absorption, despair, anger—and worst of all, fear. Why do you suppose that is?"

"Because it was a terrifying experience, being kidnapped that way," said Edward.

"Feeling so helpless," I added.

"Helpless or hopeless?" said Arthur pointedly.

"What are you getting at?" asked Jonathan.

"In the first chapter of St. Luke," said Arthur, flipping the pages of Jonathan's New Testament, "John the Baptist's father exhibited fear until the Angel who appeared before him said, 'Fear not, Zachery, for thy prayer is heard.' Later in the same chapter, when the Archangel Gabriel appeared to the Blessed Virgin, he said, 'Fear not, Mary, for thou hast found grace with God.'"

"So?" quipped Edward.

"Aboard the spaceship," said Arthur, "our abductor only said, 'Patience, stand perfectly still,' and 'the effects of teleportation will wear off sooner if you stop struggling.'"

"All that proves is that he wasn't an Angel," said Edward.

"To be sure," said Arthur. "And then he voiced something utterly insidious, of paramount significance, the point I'm getting at: he said that their scientists planted the seed of life on this planet a billion years ago, that we human beings are the evolutionary outcome of that experiment. Think back, all of you, to that moment. How did you feel when he uttered those words?"

"Rather small," admitted Jonathan.

"Smaller than small," I said.

"I don't know," said Edward. "I think I felt rather honored that they'd come to look in on us."

"Honored?" said Pierre. "Like an amoeba under a microscope?"

"Well," said Edward. "Maybe honored isn't the right word."

"Try humiliated," I said. "Or embarrassed."

"Teensy weensy," said Pierre, holding up his hand and pinching his thumb and index finger together.

"Okay," said Edward. "Perhaps I felt a bit on the weensy side of honored."

Jonathan cleared his throat. "I remember thinking I hoped they'd got their planets switched—that they were wrong."

"I thought of that movie," said Pierre, "the one with the big black monolith and the apes and the spacemen with the computer that goes haywire."

"*2001: A Space Odyssey,*" said Arthur.

"Actually, I preferred *Mad Magazine's* satirical version," said Pierre. "'201 Minutes of a Space Idiocy.' Either way, it's an overused Sci-Fi theme."

"Overused or not," said Arthur, "on some level—Heaven help us—we all believed the alien. What was his name—Klargook?"

"Close enough," said Jonathan.

"We knew nothing about him," said Arthur. "His kind, his society, his origins, his intentions—but we were so impressed by his whiz-bang technology that we all felt puny and overwhelmed. Like the Polynesian natives who fashioned replicas of propeller-driven planes out of palm fronds after the Americans withdrew at the conclusion of World War II, we were wowed by our invaders. They came out of the sky in a vessel beyond our comprehension, utilizing gadgetry we thought impossible, and—Yes, Bwana!—we, in effect, fell down on our knees and worshipped."

Several mouths opened to speak, but no words came out.

"And at that moment we lost our Faith," said Arthur, his tone dire and severe. "Not the trappings—we still prayed for guidance a few minutes ago. Not the details—we called upon Christ Jesus and the Virgin Mary for guidance, and St. Michael the Archangel for protection." He pointed to his heart. "But deep down where the soul and spirit meet, our Catholic Faith had been uprooted and cast into the fire."

"How can you say such a thing?" I gasped, appalled.

"Because, my dear Sister," said Arthur. "If aliens seeded the earth, then God did not make Man in His Image. If evolution is true, then Adam and Eve never existed. If there were no First Parents, there was no Fall. If there was no such thing as Original Sin, there was no need for the Son of God to come and save us from it. If there was no Nativity, there was no Resurrection. If there was no Last Supper, there is no Sacrifice of the Mass. If there is no Holy Eucharist, there is no Catholic Church. Once the first domino is knocked over, the rest tumble until none remain standing."

"All because we were lulled by gizmos," said Pierre, shaking his head thoughtfully.

"I've never played with dominoes," said Edward. "But granting all you're saying, Arthur, it's hard to argue with what we saw with our own eyes, what we experienced with our whole bodies. How do we dismiss all that?"

"When I was very young," Arthur answered thoughtfully, "Mom took me shopping at a place called Montgomery Ward. In the appliances section there was a man demonstrating a new kind of oven. He wrapped a wiener within a paper napkin and placed it inside and closed the door. A minute later he took it out, and the wiener was thoroughly cooked—swollen to bursting, steaming as though held over a flame—but the napkin wasn't charred. He then put inside a Pyrex measuring cup filled with water. When he removed it the water was boiling, but the handle was cool to the touch. 'Ladies and gentlemen,' I remember him saying, 'Heat without fire. Welcome to the space age!'"

"Microwaves," conceded Edward.

"Mom suspected witchcraft," said Arthur. "Many things seem impossible if you don't understand the principle behind them."

"And remember the stage magician," said Pierre. "He distracts his mark from what he's really doing."

"You're suggesting that all we've experienced is merely a distraction?" scoffed Edward, waving his arm in the general direction of the submerged flying saucer. "Who's doing the distracting, and from what?"

"That is the question," said Pierre. "From what? I would say from our convictions."

"But who?" insisted Edward.

"Who would benefit from our losing our Faith?" asked Arthur, looking as though he knew the answer to his own question. "Who rejoices when anyone loses Hope?"

"Surely you don't mean—" said Edward.

"He does," said Pierre, "and I agree. Our frail senses are limited and consequently easily bamboozled by so adroit a hand."

"You mean Satan," said Edward.

"The Father of Lies," affirmed Arthur.

"Why would he go to so much trouble for the likes of us?" asked Edward.

"Him bein' so powerful and all," said Grayburn, "maybe it ain't so much trouble."

"Come again?" asked Jonathan as all eyes turned again toward the fireplace.

"To a buncha ants," said Grayburn, waving the poker around, "a tossed marble is what they would calls a catty-strofy; to a youngster it's a darn good shot; to a grownup maybe it's somethin' they dug outta their shoe and tossed away. Wasn't Lucyfur s'posed to be the second honcho only to God way back when? Maybe what y'all're talkin' 'bout don't amount to more than a kid's science fair project to the likes of him. Besides, everyone knows the Old Goat don't always do his own dirty work."

"You mean he's powerful enough," said Jonathan, "and sometimes he employs wicked men."

"Or stupid idiots," said Grayburn. "Dumbbells does as much
harm as smart folks when it comes to doin' wrong."

"Thank you, Grayburn," said Pierre, smiling appreciatively.

"So if not Satan directly," said Jonathan, "someone under his
influence."

"Seems someone's pulled a fast one on y'all," said Grayburn.
"I, for one, am glad I weren't there to see it."

"A fast one?" said Edward. "I can't see how what we saw was
just some parlor trick. It took power, and applied science—years
beyond anything on this planet."

"Science," said Pierre, thoughtfully. "The new religion.
We've discussed among ourselves on many occasions the tendency of scientists to present their theories as established fact
while the populace bows and accepts. Science, once the study of
God's handiwork, has increasingly become the tool of spiritual
detraction, erosion, and compromise."

"All the worse," added my big-brained Big Brudder, "when
theologians, who should consider their discipline the highest activity of human reason, bow to the notion that knowledge must
be restricted to what can be observed through the senses, thereby
denying science the very principles it needs to function properly.
Sadder still, when such capitulation leads to the abandonment of
the tenets of metaphysics and the wholehearted embracing of
flawed, even patently erroneous, hypotheses."

"When the who leads to what even of the which?" asked Jonathan, crossing his eyes.

"Was that last bit intended for me?" asked Edward stiffly.

"Are you a theologian?" asked Arthur.

"No, but still," said Edward.

"Ah, well if you perceived yourself running parallel to my line
of thought, perhaps it was," said Arthur. "If so, you're in good
company. Dare I say it, but Fr. Baptist has been catching flack
lately for pointing out that St. Thomas Aquinas was wowed by
Aristotle, who represented the fashionable science of his day."

"Come again?" asked Jonathan. "Oh, yes, that series of ser-
mons that sent old Mr. Turnbuckle blustering through the roof."

"Thomists are sensitive that way," said Pierre.

"They can huff and puff all they want," said Arthur, "but one of the reasons St. Thomas denied the Immaculate Conception in the *Summa Theologica* was his acceptance of Aristotle's hypothesis that the soul doesn't enter the fetus until the quickening, which he claimed didn't occur until ninety days after conception for females. Aquinas reasoned that grace could not be applied until a rational soul was present, hence the Virgin Mary couldn't have been sanctified at conception."

"Didn't he also appeal to St. Matthew and St. Paul?" asked Jonathan, struggling to hold his own. "Something about Jesus having to save all mankind, therefore Mary was not exempt?"

"Correct," said Arthur, "and to St. Augustine as well: 'All flesh born of carnal intercourse is sinful.' But that was not St. Thomas's primary argument. He appealed to Aristotle first. It was a silly biological argument based on unsupportable supposition beyond the scope of the technology of the time. The matter was later sorted out by Blessed Duns Scotus, but we're getting off the track. My point was that St. Thomas Aquinas, one of the greatest minds the Church has ever produced—not to mention a model of heroic holiness—was not above a bit of waffling. This is what I meant by theologians holding material science above metaphysics, in effect forcing the proverbial square peg into a round hole. The claims of science are forever changing while transcendent Truth remains steadfast. In fact—"

"Excuse me—Pierre, everyone," said Jonathan, rubbing his temples. "I don't know about you, but my brain is about ready to burst. Do you think we might take a ten-minute imbibulatory breather? Some of us are still dry."

"A thousand pardons," said Pierre. "But of course. Drinks all around!"

∞§[Martin]§∞

GARDENING TIPS: If you want to read up on Ar-

istotle's prenatal theories, see his History

<u>of</u> <u>Animals</u>, Book VII, Chapter 3. If not, I'll
just recap that the esteemed--dare I say
"chic"--Greek philosopher asserted that the
first movement of males occurs on the right
side of the womb forty days after conception,
whereas for females it occurs on the left
fifty days later. I'll give him this: Aristotle was honest enough to add: "However, we
must by no means assume this to be an accurate
statement of fact, for there are many excep-
tions . . ." Would that modern scientists
were as candid.

--M.F.

N.B.: Oh, and just to keep the record complete, the verse Pierre quoted, "For where
there are two or three gathered in My name
. . ." was from the Gospel of Saint Matthew,
chapter eighteen verse twenty.

∞§[†]§∞

∞§†§∞

28. Wherein We All Stand

∞§[Martin]§∞

"I SECOND THE MOTION," said Edward. "I could sure use an im-bibulatory breather."

"I'd love to third it," said Father, "but the time of fasting before receiving Holy Communion will soon be upon us."

"'Tis sad," said Jonathan, "but at least we can enjoy a swig or two vicariously with ourselves through Beth's journal."

"Ever heard of Black Sambuca?" said she, looking the next page over. "That's what Arthur was drinking."

"Ew," replied Jonathan. "What about me?"

"I didn't notice or just didn't say," she said as she scanned a couple more. "Grayburn's poison was peppermint schnapps."

"Egad," said Jonathan, making a face. "Drat and double drat."

"Swing low, sweet chariot," said Kahlúa, throwing up her hands. "The padded one with the guys in white. Excuse me for pointin' out the obvious, but you guys is obsessed! There you are in a creepy house with a bug-eatin' doc, a killer on the loose, and a flyin' saucer hanging over your heads, and you're all sittin' around big as you please discussin' theology!"

"You don't know the half of it," said Millie, resting her weary chin in her upturned palms. "You should see the mess they always leave behind."

"Doesn't surprise me," said Joel. "I mean, from the first moment I met these guys it's been one uninterrupted metaphysical discussion."

"Usually fueled by booze," said Pierre, sadly. "Unlike now."

"Why was you gangin' up on Eddie?" asked Kahlúa. "He was the only one with his head on level, to my way of thinkin'."

"Laid him out flat," agreed Millie.

"I'm used to it," said Edward. "Around these guys, as has been pointed out, you develop a thick skin."

"Or one heckuva thick skull," said Kahlúa.

"I beg your pardon," said Arthur, shifting in his chair. "I thought I was making a valid point."

"You're always making valid points," said Beth playfully. "Since I can remember, whenever you're nervous or anxious about something, you start explaining the cosmos. You guys should have heard him during final exams!"

"I think we're all a bit like that," said Jonathan, patting his chest. "Barstool theologians: the more trouble we're in, the more we spin—metaphysically speaking, of course. You gotta love us."

"And love us we do," said Pierre. "But time's a'wasting and we've got miles to go yet—literally. Beth, do please continue."

"Sure thing," said Beth, clutching her pages and taking a deep breath.

∞§[*Beth*]§∞

"Only the other day," Arthur was saying between volumes he was removing and replacing from the shelves and sips of something dark and viscous called Black Sambuca from Dr. Horehound's liquor drawer, "a rattled young man who'd come in looking for a copy of Jules Verne's *The Mysterious Island* told me he'd just been fired from a Catholic high school."

"What unspeakable sacrilege did he commit?" asked Jonathan.

"He said he was teaching Earth Science," said Arthur. "He had just presented the second law of thermodynamics, when a sullen girl in the third row, who rarely asked questions, wanted to know whether this didn't pose an obstacle to the theory of evolution. He answered that indeed it did, and that it had been raised as such shortly after Darwin published his book. He assured me that was all he'd said. The girl didn't pursue the matter further, and he went on with the lesson. The next day he was summoned to the principal's office—a nun, of course—who told him it wasn't the school's policy to teach creationism. When he told her he had merely answered a question in his field of expertise as his job description required, the sister told him in future he was to refer all such questions to her. He made the fatal mistake of commenting that he hadn't realized her job description included playing God. His name was peeled off his locker before the end of the period."

"The science editor at the *Times* was forcibly retired," said Pierre, "because he admitted in his column that he believed in God. Kahlúa knows him and told me about it. The paper was inundated with complaints from an organized contingent of professors in the Geology, Chemistry, and Astrophysics Departments at South Central University."

"'Scuse me," said Grayburn, elbowing amongst them with a glass of peppermint schnapps in his gnarled hand. "I knows 'bout you bein' a reporter, Mr. Bon-Ton, but what're the rest of y'all—college perfessors?"

"Hardly," said Jonathan, "though I suppose Arthur here is closest."

"But not by much," said Big Bro. "I clerk at an antiquarian bookstore—old, rare, hard-to-find books, a fitting position for someone who loves to read as much as I. The discount Mr. Gilbert gives me is worth more than my salary."

"I manage the all-women clerical staff at a Brackmore's Hardware Emporium while doing accounts receivable," said Edward, shrugging sheepishly. "Believe me, my radar is searching for something less frustrating and more stimulating. Jonathan here has it worse. He clerks at Tallulah's on Rodeo Drive. Very upscale, you know."

"Tallulah's?" I asked. "What's that?"

"A ladies' shoe store," mumbled Jonathan, his facial hair bristling.

"Really," I couldn't help saying playfully. "I suppose that's one way of meeting eligible females."

"Not in that part of town," said Jonathan, shuddering. "I, too, am looking for another position."

"And you, Missie?" asked Grayburn before I could comment on that.

"I'm helping my friend get her seamstress shop established back in Ohio," I said. "Sally Singer's Sewing Circle. I do embroidery on some of her gowns and I teach a crocheting class in the front room on Monday nights."

"Funny thing," said Grayburn. "The reason I asked is that most people who comes here talks 'bout their work more'n theirselves. You folks're sure differ'nt."

"For Jonathan and me it's just income," said Edward. "For Arthur it's something more, and for Pierre, well, it's—"

"Yes, well," said Pierre. "I think we've given our gray matter enough of a breather. Serious matters are still looming before us."

"Right," said Jonathan, heaving a sigh. "It just goes to show how utterly outclassed we are by whatever's lurking in the lake."

"You can say that again," said Edward, pounding the desk with his fist. "Look at us! A hardware store manager, a bookseller, a reporter, a seamstress, a groundskeeper, and—no offense, Jonathan, but really—a ladies' shoe salesman!" He waved his arm again to indicate the spaceship. "Whatever it is, what are we against *that?*"

"But isn't that the way of things?" insisted Arthur, setting down his glass and hefting a thick volume which he'd prepared with scraps of paper as bookmarks. "Might I be so bold as to read from Tolkien? I'm referring to Frodo's cry of 'Why did it come to me? Why was I chosen?' when he learned the nature of the Ring in his possession. To which Gandalf replied: 'Such questions cannot be answered. You may be sure that it was not for any merit that others do not possess: not for power or wisdom, at any rate. But you have been chosen, and you must therefore use such strength and heart and wits as you have.'"

"That's all fine and good," said Edward with renewed anger and frustration. "But may I point out: that's a bloody book! A novel! We're up here in the mountains, miles from help. What are we supposed to do against, against—?"

"'Despair or folly?'" read Arthur from another place: "'It is not despair, for despair is only for those who see the end beyond all doubt. We do not. It is wisdom to recognize necessity, when all other courses have been weighed, though as folly it may appear to those who cling to false hope.'"

"False hope?" said Edward. "Frankly, I see *no* hope."

"Then you are determined to leave?" asked Pierre.

"I can't see any other option that makes sense," said Edward. "Sorry, but you're not Gandalf, Pierre. Neither is Arthur. You said we should speak our minds, and I'm sorry if I offend. We call ourselves Knights, but this isn't a game. This is real life, real stakes—the danger is all too genuine."

"Exactly," said Pierre. "As you say, this isn't a game. We call ourselves Knights, and the time has come to test our mettle. If you decide to leave, I cannot and will not stop you, Edward. Be advised that it will shatter our fellowship if you go, and things will never be the same between us again. But I choose to stay and fight this thing. I will not leave a comrade behind, no matter how frail and spiteful and disappointing he has proved himself to be; for what is my friendship worth otherwise? In good conscience, no matter the consequences, no matter the odds, there is no other course for me to take."

"So that's it," said Edward, squaring his shoulders. "Jonathan? What do you say?"

Jonathan stood perfectly still, the weight of the moment crushing his shoulders. I wanted to scream, frankly, but I knew I mustn't—maybe later, but not just then. Grayburn looked like his name: gray and charred, but with the glow of stirred embers in his eyes.

"Hold on, Edward," said Arthur. "Before you render your decision final, allow me one more word. For the sake of our friendship, I ask you to hear me out."

"All right," said Edward, clenching his fists. "For the sake of our friendship, which I would hate to see shipwrecked."

"Good," said Arthur, taking up the little pocket New Testament. "Permit me to read from St. Paul's First Epistle to the Corinthians, chapter fifteen. Everyone, please attend, for everything, I say *everything*, hangs upon this:

Now I make known unto you, brethren, the Gospel
which I preached to you, which also you have received,
and wherein you stand; by which also you are saved, if
you hold fast after what manner I preached unto you, unless you have believed in vain. For I delivered unto you
first of all, which I also received: how that Christ died
for our sins, according to the scriptures: and that He was
buried, and that He rose again the third day, according to
the scriptures: and that He was seen by Cephas; and after
that by the eleven. Then He was seen by more than five
hundred brethren at once: of whom many remain until
this present, and some are fallen asleep. After that, He
was seen by James, then by all the apostles. And last of
all, He was seen also by me, as by one born out of due
time. For I am the least of the apostles, who am not
worthy to be called an apostle, because I persecuted the
church of God. But by the grace of God, I am what I
am; and His grace in me hath not been void, but I have
laboured more abundantly than all they: yet not I, but the
grace of God with me.

Arthur closed the book and set it on the desk.   As well as I
know my brother, I can't explain the emotions that played upon
his face as he summoned the courage to say what needed to be
said. "The Gospel," he spoke at last, "which you have received,
and wherein you stand. Wherein we all stand. That is the point
of our fellowship, of our very lives. St. Paul considered himself
unworthy, too: born out of due time, a man who had persecuted
the followers of Christ. What he and Tolkien are telling us, each
in his own way, is that regardless of who we think we are, a task
beyond our means, strengths, and talents has been set before us.
If we accept the challenge, it will not be we who will succeed,
but the Grace of God within us. As Catholics, we honor hundreds of Saints who died in the attempt. They are heroes because they tried, they strove, they kept the Faith, even if their
endeavor ended in death. Gentlemen, Beth, this is our commis-

sion. We didn't seek it, and we surely don't want it, but it has been handed to us nonetheless. Pierre, would you be so kind as to read the First and Second Commandments again for us?"

"Of course," said Pierre, blinking as if wakening, then referring to the paper in his hand: "'One: Thou shalt believe all that the Church teaches, and shalt observe all Her directions. Two: Thou shalt defend the Church.'"

"It seems to me," said Arthur, "and I think it should be obvious to all present, even Grayburn who is not a prayerful man, that the primary, fundamental, and insidious attack we face is not upon our persons, or upon our pride, or upon our claim to be Knights, but upon the One, Holy, Catholic, and Apostolic Church. That alien being, whatever or whoever it is, has attacked that which we consider Holy and Perfect, given to us by Jesus Christ Himself, handed down to us through His Apostles, and defended by countless martyrs. The question we must ask, and which we must answer here and now, is: where do we stand? Do we defend the Gospel, or do we worry about our safety? As Jesus Himself said; 'Fear ye not them that kill the body, and are not able to kill the soul: but rather fear Him that can destroy both soul and body in Hell.'"

"You mean we must fear God, first and foremost," said Edward.

"Above and beyond whatever's in the lake," said Pierre.

"Exactly," said Arthur.

"You really mean—?" said Jonathan. "Can it really be—? It's like something out of—"

"*The Roman Martyrology*," said Pierre intently. "Our Faith, our resolve, put to the test."

"Oh my God!" said Edward, clasping his hands to the arms of a chair and sinking slowly into it. "I didn't realize. I still don't see—Good Heavens!—maybe you're right, Arthur. Was this what it was like when St. Cecilia was brought before the Prelate of Rome?"

"Or when St. Thomas More was summoned by Thomas Cromwell," added Jonathan.

"Or when Don Juan of Austria and his small European fleet sighted Ali Pasha and the mighty Turkish fleet, just out of Lepanto," said Arthur.

"The sting of fear," said Pierre. "Many of our forebears have felt it, and faced it head on."

"Who would have thought?" said Edward. "I certainly didn't. And to think I almost—what must you think of me?"

"That you've come around!" said Pierre, clasping a hand on Edward's shoulder. "My dear Fellow!" he exclaimed. "My good Friend, and fellow Knight!"

Arthur, too, sank into a chair and buried his face in his hands. I wanted to rush to him, but knew I had best stay put. Jonathan leaned against the desk for support. I hoped he might look at me, but then I realized this was a critical moment for these men. Truly, I was but an observer—thoroughly involved, but an observer all the same. One very frustrated ready-to-burst observer! Grayburn, after several seconds of befuddled blinking, turned to the fire, grabbed the poker, and began noisily jabbing the logs.

After a minute that seemed like an hour, Arthur roused himself for one more scriptural reading, this one to seal the deal. Taking up the New Testament he said, "St. Paul's Epistle to the Romans, chapter fifteen:

> What things soever were written, were written for our learning, that through patience and the comfort of the Scriptures, we might have hope. Now the God of patience and of comfort grant you to be of one mind one towards another, according to Christ Jesus; that with one mind, and with one mouth, you may glorify God and the Father of our Lord Jesus Christ.

I suppose that would have been a fine moment to end this chapter, but something remarkable happened which caused everyone to jump and take notice.

There was a loud, rubbery pop—a sound we knew and dreaded so well—and suddenly a sphere of light appeared.

"Gadzooks!" exclaimed Pierre, leaping to his feet.

"What now?" gasped Jonathan.

"Land sakes!" said Grayburn, holding the poker like a weapon but keeping his distance.

"Stand fast!" commanded Pierre. "Attend!"

The orb hovered steadily, silently, ponderously, about three feet above the desk. It did not crackle and spew red sparks like the one that had chased Joel, nor the ones that attacked the vehicles outside. This one struck me as being like a miniature moon: blue so pale it was almost white with hints of green, silent and somehow reflective—perhaps thoughtful—in nature. The idea occurred to me, although I didn't think to voice it, that this sphere didn't seem angry or ready to pounce. Something about it seemed—I don't know—serene, somehow, or even kindly.

"What do you think it wants?" asked Jonathan.

"What should we do?" asked Edward, rising to his feet and brushing his hair from his face.

"I don't know," said Pierre. "Keep perfectly still."

This we all did, our eyes riveted on the ball of light. If it was regarding us, it did so for quite some time. Then, without warning, it collapsed—not with a burst of light, and not into nothingness, but into a something rectangular, thin, and no longer glowing—a piece of brown parchment which fell unceremoniously onto the desk.

Curious, we all gathered around.

"What are those markings?" asked Edward.

"It looks like a message," said Jonathan.

"Don't touch it!" I gasped.

"It's a note of some kind," said Pierre, gingerly picking it up. "Arthur, are these runes?"

"Yes," said my brother, bending close. "Definitely runes."

"Can you decipher them?" asked Pierre, handing it to him.

"Let me see," said Arthur, accepting it and easing himself into Dr. Horehound's chair. He set it on the blotter and examined it, his forehead gathered in furrows of concentration. "Oddly," he said, "although this is written in an ancient alphabet, the language seems to be modern English. The first line seems to be one word: D ... A ... the next figure, shaped like a diamond, represents the sound we write as 'NG,' then ... E ... R. I believe the word is DANGER."

"You got that right," said Jonathan, looking around warily.

"Danger," said Pierre. "Is it a warning? A threat?"

"I don't know," said Arthur. "The writer is inconsistent."

"How so?" asked Edward.

"Runic is a phonetic alphabet," said Arthur. "Each symbol represents a specific sound."

"Isn't our alphabet like that?" asked Jonathan.

"Somewhat," said Arthur, "until you get to words like 'Knight' with three silent letters. This symbol for 'NG' shouldn't be used here. It's a single sound made by the back of the tongue pressed against the roof of the mouth, normally used as an ending, as in the word 'ring' or 'turning.' Phonemically, in this context, N and G are in separate syllables, and the G is soft rather than hard. Their sounds are distinct, so they should have been rendered as two discrete letters, N and J. It's as if the writer is forcing English spelling into an alphabet in which he is not fluent, resorting to the use of a chart, perhaps."

"You got all that out of one word?" asked Jonathan.

"This system also lacks lowercase letters, as well as commas and periods," said Arthur. "It makes for a lot of guesswork."

"Well," said Pierre, "do your best."

"Of course," said Arthur. "The second line is composed of three words: SAIL ... AT ... ONCE."

"Sail?" said Jonathan. "Like on a boat?"

"Maybe it means to flee," suggested Edward, then caught himself. "Or not."

"The third line makes no sense," said Arthur. "I may be mistaken, but it seems to say, MEN WHO GNAW THE FLESH."

"'Danger,'" repeated Pierre, "'... sail at once ... men who gnaw the flesh.'"

"Maybe it saw us attacking the prime rib at dinner," said Edward.

"A rather crude way of putting it," said Pierre. "But it seems to mean us."

"We didn't all eat dinner," said Jonathan. "Still, it sounds like a command."

"Unless it means the flesh-gnawing men are the danger we should sail away from," said Edward.

"I sure hope not," said Jonathan.

"What's next?" said Pierre.

"Hmm," said Arthur. "C and K share the same rune, hence the odd spelling of 'back.' The first symbol in the last word is our 'TH.' I have it: GO BACK FOR NO THING."

"No thing?" asked Edward. "Go back for no thing?"

"Like take nothing with you?" said Jonathan. "Travel light, when you go sailing?"

"Somebody wants us to go sailing?" said Edward. "On the lake? With that saucer out there? Nuts to that!"

"Could be," said Arthur. "The next line is AVOID DEEP WATER."

"Where the spaceship lies," said Pierre. "Avoid the saucer."

"Good advice," said Jonathan.

"Damn good advice," said Edward. "Better would be to avoid the lake altogether."

"The first word in the next line is NOWARD," said Arthur. "That's not a word."

"Maybe it's like 'no thing,'" said Jonathan. "No ward."

"Like a hospital ward," said Edward.

"Or a minor under a guardian's care," said Pierre. "Or not to ward something off."

"NOWARD BY EAST SHORE," said Arthur. "That's the whole line."

"Could it be a name?" asked Jonathan. "A guy name Noward is waiting by the east shore?"

"Or it's a place by the east side of the lake," said Edward.

"Sail at once," reasoned Pierre. "Sail noward ... *northward* ... 'by' as in 'alongside' ... the east shore."

"Bravo, Pierre," said Arthur. "I do believe you're right. The next line is: WESTWARD BY NORTH."

"A series of nautical directions," said Jonathan.

"Northward alongside the east shore," said Pierre. "Westward along the north shore?"

"Why?" asked Jonathan. "Where to?"

"Good Heavens, Gentlemen," said Arthur, tapping the next phrase with his finger. "TO WHERE YOU BEHELD THE CROSS."

"The campground!" said Pierre, Jonathan, and Edward together.

"That makes sense," said Pierre. "If we sailed up the east shore, then turned west along the north shore—it's the long way around, but we'd come to the campground."

"But the spaceship!" said Edward.

"Avoid deep water," said Pierre. "Is that all of it, Arthur?"

"It's signed," said Arthur. "YOUR SERVANT FAWNSKIN."

"Fawnskin," said Edward. "That's a town somewhere—over near Big Bear Lake."

"YOUR SERVANT FAWNSKIN," repeated Arthur. "Then: EMISSARY OF ... something odd here ... FORKBAERD. I suppose that's like 'Fork-Beard'—archaic spelling."

"Colorful name," commented Pierre. "I rather like it."

"And it concludes," said Arthur, "PRINCE OF THE FILAXEEN."

"Filaxeen," said Pierre. "Ever hear of the Filaxeen?"

"No," said Arthur, pushing the parchment away. He folded his hands on his paunch. "Gentlemen, I would say that we've just been offered a course of action."

"To sail up the lake and over to the campground," said Jonathan.

"Where we first saw the lights," said Pierre.

"At the behest of this Fawnskin," said Arthur. "Emissary of Forkbaerd."

"A prince," said Pierre, looking loftily up at the ceiling.

"If you can believe this Fawnskin," said Edward. "Arthur, didn't you say you found it odd that this message is made of modern words transcribed into an ancient alphabet?"

"I find it more intriguing that whoever wrote this knew one of us could decipher it," said Arthur. "So, are we going to accept the invitation?"

"To sail to the campground?" exclaimed Edward. "Why don't we just hike up the western road? I should think that would be a lot more practical—not to mention safer."

"You said it was washed out," said Pierre. "And the message specifies that we go by sail. Grayburn? What do you think? Would there be enough wind this time of night?"

"Hard to say with the storm and all," said Grayburn. "There's usually an evenin' breeze outta the north. If so, we could tack against it. 'Course, you're talkin' 'bout takin' one of the Master's boats—lackin' his permission, I might mention."

"He said we should follow our instincts," said Pierre. "He was adamant about the point."

"Doesn't one of the boats have a motor?" asked Edward.

"One do," said Grayburn. "But your note there says to sail. Seems to me if y'all don't wanna wake up whatever's in deep water, silent sailin's the ticket. Might any of you knows how?"

"I do!" I chirped, glad for something to contribute.

"Don't take me wrong, Missie," said Grayburn. "But I don't cater to the idea of tellin' the Master I let a lassie take out one of his sailboats on her say so."

"I like that!" I said. "I'll have you know—"

"'Course," said Grayburn, rubbing his chin. "If I was to captain 'er, I don't think he'd mind—least not as much. Dang if this couldn't mean my job."

"You'll take us?" said Pierre.

Grayburn let out a big breath of air, puffing his cheeks as he did so. "Oh peacock feathers! This place is goin' to pieces anyway. Okay, I'll do 'er."

"Hurrah!" cheered Pierre and Jonathan.

"A point," said Edward. "We agree that we can't stay here like sitting ducks. But is fleeing across the lake any different than fleeing to town?"

"I should think so," said Pierre. "We're avoiding the spaceship, yes, but we're not fleeing. We'll be heading *toward* something—someone, I should say, who has invited us."

"Commanded us, you mean," said Jonathan.

"The command of a prince or his invitation," said Pierre, "is a difference without a distinction."

"What about Beth?" asked Arthur.

"What *about* me?" I huffed. "You're not going to suggest that I stay here!"

"Not me," said Arthur, throwing up his hands. "But the message said *MEN* WHO GNAW THE FLESH."

"I'll assume the epicene," I said. "And I've had my share of prime rib in my time."

"Then it's settled," said Grayburn. "Missie, I'll count you as my first mate."

"Aye-aye," I replied. "And the best with whom you've ever sailed."

"I believes you," said Grayburn, smiling broadly.

"What about Thorndale?" asked Pierre, taking up the parchment and folding it into his pocket. "Should we wake her? Take her with us?"

"She sleeps with a 10-guage pump-action shotgun," said Grayburn, shaking his head. "I ain't 'bout to try and waken her."

"*10*-guage?" marveled Edward.

"We'll bolt the front door on our way out," said Grayburn. "If anyone can take care of herself, it's Thorndale."

Just then we heard a howl. It was ferocious, and ravenous, and very near. The sound reverberated off the walls and ceiling, rattling the French doors.

"That's outside, isn't it?" said Jonathan. "Not inside the house, I mean?"

"Don't ask me how, but it sounds inside to me," said Grayburn, pointing straight up. "Maybe upstairs. If we's gonna get to the docks, we'd better run."

And run we did.

∞§[Martin]§∞

GARDENING TIPS: With Arthur's help I have re-

constructed the message left by the sphere of

light.

ᚺᚨᚠᛟᛏᚱ
ᛋᚨᛁᛚ ᚨᛏ ᛟᚾᚺᛖ
ᛗᛖᚾ ᚦᚹᛟ ᚷᚾᚨᚹ ᚦᛖ ᚠᛚᛖᛋᚺ
ᚷᛟ ᛒᚨᛚᛚ ᚠᛟᚱ ᛏᛟ ᚦᛁᛟ
ᚠᛟᚱᛁᚾ ᚺᛗᛗᛖ ᚹᚨᛏᛖᚱ
ᛏᛟᚱᚹᛖᚱᛁ ᛒᚻ ᛖᚨᛋᛏ ᛋᚺᛟᚱᛖ
ᚦᛖᛋᛏᚹᛖᚱᛁ ᛒᚻ ᛏᛟᚱᚦ
ᛏᛟ ᚦᚺᛖᚱᛖ ᚻᛟᚢ
    ᛒᛖᚺᛖᛚᛗᛁ ᚦᛖ ᛚᚱᛟᛋᛋ
        ᚻᛟᚢᚱ ᛋᛗᚱᚹᚨᛏ
            ᚠᛖᚹᛏᛋᚺᛁᛏ
        ᛗᛗᛁᛋᛋᛖᚱᚻ ᛟᚠ
            ᚠᛟᚱᛚᛒᚨᛖᚱᛁ
    ᚲᚱᛁᛏᛚᛖ ᛟᚠ ᚦᛖ ᚠᛁᛚᚠᛖᛗᛗᛏ

```
    DANGER
SAIL AT ONCE
MEN WHO GNAW THE FLESH
GO BACK FOR NO THING
AVOID DEEP WATER
NOWARD BY EAST SHORE
WESTWARD BY NORTH
TO WHERE YOU
  BEHELD THE CROSS
    YOUR SERVANT
      FAWNSKIN
    EMISSARY OF
      FORKBAERD
  PRINCE OF THE FILAXEEN
```

                                    --M.F.

∞§[†]§∞

∞§†§∞

29. No Room for Watchmakers

∞§[Martin]§∞

"WOW," SAID JONATHAN, as Beth passed her pages to me. Rather than hand them to Pierre, I took the liberty of leaning awkwardly forward and depositing them on the pile at his feet. He was already digging the next batch out of the chest at my elbow.

"We ran to the docks?" asked Edward incredulously.

"Apparently," said Arthur. "If the beast was in the house, we had to go somewhere."

Edward scowled. "And just how do you suppose it got in there?"

"Good question," said Jonathan. "It had to be Horehound's doing."

"He gives me the heebie-jeebies," said Beth, rubbing her arms.

"Hold on," said Edward, rubbing his temples. "Am I remembering, or just thinking now as I surely did then, what a foolhardy thing to do?"

"Heading for the docks, foolhardy?" mused Arthur. "When it's the only option?"

"Sailing into the arms of the aliens we just escaped from?" countered Edward.

"Loonytoons," said Kahlúa. "That would be my word for it."

"We already agreed heading for town was out of the question," said Beth.

"Why didn't you barricade yourselves right where you were?" asked Millie.

"French doors," said Monsignor Havermeyer. "Glass panels. Not very strong."

"And no weapons," added Jonathan.

"And we did have this Fawnskin's invitation," said Beth, helpfully.

"Oh, now that makes perfect sense," said Edward, sarcastically.

Jonathan took a deep breath and let it out nervously. "This may sound prideful, but I must say, well, I'm rather proud of us."

"As am I," said Father, as he removed a frayed book on European history from the shelf and opened it in his lap.

"Manly hug-fest ensues," snickered Kahlúa.

"I should hope not," blustered Millie.

"Proud of us, for what?" asked Edward.

"Oh, grappling with serious issues," said Jonathan, "deciding to pursue a courageous course, that sort of thing. Say, I thought you'd got your head back on straight."

"That was the me in Beth's story," said Edward. "The me sitting here is still unconvinced."

"Maybe your head's still on crooked," said Millie.

"Well," said Pierre, "let us see what we can do to change that."

"Sure, sure," said Edward. "So who's going to tell the tale of the valiant or insane voyage—take your pick—across the lake? Or should I say the longest way around without walking on dry land?"

"For all that, the honor falls to you, Edward," said Pierre, handing a clutch of pages to Monsignor Havermeyer, who gave them to Jonathan, who passed them to the nuts-and-bolts man.

"Poetic justice strikes again, O Contrary One," said Jonathan.

Edward eyed the words before him. "I can't help being skeptical. It's not something I can turn off like a light."

"To be honest, I must admit that I'm confused," said Jonathan. "I may be in the dark as to these events, but I'm imagining them more and more vividly. I can't tell if I'm visualizing or remembering." He caught himself, then glanced at Beth and Arthur to see if he had crossed the eidetic taboo line. Apparently, he hadn't.

"An excellent point," said Arthur. "I, likewise, can't be sure. But I must say I find myself gripped with a sense of dread. Whether real or imagined, I can't tell. But I fear for my sister's safety—that she's moving toward some terrible, unforeseen peril."

"But I'm here, Big Bro," insisted Beth, her face intense. "Whatever it was, I must have survived it."

"But at what cost?" asked Arthur.

"We'll never know if we just sit here wondering," growled Millie.

"Never knowing if you're imaginin' or rememberin'," said Kahlúa.

"The ladies are right," said Pierre.

"Of course," said Arthur, shaking the gloom from his sleeves. "Pay no attention to me. Edward, everyone, to the oars!"

"Well," said Pierre. "First, we had to get to the boat."

"Then stop beating yourselves to death with your lips!" snapped Millie. "Get moving!"

"That's tellin' 'em," said Kahlúa.

Edward cleared his throat, and with a tense voice, continued the tale.

∞§[Edward]§∞

The thing howled again. By some trick of the wind, the shape of the house, or acoustic factors with which we were unfamiliar, it was impossible to tell which direction the sound came from— inside or outside. Worse, it seemed near and far at the same time. Nonetheless, we had all squeezed through the front door-way and spread out on the front porch before it halted its unnerv-ing wail.

"Maybe this isn't a good idea," said Beth.

"You think?" I quipped.

"The sick call kit!" exclaimed Arthur. "I wish I'd fetched it."

"Not with that creature up there," countered Beth.

"If that's where it is," I said.

"'Go back for no thing,'" quoted Jonathan.

"But holy water, surely," said Arthur.

"There's no turning back now," said Pierre.

"Perhaps," said Arthur hopefully, "while we're still this close to the door."

"Lan' sakes!" exclaimed Grayburn as he turned a key in the lock. The tumblers rumbled into place like bowling balls. "Never heard nothin' hereabouts howl like that before."

"Well?" said I. "What are we waiting for?"

"Stick together," said Pierre. He gave my shoulder another brotherly hand squeeze, the third since I'd agreed not to head for town on my own. He added encouragingly, "Safety in numbers and all that."

We moved in a tight group, bumping into each other as we crept northward along the front of the lodge, then eastward along the north side. The docks, pier, and boats came into view beyond the fluttering porch lights, all pale white in the moonlight which—according to Pierre, Sheriff Brumus, the moon clock at Hal's Groceries, and the calendar on Dr. Horehound's desk— couldn't be shining. From under the cover of the porch I could not as yet look up to judge for myself.

The creature howled again, a prolonged cry that cracked mid-wail.

"Now it's definitely outside!" groaned Beth.

"Where?" asked Pierre.

"Over there!" said Jonathan and Arthur, pointing in opposite directions.

"Great," I said to myself.

"Maybe we should go back inside," said Jonathan. "Wait for it to go away."

"No," said Pierre. "'Thou shalt not recoil before thine enemy.'"

"What 'bout for a shotgun?" asked Grayburn. "There's one in my bedroom. I could slip 'round back—"

"'Go back for no thing,'" grumbled Arthur. "If holy water couldn't help, neither would a gun."

"Y'all're jokin'," said Grayburn.

"We're a weird bunch, remember?" said Jonathan. He shrugged his shoulders as if he didn't completely understand us himself.

At that moment, I admit, I didn't either.

"Hurry," said Pierre as we crept down the steps to the graveled walkway.

At last I could look up at the moon. It was directly overhead. Trouble was, with all the jostling and scuffling, I couldn't get a steady view, and I wasn't about to stand still.

We were halfway to the boardwalk when the thing cried out again. This time I thought it was behind us—no, not somewhere back there around the front of the lodge behind us: *right behind us!* I pushed the others ahead and fell behind—guilt over almost leaving, not courage, being my motivating factor—and turned to greet my fate. To my surprise there was nothing there. The graveled path, the steps up to the porch, the posts, the fluttering gas lamps, the outside furniture—all as they should be.

"Thanks for the impetus," said Arthur.

"Impulsion is the mother of momentum," said Pierre.

"What?" I asked, still facing the lodge.

"Sounded close," said Jonathan.

"Where is it?" asked Beth. "I don't see anything."

"Just keep moving," said Pierre. "Which one, Grayburn?"

"What's that?" asked Grayburn.

"Which boat shall we take?" said Pierre.

"Ah," said the old codger, "that'd be the beauty closest to the boathouse. She's called the *Queen of Hearts.*"

"Imagine that," said Arthur. Knowing him, if he'd had a paintbrush, he'd have daubed the word "All" before "Hearts."

Just as our footfalls changed from crunching on gravel to thumping on the boardwalk, there was a sudden flash of light. Then another and another.

"Not another sphere!" said Jonathan. "I've had about enough of—"

"It's not," said Arthur, pointing up at the lodge. "Look!"

I followed his line of sight up to—not the porch, not the second story windows, nor the third, but all the way up, up, up to the surveillance turret at the top of the watchtower. Just as my eyes focused on the transom, there was another burst of shrill light through the glassless windows. It flashed several times, died down, flickered, flashed, flickered, flared intensely, then went out. It was just like what Pierre, Jonathan, Joel and I saw the first night from the side of the lake, which in turn was like a clip from one of Arthur's beloved Frankenstein movies. Knowing that there was a genuine Tesla coil up there would have sapped the urgency out of the moment, except this time, there was something new. Poised on the widow's walk, gripping the wrought-iron railing, framed by the crackling electric arcs, crouched a shape. It was black—or rather blank—against the blazing corona behind it. From its outline I had the impression that it was lithe, muscular, and hairy all over. When the flashing behind it ceased, so did it—blending as it did into the darkness of the open window.

"What the heck was that?" asked Jonathan.

"Is it still there?" asked Pierre.

"Don't rightly know," said Grayburn.

"It's not a bear, is it?" asked Beth.

"Or a mountain lion?" asked Arthur.

"Wrong shape, wrong size," said Grayburn.

"How'd it get all the way up there?" asked Pierre.

"Good question," said Grayburn.

The Tesla coil exploded into buzzing, dazzling activity again. The thing was still there on the widow's walk, outlined by the zigzagging discharge. Whatever it was, it slowly and purposefully expanded its upper portions, froze motionless for several long seconds, then contracted all its muscles, hurling a shriek at us with all its might. I actually felt the fibers of my waistcoat vibrating against my chest as the yowl buffeted us.

"To the boat!" commanded Pierre.

"You said it!" said Jonathan.

"Quick, now," said Grayburn as we came to the easternmost dock. "Watch yer step. Missie, be a good lass and get yerself up to the bow. The rest of you, untie the lines and get ready to push us off."

"What about you, Captain?" asked Pierre as Jonathan and I began unraveling the ropes from two cleats on the starboard side of the boat.

"I'll man the tiller," answered Grayburn as another blast of light erupted from the watchtower.

"Don't look now," said Arthur, gazing up at the lodge, "it's not up there anymore."

"Where'd it go?" I asked, not daring to turn my attention from the damp, smelly rope that had become entangled in my haste to get it off the rusty metal prongs.

"Just before that last bit of flashing stopped," said Arthur, "it looked as though it was preparing to lunge."

"From the widow's walk?" I scoffed, my fingers scrabbling furiously. "To where?"

"The porch roof, I assume," said Arthur. "Then to the ground, most likely."

"There!" said Pierre. "I think I saw its eyes—on the roof overhanging the steps."

"Good Lord," said Jonathan as he got the last loop of rope free of his cleat. "If it can leap like that, it can be here in seconds."

"Darn," I grumbled, fumbling with the line. "I may be good with nuts and bolts, but not with rope."

"Here, Edward," said Jonathan, elbowing me aside and attacking the mess I'd made.

"It's coming!" exclaimed Beth from the bow. "It's jumping off the roof!"

"Hurry it up!" barked Grayburn.

"Done!" said Jonathan, flinging the rope aside.

"Okay," said Grayburn. "Let's shove off!"

"Don't you need to unfurl the sails or something?" asked Pierre as Jonathan, Arthur, and I crouched, grabbed the handrail along the edge of the boat, and pushed with all our might.

"Not till we clears our moorin's," said Grayburn. "Stop jabberin' and push!"

"One—two—three—HEAVE!" ordered Pierre, standing behind us.

Another ferocious howl spurred us on. I could hear panting, slavering, and slurping interspersed with the scratch and clatter of paws against loose pebbles on the path.

"Harder, gents," urged Pierre.

"Don't hurt yourself," grunted Jonathan.

"C'mon you landlubbers," said Grayburn. "Put yer backs into it!"

Claws scraped the planks of the boardwalk.

Once she started moving, the boat glided smoothly, like a bar of Ivory soap in a bathtub. A moment later we leapt—or in Arthur's case, clawed and crawled—onboard as the boat cleared the dock. I distinctly heard the swipe of a paw through the air inches behind my head. I turned to see a huge dark shape teetering on the edge of the pier, its muscular forelimbs waving frantically to regain its balance. If we had been a half second slower it would have made it onto the boat. As it was, it dropped on all fours and glared at us with furious, glowing eyes. I wondered if it might try to jump, but instead it began pacing back and forth, its long, hairy tail brushing its face as it made its sharp turns, all the while its eyes trained wickedly on us.

"What in heck *is* that thing?" asked Jonathan as the boat rocked, its momentum easing about thirty feet from the dock.

"Too big to be a wolf," I said.

"Too shaggy to be a bear," said Grayburn, seating himself with his hand resting on the arm of the tiller. "Missie! Prepare to raise the jib!"

"Aye-aye!" answered Beth, deftly fiddling with something at the front of the boat. "And the name is Beth, Captain," she said between tugs, "if you please."

"Fair 'nuff," agreed Grayburn.

"Can I help you with that, Beth?" asked Jonathan.

"Do you know how to affix the jib to the forestay and attach it to the halyard?" asked Beth, who was clearly in her element.

"Uh, no," said Jonathan.

"Then I guess not," said Beth, smiling pertly.

"Now that that's settled," said Grayburn, "the rest of y'all sit down and keep outta the—"

The thing on the dock raised itself onto its hind legs, seemed to clench its forepaws into fists, and let out a screech that, even from the safety of the boat, was nerve tingling.

As unsettling as the moment was, compounded by the chilly breeze buffeting us from the north, it was my first opportunity to give the moon a good solid look. There was a sizable break in the clouds. Yep, there it was, directly overhead, centered in a star-cluttered sky unlike anything we see down in the glare of the city. I almost opened my mouth to say, "What do you mean that isn't the full moon?" when I realized with a start that it, in fact, *wasn't*. It was round, coldly luminous, pale gray, and the right size, but the cratered terrain was all wrong. I've spent my share of idle time looking for the Man in the Moon, comparing guesses about his facial expression with friends—the Tumblars among them—and the patterns on that disk in the night sky were completely unfamiliar. Another thing: it didn't seem to be up in the heavens, either, but closer to us, as if suspended somewhere between. There was also an uncanny suggestion of a porcelain-like shine to it.

I would have said something as I seated myself, but my attention was also drawn over the side of the boat into the dark water below. I couldn't shake the mental image of that huge spaceship skulking down there, the aliens looking hungrily up at us through their scopes, and worst of all, Joel hobnobbing with them and sharing in their condescension. If they decided to raise themselves up out of the water just then, our little sailboat would be swamped and scuttled.

Yet we were heading out into perilous waters because we received a note in stilted English written in an obsolete archaic alphabet, a note that materialized out of a collapsing ball of light. The intensity of Arthur's faith invariably left me in the dust, as did Pierre's lofty predilections; but, somehow, this mission aboard a sailboat had become our only course of noble action— something about which I was still not entirely clear. In fact, much more than appeals to faith and chivalry, the thing that kept echoing in my head was something Pierre had said back in the library: "If you decide to leave, it will shatter our friendship and things will never be the same between us." If that wasn't emotional hornswoggling, I don't know what was. I respected Pierre more than anyone else I knew. Arthur lived between the pages of his books, and Jonathan swam in his hormones. At the moment Joel was hiding in a submerged alien spaceship—go figure. But Pierre lived comfortably and confidently right inside his skin like nobody in my experience. I felt fortunate to be his friend and didn't want to blow it. Still, I didn't like threats.

But another thought came to the fore, pushing all else aside: I did so yearn to become a real Knight some day. I didn't voice my thoughts about it much, but the wish was solidly there. I sometimes pictured a king with a golden crown and royal red robes dubbing me with the flat of his sword, and me in a suit of highly polished armor—as if that were the kind of skin in which I would be confident and comfortable. It was crazy, I knew. Arthur would have called it "anachronistic," but I'd wager most of what went on in his head was just as out of step with modern times.

Oh, and speaking of armor and the chilly breeze coming out of the north, I sorely wished I'd been wearing something a lot warmer. Formal attire was completely out of place during an evening sail. In a matter of moments, all thought of my physical discomfort would be banished by my amazement at how this very wind interacted with the sails, but my initial reaction was a fit of shivering.

Because of these distractions, I can't be sure my recollection of the ensuing conversation is all that accurate. But here goes nothing.

∞§[Martin]§∞

"If I may interject," said Pierre. "In spite of Edward's caveat, I chose his version for our passage up the lake precisely because he captured the essence of what was said, if not all the details, better than anyone else."

"In your opinion," said Edward.

"As the only remaining opinion, yes," said Pierre. "Do go on."

```
GARDENING TIPS: I had considered including a

drawing of a sailboat here with all the parts

identified; but then Kahlu/a showed me that if

you typed the words "parts of a sailboat" into
```

```
something called a "search engine" in her of-

fice computer, you could see much better and

more detailed depictions than I could ever

render in a flash.  I have to admit: I wish my

Underwood typewriter had a feature like that.

                                  --M.F.
```

∞§[Edward]§∞

"Well, Gentlemen," said Pierre as we found ourselves seated facing each other behind the mast. We had to crouch to maintain eye contact because the boom was suspended between us. It was attached to the mast at one end with large bolts and extended back almost to where Grayburn sat officiously at the tiller. Along its length was a collapsed sail tied in bundles with loops of rope. Pierre clasped his hands between his knees and said, "You know what I'm thinking."

"Haven't a clue," said Jonathan.

"You know," said Pierre pointedly, "about that creature."

"I can guess," said Arthur. "Dr. Horehound."

"What are you saying?" asked Jonathan.

"The book you found the first night in the library," said Pierre. "The one by Montague Summers."

"The Vampire?" asked Jonathan. "Oh, no, of course—you mean the other one, about werewolves."

"I came across it myself yesterday morning," said Arthur.

"But," I countered, pointing straight up, "you said, and I agree. That ain't a full moon because that ain't *the* moon."

Everyone looked up and nodded.

"Don't that beat all," said Grayburn. "Strangest lookin' moon I ever seen."

"And in the wrong position," said Arthur. "This time of year the moon's path is across the southern heavens." He indicated the proper arc with his arm. "It's never directly overhead, like it is now."

"Don't think the fish'll be int'rested," said Grayburn. "Now gents, 'scuse me for interruptin' yer blatherin', but jus' for yer information, as it may come in handy, you and you is portside." He pointed to Pierre and Jonathan, who were seated on the left bench facing the right. "You and you is starboard." That meant Arthur and me, seated on the right facing left. "Got that?" We did, more or less. "Okay, Beth, up with the jib, if you please."

"Aye-aye, Captain," called Beth, who seemed very happy to be doing something other than sitting and talking. I suspect she was listening, though.

The pier from which we had shoved off was pointed due north, but thanks to the equal-but-opposite reaction to the force of four Tumblars tumbling aboard behind the mast, the boat was now aimed roughly northeast.

Here I was in for a surprise—that amazement at how wind interacts with the sails I mentioned a few moments ago. As Beth hoisted the jib—that is, the front sail—the wind caught it with a leathery pop, nudging the boat forward in a northeastwardly direction. Now, I knew a little nautical terminology, the kind one absorbs from books and movies, but having never sailed, I understood nothing of the practical particulars of wind propulsion. I would have intuited that wind blowing in a southerly direction would have pushed the boat backward, toward the pier. But here she was moving slowly but surely into the wind. I made a mental note to visit Arthur's bookshop to pick up a volume on the perplexing aerodynamics of sailing.

"Almost," said Jonathan, "but no cigar." He was still talking about the moon, apparently.

"I wonder what it is," said Arthur, scratching his head.

"Like I was saying," I said, yanking my attention away from the sail. "How could a man turn into a wolf if that isn't really the moon?"

"Some folklore connects lycanthropy with the lunar cycle," said Arthur. "The Lon Chaney Jr. movies certainly ran with the notion. They also rendered the condition indistinguishable from a communicable disease—Larry Talbot, the melancholic victim:

'He who is bitten by a werewolf and lives becomes a werewolf himself.'"

"Sort of like rabies," said Pierre, "or malaria, I suppose."

"But there are other traditions," continued Arthur authoritatively, probably to steady his nerves. "Some attribute the transformation to a curse or spell that has nothing to do with the moon, and some ascribe it to conscious desire—the resolve to descend unfettered into our animal nature."

"Like that Tarot card," said Jonathan. "The one with the lobster crawling out onto the land."

"The opposite, actually," said Arthur. "The Moon card denotes hesitancy within the wish to ascend. There is another card that hasn't come up yet, The Devil, which better represents what we're talking about—the desire to descend into the carnal depths. In the case of the willing werewolf, a man wholeheartedly surrenders and submits to Satan, who is only too happy to oblige his supplicant. After all, just as vampirism is a mockery of the Resurrection, werewolfism is a travesty of the Incarnation."

"Come again?" asked Jonathan as the boat careened gently forward, taking us further from the hairy beast that was still pacing the dock, glaring malevolently at us. "I get vampirism and the Resurrection, but not the werewolf and the Incarnation."

"If I may," said Pierre.

"Of course," said Arthur.

"In assuming human nature, the Son of God elevates us into His divine nature," explained Pierre. "Whereas the werewolf is a man who willingly descends into his beastly nature to partake of the drives and pleasures thereof. As is his wont, Satan thus sullies the point of the Incarnation by endorsing its antithesis. Did I get that right?"

"Right as rain," said Arthur. "Since animals lack Free Will, it is furthermore the abandoning of one of God's greatest gifts in favor of unbridled appetite. Still, there's something bothering me, something I read in that diary—"

"'Scuse my impert'nence," said Grayburn, "but y'all realize yer talkin' 'bout the Master—not just my employer, but the owner of this here sloop."

"I do," said Pierre, "and we'd apologize if it weren't for—"

"If I'm hearin' you right," continued Grayburn, "y'all're claimin' right here 'neath the cold moonlight—or whatever that is up there—that that animal growlin' on the dock is Dr. Horehound?" (His pitch rose steadily throughout his delivery, hence my placement of a question mark at the end.)

"I realize it's a stretch," said Pierre, "but considering that we're floating dangerously near a flying saucer—"

"I only got y'all's word for that," said Grayburn with a derisive cackle. "Whoever heard of a *flyin'* saucer *sunk* in a lake? A leaky tub like the Master's missin' boat'd be more like it. We oughta keep an eye out for that old bucket while we're out here, come to think of it. We don't have no runnin' lights, and we don't wanna risk no collision in the dark. Anyway, besides, as I was sayin', Dr. Horehound don't 'zactly kowtow to God, and I doubt very much that he'd snuggle up to the Old Goat, neither. If he's that beastie on the dock—*if*, I repeat, *if*—then he was hexed, if y'all believes in that sorta thing. Leastwise, so's it seems to me."

"Like I was saying, about the diary ..." said Arthur, his voice trailing off as he realized everyone had turned to gaze at the receding pier.

By now we were maybe a hundred yards away, moving steadily northeast. The boathouse was due south of us, drifting gradually to the right from our perspective. The creature on the dock, backlit by the lodge's ever-burning porch torches, had stopped pacing. It was sitting doglike on its haunches, its tongue lolling out the side of its mouth, its tail whipping catlike from side to side. The freezing glow of its malicious red eyes blinked off and on, off and on. I got the impression it was considering its options.

"Prepare the mainsail!" called Grayburn to Beth, who saluted in return.

"Dr. Horehound seems so self-controlled," said Jonathan. "Not a man of—how did you put it?—unbridled appetites."

"You're wrong there," said Beth, who had jumped down into our midst and was busy freeing the sail from its bonds along the length of the boom. It was strange seeing her going about man's work in a damp, clinging dress. As she finished her task, she slapped the boom and said, "Have you noticed the way he eats?"

"Beth has a point," said Arthur. "Dr. Horehound doesn't masticate food, he sucks the life out of it, nibble by nibble."

"I 'sumed he was jus' bein' prim and proper," said Grayburn.

"If I were a clinical psychologist," said Pierre, "I'd say he's overcompensating."

"And for this yer sayin' he's a werewolf?" scoffed Grayburn.

"No," said Pierre. "Because twice he became ill and excused himself from our midst. Both absences coincided with the appearances of that wolfish thing."

"Three times, actually," said Jonathan. "The first night we were here, the night before you arrived, Arthur—remember us telling you?—we heard it howling when we were coming down the western shore in the van. When we made our way to the lodge, Grayburn here showed us into the library. Dr. Horehound came in shortly afterwards. Did anyone notice that he was barefoot? He tried to appear calm and in control, but he was all sweaty."

"So?" snorted Grayburn. "It's his house. He can go without shoes if he's gotta mind; and a little sweat never hurt nobody."

"After he excused himself," said Jonathan ponderously, "I saw mud on the carpet. It was gone the next morning."

"Just Thorndale doin' her job," said Grayburn, pointing back over his shoulder. "Y'all coulda tracked it in."

"I distinctly remember wiping our feet on the doormat," said Jonathan, whacking his knee, "at your insistence."

"So his transformation preceded the séance," said Arthur thoughtfully. Then he muttered something that sounded like, "Wolf's heart and no soul."

"What was that?" I asked, thinking I'd heard that phrase before.

"According to the sheriff," said Pierre, "animal attacks have been going on in the area for months."

"Flurries separated by lulls," said Jonathan, "or so Dr. Horehound told us."

"It would be interesting to know if those flurries coincided with recent reenactments," said Arthur. "Repeated exposure to the Revealing Star with a substitute deck in the hands of a surrogate medium was likely bringing this on gradually for some time—unlike the one evening it took in 1896. Diluted application versus full strength, you might say."

"Substitute deck?" I asked. "Diluted application? I'm not following you."

"It's also possible," said Arthur, more to himself than to us, "that poring over wicked books, like the ones he ordered from Luxembourg through Lenore Poe, exacerbated or accelerated his tendency to metamorphose."

"That's an awful lotta maybes, mights, and poss'blys," said Grayburn. "Too many for my taste."

"I'll add to them," said Arthur, now more to us than to himself. "These bursts of Tesla coil activity, the night you arrived and just now: maybe he has been attempting to use it as—what did Madam Douceur call it?—a 'subvection countermeasure'—when he feels the lycanthropic transformation coming on."

"Somebody better tell him," said Jonathan. "It doesn't work."

"Perhaps it does," said Arthur. "Within limitations—maybe as long as he stays within the coil's electrical field. How big an area might it encompass? I'm afraid I don't know much about how it works."

"Basically," I felt compelled to contribute, "the Tesla coil is an air-core resonating transformer." I enjoyed saying something that Pierre and Arthur didn't already understand for a change. "It was the forerunner of the radio frequency coil that made radios possible. Last year Mr. Brackmore decided to build one to dazzle customers. He spent several thousand on materials, and two weeks of overtime hours—mine—constructing it. It was taller than a sixteen-foot ladder. We finished it late one night when the store was closed. He turned it on, sparks filled the showroom, and every fluorescent bulb in the place lit up."

"Yes," said Jonathan. "I once saw that demonstrated at the Griffith Park Observatory."

"It's a cool effect," I agreed. "It doesn't affect incandescent bulbs, but a fluorescent held in your hand will, well, fluoresce. So yes, in answer to your question, I can see how a coil the size of that tower might generate a field large enough to encompass the entire building. Whether it would repel spirits or cause a subvecting counter-whatever, I don't know."

"Grayburn," said Arthur, "surely you know about the coil in the tower? Did you ever see Dr. Horehound fire it up?"

"Yessir to both questions," said he. "Yep, he'd take this here measurin' gadget with a wigglin' needle all over the house. Also one of the tube lights from the basement. Lit up everywhere he went."

"How about the séance room?" asked Beth.

"'Spesh'ly the séance room," said Grayburn.

"How about outside the building?" asked Pierre.

"I never seen him checkin' outside."

"The field likely covers part of the island," I said. "The western end around the lodge, anyway. I don't know about the garden. But in any case, Jonathan's right. It doesn't work—at least, not against werewolfery. That creature was up in the turret, right at the heart of the Tesla field."

"All the more reason I wish I'd gone back for the sick call kit," said Arthur. "Truly, we are defenseless."

"The discharges from the Tesla coil seem to have ceased," I observed. "I wonder why."

"You're right," said Pierre. "The tower is dark."

"Hrmph," grunted Grayburn. "Well, Lassie—Beth, I mean— ready to raise the mainsail?"

"Aye-aye," said Beth, repositioning herself beside the mast and heaving on a line. The canvas unraveled noisily. A moment later the wind caught the sail and caused it to billow gently.

"Now watch yer heads," said Grayburn. "The boom's gonna swing!" As he said this, he moved the tiller and pulled on a rope at the same time.

The boom had been lolling to starboard. Suddenly, with a long creaking squeal, it swung portside. At the same time the boat gently swerved until the bow was pointing somewhat west of north. Water slurped and gushed around the bow as the boat surged forward into the wind. We weren't racing by any means, but we were definitely making progress.

In addition to a warm jacket, I wished I had a compass.

We sailed in this direction for several exhilarating minutes in silence. Then Grayburn reversed the process, swinging the boom to starboard again and turning the boat slightly east of north.

"Whoa!" exclaimed Pierre as we all ducked.

"This is called 'tackin'," said Grayburn.

"Tacking?" asked Jonathan.

"Well, I call it amazing," I said, but I don't think anyone heard me.

"The message said to 'void deep water, which I surely can do," said Grayburn after several minutes. "I know this here lake like the back of my hand. That's why we can't get too close to shore, neither. The keel on this beauty goes down more'n five feet below."

As I considered this, the eastern shore came into view in the somber moonlight. With a grunt of warning, Grayburn repeated the tiller/rope routine, bringing the bow gently to port and away from shore again.

"I say," said Pierre, pointing to the boom, "is that thing going to keep swinging back and forth like that?"

"Sure 'nuff," said Grayburn, "'cause that's what tackin's all about. Jus' watch yer heads and y'all'll be fine."

"If you can't go close to shore," said Jonathan, "what are we going to do when we get to the campground? There isn't a dock there."

"I 'magine you'll get wet," said Grayburn.

"Don't look now," said Beth, swaying beside the mast and pointing toward the dock which had receded to a small structure in the distance. "Whatever or whoever it is, it isn't there anymore."

We all turned to see that indeed it wasn't.

"Did you see where it went?" asked Jonathan.

"Sorry," said Beth, shaking her head.

"It better not pester Thorndale, that's all I gotta say," said Grayburn, leaning back and enjoying the wind in his face. "Now I've got somethin' to ask you fellers, if you've a mind. You was sayin' back at the lodge that evil-lution nixes Jesus, and that just don't sit right with me. Last March there was this priest feller in one of the Master's groups. He believed in it. He said that knowin' him and his golden retriever shared common ancestors gave him a special sense of connection. I kinda liked that."

"So this priest actually admitted he was a son of a—" said Arthur.

"Stop right there, Big Bro," said Beth, one arm wrapped around the mast, strands of her drying hair fluttering in the wind.

"That's what we call sentimentalism," said Pierre, suppressing a chuckle. "Substituting a warm feeling for the truth."

"It's all too common these days," said Jonathan.

"But I thought evil-lution's a done deal," said Grayburn. "Everyone says so."

"Hardly," said Arthur. "Lately during the lulls between customers I've been reading about recent discoveries in microbiology."

"Arthur working in a bookstore," said Pierre, placing his hand on his heart. "It's like throwing kerosene on an open flame."

"You would know," I quipped, but not loud enough to be heard.

"When Darwin examined a cell through the microscopes of his day," said Arthur, oblivious to us, "he could see a nucleus floating in transparent goo—basically what you see when you crack an egg. It was easy for him to visualize such a simple thing becoming gradually more complicated through the ongoing process of mutations and natural selection."

"He always talk like this?" asked Grayburn to no one in particular.

"If you only knew," I answered, shaking my head.

"But now, with today's technology," continued Arthur, "we're discovering that living cells are anything but simple. Each one is a complicated factory where proteins take on the roles of suppliers, loaders, switch-throwers, copiers, toolmakers, crane operators—and all of this managed by tiers of foremen and supervisors signaling orders like traffic control officers."

"Now there's an image for you," said Jonathan. "And all that's going on in every little cell inside me?"

And in every single cell inside Arthur's head, I thought to myself. That explains it. I mean, sometimes his well of knowledge seems endless—which I admit can be intimidating, sometimes even annoying. But as with Pierre, I'm grateful to know him. He reads and I listen. I get the benefit of his intelligence without having much of my own. Such a deal. And he's certainly not stuck up about it like some geniuses.

"The complex operation within a cell has been compared to the construction site of a high-rise building," said Arthur, "only more efficient because the workers are self-repairing and self-replicating. The deeper scientists probe into the process of life, the more complicated it becomes, to the point where some researchers are starting to scratch their heads and say, 'This is no accident. This didn't happen as the result of random mutations. This must be the product of *intelligent design.*'"

"Y'all lost me 'long the way," said Grayburn. "Watch yer heads, I'm turnin' her again!"

∞§[Martin]§∞

"Hold your loquacious horses!" clamored Kahlúa. She leaned forward, her brow crinkled. "Toolmakers, switch-throwers, crane operators, all managed by tiers of traffic control officers! I've heard it before, and I know I've never read any such book!" She aimed her index finger accusingly. "Pierre! You gave the *Artsy* staff that same speech around the coffeemaker. It was the day you came in to sign your contract. We were discussing the microbiologist that got tarred and feathered by his dignified colleagues at C.I.S.T. for saying he no longer believed in evolution."

"Cyst?" asked Millie.

"The California Institute of Science and Technology," said Pierre. "Madam Hummingbird, I assure you—"

"Here I thought you were this amazing scholar," said Kahlúa.

"Amazing scholars have their research assistants," said Arthur.

"You mean you don't care if he steals your thunder?" asked Millie.

"Why should I mind?" chuckled Arthur. "I've no professional stake to defend. I just dig up the information because I'm hungry for it. I leave it to more proficient mouths to spread it around. I may be annoying at times, but apparently I'm not stuck up like some geniuses."

"Sorry about that," said Edward.

"Not at all," said Arthur. "I regard it as a compliment."

"Whatever you say," said Kahlúa, leaning back in her chair. "Methinks you should demand a cut of Pierre's paycheck."

"Methinks Edward should continue with his story," said Millie.

∞§[Edward]§∞

"Some scientists, perhaps," said Pierre after ducking as the boom swung from port to starboard again—

∞§[Martin]§∞

"Hold on," said Edward, glancing further up the page. "What scientists is he talking about?"

"I think the ones who probe into the processes of life," said Jonathan.

"And conclude that they are witnessing the product of *intelligent design*," added Arthur.

"'Aha!'" said Jonathan, whacking his brow. "'So maybe there really is a God'—duh, yuh think?"

"Ah," said Edward. "Of course. Okay, one more time."

∞§[Edward]§∞

"Some scientists, perhaps," said Pierre, after ducking as the boom swung from port to starboard again and we veered toward the shore. "As I understand it, Arthur, most still insist on Darwin's principle of step-by-step variations that take hold because they help the organism survive better."

"But they can't explain how these fantastically complex, integrated systems came about in the first place," said our resident scholar. "Life started out multifarious or it wouldn't have worked! Yet most researchers continue to cling to a theory that predates the phonograph—and we know how far the recording of sound has come since Edison's wax cylinder! Mesmerized by Darwin; lulled by outdated science."

Pierre suddenly adopted an overdone Austrian accent with female overtones: "Wot does it mean, doctah?"

To which Arthur responded, with a heavy-handed European inflection: "It means there are times when a mere scientist has gone as far as he can—" Naturally the rest of us were required to join in for the well-rehearsed next part: "—when he must pause and observe respectfully while something infinitely greater assumes control." Then we dropped our voices to a profound rumble: "I believe this is one of those times."

(We were quoting an exchange between Osa Massen as Dr. Lisa Van Horn and John Emery as Dr. Karl Eckstrom in *Rocketship X-M*, one of Arthur's favorite movies from the early nineteen fifties. He loves to point out that the musician who composed *The Grand Canyon Suite* wrote the score for this film.)

"Ah well," said Pierre, "that was why it was called science *fiction*. The fundamental tenet of modern science *reality* is that all explanations about everything-that-is must exclude the notion of God."

"They sure got that backwards," commented Jonathan.

"No room for watchmakers," said Arthur. "Only watches that not only put themselves together, but also wind themselves, repair themselves, and randomly make mistakes in doing so that gradually change themselves into motorcycles."

"Uh ... right," said Jonathan.

"Talking about watches to motorcycles," I said. "I wanted to ask you—"

"Watch yer heads," warned Grayburn. "Time to turn!"

The boom let out a tortured groan as it careened from starboard back to port. The mainsail ruffled and sagged, then billowed full again, and the boat gracefully veered away from shore.

"What was that, Edward?" asked Arthur. "I'm afraid I don't really know much about motorcycles. I was speaking by way of analogy."

"I gotta nuther question, if you don't mind my buttin' in," said Grayburn.

"Of course," I said, figuring at the rate we were going, I'd eventually get my question asked in an hour or two.

"Who's Dumb Otis?" asked Grayburn.

"Who?" asked everyone together.

"Back in the lib'ary," said Grayburn, pointing to Arthur. "You said Dumb Otis sorted things out."

"I did?" asked Arthur.

"Duns Scotus!" laughed Pierre. "What you thought you heard—"

"—is always better than what was actually said," chimed in the rest of us.

"Oh," said Arthur good-naturedly. "We were discussing the objections of St. Thomas Aquinas to the Immaculate Conception of the Blessed Virgin Mary. Blessed Duns Scotus was a scholar of considerable renown who clarified the situation by circumventing the whole quickening business. It's a beautiful example of what happens when theologians stand their ground. As such, he cited St. Anselm of Canterbury: *'Potuit, decuit, ergo fecit.'* Duns Scotus posited that while the Blessed Virgin was in need of redemption as were all human beings—"

"Hold on," said Grayburn. "Po-too-eet day-coo-eet what?"

"'God could do it,'" translated Pierre, "'it was appropriate, therefore He did it.'"

"Did what?" asked Grayburn.

"As I was saying," said Arthur, smiling patiently. "Duns Scotus explained that the Mother of Jesus was prevented from contracting Original Sin through the foreseen merits of her Son's Crucifixion."

"I'm losing you," said Jonathan.

"I fell overboard a ways back," cackled Grayburn.

"God transcends time," said Arthur. "He is not bound by it. The redemptive grace of the Bloody Sacrifice of Calvary flows backward as well as forward in time because all times are *now* to

Him. Therefore He applied that grace to His Blessed Mother at the moment of her conception, even though the event preceded the Crucifixion in linear time."

"That's either deep or screwy," said Grayburn. "Darn if I don't know which."

"Perhaps a little of both," said Pierre, folding his hands as if in prayer. "I mean that respectfully, of course. We are, after all, trying to explain a theological mystery."

"None of the Master's guests ever talked like you guys," said Grayburn.

"I should think not," said I.

Just then, as the dimly lit shore began to recede—

∞§[Martin]§∞

"I'm sorry," interrupted Kahlúa with a long, protracted sigh, "but I said it before and I'll say it again—you guys is obsessed! No, I take that back. You's whacked!"

"Kaputsky," I quipped, "as Doctor Yomtov would say."

"I like that," said she.

"Perhaps I should have edited some of the discussion out," said Pierre, "but it's so indicative of what we are."

"I was kind of enjoying it," said Jonathan. "I can picture us on that boat, sailing into danger, expounding like that. It's us all over. The more trouble we're in, the more we spin!"

"You gotta love us!" laughed the Lads.

"Only you guys could go from lycanthropy to evolution to the Immaculate Conception in one conversation," said Beth.

"It doesn't exactly move the story along," grumbled Millie. "I'm waiting for gore, horror, and worse."

"You should join us for late night movies at Arthur's," said Joel.

"Well," said Pierre, "for what it's worth, things are about to start cracking."

"Please," said Kahlúa. "It's them or me."

"I assume I'll come back into the story eventually," said Joel dejectedly.

"You're here, aren't you?" said Jonathan.

"More or less," said Joel. "Mostly less."

"I know, Joel," said Arthur. "This whole business has been hard for you."

"What about me?" asked Millie. "I could have been over at Muriel's watching the Pope say Christmas Mass on television, but nooooo."

"You be kidding, isn't you?" asked Kahlúa. "Whatever happened to *How the Grinch Stole Christmas?*"

"That was on last night."

"Who's next?" asked Monsignor Havermeyer, readjusting his bathrobe and finding it wanting.

"I've still got more pages," said Edward.

"Then by all means," said Father, "please continue."

∞§[†]§∞

∞§✝§∞

30. We're All Going
To Act Like Knights

∞§[Edward]§∞

JUST THEN, AS THE DIMLY LIT SHORE began to recede, we heard thrashing sounds in the brush beneath the stately pine trees. Something was fiercely tearing its way through the underbrush.

"You don't suppose—" said Pierre.

His thought was proved true by a ferocious howl.

"Dear God," said Beth. "It's following us!"

"How could it get so far around the shore so quickly?" asked Jonathan.

"Do you think it might follow us all the way to the campground?" asked Pierre.

"It sounds mighty determined to me," I said.

"What are we going to do?" asked Beth.

"Fer now," said Grayburn, "all we can do is keep on goin'—leastwise, that's all I can think of."

"No help for it," said Arthur, as we slumped low on our benches.

Just then the boat heaved unexpectedly to portside, then rocked to starboard as a swell rolled under us. We all grabbed onto the rails as the boat tilted back to portside then gradually straightened, except for Beth who clutched the mast and Grayburn who held fast to the tiller.

"Whoa ho!" said Pierre. "What was that?"

"Shhhh!" shushed Grayburn. "Listen!"

Listen we did. The thing in the underbrush continued its hacking and tramping. Otherwise there didn't seem to be a sound, and then we heard the surge of water slop and slosh on the shore.

"That there wave come from the center of the lake," whispered Grayburn. "Somethin's stirrin' in the deep."

We all turned to peer in that direction. The lake was a flat expanse of blackness with zillions of dots of moonlight playing on its rippling surface. Other than that, we saw nothing. A few moments later a second, less powerful swell rolled under us, rocking the boat less wildly.

"Is that my heart, or do I hear thumping?" asked Arthur.

"I think it's your ticker, old chum," said Pierre.

"Something displaced all that water," I said. "Something big."

"The saucer," whispered Jonathan. "It's rising up again."

"Maybe," said Pierre. "Stand fast."

We continued watching and listening. Unaffected, the creature on shore continued its thrashing. A minute passed, maybe two, and then we heard that all too familiar pop. A brilliant blue-white sphere appeared about ten feet in front of the bow—well, actually a few degrees to starboard. It hovered about fifteen feet above the surface of the water.

"Not another one," exclaimed Jonathan.

"It's just floating there," said Pierre.

"That's what they always do—at first," whispered Jonathan.

"It's blue," said Beth. "Like the one that gave us the message."

"Hold on," said Grayburn. "I'm gonna try somethin'. Watch yer noggins." With that he pulled the rope and shifted the tiller, swinging the boom to starboard and veering the boat toward shore. "There, you see? It's holdin' its position due north of us. I need to 'void the shallows, so I gotta turn 'er again right away. Here we go."

The boat swung northwestward once more, and the sphere indeed held its position due north of us.

"Maybe it's here to guide us," suggested Beth. She stepped down onto the foredeck to get a closer look.

"Careful, Sis," said Arthur.

"It's beautiful," said Beth, holding out her right hand. "I think it wants us to follow it."

"Then it's leadin' us where we're already headin'," said Grayburn. "'Though we gotta zigzag. You s'pose it understands that?"

"Who knows?" sighed Pierre. "But I think Beth may be right. It's not doing anything threatening."

"Let's hope it stays that way," said Jonathan.

We went on like that for another minute or so, and then we heard the humming. Arthur was the first to say something:

"Uh-oh. Do you hear that?"

"What's happening now?" said Jonathan, looking all around.

It was a deep, growling hum. It was hard to tell which direction it was coming from. I could feel it through the rail I was clutching and the bench on which I was sitting.

"The light!" said Beth, still holding out her hand.

The sphere was glowing brighter, perhaps larger—it was hard to tell. Swirls of radiant blue and green started peeling off its edges. It drew closer to the bow, to Beth's outstretched hand.

"Beth!" said Arthur.

"It's okay," said his sister. "I'm sure it's okay. See? It's not attacking."

"Oh dear," said Jonathan, rising to his feet. "Beth, don't!"

The orb was now inches from her hand, and it was definitely pulsing and sparking. Like a trained bird it seemed to be preparing to alight upon her palm.

Then, from where I was seated on the starboard bench facing portside, I saw the other light. It was way out over deep water, coming toward us at a terrific speed.

"Look!" I said, but everyone but Beth was already aware of it.

"My stars," said Grayburn. "Don't that seem wicked."

That described it to a T. It reminded me of an artist's rendering of an early N.A.S.A. space capsule plunging through the earth's atmosphere upon reentry, orange and yellow flames pouring from the heat shield and fluttering in the turbulence behind. Only this thing was flying horizontally over the water, about twenty-five feet in the air—and it was heading straight toward us. Its glare played on the sails and outlined our faces. That low grumbling hum grew louder and angrier as it approached.

"What in Heaven's name—?" gasped Pierre.

"What should we do?" groaned Jonathan.

"Ain't much we *can* do," said Grayburn. "Can't outrun it. Only a slight breeze, and we'd need one heckuva gale. More like a hurricane. We're sittin' ducks."

"Maybe we should head for shore," said Arthur.

"Can't," said Grayburn. "We'd go aground—"

The beast in the underbrush shrieked and howled, reminding us that abandoning ship and swimming to dry land was out of the question.

Suddenly remembering Beth, I turned to look at her. The sphere she thought so friendly suddenly flared and darted away from her, shooting in an intercepting course for the approaching fireball. Surprised, Beth stumbled backward and landed sitting on the foredeck.

The fiery thing was almost upon us. The hum had become deafening. Suddenly, purposefully, it swerved southward, avoiding the small blue-white sphere, then flew in a smooth circle with the diameter of a football field counterclockwise around our boat. When it had gone completely around us, it came to an abrupt halt a frightening stone's throw to port. It hovered there, about twenty feet in the air, the flames sputtering and falling away to reveal a long, slender vessel that vaguely resembled a shovel, the blade part in front with a thin pole behind. The nose section, upon closer inspection, reminded me of the head of a platypus, a thin flat beak in front that swelled smoothly back toward the cranium in which the pilot and crew probably sat. This front section was about the size of a double-wide mobile home, with a thin cylindrical rear section, minus fin or strut about three times its length, extended behind. This bizarre shuttlecraft—I assumed it came from the mother ship we knew so well—was smooth and eerily white, like polished alabaster, with whirls of demon red and inky black rippling over its surfaces. As with its larger cousin, it had no windows; but I think we all felt that whoever or whatever sat at the controls was glaring at us malevolently. That infernal humming dropped to a lower pitch, as though its engines were idling.

The small blue-white sphere maneuvered to a position between us and it, a pathetic David standing up to a mighty Goliath.

"Oh no!" cried Beth, scrambling to her feet. "The poor thing doesn't stand a chance!"

"And you think we do?" groaned Jonathan.

"Do something!" cried Beth, leaning over the rail.

"Like what?" asked Pierre.

"I'd say this is a good time for one of your prayers," said Grayburn.

I opened my mouth to say something—I can't remember what—when a beam of concentrated purple light flashed out from the nose of the vessel. For a fraction of a second the little blue-white sphere was overwhelmed in a blaze of crackling sparks, then exploded into nothingness.

"No!" screamed Beth. "You freaking alien sons-of-bitches!"

The awesome hovercraft's engines surged and rumbled, producing a deafening parody of a sadistic laugh.

"I guess this is it," said Pierre. "Lads, it's been an honor knowing—"

But his words were subsumed by an ominous hum, an unnerving sound we knew too well. Suddenly Beth was engulfed in an aura of fuzzy yellow light. She struggled within the hazy cocoon, her eyes wide and her arms pinned at her sides.

"Big Bro!" I heard her cry, but her voice was muffled, as if she was wrapped in cotton wadding.

"Good Lord!" gasped Arthur. "Beth! No!"

There was a brilliant flash at the bow of the boat, and Beth was gone.

"Oh my God!" cried Arthur, lunging across the deck. "Li'l Sis!"

∞§[Martin]§∞

"They snatched me?" said Beth with a gasp. Then her eyes narrowed. "They *snatched* me!" she exclaimed angrily. "Those alien bastards killed that poor little light ball, and then, and then—"

"Puddin'!" soothed Kahlúa, reaching across Arthur to give her hand a reassuring squeeze. "You're here now, remember?"

"But it's as if," shuddered Beth. "I can almost—" She straightened in her chair. "Darn! It was so real for a second, and now it's gone."

"I was right," said Arthur as Kahlúa withrew her arm. "I knew something bad was about to happen. It's almost as if—" He blinked and rubbed his temples. "I can almost see it, feel it—but it keeps slipping away."

"I think we're making progress," said Pierre. "Edward, don't stop."

∞§[Edward]§∞

A moment later, that deadly purple ray flared out again, this time aimed at the jib. The foresail exploded into flame. Blackened canvas curled away from the expanding hole, and various ropes sprang and went limp.

"Hey!" yelled Grayburn. "That'll be enuffa that! Fire on deck!" He released the tiller and fumbled for an extinguisher strapped under his seat. Moving faster than any of us thought his spindly legs could carry him, he charged to the bow and deftly sprayed the smoldering tatters of the foresail with bursts of white powder. Within seconds the fire was out. "The Master's gonna kill me!" he muttered as he strutted between us back to his perch. In a burst of rage, he flung the canister at the shuttlecraft. It plopped uselessly into the water well short of its target and disappeared. The vessel's engines responded with another round of taunting horselaughs.

During all this, Arthur had managed to heave himself halfway over the portside rail. "Beth!" he screamed. "Li'l Sis!"

Pierre and Jonathan grabbed him and pulled him back into the boat.

"Oh, God!" cried Arthur as he sank to his knees on the deck. "They've got her! I never should have brought her here. Oh Lord, what have I done?"

"Steady," said Pierre, slipping off the bench and throwing an arm around Arthur. "We'll get her back."

"How?" said Arthur with a shudder. "What was I thinking? What are we going to do?"

"You were thinking like a Knight," said Pierre, "and we're all going to act like Knights." He looked up at us. "Right?"

"Right," we all answered, unconvincingly.

"Beth chose to come with us," I said. "You couldn't have stopped her."

"All of us combined couldn't have stopped her," said Jonathan.

Its mission complete, the damage done, the shuttlecraft's engines accelerated to a roar. The sinister vessel burst into motion, careening up into the sky in a graceful arc, turned, then nosedived into the lake a hundred yards to port. There was a momentary sucking sound as water rushed in behind it, then a churning wave came roaring toward us. We held on helplessly as it knocked the boat sideways. For a terrifying second, I thought we were going to capsize, but to my relief the boat righted itself, rolled to port, then finally straightened, the mast pointing accusingly at the weird moon overhead.

Jonathan, Pierre, and Arthur untangled themselves from the heap they had become on the water-splattered deck. Stunned and silent, they regained their positions on the side benches. I had managed to stay put by gripping the rail until my hands ached. Grayburn sat stoically at the tiller, his face grim. We hunched there wordlessly for several minutes, grateful to be alive, bewildered by the gaping unknown that lay before us.

And then, as if in answer to our wordless prayer, the blue-white ball of light popped back into existence a short distance from the bow. True to its nature, it hovered due north of us.

"Will you look at that?" said Grayburn. "It ain't killed after all. I s'pose it wants us to keep on goin'."

"But we can't leave Beth," said Arthur.

"We can't do anything for her here," said Pierre.

"But, but—" stammered Arthur, tears running down his face.

"Look," I said in a voice that took me by surprise. "Arthur, I know I almost made a mess of things back there at the lodge. But you were right. That ball of light gave us a message, a course of action, when we had no idea what to do other than to

stand fast and hope for the best. Well, it seems to me that following it is still our only hope."

"Frankly, I'm shocked," said Arthur, looking at me with eyes
that had aged a hundred years. "Edward, I would have thought
you'd be saying that message led us into a trap." He took a deep
breath, and as he let it out he added, "And I would have agreed
with you."

"I'm a bit bewildered myself," I admitted. Indeed, my primary
emotion was no longer fear but conviction. Somehow these
events had forged a solid-steel change in the furnace of my heart.
"I have no idea what we'll find at the campground," I found myself saying, "but no one else is making any offers. We started
our council with a prayer, trusting in Our Lord and Lady to give
us an answer." I pointed to the ball of light. "Well, there it is."

The beast in the underbrush let loose an angry screech.

"Another country heard from," said Pierre.

"I thought you fellers might wanna turn back," said Grayburn.

"To what?" asked Jonathan. "Seems we've got the same problem we discussed in the library. We can't run away from them.
We can't just sit and wait for them to come and get us. Now
they have Beth—Heaven help us!—but essentially we're in the
same position. We don't know how to fight them. Maybe this
Fawnskin can help. Or Forkbaerd, or whoever. I say we find
out."

"Well said," said Pierre. "Jonathan, Edward, Arthur: for what
it's worth, I am proud to be in your company. Grayburn, can we
still make progress with just the one sail?"

"Sure thing," said Grayburn, rubbing his chin. "I'll have to
tack at a wider angle, and the goin's gonna be slower, but I can
still get y'all there if that's what you want."

"We do," said we all as one. It felt good. In spite of all, it felt
very good.

"Then that's what we'll do," said Grayburn. He hawked up
something and spat it over the side. "I pro'bly won't have a job
to go back to, and I still think y'all're bonkers, but we may as
well see it through. Besides, with all the weirdos that've come to
the Master's creepy shindigs, I ain't never had so much excite-

ment. I don't 'spect I gotta lotta years yet to live, but this here's one night I'll remember to my dyin' day!"

∞§[Martin]§∞

"Gentlemen, if I may," said Father, as Edward's pages were relegated to the pile on the floor. "I'd like to second Pierre's sentiment. I am indeed honored to know you."

"Group hug!" piped Jonathan.

Everyone looked at him incredulously.

"Kidding!" Jonathan assured them.

"So you left me," said Beth.

"It's what men do, Sweetie," said Kahlúa.

"Given the circs," said Millie, "I think they did the right thing."

"Watch out, Fellows," I said. "I think Millie's vying for that position you posted in the *Artsy*. Tumblar Den Mother, wasn't it?"

"Bah!" said Millie. "I've been cleaning up after you rascals till my fingers are raw and my hair's gone gray."

"I say she gets the position!" said Jonathan and Edward together.

"Carried," said Pierre. "I guess."

"Keep it up, all of you," said Millie.

"That's what they do," said Kahlúa.

"Don't I know it," said Millie.

"Come on, everyone," said Arthur seriously. "So Pierre, what *did* we find at the campground?"

"You still don't remember?" asked Pierre.

"I'm afraid not," said Arthur. "Does anyone?"

The Lads shook their heads.

"I'm afraid it will have to wait," said Pierre, delving into the antique chest. "In the immediate hangs the matter of the abduction of Arthur's seaworthy sister."

"And me," said Joel, raising his hand like a school kid. "I'm still aboard that spaceship, apparently."

"I was just about to ask about that," said Kahlúa. "Beth'll likely hook up with Dr. Jekyll and Mr. Maruppa."

"Thanks," said Joel.

"Oh goodie," said Millie. "Here comes the gore and the horror."

"What *do* you watch over at Muriel Cladusky's, Millie?" I chided.

"Nothing worse than the Saint Philomena's Chainsaw Massacre I see through my kitchen window," said Millie, "every Sunday after Mass."

"I do believe she's referring to your flock, Father," said Jonathan.

"Santa's sweet, busy little helpers all," said Edward.

"More like *The Attack of the Mole People,*" said Millie.

"Millie!" said Arthur. "You know that film?"

"Friday night's *Creature Feature*," said she.

"The truth will out," said I.

"As will Beth's story, I hope, before I'm wrinkled and gray," said Kahlúa.

"I second Kahlúa," said Father Baptist.

"Ayes have it," said Jonathan. "Motion carried."

"Lights, camera—" said Edward.

"Reverend Fathers," said Pierre ceremoniously, as he reached across me to hand another clutch of pages to Beth. "Ladies and Gentlemen: 'The plights and perils of Beth von Dershmidt.'"

∞§[To be continued . . .]§∞

∞§[†]§∞

Made in the USA
Middletown, DE
14 March 2021